CARRIED BY SIX

To Tamu Mno—
With My Very
Best Wishes.
Thanks For All
Your Support.
Allen
Nov. 17, 2009

CARRIED BY SIX

Allen Ballard

Seaforth Press

Carried by Six is a work of fiction.
Names, characters, places and incidents are the products of the author's imagination or are used ficticously. Any resemblence to actual events, locales, or persons, living or dead, is entirely coincidental.

To order additional copies of this title, contact your favorite local bookstore or visit www.tbmbooks.com.

Book and cover design by Melissa Mykal Batalin.
Author photo by Phyllis Galembo.

Published by Seaforth Press
Printed in the United States of America

ISBN: 978-1-935534-181

For my students, past and present.
May God bless and keep you one and all as you journey through life!

ACKNOWLEDGEMENTS

I'd like to thank Renni Browne for putting her unmatched editorial skills to work on the manuscript of this book. Thanks also to my good friends, Dr. Carson Carr Jr. and Deacon Ernest Williams of Mt. Calvary Baptist Church, Albany, New York, for being there for me in fair weather and foul.

The same goes for the Rt. Reverend Robert W. Dixon, his wife, Georgia Dixon, and my entire Mt. Calvary church family whom I love dearly. My brothers, Walter and Forrest, and their families have been staunch supporters of my work as has been my son, John. I'd like to make a special note of my gratitude to the late Geraldine Ballard, who was always the very first person to read drafts of my books and did so with alacrity and great empathy for the travails of a writer. In this and more ways than I can count, her great loving spirit, compassion, musical artistry, and zest for life is sorely missed.

Thanks also to Professors Leonard Slade, Darlene Clark Hine, and Lillian Williams, Staff Inspector (Ret.) John Herritage, New York State Police, and Diane Turner, Suzanne Lance, Greta Petry, and the late Gartrell Turman, all of whom have been great supporters of my writing. I thank finally, Velma Cousins, for being such a good friend over the years and for all of her help and support.

CHAPTER 1

OBIE BULLOCK PULLED HIS BATTERED OLD CHEVY SEDAN in front of the Joseph E. Hill projects, checked the sign, and double-parked. He got out of the car and mopped the sweat from his brow with a big red handkerchief. It was only eight in the morning, but the pavements in North Philly were already warming up, just like every other day this week. He began the short walk to his building, past the graffitied concrete tables. The old men were already out playing cards.

One looked up. "Just getting in from the job?"

"You know it. Any of you see Dora Lee yet this morning?"

"Heading towards the bus about fifteen minutes ago," another player said. "Looking good, too, man. Go figure. Prettiest woman in the place and married to somebody ugly as you."

Obie laughed and aimed an air punch at him.

The older man stood and threw up his arms. "Come on if you dare. These the fists destroyed Bucky Jackson."

"Man, I know I can't stand against the mighty Tyrone Waters."

With that, Obie took off at a run towards the building entrance. The entire table collapsed in laughter, the other men clapping their hands and encouraging Tyrone, a bent-over senior citizen.

"Go get him. You know Obie ain't nothing for you."

"Show him, Tyrone. Do your bad thing on him."

Tyrone stood and shouted after his disappearing foe. "Don't mess with me, man, thunderbolts in these fists."

Still laughing, something he hadn't done a lot of lately, Obie entered the lobby. He looked up and down the corridor for Roy, who was away from his desk. Damn, the house committee had met with the police just three nights ago and agreed that two officers would be assigned to the building—and that one would always be on duty at the front desk, no matter what.

You'd think the rape and murder of little Shakeisha a month ago would be enough to make them keep their promise. And it wasn't like Roy to leave the desk unattended. When he had to take a break, he'd go ask one of the men outside to take over for a few minutes. Obie sighed. This was no way to help make this place safe for the kids and the old folks, much less stop Son Teagle's gang from taking over the building.

He walked to the desk. A copy of Ebony lay half opened on it, like Roy had been interrupted while he was reading. He pulled out the chair and sat down, ready to stay there until he came back. Probably had just gone into the recreation room to take a leak.

"Morning to you, Miss Taylor, that dress fits you just right, ought to knock them out in the office today." Obie smiled up at a tall, graceful woman whose body was snugly wrapped in a yellow dress speckled with Yoruba symbols. "Yes, ma'am, you'll surely be the queen of Chestnut Street this beautiful day the Lord has sent."

She grinned and blew him a kiss on the way out the door. "Oughta be 'shamed of yourself, Obie, way you be sweet-talking us all the time."

He had a snappy comeback ready, but just then four kids, followed by their twenty-six-year-old mother, burst out of the elevator and were all over him before he could even say hello.

"Where's the candy?"

"When you going to ride me piggy-back again?"

"He promised me first, didn't you, Obie?"

Their mother, Serena, quickly reined them in. "Obie, you spoil them rotten, one day I'm going to leave them with you for good."

Obie laughed. "I wouldn't mind, one bit." He looked at the kids. "We'd have us a ball, wouldn't we?" They nodded unanimously, thinking perhaps of the homemade oatmeal raisin cookies and fruit punch that always awaited them when they stopped in at the Bullocks' apartment. Then they were off, propelled through the door by Serena.

Obie turned back to Ebony, where Roy had apparently been reading an article about the fifty leading eligible bachelors of the year. Maybe his good buddy, stationed in the Hill project for the past four years, had been hoping he'd make the list some day. Obie didn't get a chance to look at much of the article, what with the elevator banks constantly disgorging folks. All of them had something to say to Obie, who by this point was hurting for sleep.

Around eight-thirty, the elevator traffic slowed down. The building had just about emptied itself out, leaving only the old, the unemployed, and three or four of Son's gang members, embedded in the apartments of decent folk. They'd come back from prison—most of them—settled in with their mothers or grandmothers, and proceeded to sell drugs. That's what the meeting the other night had been all about.

ROY STILL HADN'T COME BACK, and Obie was worried. Given all the problems with security lately, he hadn't wanted to leave the desk unoccupied and go off looking for him. But freed now of the distraction caused by the comings and goings of the residents, he took a careful look at the recreation room door and saw that it was slightly ajar. And wait a minute—Roy's key ring was still in the lock. Yet the room was dark.

Something wrong here.

He quietly pushed the door open and turned the light switch on with his left hand. As he walked, he reached for the gravity knife he always carried in his pants pocket. Might be illegal, but it sure made him feel better. He pulled the knife from his pocket and with a quick flick of his wrist snapped the blade into its locked position.

"You in there, Roy?"

Silence.

"Roy, I said are you in there, man?"

He moved down the wall of the room at a half-crouch, easing towards the still darkened alcove where the restrooms were. When he reached them, he burst into the men's room, knife forward.

He looked into the corner of the bathroom.

Roy's inert body lay sprawled between the corner and an overturned trash can. Blood was still coming from a wound in his throat and spreading over his white shirt with its silver badge. It was all over his blue pants and forming a pool on the floor.

On his shirt lay an envelope addressed to the Men of Africa United. Obie picked it up and was about to open it when he heard what sounded like a stall door opening.

The killer was still there.

Obie reached down and pulled the Glock .9 mm weapon from Roy's holster, then slowly opened the men's room door and walked out.

The sound had come from the ladies' room.

Standing at the side of its door, his body pressed against the wall, Obie knocked real hard.

"Whoever's in there, come on out. You got any shit, drop it."

Silence.

Should he just bust in? No sir, buddy, too old and too smart for that. Good way to get blown away. But if he tried to get to the phone, the killer might come out and fire at him before he reached it. The son of a bitch only had one way out, and that was through him. Shit.

He tried again. "Come out! Hands up."

Through the rusted vents at the top of the door, Obie heard the distinct sound of metal against metal—the killer was locking and loading a clip of bullets into some kind of a machine pistol.

Which meant that Obie was in very deep water.

Whoever was in there would come out soon. No way he was going to stay and wait for the cops to come get him. Obie had to find a way to get out of the rec room. And quick!

What the eye could not see, the eye could not shoot. He'd just turn the tables on the guy and put him in a trap.

He quietly made his way back to the light switch and turned it off, plunging the entire room into darkness. He slammed the door shut, locked it with Roy's keys, and inched his way along the wall towards the security guard desk some twenty-five yards away at the other end of the hall. Just make that phone, let the cops flush the killer out.

With his gun trained on the shut and latticed door, he backed down the hall. An image of house-to-house fighting in Ramadi flashed in his mind. Could surely use some of them mean-assed boys from his old squad right about now. At age forty-five and still hurting from his abdominal wounds suffered in Iraq, he was definitely getting too old for this kind of stuff.

But just a few more feet, and it would be all right.

The door of the recreation room exploded before Obie's eyes—glass shattering, wood splintering. The noise from the killer's machine pistol, an Uzi, reverberated along the painted concrete walls of the hallway.

A boy in his teens kicked the remnants of the door open. He wore dungarees, a red turtleneck shirt, and a blue bandanna tied around the lower part of his face to conceal his identity. The gold chains around his neck were so thick they looked like they belonged to an Egyptian pharaoh. Gold was on his wrists and ring fingers, too.

His machine pistol was raised and pointed towards Obie.

"Drop that gun, son," Obie said. "Drop it and live!"

The Uzi exploded once again, the bullets spewing all over the walls, floors, and ceiling of the hallway. The kid didn't even know how to control the firepower he had in his hands. Obie hit the ground hard, rolled, took aim, and fired to kill. Anger at Roy's death and months of infantry fighting in Iraq left no room in his heart for halfway measures—aim for somebody's legs and they just might shake it off and kill you.

His shots ripped into the boy's chest.

As the teenager fell, he squeezed the trigger. The Uzi sprayed bullets in a chaotic pattern all over the room.

Obie fired again, and the slender body lay silent on the floor. The Uzi clattered onto the blood-soaked tiles.

Obie stood motionless in the hallway for a few seconds, then heard shouting outside and distant sirens coming closer and closer. He went over to the desk, threw the service pistol on it, and walked back down the slippery hallway floors towards the body. On the way, he kicked the Uzi with his foot, sent it flying down the corridor. He reached the corpse and tore the blue kerchief from the face—

"No. Oh, no!"

WHEN THE FIRST COPS ENTERED THE BUILDING and trained their guns on Obie, they found him holding the boy's head in his arms. Obie's face was wet with tears, and great moans came from his powerful body. He was mourning the death of Trevon Teagle, the best center fielder he'd ever coached on the Joseph E. Hill pee-wee baseball team.

When Obie first met him, Trevon had been nine years old, small for his age, angry and hungry all the time. But he'd blossomed into the best. Boy, that little fellow could fly! See him running, eyes turned round on that ball, both arms pumping, twelve years old, glove up in the air. Then that leap towards the sky and the ball. Sudden shrieks, little boys throwing each other all around, happy brown-faced mothers hugging, shouts of "Trevon!" Then off to McDonald's for burgers, fries, and all the milkshakes they could drink, everybody coming over to tell Trevon what a great catch he'd made, what a great future he had. Liquid mercury, that's just what he'd been like on the field. And maybe, just maybe, those first shots of his that had missed Obie—that was on purpose?

"What's your name?" A policeman, shotgun in hand, stood over Obie. "What happened?"

"I just killed this boy here and he used to play Little League for me. He's Son Teagle's baby brother."

"Teagle? Oh, Jesus, you better sit down. You're in a whole mess of trouble."

"Don't worry about me, I been through worse. But my friend Roy, one of the project cops, he's in the bathroom. I can't believe it, but the kid slit his throat." Obie didn't even bother to wipe away the tears on his face. And didn't even know who or what he was crying for—Roy, Trevon, Shakeisha, himself, his family, or the whole sorry state of affairs in this project that had once seemed to him and Dora Lee such a fine place to raise children.

JOHN SARNESE, POLICE CAPTAIN AND COMMANDER OF THE 89TH PRECINCT, had just walked into his office and smelled the coffee brewing when the call came in that an officer was down at the Joseph E. Hill project. The dead cop was Roy Cobb, a great guy and a stellar officer, and of course it had happened at the projects. Damn it all!

He hit the intercom button. "Miss Rutherford, tell Robbie to bring the car around front, I'll be out in two minutes flat." He poured what little coffee had already brewed into a mug, took a swig, and walked over to the mirror. He straightened his tie, put on his cap, patted the blackjack in his back pocket, and headed out into the precinct room.

He looked at the desk sergeant. "Get somebody to sweep the floors, for Christ's sake, and make sure it's done before I get back. I'd like to take a step without feeling things crunch under my feet. And don't forget to make those corrections in yesterday's morning reports. I'm getting tired of having to check over those things after you guys. That's your job."

With that, he was out the front door and hurrying down the concrete steps and into the big black unmarked Chevy with its leather-covered red light inside and the small radio antenna extending from the center of its roof.

He turned to Robbie, the slim, light-brown-complexioned plainclothesman who was his driver for the month.

"Let's get going. The car looks good this morning."

Robbie pulled the cover off the red light, hit the siren switch, and drove slowly down the street. It was blocked by illegally parked civilian cars belonging to the precinct cops.

Once on Cecil B. Moore Avenue, Sarnese's car hit a traffic jam at the corner of Fifteenth Street, where a delivery truck was triple-parked in the midst of a swarm of horn-blowing cars. The driver and his helper were pushing a hand truck loaded with cases of Campbell's chicken noodle soup down a ramp. There the captain's car waited, jammed in on three sides, its siren blaring and red lights and headlights flashing. Sarnese watched other police cars, drawn by the call "officer down," speed past the intersection on their way to the Hill project.

"Enough of this," he said. "Back her up, then pull up on the sidewalk. That's the only way we're going to get out of here."

When his car finally arrived at the project, Sarnese saw about ten empty police vehicles parked at all kinds of awkward angles in the street. It reminded him of the mess outside his station. He'd fix that problem, all right. Just wait until he got back. But right now he had more important things on his mind—one of his cops had been killed, and it shook him to the very core of his soul, almost as much as the death of that little girl Shakeisha a month ago. He'd break that gang if it was the last thing he ever did in his life.

When Sarnese came up, the police guards snapped to attention and saluted. Sarnese walked down the ground floor corridor and saw white-jacketed African-American and Hispanic medical emergency workers waiting while the detectives marked the area with chalk. The police photographers were already snapping pictures.

The captain went straight to the recreation room, where a group of men—some white, some black, some with wild-colored bandannas around their heads, others wearing Phillies baseball caps or Eagles Football T-shirts—sat around a ping-pong table with papers strewn all over it. All had police badges pinned somewhere on their clothes.

Just as the captain entered the room, the precinct's chief detective sergeant looked up from the table.

"Will somebody please turn on the fucking fan?" A younger officer jumped to obey his order, but it was already on, probably running at the highest speed it could.

Obie Bullock sat at the table, his muscular arms propped on either side of the ping-pong net, which was lying flat because its clamps were broken. His yellow short-sleeve shirt was half open at the collar, and he looked dazed.

In the past, Obie had led marches protesting police abuse. And several times he'd called Sarnese himself to report cops sleeping on duty in the parking lot behind the projects. At first Sarnese had been irritated, but then one evening, just on a whim, he'd invited Obie to have a cup of coffee with him down at the local Dunkin Donuts, and before he knew it, their common military service and love of bass fishing had bonded them. Wasn't long before they'd become good friends. And when Obie's stepson, Jason, had been arrested for driving an unregistered vehicle with a suspended license, Sarnese, awakened by a post-midnight call from Obie, had come into the precinct, released the kid with a stern warning, and vacated the arrest. He figured Obie would have done the same for him if the shoe had been on the other foot. They had each other's backs.

Just the other night, Obie had stood up in that meeting about Shakeisha's killing and pledged the support of his organization—the Men of Africa United—to root out the dealers who'd infiltrated his building and the project. And Sarnese had sworn to back them up, so he was feeling pretty bad now. Shit, Bullock wasn't even a cop, wouldn't have the protection of the uniform. And even that didn't mean much these days. If the thugs wanted to kill somebody, they did it.

It wasn't a week since they'd shot a witness dead who was ready to testify against some members of the gang. The detectives heard that Teagle had sent a message from prison to the witness telling him he could either "take his money and lie, or take my bullet and die." The guy had said he didn't care what happened, he wasn't going to stop talking until the last of the gang was locked up. Three days later they found his bullet-ridden body crumpled up in a dumpster outside a deli. As usual, nobody had seen a thing. And Sarnese couldn't even blame them for not talking, because when all was said and done, the folks in the community had to live with Son Teagle's thugs, meet them in the stores, run into them on the streets, cross their paths in the playgrounds, and take their kids to school through groups of them standing on the corners selling drugs. If he had to live in that situation, he'd be scared too.

His brusque nod to the detective sergeant signified that the captain would take charge. He grabbed a folding wooden chair, turned it around so he could rest his arms on its back, then sat down across from Bullock.

"You did a hell of a job this morning, but I guess you know it wasn't exactly the smartest thing you ever did."

"Just what I had to do to get out alive, captain. If I'd seen my way clear to getting to that phone, I would have—"

"We'll cut this interrogation short here and get you down to the station, it'll take a while to get things straightened out."

Bullock, his face grim now, said, "Before we go over, I'd like to call Dora Lee and let her know what's happening. And I'd appreciate it if you could have somebody contact the schools and let my kids know about this, so they don't get the news from nobody else."

"You can call her from my car." Sarnese called out to Robbie. "Find out where the kids are and go over and let them know. After that, you can go down and pick up Mrs. Bullock from work and bring her home. Take one of the precinct cars."

Sarnese and Bullock returned to headquarters, a weather-battered gray stone building with granite steps that had been worn down in the middle.

The television cameras were already there. Reporters elbowed each other, trying to get their microphones and tape recorders close to the two men. Bullock, his shirt stained with sweat, blood, and dirt from the morning's events, kept his face straight ahead and ignored the crowd. Sarnese just pulled his hat down more firmly on his head and kept on walking. When he made it to the top of the steps, he turned to the reporters.

"Just a little bit of silence for a minute, please. We haven't got all the facts yet on what happened over at the Hill project, but in about two hours I'll hold a news conference and tell you everything we know. You'll just have to wait." He and Bullock disappeared into the station house as policemen barred the reporters from entering the building.

Sarnese stopped for a second at the precinct sergeant's desk. "Get somebody out there in the street this minute—I want tickets put on every one of those illegally parked cars. That includes the car of the guy who's going out to give the tickets. No exceptions, and that means you too. I'm sick and tired of this shit. Now I'm going into my office with Mr. Bullock here, and I don't want to be disturbed by anybody, except the detectives when they get back. Hear that!"

TWO HOURS LATER, Captain Sarnese stood quietly by the mayor, the commissioner of police, and Obie Bullock as the mayor opened the press conference. An officer had been killed and his assassin fatally shot by Obie Bullock, the outstanding citizen and army combat vet who now stood by his side. All was in order, the mayor said, and although there would be an inquest as required by law, there would almost certainly be no prosecution of this man who'd seen his duty and done it.

The mayor, a tall, dark-brown-skinned man with streaks of gray in his hair, turned to the commissioner.

"Tell them why this killing took place."

"It was a political assassination, pure and simple." The commissioner raised his arm to show a photo of a bloodstained letter. "This was found pinned to the body of the dead officer. It says, 'This is what awaits every man of the Mau-Mau—that's the abbreviation for the Men of Africa United—especially Obie Bullock.'" He turned and said, "Mr. Bullock, as the founder and head of that organization, might like to comment."

Bullock, looking for all the world like a retired linebacker, moved to the front of the steps at the top of the station house.

"I didn't expect things to be this bad when we started our drive against drugs in the Hill projects and in our community. But I'll be damned if I'm going to let the bad guys take over. Decent folks got a right to live without fear, and with God's help, I'll do my best to see they do." His voice shook slightly. "I loved Roy like a brother, and Trevon...Trevon, he was like another son to me, and I will forever fault myself that I couldn't save him from becoming a thug and a killer. But the pull of the streets and all those gold chains and Cadillac Escalades and five-hundred- dollar sneakers—hey, I just couldn't compete.

"And now look what's happened. One of the best men I ever knew, Roy, is stone cold dead, and Trevon is lying in the morgue next to him. I don't know if the good Lord has ever sent me a worse day than this one, but I'm determined to stay in this fight. Ain't never run from one yet." He shook his head slowly and handed the microphone back to the commissioner.

At the rear of the crowd of reporters, in a sweat-soaked gabardine suit, a short, balding, trim man was scribbling away on a notepad. Sarnese recognized him as Walter Shapiro of the Philadelphia Gazette. He'd been chronicling the activities of the Mau-Mau for the past several months.

"Obie, can you answer one question? Do you have any fear for yourself?"

"Sure I do, Mr. Shapiro—I'm no fool. But I ain't going to let it get the best of me."

"Have you asked for police protection for you or your family?"

Bullock turned to the commissioner. "That's for him to answer."

The commissioner, a Puerto Rican, said all necessary protection would be provided.

The mayor stepped forward. "I just want to emphasize that fact. There'll be no intimidation of good citizens in my administration. That's all for now, the news conference is over."

The television cameramen and reporters followed him and the commissioner, peppering them with questions, until they got into the mayor's black Cadillac and drove off slowly down the street.

It was still partially blocked by the policemen's private cars. But a ticket was tucked under the windshield wipers of each vehicle. Not that this made John Sarnese happy. At any other time, he'd have hoped the commissioner would notice the tickets. But now, what with the killings and all, he was just going through the motions of being his usual hard-nosed self. Somehow he had to find a way to bring some measure of peace to the Joseph E. Hill project and protect those people over there—that was his sworn duty.

And with Teagle, you never knew when or where he would strike next. Nothing was out of bounds for him. Seemed like the prison walls couldn't hold him. Or stop him.

CHAPTER 2

DORA LEE SAID GOODBYE TO OBIE, hung up the phone, and sat unmoving at the receptionist desk at the Spruce Street firm of Raleigh and Waterbottom. Her black hair, done up in cornrows, was only a shade darker than her glistening ebony skin, and her eyes had a slight slant to them. She wore a pale gray linen dress that was sparkling clean, ironed, and starched to perfection. It seemed to deepen the rich blackness of her skin.

A single tear coursed slowly down her cheek. So much trouble.

Just the other morning, she'd dropped a plate of hot cornbread off for Roy on her way out to work, and you'd have thought it was a five-course breakfast from the way he'd thanked her. Just a nice Georgia man, with two grown kids and lots of friends amongst the card-playing old men who hung around in the rec room and swapped jokes with him when the weather was too bad for them to go outside.

And Trevon! She couldn't believe he'd gone so far down the thug road as to kill a cop—one he knew, one who'd tried to help him go straight. Lord knows Obie had done everything possible to help that boy out. Took him on team trips upstate and over in Jersey, attended his graduation from elementary school, bought him a bookpack when Mrs. Teagle couldn't scrounge up the money, gave him books on Jackie Robinson, Ken Griffey Jr., and Tony Gwynn, and now this...it was all just too sad to think about. Like some curse had put been put on black children so they'd vanish from the earth.

Dora Lee turned away from the typewriter and began to sort the mail. About halfway through the pile of letters, her eyes fell on an envelope addressed to her. It was green with borders of red.

She opened the envelope, then screamed.

It contained two sheets of paper and a picture. A message,

written in what looked like blood, was on one sheet: "Bullock, stop fucking with us." The second sheet was a crude map of the route Dora Lee took to get to work. The photo was a snapshot of her, dressed in a springtime paisley dress, as she exited from a nearby subway stop.

Dora Lee was quickly surrounded by white-shirted executives clamoring to know what had happened. Then she saw her best friend, Ruth Lenhardt.

"Dora Lee, why'd you holler like that?"

She put her arms around Dora Lee, who sat stock-still at the desk, the green envelope and its contents resting under her hand.

Dora Lee slowly turned her head towards Ruth. "They want to kill us. Those rotten gangsters think they can run us out of our home. They got another think coming."

She wondered if she sounded brave. She felt terrified.

DORA LEE SAT IN THE FRONT SEAT OF THE CAR as Robbie—such a nice young policeman—headed straight up Broad Street. He was quiet, like he sensed that she needed some time to sort things out. And she really did. She had a lot to think about.

First, there were the children, just two of them at home now. They had to be made safe, and that would be no easy task what with all the activities they were involved in. Sabaya, in her senior year at the High School of Creative and Performing Arts, had the promise of a scholarship to Oberlin College in the fall. But how was she going to concentrate on her piano and keep those fine grades up with all of this violence going on around her? From today on, every time she walked into the recreation room she'd see traces of bloodstains—the janitorial staff would scrub and scrub to get them out, but the walls would never come all the way clean. Dora Lee knew that from the time when the Thompson boy was shot near the eighth floor stairwell. More than that, she knew Sabaya was secretly seeing Hashim, her long-time friend from elementary school who now floated on the fringes of the Teagle gang. Play with fire…

As for Timba, their fifteen-year-old, today's events were bound to twist him inside. He and Trevon had been good friends until a few years back when Trevon tried—unsuccessfully, praise the Lord—to recruit him as a drug runner. Not long afterward Trevon put his hands on Sabaya's butt, propositioned her, then called her a cock tease when she told him to get lost. Despite being younger, Timba sought him out and whipped him good. Don't mess with his sister! But though he was a great athlete, strong and quick like his Dad, Timba was doing poorly in school. He was already walking a narrow path between the streets and the books, and she didn't want to see him fall off like her son Jason had before Obie came into their life eighteen years ago.

And Obie, sweet and impossible man! He would take everything that had happened today real personal-like, and there was no telling what he'd do now that Teagle had crossed the line and threatened his family. Wouldn't surprise her one bit to see him sweep through the stairwells by himself one night and toss any dealer he could get his hands on right down the steps. And that just wouldn't do, what with him being the head usher at the church and all. It had taken a long time for her to get him going to church regular and trying to keep that temper of his in check.

Most of all, Dora Lee was worried about Obie and her. Credit card bills that had somehow piled up, the coming college tuition, his night shift work, and all of his anti-drug activities were eating away at the comfort between them, the closeness. She loved him too much to see that happen.

And she had final exams coming up in her secretarial science and computer courses next week. She was already behind in the reading. And what were they to do for dinner tonight?

Lord, Lord. Lord!

She looked out the window and then up at the blue sky.

Jesus, please help me. A hymn flowed through her mind:

You just ask the savior to help you,
Comfort, strengthen and keep you.
Jesus is able to help you,
He will carry you through!

The verse repeated itself in her head, over and over again. Just that one verse. She saw Reverend Johnson, short and dark, singing that song in his husky voice from the pulpit last Sunday. The power of the music had lifted her soul then, and she decided now that she would face this problem as she had faced every other one in her life. She would continue to praise God and thank him for her many blessings. Yes, she would! He will carry you through.

The patrol car pulled up in front of the police station. The polite young officer said, "Mrs. Bullock, good luck to you. You and your husband have made us real proud." Dora Lee knew what he meant. African-Americans around the city had been uplifted by the Bullocks' struggle against the drug dealers.

Little did he or they know the cost. And some of it was real personal. It had been a month and a half since she and Obie had made love.

WHEN OBIE DROVE UP in front of the Joseph E. Hill project for the second time that day, he was bone-weary. Just that morning, things had been looking up a bit—kids fine, Babe Ruth league about to begin, Sabaya all set to take a special summer music course. And then there would have been the August church picnic, and the annual family reunion trip to Pine Hill, just outside of Gastonia, North Carolina. And things with Dora Lee might have gotten sweeter once they were down there.

It had been all too simple, too good. Now everything had crashed down around him. He'd already been in trouble. Now, just like that, he and his family were in serious danger.

It was five o'clock, and as Obie and his family walked into the courtyard of the project, the old men were still out playing cards and checkers. But this time nobody greeted Obie warmly or teased him. For one thing, he and his family were accompanied by two white officers, their assigned bodyguards.

For another, about a hundred yards away from the playing tables, sitting on the swings and playing loud rap music on a gigantic ipod box, was a group of seven or eight teenage boys. Their bodies were swaying to the music of the M.C. Rappers, and as they danced, they kept pointing towards the Bullock family. They were friends of Trevon and junior affiliates of the Teagle gang.

Obie knew them all by name. Wasn't one of them he hadn't tried to set right, but the dealers had too many things to offer them and he'd lost the contest for what was in fact those kids' lives—five years from now they'd all be dead, crippled by gunshot wounds, or stuck away in some prison cell.

One cop turned back to Obie and said, "Want me to shut them up?"

Obie, who was holding Dora Lee by her hand while the kids walked in front of them, said, "Leave 'em be."

As the Bullocks approached the entrance to the apartment building, the boys started to shout.

"Going to get you, Timba!"

"Better watch out, faggot!"

Timba had a fade haircut and a confident walk, with just a hint of the street in his stride. He suddenly darted across the playground, and before anybody could stop him, he'd crashed into the leader of the gang and snatched up the boombox. He was about to throw it on the sidewalk when one of the cops came up from behind him, grabbed the box, and held Timba back. The other cop gave the boombox to its owner and scattered the kids.

They retreated to a far corner of the yard, where they regrouped. Their leader turned up the machine even louder and shouted, "Yo, Timba, you faggot, your ass is mine!" as the Bullock family and its police escort finally entered the apartment building.

Just as everybody was on the elevator and the doors about to close, Obie stepped out, nodded to the cops, and said, "See the family upstairs, I'll be right up. I got something to do."

He walked slowly out of the building door and towards the gang of boys. Now the group at the table came to life.

"Obie, man, what you doing, you crazy or something?"

"Don't be no fool now, Obie!"

He kept on walking across the yard. When he got within ten feet of the teenagers, he said, "Duwan, Djersha, Lumumba, and the rest of you all, come over here for a minute." His voice was low but clear—every word seemed to echo through the yard. "I want to tell you something. And turn that thing down."

Looks of astonishment and disbelief came over their faces. But at one time, when they were all younger, Obie had been one of the few caring men in their lives. Some vestige of gratitude remained. Duwan, their leader, nodded to the fellow with the boombox and he turned it off.

"Mister Bullock, ain't nothing you can tell us. You offed Trevon, and he was our brother. End of story."

Obie's eyes ranged across the angry faces of the boys, all of whom wore their hair in Rastafarian style and their balloon-style pants low on their hips. Tattoos adorned their arms.

"Trevon is dead and gone and I'm truly sorry I had to kill him. Ain't nothing to be proud of. But he cut Roy's throat, then tried to machine-gun me. So I killed him stone dead. And that's an awful waste of a human life, because Trevon could have been a lawyer or a doctor or a major league star, not just some janitor like me. The sky was the limit for him, and he never got off the ground. But that ain't neither here nor there right now, question is about you all."

Duwan looked at Obie like he was a fool. "Us?"

"Yes, you!" Obie aimed his finger dead in the center of Duwan's chest. "Because you're going to end up the same way as Trevon if you don't change your ways. Find you all a job, a school, something to do, because cops or no cops, your bosses upstairs or not"—he jerked his head up towards the apartments that had been taken over by the dealers—"I will personally hold each and every one of you responsible for anything that happens to anybody in my family, or for that matter any of the decent folks that live in this here project."

The boys were silent, and Duwan, along with the rest of them, almost unconsciously took a step backwards from Obie. They all knew what he'd done to a six foot 250-pound lunatic who'd come swinging a knife in the midst of the playground one day, threatening to kill the screaming toddlers. Had walked straight up to the man, grabbed him in a judo lock, turned him around, and busted his knife arm before he could slash even one of those children.

Obie folded his arms across his chest. "Now, you all go on home and mourn Trevon—that's the right and proper thing to do. Mrs. Teagle can use a lot of sympathy right now, and I feel sorry for her. But don't come messing with me and my family, 'cause you'll find a heap of trouble."

Out of the corner of his eye, Obie saw one boy who seemed to be trying to conceal himself behind the others. He was light-brown-skinned, wore his hair bald and was dressed in a summer shirt and regular-cut blue slacks.

"You, Hashim, don't be trying to hide from me. Especially don't want to see your ass nowhere around here. Now, all of you, get!" He turned and walked off, and when he reached the door and looked back, they were gone.

The men at the table were mute. Obie had walked into the lion's den and out again. A couple of them kids would as soon shoot a man as take a drink of water.

ON THE ELEVATOR TO THEIR TENTH-FLOOR APARTMENT, Obie felt like his mind was running a mile a minute. Never mind that his family was at risk. He had to be back at work tonight by twelve o'clock and hadn't even had one minute of sleep.

When he reached his door, the two policemen were waiting outside. The older one said, "We'll be out here till eleven o'clock, when our relief shows up. Any problems, just give us a yell. And I'd appreciate it if you could let us have a couple of kitchen chairs."

Obie thanked the men, said he'd get them the chairs, and entered the apartment. The door opened directly into a living room painted white but full of the earth colors of Africa. Hanging on the wall above the heavily upholstered blue couch was a brown and yellow Kinte cloth with pictures of African villages, and women—tall and willowy like Dora Lee—carrying water from the wells to their thatch huts. In the background, men sat smoking their pipes and pointing towards Mt. Kilimanjaro.

On another wall was a reproduction from the Philadelphia Afro-American Museum, a Nubian sculpture of an African woman's head. Whenever Obie looked at the picture, he was drawn into a stream of time that flowed back to his very wellsprings, so much did the woman's face remind him of his grandmother from Rocky Mount, North Carolina.

In another part of the room were photographs of both Dora Lee's and Obie's families, with neatly typed captions beneath each glass-covered picture. There was grandfather Conrad Bullock, standing with his family in front of a whitewashed church, straw hat in his hand. Beside him stood grandmother Bullock, dressed in white and holding a black parasol to shade herself from the fierce North Carolina sun. The boy children, including Obie's father, were dressed in knickers, and the girls, their hair plaited in long pigtails and tied with ribbons, wore white dresses and wide straw hats.

There was also a picture of Dora Lee's mother in a red blouse and black skirt, her school uniform, as she stood in a class of students in Barbados. Beside her hung a picture of her husband, immaculate in the red and white uniform of the Barbados police. The floor of the room was covered with a deep-pile red rug they'd found tucked away among remnants in the back of a store over across the Delaware Bridge in Jersey. It had been a prize find.

The centerpiece of the living room was a mahogany table Dora Lee polished most every day. A big black Bible was in the middle of the table, and either Obie or Dora Lee had read aloud from it every Sunday morning as long as they'd been married. At first they'd read to each other—Jason, Dora Lee's boy, well on his way to his first incarceration in reform school, would have none of it. But when Sabaya and Timba were old enough to understand, Obie and Dora Lee had taken turns reading to them on succeeding Sundays. The children stopped protesting when they realized it didn't do any good.

Family prayer and the Bible always came before the Sunday morning breakfast of biscuits, scrambled eggs, bacon, and grits Obie cooked himself. Dora Lee would stay in bed until time to eat. He'd never missed a Sunday, even when, in the early days of his marriage, his head throbbed from the bourbon still flowing in his bloodstream. What with the church and all, he'd hardly ever touched the hard stuff for a good seven or eight years now. Dora Lee didn't like it, and it set a poor example for the children.

But he needed a good belt of whiskey right now. The images of Roy and Trevon were running in his head like a movie he couldn't get to stop. And he had truly loved Trevon, could hear him now talking softly with Timba years ago when he used to sleep over, saying he was going to be an airplane pilot, go all over the world, then maybe one day invent his own kind of airplane, so big it could carry almost a thousand people. Timba had said it was impossible, but Obie could still hear Trevon telling him no, he could do it, he just had to keep reading those airplane books. "You just wait. You be seeing what I can do one day."

Obie definitely had to have him a drink of whiskey.

He walked straight back into the kitchen, took down a bottle from the cupboard, and made himself a stiff bourbon on the rocks.

He heard Dora Lee tell the kids to start their homework. She came into the kitchen.

"What in the world are you doing, Obie Bullock?"

"Don't be starting up with me now, baby, I ain't in the mood."

"Who is? It's been a terrible day for all of us, that doesn't mean you have to start drinking whiskey again." Dora Lee began to take pots down from the cupboard. "And I don't know what we're going to have for dinner, either."

Obie filled the ice tray and put it back in the freezing compartment. "You'll find something, baby. I'm going to sit for a while, then we can talk these things out after dinner."

"Fine, but first do me a favor and throw that stuff out."

"Nope." He headed to their bedroom, where he sat down in a scuffed leather chair they'd bought years ago at the Salvation Army store. He reclined the chair, put the drink on its arm, and watched the news for a few minutes.

Suddenly his own face appeared on the screen. Lord, it was lined. Life had really done a job on him, and it wasn't through with him yet. All them childhood years in the tobacco fields and young years of military campaigns and maneuvers—always under the hot sun—had told on him. And his fight against the drug dealers would probably have him looking like he was in his fifties by next month, if it didn't kill him dead first—

A young black woman, light-complexioned and somewhat hard of voice and look, had shoved a microphone in his face.

"Do you think, Mr. Bullock, there's anything you might have done to spare the boy's life? After all, he was only sixteen years old." Obie watched with some satisfaction as the camera cut away without recording his reply. He'd told the woman, "You got no idea what you talking about."

He picked up his glass, got up from the chair, and walked out to the patio balcony that overlooked a big water fountain in the middle of the project. The sight of the fountain calmed him under all circumstances. Almost like it could play a song for him. And he needed that water song now. That and a good long talk with his brother Boatwright down in Carolina, because all of this confusion around the killings was going to make it hard for him to continue looking after Justine and Uncle Ward, who lived up in Germantown. Justine stayed with their aging uncle, and it was Obie who took her to treatment every week and saw to his uncle's prescription needs. Boat would surely have some good advice on how he could handle that.

And home base had to be made secure. First and foremost, the dealers down below in those apartments had to be evicted—they were the real headquarters operation for Teagle's gang in North Philly. By hook or crook, the Mau-Mau had to get rid of them.

Else little black boys would keep on growing up to the point where they were shoving one another out of the way to get in line for a short life or the sure fate of a life in prison—almost begging for it every day in their songs, screaming for it with their body motions, saying I'm going to fuck with everybody's space and peace and quiet till you put my black ass in jail. Like prison was their natural home, the place God intended for them to be.

Obie was looking out at the water when he heard a knock on the bedroom door. He turned and watched Sabaya come into the room. My, how his little girl had grown up.

She was medium tall and wore her hair cut short in fluffy, shiny curls. Obie noticed how the tight dungarees and the bright yellow blouse showed off her curves. Every day brought her closer to womanhood, and every day he worried about the temptations surrounding her in these mean-assed streets.

He turned back to the balcony, knowing his daughter would come up, sit down on the little wooden bench, and talk to him while he kept looking down at the fountain.

"Daddy, I'm scared. What are we going to do now?" Sabaya fingered the cross on the gold chain she wore around her neck. He'd given it to her on her fourteenth birthday.

Obie shook the ice cubes in the now empty glass of bourbon. "Right now, we ain't going to do nothing but get us a good dinner. Go on in and help your mama. We been through a lot already, always managed to come out okay. We'll get out of this one too."

"But this time it's different, Daddy. How am I supposed to get down to J.C. Penney's this summer for my job?"

Bullock put his arm around her shoulder and led her back towards the kitchen and a fresh drink. "Just come on, now, I'll take care of everything."

"But if I don't work, where will we get the money for my clothes for school this fall?"

"Told you, don't worry yourself about it."

Dora Lee had a pot of water boiling for spaghetti and was pouring a jar of meat sauce into a pot. The counter in the cubbyhole of a kitchen was covered with salad makings.

Dora Lee stopped tearing the lettuce. "Please don't take another drink—you know you have to go to work tonight. It's already almost seven, next thing you know you'll be losing your job. Then where will we be?"

"Mama's right, what will we do then?"

Obie eased his way past Dora Lee, almost pinning her against the stove as he reached for the bottle. "You all are worse than a pack of hound dogs. Just leave me be."

He made his drink and thrust the bottle back into the cabinet. As he walked out of the kitchen, he noticed Timba on the telephone in his room, really a corner of the living room that had been set apart by wooden screens. Timba slept there on a convertible sofa.

Obie knocked on the wooden shutters—Dora Lee insisted on knocking even though Timba's space was only semi-private.

"You'll have to get off the phone," he said. "Got to make an important call."

"Sure, Dad, just give me a minute."

Obie hurried back to the bedroom. The rules of the Essex Custodial Company where he was a shift supervisor required at least three hours' notice before not coming in or they gave you an automatic one-day suspension. He had exactly three minutes to make the call.

He phoned his boss.

"Obie. Hey, big fellow, glad you called. All the folks around here are sitting around watching you on television. You had some kind of day. We're all behind you. I'll take over for you tonight, so don't even think about coming in. You want to take another day, just let the office know in the morning."

"You're a real prince, man. Appreciate it."

He went back out to the balcony, sat down on his canvas-covered picnic chair, picked up his glass of bourbon, and started to browse through a copy of Outdoors Today, not really seeing anything he was looking at. But halfway through the issue he stopped, entranced by one picture—a fisherman in high rubber boots stood in the middle of a stream where white water was splashing and foaming off the rocks. On the other end of the fisherman's line, a gray trout with brown speckles that glistened in the sunlight was leaping high in the air, its eyes wild and defiant, as if sheer will could break the hook loose from its mouth.

But the fisherman had a smile on his face. He knew that poor fish was his. The strong take the weak. Obie shook his head and let the magazine rest in his lap. Just stared off into space, remembering quiet days in the sun, toes squiggling in the muddy old pond, showing Justine how to take the perch off the hook and scale it. And far off in the distance, the sound of Pop Bullock calling, "Obie, boy, time for the evening chores." Justine, big saucer eyes fixed on him, saying, Just let me catch one more, Obie, Papa won't mind. No, he won't mind for you, 'cause you're the apple of his eye, but he will surely make me pay for it come tomorrow, don't know how, maybe a slap upside the head or some of his special kind words like, "You ain't going to be nothing, boy, never!" So he'd gather up what was left of the cornbread and cold bacon, wrap it in cotton cloth, and lead his little sister back up to the shotgun shack they called home.

Before he knew it his glass was empty again, and he faced the options of staying out on the balcony without a drink or going back into the living room to that disapproving family of his. Not only that, but there were decisions to make about their lives and welfare. Man, it had been a lot easier in the army. All he had to worry about there was a squad of men. And they pretty much knew their jobs and how to take care of each other.

The screen door opened and Dora Lee came out on the balcony, a can of Diet Coke for him in one hand, a heaping plate of spaghetti and meatballs in the other. She put the food down on the little serving table.

"I'll be back in a minute with the garlic bread and the salad."

Obie drew the serving table up beside him. Two minutes later, Dora Lee was back with the other food and a cup of tea for herself.

"Baby, we got to talk." she said. "We knew we were in for big trouble when we started to fight the drug dealers two years ago. Looks like God didn't mean for things to be easy for us. But the kids are another thing. We got to make some decisions and we got to make them now. Not tomorrow. We your family, and we're counting on you. Those children in there got to be out of here tomorrow morning. Where to, Obie?"

Dora Lee was standing with her body bent over the rail, her elbows resting on it. It was a position that made it natural for him to put his hand on her bottom, and that's what he did, setting down his knife and spoon for a second, just so he could feel that wonderful springy firmness and run his hand up and down the length of her legs.

There'd been a time when she loved that too. But now she brushed his hand aside.

"We got no time for messing around. Let's talk."

"Soon as I finish eating this good spaghetti. Get me a cup of coffee now, would you?"

Dora Lee sighed and looked at him and shook her head. "Be right back with it."

When she returned, Obie said, "Let's get down to business. What do you want to do? Any ideas?"

"We should get the kids out of here and down south within the next couple of days. As a matter of fact, we should get them packed up tonight and out of here tomorrow morning if we can."

"But baby, Timba's pitching his first game of the season tomorrow night. And there's still two weeks of school left, they'll be taking final exams in a few days."

"They're still children and it's our job to protect them. We'll just have to sit them down and tell them what's what."

Obie tightened his hand on the Diet Coke can. She wanted to move too fast. He was about to tell her that when she said, "Honey, you killed Son Teagle's kid brother. Now tell me, what would you do if you were in his place?"

Obie shrugged his shoulders. "I can't believe Son would order a direct killing of a cop like that. He'd have to know it would bring them down on his boys here like a ton of bricks. Nope, I'm thinking it was the work of some of them hotheads, must have corralled Trevon into it."

"That don't make no difference. He's dead, and you did it, not them."

Obie set the can down, reached over and put his hand under Dora Lee's chin. "Son knows how I thought about Trevon, many's the time Mrs. Teagle thanked me for all I done for that boy. Not that it really matters now, 'cause it just adds one more log to the fire and Son is one crazy son of a bitch—you're right, got to get the kids out of here, come hell or hurricane."

Dora Lee caught hold of his hand. "Honey, you know I'm beginning to believe it's true what they say about no good deed goes unpunished. We should just get ourselves together and get out of here, like everybody else who's got any sense. Ain't worth sacrificing everything for all these ungrateful folks around here. See how many neighbors have come by this evening—not one."

"Come on, Dora Lee, kind of hard for them to get by those cops. They'll be along, just you wait and see. Now let's talk to the kids." He picked up his now empty plate.

When they got back to the living room, he saw that Timba had closed the shutter door, signaling his withdrawal from the family and the adult world. Probably a little pissed he'd had to get off the telephone. Sabaya's door was also closed. He knocked, and she said for him to come in.

She was sitting with her head bent over a biology textbook lying open on the white lacquered desk that ran the length of her bedroom wall and served both as a study and entertainment center. Piles of old CDs—now all loaded into her Ipod— were neatly stacked in cubbyholes in the wall unit. Under the far end of the desk, in another compartment, lay dozens of classical musical scores. On one wall of the room were concert posters, above her desk a church calendar with religious quotes for each month. Today it read, "God is my strength, He girds me with righteousness and maketh my way plain."

Sabaya, looking studious in her gold-rimmed eyeglasses, glanced up from the book. "Dad. I didn't mean anything by what I said in the kitchen."

"It's okay, darling, this hasn't been the easiest day for any of us. Come on into the living room now, we got to talk this whole thing over."

In the living room Dora Lee was sitting on the couch with Timba, his walnut brown features so much like his mama's.

He said, "Let's get it on, Dad."

"We'll do just that," Obie said as he took the easy chair. "But first, we'll have prayer."

After the family had joined hands together in a circle and asked God for strength, Obie began by explaining their situation and the dangers all around them. There was no way their safety could be secured under the present circumstances. Captain Sarnese had told him there just weren't enough cops. The ones outside their door would be there only for a few days.

Then Dora Lee took both children by their hands.

"We're sending you down to Uncle Boatwright's in the morning."

Timba stood up, his hands clenched at his side. "No, Mama— I've got to pitch tomorrow night, everybody's counting on me. It's not fair. And what about school?"

Tears came to Dora Lee's eyes. She leaned forward on the couch and put both of her hands on her knees. She always did that when she was upset.

"We don't have a choice. You don't have a choice. I'll deal with the schools, and I'm sure when I explain the circumstances, they'll make allowances—"

"You know how my high school is about examinations and recitals," Sabaya said. "I've got a straight-A average going into the finals, and this will wreck it, and I'll lose my scholarship. Let me stay at Big Mama's house till graduation. She's way downtown, nobody knows where she lives."

Obie looked at Dora Lee.

Timba said, "I'm staying if she stays. My baseball and grades are just as important. Besides, I'm a man, and you may need my help. No way she stays here and I go to North Carolina. Fair is fair, and—"

"Calm down, you two," Obie said. "We already know everybody isn't always going to agree when we have family talk. So this is what we're going to have to do. Sabaya can stay at her grandmama's until school's over. Then she goes to North Carolina. Timba, you're out of here tomorrow morning. I'm sorry, son, but there's a lot more at stake with your sister, and there's baseball in Gastonia. The team here's just going to have to do without you this summer. This is wartime now."

"But Dad—"

"Hush, now," Dora Lee said. "Let's hold hands." She began to sing, "Jesus Keep Me Near the Cross, There's a Precious Fountain."

They sang one verse of the hymn, then all of them squeezed each other's hands. Dora Lee said, "May the Lord watch between me and thee while we are absent one from another. Amen!"

There was a hard knock at the door. Obie opened it.

One of the policemen, the older one with the decorations on his blouse and the tired eyes, said, "There's a man out here wants to see you. Leroy Merriweather, says he's in your organization."

"Sure, let him in." The policeman stood aside, and in walked Leroy, dressed in a white skullcap, a white dashiki, and a pair of red slacks.

"Uncle Leroy, they not going to let me pitch tomorrow," Timba said. "Tell them that's not fair."

Leroy put his arm around Timba's shoulder. "This is one time I can't try to change your folks' minds. Them Teagle boys don't play games." He turned and kissed Sabaya on the cheek. "How's my lady? You just get prettier and prettier every day. Beauty, brains, and talent. Don't make them no better than you, darling. Joy of your daddy's life."

Obie was all smiles. "Hey, man, where you been? Call for you yesterday, and here you come today."

"I just saw on television what happened. Already contacted all the guys and put them on alert. Figured you'd be too busy with the family to deal with that." Leroy grabbed Obie's arm.

"Let's go out on the terrace, I don't trust nobody these days. I'd swear to goodness your phone is tapped—I mean, I know it. Shit, everybody knows them dealers got snitches inside the police department."

"You're right, man. We got to walk this one all alone."

"You know they're going to be coming after you strong and hard."

"That's all right. The main thing is the kids, and we got that one handled. They be gone in the morning."

"What about Dora Lee?"

Obie had anticipated that question but hadn't quite figured out what to do about her. For one thing, they'd never been separated from one another since their marriage eighteen years ago.

But she wouldn't be safe in their apartment. And there was no way she'd be able to go to work on the subway in the morning without an escort, and even then who knew what the Teagle people might have in mind?

"You're the war counselor," he said. "What do you think?"

"I know Dora Lee," Leroy said. "She's not going nowhere if it means she has to leave her job and stop going to night school. Truth is, she should go south with the kids. But anyways, she can't stay here, not with you working nights. By tomorrow, we got to find her another place to stay."

"We'll have her out of here by the morning. I'll be holding the fort down all by myself."

Leroy said, "We'll have two armed brothers living here day and night. You still got your heat, right?"

Obie nodded.

Leroy fingered his prematurely graying beard. "One more thing, man. You know they going to bury Trevon on Friday. Bound to kick up even more trouble. Some of the folks in this project are mouthing off about you killing that thug, saying you shouldn't of shot a kid."

"It don't take much to turn your own people against you," Obie said. "But we can't let that stop us. Got to push on."

Darkness had fallen over the city. The two men stood on the balcony and watched the lights coming on in the project across the way. Had they forgotten anything? Obie didn't think so, but they talked for a long time trying to cover all the angles.

....

TWO HOURS LATER, LEROY HAD LEFT and the adult Bullocks were in their bedroom. They'd decided Dora Lee would temporarily stay with her friend Ruth, who lived out in Ardmore. They'd take the train together into Thirtieth Street Station, then the bus to work. Dora Lee was sure she'd be given a job in the inner office and thus be relatively safe while at work.

It was one o'clock in the morning. The children were asleep and Dora Lee had finished packing all their clothes and made all the necessary phone calls to relatives and friends. She'd still have to take the day off tomorrow and put Timba on the plane to Gastonia in the morning. And he knew she'd have to miss her evening classes tomorrow night, because she hadn't been able to do her homework.

Obie had taken his shower and gotten into bed. He'd thought about taking a nightcap and had decided against it. He lay in the bed leafing through a fishing magazine while Dora Lee, in the bathroom, prepared for bed.

He was deeply worried about the family's finances—the last-minute airfare to Gastonia alone was sky-high, and the credit card companies were already calling. Bastards, with their twenty-five-percent interest rates and twenty-five-dollar penalties for late payments! And Sabaya could lose her Oberlin scholarship if her grades dropped. He'd tried to make the project safe for people, and now his family had to leave. It wasn't fair, but then neither was life itself.

Obie heard the sound of the shower going in the bathroom. Maybe, since it would be their last night together, they'd make love tonight. But he knew Dora Lee was really tired. They used to pleasure each other a whole lot, but it surely had been a while. Before she'd started night classes at the community college, before he'd started the Mau-Mau.

He looked up from his magazine. Dora Lee had come out of the bathroom, a white towel wrapped around her head and a white bathrobe covering her ebony body. She came over to his side of the bed, pulled the magazine away, bent over and kissed him. He drew her close.

He put one arm under her neck, opened the robe and let his other arm fall on the wonderful curves of her hips. Her firm breasts lay against his chest. A deep warmth bound their two bodies together. It was with great reluctance that Obie brought himself to sit up so he could take his pajamas off. Even one second away from that body was too long.

Dora Lee said, "Honey, I just want to say I'm sorry we haven't been—"

"SShhhh, baby. Only thing matters is you're here now."

He got back into the bed, once again drew her close to him, and wondered at the luck that had brought him, just a poor working man, such a woman. Her thighs were smooth as velvet, and her high, proud breasts had nipples that alternately stiffened and softened as he trailed his fingers over them.

Dora Lee quieted herself under his touch, and when he put a hand on her buttocks and gently pulled her tight against him, she slipped her arms around his neck. As their bodies first slowly and then more rapidly moved together, he began to hum his favorite song, the one she said had made her love him—"So Amazing." After a while, as was her way, she began humming the tune while he softly mouthed the words. As her body began to twist against him, he stopped singing and kissed her. Their tongues played together, then everything he had was playing with everything she had, and it seemed to him like they were one body, just all mixed up in each other. Nothing, absolutely nothing, was better than her sweet loving.

When all was over, he held her close beside him, kissed her gently on her breasts, and said, "No way I could ever tell you how much I love you, baby."

"Me too." She sounded sleepy.

He said, "Come what may in the days ahead, our strong love and God's grace going to see us through. Ain't no man, beast, gang, or force of nature going to break us."

They fell asleep wrapped tightly in each other's arms.

CHAPTER 3

OBIE HAD DONE EVERYTHING HE HAD TO DO on this sad day after the killing. Timba was on his way to Carolina, Sabaya safe down at her grandmama's, and Dora Lee had been dropped out in Ardmore at her friend Ruth's house.

But one big thing remained: to go down to the ball field, face his Ernie Banks Yellowjackets, and explain to them how the killings yesterday would affect their season. Many of his kids had known Trevon and looked up to him—after all, he'd been a great ball player, was Son's brother, and when he wasn't trying to outdo Son in his meanness and cursing, had an appealing personality. That was the hell of it—God didn't seem to discriminate too much between good and evil folks when it came to making people like you.

The doorbell rang. Must be Reverend Johnson, who'd promised to accompany Obie to the game. Said he wanted to see the new uniforms bought with Macedonia's church funds, but Obie knew he also wanted to give him spiritual comfort, just didn't want to say so knowing how Obie liked to tough things out on his own. But right now his inner core was really being tested and he could use all the help, spiritual and otherwise, he could get.

He looked through the peephole, then let the pastor in. "Glad to see you, Reverend."

They embraced, then the pastor said, "Where are the police guards, aren't they supposed to be here?"

"No, the family's safe now, and my boys will be coming over starting tomorrow night, so I called Captain Sarnese and told him to take the cops away. Just don't like the idea of having them around me all the time, makes me all jumpy and everything." He motioned the pastor towards a seat. "I'll be ready to go soon as I call my brother in Carolina and see Timba got there all right—

that boy's smart as a whip, but I wouldn't put it past him to walk right on by his uncle and not even see him. But I guarantee you he'll see the nearest hot dog stand."

The pastor smiled and picked up a book by Reverend T.D. Jakes. "Take your time, I'll just read this for a bit and see if I can't pick up some inspiration for Sunday's sermon. Sometimes the well runs dry, you know."

Obie laughed. "Not with you, pastor. I'll be right back."

Assured by Boatwright that Timba had arrived safely—after fifteen minutes of panic, they'd found him eating a hot fudge sundae at a Ben and Jerry's counter—Obie and the pastor went downstairs. The police escort might have been removed from his apartment door, but the lobby was flooded with police and the recreation center guarded by the two officers who'd been relieved from duty upstairs. A new officer, a young Dominican woman far too pretty to be a cop, sat at the table where Roy had been. Obie noticed that she too was reading the article on eligible black males. He sure wished somebody had gotten rid of that magazine by now.

The courtyard, except for the card players, was empty. The heavy police presence had driven the teenagers away, and the ordinary residents of the Hill project were all inside their apartments, gun-shy by now, frightened of being caught in some crossfire—any crossfire—from God knows who firing the weapons for God knows what reason. Just practicing self-preservation, using good common sense, he figured.

In the car, the pastor said, "How's Dora Lee taking all of this, seems to me it's an awful lot for her to bear—she had such high hopes when she first came to live here with Jason."

"I got to tell it straight, Reverend, she can't take too much more of this stuff. See, she really had her fill of violence when Jason got involved with those gangs, and I sometimes wonder how our marriage ever survived all of that, him getting sent away and all. Thing is, she just has to leave now, no matter what, and I'm not about to give up, no matter what." He drew his hand across his throat. "She's had it up to here."

"You got to keep praying, Obie, and things will work out for you all. God is with you in this, and he's not going to cut out on you."

Obie, stopped now at a red light, leaned forward to look up and see when the light changed.

"The thing is, I practically weep every time I see one of these kids of mine out there go wrong, because I know all of the good that's in them, and I know what they had to go through just to graduate from elementary school. And it's like I'm their only hope. When's the last time you saw a black man walking with his kids somewhere—just walking, that's all I mean, leading them by the hand, having fun with them, being a kid along with them?" He was so carried away that he took his hand off the steering wheel. "Never, practically never! Nobody's left to carry the load. And Dora Lee don't understand that!"

"She does, Obie, she saw how you finally turned Jason around. You got to remember how hard she struggled when they were all alone. That's one strong hard-working woman, but you can only ask so much of one person—she just may not have enough strength for the battle any more. Like I said, prayer has got to be the answer. And you love her. That, too."

"More than anything in life. And I need her now more than ever. 'Cause, truth is I got more on my plate right now than I can handle, what with everything here and my sister and uncle up in Germantown." He sighed. "But right now I got to face these kids, and that should be something, what with how they thought about Trevon." They'd arrived at the ball field. He parked the car and opened the door for the pastor.

It was six o'clock and most of the players were already there, although some few were just getting in from school or from their after-school jobs. A cluster of yellow-and-white-clad boys from his team were gathered off to the side of the dusty field. His assistant coaches, Shaka and Sonny, were already there talking to the kids, who were seated in a circle on the ground, some holding bats, others with their treasured leather gloves already on.

Obie turned to the pastor. "Reverend, if you don't mind, I'd like to talk to them myself. Afterwards, maybe you can come over and I'll explain to them about the contribution the church made for the uniforms."

"I'll wait for you here by the car till you're ready for me."

The walk from the car to the benches—maybe a hundred yards—was one of the longest Obie had ever made in his life. Many's the time he'd walked it with Trevon at his side, because he often drove him over to practice. And for a second it seemed he was still there, only this time just a quiet presence whispering, "Coach, I missed you on purpose, I really did."

As Obie approached the team, the coaches and the boys fell quiet, like he was walking towards them with Trevon's name traced out in blood on his white T-shirt. You could tell the team hadn't expected him to show up.

"Finish up your stuff, Shaka," Obie said. "When you're done, I'd like to say a few words to them." He moved off to the side so that he stood, arms folded, halfway between the coaches and the boys.

Their eyes never left Shaka's face, as if they were deliberately avoiding looking at Obie, trying to postpone the moment when they'd have to reconcile in their minds two different Coach Bullocks. The first had comforted them when they struck out, cheered them when they hit a blooper single, and routinely paid for their equipment out of his pocket when they didn't have the money to pay for it themselves. The second was the man who'd put four shots in Trevon's chest, so closely spaced that an ice cream container lid could have covered them all—"expert military marksman," one of the papers had said.

Shaka, sweating from the June heat and humidity, wrapped up his remarks. "So that's the game plan. You guys have had a good pre-season, gone through a lot of conditioning, and are about as ready for this as you'll ever be. I'm going to turn things over to Obie now, and afterwards I'll give you the starting line-up cards."

Obie stepped up. "Good afternoon, ErnieBanksmen!"

"Afternoon, Coach!"

Obie pulled his baseball hat down tight on his head. "You

all know what happened yesterday. Me and Dora Lee had to send Timba away, he won't be pitching this season. It was against his wishes, and he feels mighty bad about it and wishes you boys the best."

Not a word.

"And me, considering all that's happened, I'm going to have to turn over the coaching responsibilities this summer to Shaka and Sonny here, they'll do a good job...."

A low undercurrent of protest began.

"That ain't fair."

"No, Coach, that ain't right."

"We never played that way before."

Obie raised his hand. "That's the way it's got to be, fellows. I don't have to draw no chart for you to see the reasons why it just wouldn't work out. This thing has hit me pretty hard, and I hope you all see where hanging out with the wrong people and in the wrong places can get you. It don't take much—you boys are young and there's folks out there just waiting to tempt you, make you cross that line, carry guns and run drugs for them. Next thing you know you'll be upstate like Trevon was, up in one of them youth camps and on your way to state prison. Or worse, shot dead and laying in the street with your mama crying over you. So even though I won't be coaching this summer, I want you to stay focused and walk that straight line we always talk about. And I'll keep praying for you all every single night."

Ahmed Johnson, the team captain, a fast-moving shortstop already touted as a professional prospect, said, "Are you going to stay around for the game today?"

"For a couple of innings, I just wanted to come over and explain how things are going to be."

"We're dedicating today's game to Trevon, you know." He pointed to the black armbands on their uniforms. Obie had noticed them when he walked over.

He looked over at Shaka, who shrugged. "Ahmed came up with the idea and they all voted to go along with it."

"He killed a good and decent man and slit his throat wide

open, no way they're going out on that field with those armbands on." He looked at Ahmed, then at the rest of the ballplayers. "Get them off or the game's off. I meant it just now when I said you've got to walk a straight line. You can mourn Trevon in private all you want—but not on that ball field."

"We thought you'd say that, coach, but much as we respect you, we all got a lot of hurt now. Trevon was an ErnieBanksman, you made him one, and you said once a Banksman, always a Banksman." He turned and pointed to his teammates. "Trevon taught us a lot of things you didn't even know about. Even told us to follow your example, try to be like you—don't know how many times he told me that. And now look how you done him."

Oh boy, it was definitely coming out now. Down deep, these kids were blaming him for all the trouble in the projects and the neighborhood. Obie glanced over his shoulder and saw Reverend Johnson standing there. Now, with a nod from Obie, he entered the conversation.

"Young men, keep those armbands on for a few minutes while we pray silently for the souls of Trevon and Officer Cobb, that's the right way to do things. And when prayer is over, take them off, but I expect to see each and every one of you at Trevon's service. I'll be there too. Now take off those caps and let's pray together."

Way to go, Reverend. Loved and respected by all in the community for his tireless efforts on behalf of the poor—there wasn't a needy family that didn't receive a Thanksgiving basket from his church—the pastor had given the kids and Obie a graceful way out. After two minutes, he said, "Amen" and amidst some grumbling, the team members removed their armbands and went out on the field, every one of them, includimg Ahmed, shaking Obie's and the pastor's hand.

In the meantime, spectators, including some members of Teagle's youth gang, had filtered onto the sidelines, well away from the Banksmen, Obie, and the pastor.

Together, Obie and Reverend Johnson watched the first two innings of the game, then started walking back over to the car. As they approached it, Obie thought it seemed to be leaning. When he walked around to get in the driver's seat, he saw the two tires on that side had been slashed deeply with a knife. He looked back over at the ball field, where the Teagle boys stood innocently watching the third inning.

By the time he and Reverend Johnson had summoned help and gotten the tires replaced, the game was almost over, with the Banksmen ahead, 9-5. The kids had settled down and decided to play ball. He figured he'd do the same thing, but on another front.

....

Kevin O'Brien, the beat officer in the area around the Hill project, dressed in blue slacks and a white polo shirt that showed off his gym-developed muscles to their best advantage, walked into the bar in the small South Jersey town of Linwood and nodded to the bartender, who motioned him towards a back room. It was around seven o'clock, and the tavern was filled with its regulars, a mix of white, black, and Hispanic working people—waiters from catering services, bus drivers still in their uniforms, mechanics from the nearby Toyota dealership, and secretaries, receptionists, and saleswomen from Wal-Mart and J.C. Penney. They all knew what kind of business went on in that back room and considered it a privilege to know about it and yet keep its secrets. Like some people belonged to the Saved by Christ Apostolic Church or the New Testament Baptist Church, these folks belonged to Tracey's Bar and would never let the world know what went on there.

So Kevin felt perfectly safe—if not at ease, for he was waiting for Raschid, second-in-command of Son Teagle's operation in and around the Hill project. While he waited and listened to the piped-in oldies music, he wondered how he'd gotten himself into this mess. Great football player, two years of community college criminal justice, MP service with the National Guard in Afghanistan, and now this—waiting for a criminal who held his fate in his hands. What would the bastard want this time?

Oh, at first he'd had a good thing going, supplying Raschid with a little protection, just promised that on his police shift and in his area, he'd look the other way when he saw deals going down. The money, five hundred dollars a week, had been left for him in a designated post office box every week.

Kevin didn't consider this a bad thing, since as part of the deal he was fed with information about other gangs intruding on the Teagle territory. He and his eager partner in crime, Omar Robinson, would arrest any interlopers or call down the detectives on them, and get credit for diligent police work. It was, he figured, his way of keeping down violence—just let one gang control the territory and there'd be less gunfire, fewer lives taken.

But he had reckoned without the cunning and ruthless nature of Raschid. Slowly, like a hapless fly caught in a web, Kevin had been drawn deeper and deeper into the operations of the Teagle gang. He'd watched as Raschid moved in with his ailing grandmother and then, with his associates, gradually took over one, two, then all three apartments on a floor of the Hill project, spreading like a cancer from there to drive family after family out of the building. Now only the Bullocks and a few others stood between the remaining families and Teagle's total control of the project and the neighborhood. Raschid had recruited neighborhood kids, dropouts, and anybody back from prison, calling himself an equal opportunity employer. And now he was Kevin's boss too.

Well, that was about to change. Where the hell was Raschid?

He fingered the revolver in his ankle holster and took a long drink from the glass of rye and soda the bartender had brought him.

Twenty minutes late, Raschid showed up, dressed in a light blue golfer's jacket, a gray shirt, and an Eagles baseball cap. He loomed over Kevin, who was slumped on a scuffed leather couch. Much as Kevin loathed the man, he had to admit he was one sharp-looking son of a bitch. Plus he could probably outmaneuver Donald Trump in a business deal.

"What you looking so down about, Officer O'Brien? Ain't the end of the world, things will calm down in a few days." Raschid seated himself in the brown leather easy chair directly across from the couch. "Matter of fact, things are just the way I like them, all confused."

"I told you I didn't like meeting over here, too dangerous. And definitely don't be calling Doris's cell phone—she had a fit over it. Just leave her out of it."

Raschid smiled. "Don't sweat the small stuff, we had us a nice little conversation, even talked a little bit about the weather."

Kevin winced. That bastard didn't talk about things like the weather, was probably trying to get some information out of her about his habits. Nothing was too small for Raschid not to know—where and when he exercised, his favorite bar stop afterwards, the name of the marina where he kept his boat. And calling his fiancee might turn up information that could be used to blackmail him should the need ever arise, which Kevin was sure it would.

"All right, what do you want from me?"

"First, I want to let you know how sorry I am about what happened to Roy yesterday. You got to know it was nothing I had any control over, nothing Son would have wanted—he knows as well as I do what killing a cop means. Trevon went ahead and done that thing on his own. Wanted to show he was a man, impress his big brother." He shook his head. "Too bad, that was one decent cop, and I know he was your friend."

"More than a friend, he taught me everything I know about foot patrolling." Kevin looked Raschid straight in the eye. "You had nothing to do with it?"

"Hell no, man, you know me, I'm cool with everything. Making too much money to fuck up that way And you know Son don't like that kind of stuff, noways." He stroked his chin. "Really think it was about Trevon and Hashim—they both young bloods, and both of them were trying to see who could make a rep for himself quicker. You know, like that old custom the Indians had of striking coup."

Kevin smiled in spite of himself. Raschid had never finished school, but he had this way of coming up with things you wouldn't think about in a million years. "Striking coup" was when the Indians would lift a white man's scalp, or even just wound him, then go back to the tribe to brag about it—the more coups you made, the greater the warrior you were. That kind of thinking might explain how some of these young gang bangers acted.

"Okay, so you're sorry," he said. "Well, I've got news for you, I'm even sorrier and so will you be—Captain Sarnese wants to wipe you out, eliminate you, empty every one of your three apartments even if it means putting out all the relatives and kids living there." He looked down at the floor, then back up again. "I've never seen him so mad, and everybody in the precinct feels the same way. It's going to mean I can't protect you any more, too many eyes around looking for something wrong."

Raschid said, "We going to need you more than ever."

"I'm through." He was going to get out, try to straighten his life out and be a good cop again, one his retired detective sergeant father would be proud of. That's what he'd promised Doris and that's what he was going to do, Raschid or no Raschid.

"We not asking you for much now, just keep letting us know what's going on. I'm changing the number to call—it's another answering service—and everything will be fine."

"I want out." He downed the last of his drink and got to his feet. "I've made up my mind, and you're just—"

"Sit down. You ain't going nowhere till I tell you to, 'cause you ain't wanting what happens if you walk out now." Raschid glared at him. "Sit right there, right where you was."

Keven remained standing for a second, then sat back down heavily.

"Want another drink?"

Kevin nodded.

"I'll get it for you, be back in a second."

When Raschid returned, he said, "First of all I don't want to make you think I'm pressuring you or nothing like that, you're our main man and we appreciate it. You're getting married soon and you going to need some cash for that pretty lady of yours, so here's three k to help you out a little bit—one hand rubs the other, you know."

Kevin slowly reached out a hand, then pocketed the money.

"That's a lot better, Kevin, we all businessmen together now and we don't want no misunderstanding or nothing. Just keep on doing things the way they are and everything be fine. See how much we need you and how much we all appreciate what you do." He reached into his leather pouch, pulled out a cellophane bag, and passed it to Kevin. "And I didn't forget this, either. Things going to be just fine with us."

Kevin took the bag and put it into his briefcase.

Raschid opened the door and pointed to the way out. "Oh, and by the way, I want you to do one more little thing for me." He whispered something into Kevin's ear, then said. "Peace go with you."

Kevin wanted to pull his revolver and shoot the bastard. Instead he walked out without a word, without a protest, without a threat. He hated them all, every stinking last one of them.

Almost as much as he hated himself.

CHAPTER 4

SON TEAGLE PULLED THE BARBELLS DOWN from their rack, held the weights over his chest for a minute, then with a harsh grunt thrust them upwards. His muscles strained as he reached the midpoint of the lift, then with a mighty thrust he extended his arms and pushed all the way up.

Homicide Jones said, "You done it. Two hundred and fifty pounds."

Son slowly let the barbells down and Homicide returned them to the rack. Son was sitting up on the bench, sweat rolling off his coffee-colored body, when he noticed that the African-American deputy warden was looking around the room for somebody. His eyes fell on Son, then he said something to the guard and left the gym. The guard came over.

"Get yourself washed up and shaved, Teagle, the deputy warden wants to see you in a half-hour."

Son accompanied the guard through winding corridors, clanging gates, and manned security desks back towards his cell. What could have caused this unexpected summons to Mr. Richardson? Son hadn't done anything to break the agreement with him. Everything was cool in the prison, hadn't been any fights or nothing. And wasn't no way they could of busted the code on his phone calls.

Twenty minutes later, after he'd showered and put on a clean uniform, the guard ushered Son into the warden's office. Stacks of old prison manuals lay on the floor, correspondence and records were piled up on a battered wooden bookcase. The sole decoration on the wall was a faded color picture of Martin Luther King, the words, "I have a dream" barely legible.

"What's happening, warden, parole board decided to give me an early hearing?"

"No, Son, you know that's not the way we do it. All those notifications go out at one time. I'm afraid it's about something else, something personal." Mr. Richardson pursed his lips. "Your brother Trevon is dead. He was killed in some kind of shootout in the Hill project. The television reports say he killed one of the guards there. I wanted to tell you myself, so you wouldn't get it second-hand."

"What?" Son stood up so abruptly that a look of alarm flickered over the face of the warden. Then, just as suddenly, he sat back down and let his head slump onto his chest. Baby brother dead! The one he'd helped with his multiplication tables and taken out to Fairmount Park to throw footballs around. He felt tears coming to his eyes. Just couldn't help it.

"Take your time." The warden folded his hands together and looked at the ceiling.

Son wiped his eyes, then slowly began to shake his head back and forth. What the fuck had Trevon done? Told him a million times not to go my way, said I'd kick his ass if I ever caught him running shit. Had everything in the world going for him, and done gone and got himself killed. Poor Mama!

"I'd sure like to go to the funeral if I could, warden. He was my little brother, and I raised him like a daddy. I don't suppose you could do something for me?"

The warden tossed his pen onto the desk. "I might could, if you weren't up here for felonious assault and drug trafficking. It's true you're coming up for parole, but your brother killed a cop. No way we're going to be able to get you there, and I'm not even going to tell you I'd recommend it to the head warden, because I won't."

"I understand." Son leaned forward. "Can I go now? And can I call my lady, and my mother?'

The warden nodded, then buzzed the guard who'd been standing outside during the conversation.

"THEY KILLED HIM IN COLD BLOOD," Mammie Teagle said when he called her, "right there on the first floor of the projects. Shot him full of holes, blood all over the place. Killed my precious last-born child. Have mercy, Jesus!"

"Who killed him? The cops?"

There was a pause on the other end of the phone as his mother wept. Finally she calmed down enough to say, "Just take one guess."

"Bullock did it? That big ugly bastard did it?"

"And got on television and said how sorry he was he'd had to do it, Trevon was shooting at him, then said he'd do it again if he had to."

"Don't you worry about him, Mama, now get hold of yourself. What's the doctor say about your heart?"

"He give me some drugs the other day, think I'm going to be all right. Folks from the church been in and out already."

A voice clicked onto the line. "Teagle, your time's up."

"Hey, man, don't you know this is my mama? I need another minute."

"You got it, but that's all."

"Mama, put Malika on the line." Teagle's wife picked up. "How's Mama taking this, and how's Ashanti?"

"Honey, ain't nothing to worry about. He's fine. Your mama's going to be all right, but you know how she was about Trevon."

"All right, baby," Son said. "I got to split now. Tell Ashanti I love him. And make sure Mama stays with you."

"You know she won't, she'll go right back to her sister in West Philly. I love you and I miss you. I'll be up next month."

Son told her goodbye.

IT WAS SEVEN O'CLOCK in the evening. Some of the prisoners in the Delaware Correctional Facility were playing basketball on the outdoor court. Watching them from seats on the ground were Son and Homicide.

At other times, this had been Son's favorite spot in the prison. He liked to stand up here and look out over the valley down below. If he strained his eyes and looked real hard, he could see the Delaware River in the distance. It was a narrow, meandering stream from up here. But it was the very same river that flowed into the city where he was raised.

It made him sad to even think about it. Once a friendly guard, intrigued by Son's interest in the river, had brought in a map and a little guidebook to show him exactly where the prison lay in relation to the city.

"I got to get out of this place, Homicide," he said. "Got to deal with Bullock and the Mau-Mau before they wreck our whole operation."

Son started to talk fast, punching his fist into his hand to emphasize his points.

"Wasn't bad enough he put my mama out on the street, made her stand there in front of all her neighbors and church folks with her bags and furniture and all that shit from my room. And pigs laughing at her, making fun of that poor black lady with no place to go. No, that wasn't enough. Had to go and kill my brother."

Homicide, a dark-skinned man with almost-white patches on his face from acid burns, said, "Your hearing's only three months away. They might let you go."

"Not after this cop-killing they won't, got to think of some other way."

"You always was hard-headed, man, but whatever you decide to do, I'll help you any way I can."

"Appreciate it," Son said. "Now, what we going to do about that Frank Jennings? Been working with the guards and bringing some stuff in outside of channels."

"True."

Son's eyes narrowed. "Here's what I want you to do."

THREE HOURS LATER Son sat among a circle of men looking at television reruns in the recreation room. Scattered around the yellow-walled room were some thirty prisoners, the African-Americans together, the Hispanics together, and the few whites all sitting with the Hispanics who gave them protection. Son had decreed what the programming would be for the night: first "The

Jeffersons," then "Cops," and finally "Miami Vice." The Oldies-but-Goodies channel was the only one he let them watch.

Son really liked George Jefferson. He liked the cockiness of the brother, the way the short man was able to stand up to big people and defeat them with his wits and his sharp tongue. Nigger could be dead wrong, but that just made him more bodacious with his shit. And besides, the fellow who played George Jefferson was a homeboy, straight out of South Philly.

Son was in his usual spot at the front of the room, but Homicide wasn't next to him in his regular place. He was seated in the rear.

Periodically, a guard looked into the roomful of green-uniformed men to make sure everything was okay.

In the rear of the room, not far from Homicide, sat the target of Son's vengeance. Frank Jennings was an older prisoner with a quick mind and a great storytelling gift. He'd been known to keep his fellow prisoners entertained for hours on end with tales of his crimes and escapes from the police in practically every northeastern state.

He was also a big flatterer, and barely a day passed without his telling Son how smart and clever he was. Pissed Son off. The fat bastard sneaks coke into the prison through some guards who aren't on my payroll and thinks I'm dumb enough to let him get away with it? Adding insult to injury.

The guard walked into the room once again, looked quickly over its occupants, then left for the next television room. When he was well down the corridor, Son snapped his fingers and a young Jamaican prisoner leapt up from his seat and took his position as a lookout. Son snapped his fingers again, and another prisoner turned up the volume on the old television set.

Son went to the back of the room, where Jennings sat between Homicide and another prisoner. He walked up to Jennings and slammed his fist hard across the bridge of his nose. The man screamed, but Homicide grabbed his arms and held them behind his back in a vise lock.

Homicide kept pushing the arms upwards.

"Not too hard," Son said. "You'll break them."

He signaled to another of his men, who in a flash twisted a bandanna around Jennings's mouth. It would soon be damp from the sweat pouring down the man's face.

Only now, when his eyes were rolling upwards and his screams could be heard through the cotton bandanna, did Son speak to him.

"You know this is my prison. I own it, not no motherfucking governor. You got to pay the price. I really used to like you, but you done me wrong. And you surely know my middle name."

Son motioned to another prisoner. Jennings' eyes looked like he'd seen a rattlesnake a foot away from him, fangs out and arched high, ready to strike.

Son nodded his head. The prisoner grabbed Jennings' head and began to pull and twist his ears.

The other inmates gathered around in a circle.

"Pull em' hard," Son said, "We'll see if he wants to do this dealing shit any more." He looked at Homicide. "Just because I told you I don't want his arms broke don't mean you ain't suppose to hurt the motherfucker. He needs to feel pain."

Son "He ain't hurting enough, man."

The prisoners drew tighter around Jennings.

"Tear his ears off, Son."

"Break his arm, Homicide."

So excited were the prisoners that their voices were as loud as George Jefferson's on the TV, George at the moment being engaged in a shouting match with his landlord.

Suddenly the Jamaican on guard at the door signaled. "Be cool. He's coming."

One prisoner removed the bandanna from Jennings' mouth and Son returned to his seat in the front of the room.

The guard said, "You two guys back there, what's the matter with Jennings? He don't look right."

Son jumped up from his seat. "Where you been? Jennings got a bad heart and it looks like something's happening to him. He started sweating all over, next thing you know he fainted.

Homicide and Roscoe been trying to help him."

The guard took one more look at the men and called the captain of the guard on his walkie-talkie. Seconds later, a squad of guards, nightsticks at the ready and led by the warden, burst into the room. The warden took one look at Jennings and called for medical assistance. He turned to the captain of the guard.

"Lock them all in their cells until we can get to the bottom of this."

From the look on the warden's face Son knew this marked the end of friendly relations with him. But shit, a man had to do what he had to do. Couldn't let people get away with things and stay in control of the prison. Didn't matter, he had some pretty good ideas going around in his head. Bullock had messed with him one time too many, and the fact that his own boys had let Trevon get involved in a killing meant that things weren't right at home. In the meantime, he couldn't let his authority weaken—people would take advantage of you.

Little boy walking down the street, Mama pulling him along, freezing day. Come on, Son. Mama, I'm cold. Come on, boy. But Mama, where we going? Shut up, boy, we just going, that's all. Can't stay around that man no more. But my hands are cold, and I'm hungry. Shut up or I'll leave your little ass right here in the middle of the street. See what you do then. But Mama... Darkness and cold and snow whipping across his face and into his shoes. Crying in the night, and clutching the woolen coats of strangers...

Oh, yes, Son knew what happened to the weak.

MAMMIE TEAGLE, ALL DRESSED IN BLACK, sat rocking her soul away in the front pew of the church. She was supported by her mother, who'd come up from Georgia for the funeral of her beloved grandson Trevon. The church, located on one of the narrow streets that criss-cross North Philadelphia, held no more than a hundred people. Its first two rows were full of Mammie's sisters, brothers, and cousins, most of whom lived in West Philly and Germantown.

The men wore black suits with white shirts and black ties. The women wore black dresses, some of which may at one time have served as party wear, for they revealed on this solemn occasion a considerable amount of bosom. Everybody was sweating, the men mopping their brows with handkerchiefs and the women fanning themselves in rhythm with the background gospel music the organist was playing.

Behind the front rows and sitting in their basketball jackets were the members of the Hill Hornets, the basketball team Trevon Teagle had played on the year before. Just behind them were the Ernie Banksmen. Reverend Theodius Johnson, a box of Kleenex in his hands, was seated with them. Further back in the dimly lit church sat another group of teenagers, junior members of the Teagle gang. In the rear sat a group of men with hard faces and sullen expressions. They were well dressed in casual summer clothes, but most had on slacks and sports shirts with the shirttails out. Underneath the shirts they wore beepers and gun holsters.

This had been Mammie Teagle's church since she'd found a home in the projects some twenty years ago, and so, even though it was a Monday morning and they could scarcely afford to lose any pay, some members of the church had taken a half-day off from their jobs to console her as she buried her boy.

Despite all the support, Mammie Teagle's full, round face was wet with tears and her body trembling as the pastor came to the end of his sermon. The short, light-skinned man had truly preached out of his heart, punctuating almost every sentence of his message by stomping his feet and clapping his hands. Now he grabbed the microphone from its stand and paced from one side of the elevated platform to the other.

"Well, Trevon, you've left these mean streets at last. May a gracious and ever-loving God have mercy on your poor soul and forgive you your sins."

Mammie Teagle's eyes followed the minister as he left the platform and walked down the red carpeted steps to the white gold-inlaid casket in which the body of her son lay displayed. The preacher, his red robe damp with sweat, turned towards her.

"Sister Teagle, be comforted. Trevon is far better where he is.

"No more fighting, Mammie!

"No more guns!

"No more drugs!

"No more tears in the midnight hour!

"Ain't going to be worrying no more about where that child is. He's gone where the wicked shall cease from troubling and the weary shall be at rest. Done found him a better home."

The choir began to sing softly about that "old ship of Zion" that had landed "many a thousand." Mammie let the rhythmic clapping of the congregation and the centuries-old woe in their chanting voices wash over her.

The preacher nodded his head to the funeral attendant, who moved forward to close the casket. Six heavy-set pallbearers from the church deaconate started down the aisle.

"No!" Mammie got up and headed towards it. "That's my boy! Killed my baby! Have mercy, Jesus."

Saw herself in that beat-up hotel room downtown, and Trevon, in short pants, running across the worn carpet to her. "Mommy, I love you. I'll take care of you."

Saw herself holding the boy, fever burning up his body, doctor saying sorry, only God can save him now. Prayed all night long for the Almighty to spare the boy's life. And he did. For this.

She leapt into the air, shouted "Trevon!" and fell to the floor in front of the casket, where she rolled from side to side. Two white-clothed women ushers came up and helped her out of the church and into a car.

Mammie Teagle left behind a shouting, crying, angry church. Outside the building stood a crowd of about a hundred people. They carried banners that said, "Stop the police killings!" and "African-American Youth: Endangered Species!"

As her car drew away from the curb following the big Cadillac hearse, Mammie could see Raschid, already gathering people together to make a march on the police station. He'd told her yesterday it would begin right after the burial service. That Obie Bullock, pretending to help Trevon and all, was nothing but a tool of those white cops. If they thought they could get away with this killing of her boy, they were dead wrong.

The funeral procession cars had barely made the turn out of the street and onto Cecil B. Moore Avenue before the street behind them filled with people. It was just twelve o'clock, the temperature was ninety-eight degrees, and the humidity ninety percent. The march on the precinct building and Captain Sarnese, the Mau-Mau and Bullock's big supporter, was beginning. They were heading towards Sarnese's station house.

CHAPTER 5

CAPTAIN SARNESE SIGNED another vacation leave authorization and let his mind drift off to his upcoming two weeks with Angie over at Lake Piney Grove in the Poconos. This year, for the first time, it would be just the two of them up at the lake. Erin, a senior at Penn State, had decided she wanted to spend her summer working down at the Jersey shore. He worried about her a lot, so pretty and so trusting of people. Bound to be rotten kids who worked down there, and she just might fall for one of them.

Damn, he hadn't even let her move into a single room in the dormitory, and at the shore she'd be living in an apartment house that might even have boys living on the same floor. He'd find out about that when he drove her down, and—

Someone knocked at the door, and Sergeant Lake came in. "Captain, I'm sending somebody out in a few minutes. It's the Chinese day."

"Couple of egg rolls and shrimp chow mein."

"He should be back in about a half-hour."

Sarnese glanced up at the sergeant from his computer. "That just about gives me time to get all these vacation leave forms done. Why the hell does everybody want to go in July? I've been on this force for thirty years and I still can't understand why they never want to go in August. Makes me look like the bad guy when I give them the last week before Labor Day."

The sergeant closed the door. Sarnese wasn't looking forward to his egg rolls and chow mein. He had a real taste for some lasagna from the little place up on Broad Street. Well, at least Monday would be Italian.

There was a knock and Lake came back in.

"I don't suppose they want to make it an Italian day?"

"No, I already sent out for the food. Some troublemakers must have been at work at the funeral today—we just got a radio call demonstrators are on their way here to picket the police station."

"That doesn't make sense," Sarnese said. "Bullock shot the kid, not a cop."

"Like that matters. You know how they are, blaming us for everything."

"Put the station on alert, get some squad cars back here and the barricades up. Make sure the whole street's blocked. And don't forget the riot helmets. Get a move on."

After the sergeant had left the room, Sarnese sat quietly for a moment. He'd been through these demonstrations time and time again and knew their potential for trouble. Other than dirty or sadistic cops he had to run to ground and clean out, protests and picketing were the worst part of his job, and another reason he wanted to retire next year.

He picked up the red telephone on his desk and dialed four numbers. Nobody answered. Shit, you'd think if they set up an emergency phone somebody would—

"Inspector's office." Sandy's velvet voice.

"Hey," Sarnese said. "It's me. Is he in? Got trouble coming my way."

"Sorry, dear, he just left to go downtown to have lunch with the chief."

"Get hold of him, tell him to get over here quick. Demonstrators are on the way. I need help."

Sarnese put down the phone, took one of his blood pressure pills out of the bottle, walked down the now bustling corridor to the water fountain, and drew a cup of water as the station house began to prepare itself for the demonstrators.

The desk sergeant had opened the armory and was busy distributing shot guns, long batons, white helmets, and tear-gas guns to officers who'd been taken off patrol for the defense of the precinct. Sarnese looked to see that all was in order, went back to his office and took his pill, then called Sergeant Lake.

"Frank, I want everybody lined up in the precinct room in five minutes. We don't have a lot of time, and I want them to get their orders right from me, don't want no fuck-ups. I intend to go into my retirement quietly. Got it?"

A few minutes later, Captain Sarnese, wearing a starched white shirt with two gold bars on his collar, sharply creased blue pants, and a shiny black holster holding his pistol, stood before the thirty officers Sergeant Lake had assembled in the precinct room. Cradling his nightstick in his hand, Sarnese looked them over, then began to walk back and forth along the line. They were white, black, Asian, and Hispanic, but he didn't see color, only strength or weakness.

He stopped at Kevin O'Brien, a young cop of five years' experience known around this section of North Philly for his toughness on the streets. That and something else, something bad. Was making way too many collars for a plain foot patrolman. Lots of rumors circulating about him, and where there was smoke, there was fire. The guy had to be on the take, and Sarnese had to get to him before internal affairs did. He stood in front of O'Brien for a second, then turned and walked back to the front of the room, where he ordered the men to stand at ease.

"I got no time for speech-making. You'll have to be responsible for the security of the precinct until the reinforcements from the flying squads get here. And I don't know when that'll be. Force is only to be used to protect yourself or a fellow officer. Most of all, don't react to verbal threats. I don't care what they call you—no force in reaction to words. Got it?" He turned to Sergeant Lake. "Take over."

Sarnese returned to his office. His red phone was ringing. It was Sandy.

"I've got the inspector on the line. He's pissed because he thought he was going to have a good meal. Here he is."

"Sarnese, I hear you've got a little problem up there. I'm way downtown, but I'm coming up right away, so you can figure I'll be there in a half-hour. In the meantime, the chief told me to tell you he's counting on you to avoid any casualties or rioting. The mayor's sending somebody from his office to represent him there and talk to the crowd if necessary. Be cool, keep your damn temper, you hear? See you in a little while."

THE PRECINCT STATION STOOD ON A STREET so short you could throw a football from one end of it to the other. In fact, on some brisk days in the fall, the precinct cops would have a pick-up football game in the street during lunch breaks. Most of the working class black people who lived there were out of their houses and on the way to jobs downtown by seven-thirty in the morning.

But there were still plenty of people around as Sarnese walked out of the station house. He put on his white metal helmet and glanced down the street in the direction he expected the protestors to come from. The barricades had been set up at both ends of the street, a police car with its light circling behind each of them.

Sarnese, accompanied now by his driver, Walker, strode up and down the street, looking not only at his paltry thirty policemen but also up at the windows and fire escapes of the buildings from which some residents were looking down at the unusual activity in front of the station house.

A few were dressed only in their underwear, while some teenagers, bare-chested, had their iPod boomboxes blaring out that loud hip-hop music that rattled his brain. Leaning out of windows were some old men and women, one ancient lady smoking a pipe.

In the distance, Sarnese began to hear the sound of a drum. Thump, *thump*, thump, *thump*! It was almost like the roll of the funeral drums in the Italian town his grandparents were from. He'd visited there as a youngster with his folks.

The booming sound came closer and closer. Damn, they sure had some big-assed drum. Sarnese and Walker walked rapidly down the block in the direction of the sound. When they reached the barricade, Sarnese spoke into his walkie-talkie to Sergeant Lake in the station house.

"They're coming, get on out here and take command of the roadblock. I want to stay near the station house so I can get reinforcements to you if you need them." He turned to Walker. "You stay here and wait for Sergeant Lake. Give him a hand, and keep an eye on O'Brien. You know how he is."

"Sir, if you think he's going to cause trouble, why don't you just put him inside the station house?"

"I need everybody." He headed back to the precinct, passing Lake on the way. When he got there, he stood on the top step and wiped the sweat from his face. The demonstrators had arrived.

Down the street, some fifty yards away behind the barricades, a tall, lean, very dark man dressed in a white caftan and a multicolored cap was beating on a cylinder-shaped drum strapped across his chest. He would shout a few words—"The people united!"—and then pound the drum with both the palm and the back of his hand, flipping it back and forth.

Beyond the man and surrounding him was a crowd made up mostly of teenagers and the unemployed middle-aged men usually found loitering on the corners. But among them were some people Sarnese recognized immediately as part of the Teagle gang.

As a matter of fact, right there in the center of the crowd and urging them on was Raschid Tucker, a Teagle hit man and a longtime resident of the upstate prisons. That son of a bitch sure had some nerve being out here. Had committed at least three murders, all of black people, and had the audacity to come picket the station house. One day he'd catch him in the act and get his ass put away for good.

Another drum began to beat elsewhere in the crowd, and groups of teenagers started to form in little circles in front of the barricades, where they egged each other on and taunted Sarnese's cops.

"Your mama was a pig, means your daddy was a hog!"

"Stop the killing, honky motherfucker!"

The front stoops and fire escapes of the buildings facing the precinct began to fill with people. They swayed back and forth and clapped their hands to the rhythm of the drums and the rap music. Sarnese, who in his teens had been with the marines in Vietnam, began to have that funny feeling he was once again surrounded. He spoke into his walkie-talkie and ordered the barricades moved back, closer to the precinct house.

The shouts from the people on the fire escapes and in the windows grew louder. Some had put loudspeakers on their sills. The music careened from wall to wall, from apartment house to apartment house. The noise was awful. They were engaging in psychological warfare.

These kids under his command might panic under the bombardment of the music. As if the music weren't enough, debris began to rain down on the cops as they moved back down the street towards the station house.

"They running now!"

"Motherfuckers better get back to the station house while they got time!"

Sarnese walked quickly down to the patrol car that had been parked behind the barricade and turned on its loudspeaker. He turned the volume full up and warned the crowd to disperse and stop throwing stuff at the cops. But the barrage only increased—television wagons were pulling up, and his friendly neighbors obviously wanted to make the six o'clock news. And his strategic retreat had only served to bring the crowds closer to the precinct.

The small band of cops was now holding up riot shields to stave off the eggs flying through the air and splattering all over them. Sarnese ordered yet another retreat, hoping to form a protective circle about twenty yards from the station house. Where the hell were the flying squads?

That guy in the funny hat beating the drum was sitting on the shoulders of a giant with a gold earring. He was beating even harder on the drum and his head was shaking back and forth in time with the music. Other drums, scattered through the crowd, echoed his sounds.

Sarnese figured the protestors to be about one hundred and fifty strong and growing steadily. He walked over to O'Brien and patted him on the shoulder.

"Keep your cool."

An egg thrown from the crowd struck Sarnese in the chest, just below his gold badge. He took a handkerchief from his pocket, wiped away the yellow as best he could, and threw the handkerchief on the ground. But the mess was still on his hands, and he rubbed them together trying to get rid of it.

O'Brien said, "What the hell!" In a flash he was behind the barricade and grabbing hold of a black man.

"Boy, you're under arrest for assaulting an officer. That's the captain." He started pushing him back towards the police lines.

The man said, "Get your motherfucking hands off of me before I kill your ass."

"O'Brien!" Sarnese called out. "Let him go, he *wants* us to react!"

Sarnese knew O'Brien heard him. So he was furious when the young officer lifted his nightstick and slammed it hard across the man's head.

"You coming with me, nigger."

That did it, that set them off. In seconds O'Brien and cops in general were being called every name in the book. The prisoner disappeared into the crowd, and O'Brien was knocked to the ground, in danger of being trampled by what was now a mob.

"Batons out," Sarnese said, "but don't get nuts with them, we're going to get that dumb O'Brien out and then we're going to retreat into the station house."

At the sight of the police picking up the batons from a storage cart, the mob parted just enough for Sarnese to make his way to the fallen policeman. He lay on the ground, his blouse shredded, gun and blackjack gone. Blood flowed from a deep gash in his right temple. Sarnese bent down over him.

"You son of a bitch, I don't know why, but you did that on purpose. Your ass is finished on this force, that's a promise."

Dazed, O'Brien looked up at him. "I was only trying to—"

"Shut up!" He reached down, took O'Brien's arm, and retreated with him towards the station house. When he reached the barricades, he handed O'Brien over to an officer and took command of his patrolmen, telling them to be calm and slowly move back to the station house.

He himself was anything but calm and could see it would be a miracle if they ever got back into the precinct. Rocks were being tossed from the crowd, bottles and cans of food thrown from roofs and fire escapes. The path to the station house was filled with people, so that he and his men were adrift in a sea of rioters. A rock hit a cop in the shoulder. Sarnese ordered his men to pull out their pistols.

"Aim them in the air, and when I give the command, fire warning shots."

Jostled by the crowd, Sarnese managed to pull his own weapon from its holster. He raised the gun above his head and gave the order.

"Fire!"

A ragged series of loud reports resounded in the street. The crowd quieted, and suddenly you could hear the sound of traffic.

"Oh, Lawd, they done shot my baby!" The woman's cry came from an apartment building window.

Shit, if something could go wrong, it would. Sarnese didn't know how the hell it had happened, but one of his men must have been jostled while firing and accidentally sent a bullet through a window.

The crowd melted away. First people moved slowly, then as shouts of "They killing folks!" arose, they panicked and fled down the narrow street.

Sarnese looked up and saw the fire escapes were now empty except for one woman, dressed in a pair of green slacks and a white blouse. She held a small child in her arms and was crying, "Katea!"

Sarnese turned the command over to Sergeant Lake and motioned to Robbie Walker to follow him over to the apartment building. As he ran across the street, the sounds of police sirens filled his ears. He glanced down the block and saw the first of the buses containing the riot squads turn into the block. He glanced over his shoulder at Sergeant Lake.

"Get a doctor up here soon as you can."

With Robbie at his side, he entered the building, which had polished doors and brass doorknobs. The door was locked. Sarnese kicked it open and leapt up the stairs two at a time despite a warning from Robbie to remember his heart condition. When he reached the third floor, he ran down the hall to the front apartment, hurled himself shoulder-first against the door, and burst into the room.

The woman was rocking back and forth in an oversized chair, her white blouse darkened by bloodstains. In her arms she held a limp-bodied light-complexioned little girl. The girl's head was slumped over, and blood was pouring from her right leg, smashed by the bullet.

Sarnese grabbed the child from her mother's arms, tore off his shirt, ripped it, and made a tourniquet. As he knelt on the floor to tighten it around her leg, he felt the child's mother beating him on his back with her fists. He ignored the blows, finished with the tourniquet, and started mouth-to-mouth resuscitation on the little girl.

He barely heard Walker's cry: "Look out, Captain, she's got a knife!" nor did he even feel at first the pain in his back, but suddenly he felt faint.

Who would remember to take the outboard up to the boat dealer to get new sparkplugs? Damn, the lake trout will be gone clear to the bottom if we don't get the motor back in time.

CHAPTER 6

OBIE WOKE UP AND REACHED over to touch Dora Lee. His hand fell on cold pressed cotton where her sweet body usually was. An old blues song his Dad used to sing came back to him: "Got rocks in my pillow where your head used to lay, Got rocks in my pillow where your head used to lay...." Dora Lee was still up at Ruth's place in Ardmore. It was only her voice on the phone.

"Hi, baby," he said. "I'm just laying here thinking about you." The ringing had also started his head throbbing. His eyes hurt too. Too much whiskey, too much thinking about Trevon and Roy. Dreams were getting to him. And a week or so ago, he'd lost his greatest ally—Captain Sarnese—when some of his men, in particular that roughneck O'Brien, had gotten out of control at the protest after Trevon's funeral and started beating on the folks and calling them niggers. Before the day was out, Sarnese had been injured, relieved of his command, and both he and O'Brian placed on suspension, with a hearing due to take place soon.

So Obie was surely glad to be hearing Dora Lee's voice now: "I miss you a whole lot too, honey. Maybe we can get together over the weekend. You can come out here—Ruth and Bill will be away with the kids. I think they're going just so we can be together. What time's your meeting tonight?"

"About an hour from now, I just got time to eat and get myself together. Leroy and Bumps are sleeping in the living room. I got to be out of here at nine, and it's already eight o'clock."

"Before you go, Timba called last night and tonight too. He's getting a little lonely down there in Gastonia, doesn't want to tell you because he doesn't want you to worry. And all the stuff that's happening up here—especially about Captain Sarnese—has been on television down there, and everybody's always asking him are you his daddy. I can't keep him from bragging, and I'm scared to death about the wrong folks finding out where he is."

"I'm worried too, but not too much. Gastonia's not that big a town, ain't nobody up here going to find out where he is. But I'll feel a lot better when Sabaya finishes up this week and goes down. I'm more worried about her than Timba."

"She's doing just fine. You know how Mama is. Nobody's going to get within a hundred yards of Sabaya."

Obie had gotten out of bed and was fishing around in the bureau drawer for clean underwear. "Hey, sweetness, I got to go. Time to get ready for the meeting. I'll call the kids tomorrow night before I go in, I was up in Germantown to see Uncle Ward and Justine last night and went straight to work from there." Best not tell her how badly things were going with the Mau-Mau, what with the Sarnese thing.

"All right, honey, I'm going to get my books together and study for a while. Ruth and Bill say hi."

Obie sat there for a minute, his mind on his uncle and Justine. His sister was getting worse, and Uncle Ward was just barely able to function. Something had to be done about them. Soon. The Bullock budget was already busted—only thing he knew to do was get another job, and what with things being the way they were... He dropped his head on his chest, said, "Help me, Lord Jesus," then put on his robe and went into the kitchen to make coffee and warm up the beef stew. Leroy and Bumps were still asleep.

Forty-five minutes later, after Obie had taken his shower, the three men were seated around the kitchen table, making final preparations for their meeting.

Obie looked across the table at Leroy. "Man, we just got to deal with this patrol situation. With Smith leaving, that's five we lost since all the stuff with Sarnese went down."

Leroy sopped up the last of the gravy on his plate with a slice of bread. "A lot of them are saying there's no way they're going to stay with the Mau-Mau long as there's any association with these honky cops."

Bumps, a short, powerfully built man with a jet black face,

said, "I think that's a lot of shit, these folks didn't leave because of any white cops. They left because they see the cops done abandoned Obie—when I come in, there was nobody at the desk. And that was the new black captain done that, not no white man. These folks are figuring if they ain't going to protect Obie, they sure ain't going to protect the little guys in the organization. Teagle got a lot of folks scared spitless and shitless."

Obie got up and poured some more coffee for the men. "Meeting's in ten minutes. Don't blame the new captain—truth is, they only got so many cops and I knew they wouldn't be able to keep up the security downstairs. Only one cop to the three buildings in the project every shift from now on. We can't be chicken-hearted ourselves. God got no room for cowards."

"You right," Leroy said, stroking his goatee. "But we're down to about fifteen members, and that's mighty few to cover everything. The men are getting tired, and they're going to want to know about a lot of things. Particularly about why the cops aren't answering their calls the way they used to when Sarnese was in charge."

Obie pulled himself up from the table, went into the bedroom, and got dressed. He looked in the mirror and adjusted his navy blue tie and the collar of his gray shirt, marked with the initials ECC for the name of his cleaning company. He reached down into a drawer, pulled out the small holster and pistol, and strapped them around his ankle. At least that new captain had let him get the gun permit.

Fifteen minutes later, he stood at the front of the same recreation room where he'd cradled Trevon's body on that fateful morning. He still didn't feel comfortable down there, didn't think he ever would again. Members of the Mau-Mau were milling around, talking. Most were in white T-shirts, what with the heat and all.

Everybody was sweating. The four or five Muslim men stood out as they talked together in a corner with Leroy, who wasn't a Muslim but served as the Mau-Mau liaison to them. Obie circulated around the room:

"How's your mama doing, Peyton, she get out of the hospital yet?

"Foster, I read in the paper about Anisha winning the hundred meters—she's definitely Division I material. And with them grades, she can go anywhere she wants.

"York, you putting on a little weight, Cherise must be feeding you real good.

"See me after the meeting, Yusef, might have a summer job for that boy of yours."

Finally he returned to the front of the room, sat down, and looked at the small cluster of men before him. He shook off the feeling that he'd somehow failed to keep the group together in adversity and started the meeting.

"I take off for work in an hour, and we got a lot of things to go over. The first thing is to make a decision whether we going to cooperate with the police or not. It just don't make no sense to have an organization to fight drugs if we ain't."

"Obie, just tell me now, how the hell we going to cooperate with people who're beating on black folks?" This from York, a man with a bullet-shaped head, close-cropped hair, and fierce, burning eyes.

"That kind of talk ain't going to get us nowhere," Leroy said. "Our problem is right here, in this project, with black folks, our own folks who're killing us with the drugs and the dealers."

Another man spoke up. "York's right, we can't be working with the police. Let's set up our own damn thing. We can tighten up the organization and deal with these bastards on our own."

"Sure," Obie said. "And your ass will be right back in jail. Have your tail back upstate so fast you won't know what happened to you. Shit, man, didn't them years inside teach you nothing?"

York said, "I been there too, and it taught me never to kiss ass. And that's what you doing with the police." He leaned forward in his chair, his fierce eyes staring at Obie. "Now, I'm going to say something been on my mind and everybody else's mind here for the last few weeks. Why did you have to stand up for Captain Sarnese and tell that Gazette guy he wasn't a racist? Why did you have to shame all of us black folks by saying that?"

Obie felt like someone in his family had hit him in the head with a hammer. He glanced slowly around the room, his eyes going from face to face. York had once stood watch all alone for three days in a row, had supported him when the first death threats came. Had walked right up to one of the thugs. "Touch him, motherfucker, and you'll be dead tomorrow, I'm as serious as a heart attack." The dealers had laid low for a while.

Obie said, "You're like my brother, man. But not even my brother can tell me who to like or how to treat people. Sarnese's my friend, and that man has backed me and you in some hard situations. Don't come to me with that stuff."

York's fists clenched and unclenched as he tried to control his explosive temper, the thing that had landed him in jail in the first place. He stood up.

"Man, I'm sorry for the way I said what I said, but I just don't know who I hate more, the cops or the dealers. And feeling the way I do, I got to leave the Mau-Mau. Sarnese's men beat on those folks, and that's the bottom line. You do what you got to do, and I'll do the same. Later." He turned and walked out the door.

Obie looked at the remaining men. "Anybody else feel that way about me or about cooperating with the cops? If so, let's get it out now."

The men, usually of good humor and quick to endorse his leadership, sat silent. Finally, one spoke up.

"We're going to back you and we're going to keep on with the Mau-Mau. But you got to know we ain't happy about all this shit."

Leroy said, "Anybody who wants to go, do it now. Because things just going to get rougher."

There was a knock at the door. Before Leroy could get to it, it burst open, and there stood Tyrone Waters, all five foot six of him. One hand, raised on high, was clenched in a fist.

The other hand held a can of beer.

"The same man who destroyed Bucky Jackson back then figured it was about time he showed up to help you men destroy this blight on the African community." Waters's face was round, and all the hair that remained on his head had turned almost pure white. He could no longer stand erect, arthritis having bent his bones one by one.

He started shuffling like a fighter. "You all need help, and I'm here to give it."

The men began to laugh and clap. Obie smiled, and Leroy moved over to spar with the old man.

The men were cheering when the door suddenly flew open again.

There was a sudden whistling noise, and the door was slammed shut. A large bottle-like object landed on the floor, sizzled for a moment, then exploded like a rocket, sending sparkling streams of fire in all directions.

Shouts and angry cries replaced the laughter and fellowship of a few minutes earlier. It was only a firecracker, but within seconds, Obie knew that the Mau-Mau was being cut off from the community. When they went outside to see who'd thrown the thing, none of the teenagers standing in front of the entrance to the apartments would say a word.

Just part of the price paid because his friend Sarnese hadn't been able to control his cops the day of the riot.

IT WAS SIX O'CLOCK in Ardmore, Pennsylvania, and Dora Lee woke up wanting Obie very badly. Her whole body was aching for him. And there were so many other things on her mind. Besides Sabaya and Timba, there was her son Jason, now a sergeant in the army fighting over there in Afghanistan on his third tour. They kept in touch by cell phone at least once a week, but U.S. casualties were rising every day.

Jason had been such a pain when he was younger, always in trouble, bucking Obie when they got married, but now he was a full grown man redeemed by his career in the army, where he served as a helicopter gunner. She sure wished he could have found his way in a career that didn't mean she had to wake up in the middle of the night wondering whether some Pashtun guerrilla was lying in wait on the ground with a Stinger missile to bring down that Yankee gunship with him in it. Oh, it seemed like the country was in endless wars since 9/11, and that it would never be over. Each and every Sunday, the prayer list for members of the congregation in the armed forces got longer and longer—two had been killed in action in the past two years. Jason, my son, may God's ever-loving arms protect you!

She showered and dressed, enervated by the smell of coffee and the sound of the Lenhardt family getting up. Why couldn't her own family live in peace in the home they'd poured so much into over the years? We pray, we work, we love our neighbors, but all we have is a war in our lives, just like Jason has over there in Afghanistan.

Her self-pity, something she disliked in others, evaporated when the Lenhardts' four-year-old daughter knocked on her door and came in.

"Dora Lee, it's time to eat, and I want to show you the picture I drew of you. Come see."

The little girl put her hand in Dora Lee's and pulled her downstairs, chattering about the hamster another of the children had brought home from school.

"It's just beautiful," Dora Lee said, looking at the picture the little girl had drawn in her tablet with red, blue, and orange crayons. "It really is, honey. You keep this up, we'll have to make up a television show just for you. We'll call it the Pam show. Would you like that?"

The child clapped her hands. "You'd have to come with me on the show."

Her mother said, "You better let Dora Lee be, darling, give her a chance to eat her breakfast."

Ruth was already seated at the table with her two junior high boys, one twelve and the other ten. Both were hurrying to make their bus. Ruth had fed Bill earlier, and he was on his way out the door, lunch pail in hand.

"Morning, Dora Lee, I'm out of here. See you tonight. You have a great day, hear?"

Dora Lee smiled. "You too, Bill. And be careful." Dora Lee

knew how much Ruth worried that some day Bill would fall off of one of those girders. It was good work, paid well, and was steady what with all the new construction going on downtown. But it was dangerous, and she really wished they'd give him an office job. He rated it with his seven years of seniority.

"I'm always careful. Now, if I can just stop all those women from running after me at lunchtime, I'll be fine."

Ruth stood at the door holding her little daughter by the hand. She hugged her husband and gave him a long kiss.

"There, that ought to keep you."

He smacked his lips and left.

A few minutes later, when the boys had gone out to wait for the bus and Pam was sitting in the family room watching cartoons, Ruth said, "Let's just sit for a while and enjoy our coffee. Mama'll be here in a few minutes to babysit, then we can get out of here. We ought to be able to make the seven-thirty train.... How did you sleep, you look a little tired."

Dora Lee said, "Oh, I had a good night's sleep."

"I don't think so," Ruth said softly.

Dora Lee suddenly broke down in tears. "The truth is, I was miserable last night. I'm just not used to being away from my family. I miss Obie something awful, and I have these nightmares about Jason and Trevon. And I told you about Son Teagle and how evil and mean he is? In some of the dreams, he's stalking me, popping up out of nowhere when I'm walking in a park or leaving a store. I'm almost afraid to fall asleep these days."

Ruth handed her a tissue. "And I'm worried to death about Sabaya," Dora Lee said. "She's so hard-headed. I've talked to her and she acted like she was listening, but I just don't know if I was getting through."

"I think she's more mature than you think."

"You don't know her, not really. And sometimes I don't think I do either. She's so talented, so smart, but there's a wild streak in her, and it scares me. One night last week she didn't come home from school until seven o'clock, and she didn't even tell her grandmother where she was."

"All teenagers do that sometimes."

Dora Lee had stopped crying. "No, I don't think she knows the danger we're really in. All three of us. One thing the police don't seem to know is that somebody who wants to kill you can really do it. It's like the only thing on their mind, day and night, is how to find you and kill you."

Dora Lee saw the flicker of fear in Ruth's face and knew then she wouldn't be able to stay long in this house. Wasn't fair to them. Good thing that in a few weeks it would be time for the family's summer vacation, and she and Obie could go south and be with the children in Gastonia.

The doorbell rang. Before Ruth could stop her, Pam had run past her and was opening the door, crying "Grandma!"

"Pam!" her mother called out, "don't you *ever* open the door like that! I'm the only one who can answer it. I'll spank you next time."

It was too late.

The door was open and there stood a short, round black man. He held a package in one hand and a handheld computer in the other. Ruth let out a little shriek. So did Dora Lee and Pam.

Ruth's mother stepped through the door behind the man. "Whatever is the matter with you all? Stop it or the Fed-Ex man will think you're crazy."

The bearded man, dressed in his immaculate uniform, shook his head slowly and said, "Listen, folks, I don't know what upset you, but if somebody will just sign for this package, I'll be on my way." Pam clung tightly to her grandmother's side. Ruth said, "It's just that we were expecting my mother, and instead you were there. I've told the child a dozen times not to open that door unless I tell her. Here, I'll sign for it."

In two minutes, the man had left in his truck. Dora Lee and Ruth got into the rusty old Ford and headed down the street to the Ardmore train station.

Both women were silent. They remained quiet all the way to work that morning, each deep in her thoughts. The image of the man's pleasant face stayed in Dora Lee's mind.

How could she have cried out? How could she?

IT WAS A FRIDAY NIGHT, the night of the senior honors concert and the last day of school for Sabaya. Only those students who had excelled during the year were chosen to play in the recital. And those who took part had their pictures placed forever on the honored walls of the Performing Arts Hall of Fame.

She had looked forward to this night for a year. She'd be playing the piano solo in Beethoven's *Emperor Concerto*, the piece she loved so much, the one that gave her the best chance to display her virtuosity. Madame Domskaya said no other student her age, in her memory, had ever played that particular piece with such vitality and authority as Sabaya.

Oh, what a night it was going to be.

Sabaya got into her white dress and posed this way and that before the mirror in her bedroom, the one that had been her mother's room when she was growing up. Downstairs, her grandmother was busy running the vacuum one more time. It was something she always did when she was nervous.

Sabaya loved her Big Mama and felt safe in the house. She loved the stories her grandmother had told her about growing up on a sugar plantation on the hills at the top of Barbados. It had always been Sabaya 's wish to visit the island with her someday, and that was supposed to have been her reward for graduation—until all this trouble started.

Big Mama called up the stairs. "Come on down, darling. If you don't hurry up, we're going to be late, and you won't be able to do your warm-up exercises."

"I'll be down in a minute, I have to make a phone call—I'll still have time for the warm-ups."

"All right, but don't stay on the phone."

Sabaya dialed the first six digits of a number uptown. She stopped and held the phone in her hand, praying for God to keep her from temptation. Her mama had talked to her from the heart about Hashim and his reputation and where seeing him could lead. She'd told her how easy it was for a young woman to lose her good name and about the dangers of contracting AIDS and herpes. Even told her how at age sixteen a sweet-talking, supposedly God-fearing young drummer in the church musical ensemble had seduced her one day in a country field in the last hours of a church picnic, and how it had wrecked the life Big Mama had mapped out for her—torpedoed her plans of being a biochemist and sent her off instead to secretarial school. All of this her mama had told her.

Sabaya was still holding her cell phone. Her eyes were closed, but she could see Hashim's mouth.

She dialed the last digit. Hashim answered on the second ring.

"Hello, who's that?"

Sabaya pushed the "end call" button.

She sat motionless on the chair for a moment, her mind warring with her body. Demons were possessing her. Hadn't she sworn, yes sworn to her mother she wouldn't tell anybody where she was living?

She called the number again.

Hashim said, "Where are you? I thought you'd left town. Even went down to the school and waited around for you. Nobody had seen you."

"We made arrangements for all of my lessons to be done at home until the concert. But you know my recital's tonight, and I just had to do my solo."

"I thought I'd lost you, where you staying?

"Down here in South Philly at grandmama's."

"Should of figured that."

"Listen, I'm leaving on Sunday, my folks are sending me down south for the rest of the summer till I go off to college. And I want to see you. Oh, Hashim, I love you and I miss you, and—"

"Sabaya, get down here," her grandmother called. "Your dad will be here in a minute to pick us up, and we got to be ready."

Sabaya said, "Hashim, I'll meet you tomorrow morning about nine o'clock. At that diner on the corner of Seventh and South. We can figure out where to go from there."

"Wear the red dress, the one I like so much."

"I'll be right down, Big Mama."

OBIE SAT WITH DORA LEE'S HAND IN HIS. Beside her sat Big Mama, dressed in black and wearing a corsage of white roses Obie had bought her for the occasion. The Bullock family was sitting in the audience at the Philadelphia Academy of Music.

The orchestra of the High School of Creative and Performing Arts was on the stand, and what a colorful orchestra it was. You could have made a United Nations assembly meeting just from the students who were playing tonight. Or a garden of flowers—every color in God's universe seemed to be represented.

Obie held Dora Lee's hand even tighter as the members of the orchestra took their seats. Among them were friends of Sabaya, children who'd sometimes come home with her after school: an Indian violinist dressed tonight in a pink sari that glistened in the powerful spotlights; a Vietnamese trombonist who'd won a scholarship to Juilliard; and the Ukranian-born brother and sister twins, both cello players, who'd been trained early on by a famous musician in Odessa.

The conductor for the evening was Dr. Nathanson, almost seventy years old now and a holdover from the days when the school had been almost entirely white. A few days ago, Sabaya had told Obie no one could ever make her hate white people, not after what Dr. Nathanson had done for her.

But it hadn't always been that way. As the orchestra warmed up, Obie turned to Dora Lee. "Remember, honey, when Sabaya came home that first day from the music composition class and said she'd never be able to understand that man's accent—how could she pass a course in composition when the teacher didn't even speak English?"

"I remember, we were sure going to give the principal a piece of our mind."

The memory made them both smile, for the principal had called in Dr. Nathanson, who'd quickly charmed the parents with his warmth and disarmed them with high praise of their daughter: "She can be among the best." Tonight, it sure looked like she was getting there.

Applause swept through the audience as it received Sabaya

Bullock, looking almost regal in her white dress crossed with a brilliant red sash. Her hair had been lovingly twisted and braided by her grandmother, and her gold-rimmed glasses were perched on her nose. She sat down at the piano, nodded to the conductor and the audience, then struck the first chords of the Beethoven concerto.

Obie sat on the edge of his seat, his left arm propping up his chin as he watched his daughter bear down on the piano, her fingers rigid—almost like drills—as they hammered away at the keys. Sabaya would anticipate the orchestra and the conductor, now moving her head rhythmically along with the melody, now bending low over the keys, like she was coaxing the music from its hiding place in the bosom of the piano.

She swept her brown hands up and down the white and black keys, humming and smiling and playing every moment of her solos as if nothing could ever give her more joy in life than what she was doing at that exact moment. When the orchestra was playing alone, she rocked back and forth on the walnut bench in time with their rhythm, and then, when it was time, she would come in at exactly the right moment, filling the hall with clear, pure, utterly beautiful sounds.

When the concerto was over, the whole audience stood up and applauded Sabaya, whose face was shiny from perspiration.

Obie jumped up and shouted, "That's my baby!"

She bowed, and Mr. Nathanson took her arm and led her forward. He wore a tuxedo that contrasted sharply with his usual costume of white shirt, blue tie, and baggy gray trousers. His shirts were always freshly pressed, the pants never.

The principal came out and handed a bouquet of long-stemmed red roses to Sabaya. She bowed, then turned to the orchestra and with a graceful lifting of her arms invited them to stand up. She turned to the audience, looked at her parents and grandmother, and tossed three roses towards the audience.

"For my folks!"

"HONEY, I REALLY DON'T WANT to spoil the evening, because it's been great. Your mama and me, we're awful proud of you. But we haven't seen you for three weeks and a lot's been happening—not much of it good."

The family was celebrating at a Chinese restaurant. Obie had enjoyed the food and the conversation. Now he had to do a hard thing.

Sabaya said, "I know, I read the papers and I can see how much danger we're in, but I'll be leaving on Monday anyway."

Dora Lee took over for Obie. "What your daddy means is, you're not going to be able to stay for the graduation party tomorrow night. We've been pushing our luck by letting you stay here as long as you have, it's just too risky for you and dangerous for your grandmother. So we've got a ticket for you tomorrow morning on the eleven o'clock flight to Charlotte, Gastonia's only a half hour away."

Sabaya looked from one of them to the other. It was a hard look, but more than that. Obie had never seen that much defiance on her face.

"No, you can't do that to me! I won't let you, I won't go! It's my high-school graduation party, the only one I'll ever have." She turned to her grandmother. "Big Mama, don't let them do this to me."

Right there in the restaurant, his darling girl broke out in tears.

"But baby—"

"Stop it, Daddy. I'm not a child any more, and I'm not getting on that plane tomorrow morning."

Everybody in the restaurant was looking at them. Obie turned away quickly from Sabaya and called the waitress over.

"Check, please, and I'd appreciate it if you'd hurry."

Big Mama put her arms around Sabaya. "Now, honey, they're just doing what's best for you. Why, at Christmastime, when you're home from college and everything's safe and sound, I'll let you have a party myself. I'll pay for it. Only just stop the crying, now. Your folks have said you have to go and you know you do."

Sabaya excused herself and went to the restroom. When she

returned she was no longer crying, and Obie didn't like the look on her face. It was calm and resolved and distant, like nothing mattered to her.

As they got up to leave the restaurant, Rita Simpson, a long-time neighbor of theirs, was just coming in with a girlfriend. Obie had never come to know her very well—she kind of kept to herself—but she was one fine-looking woman. Her skin was walnut-colored, and she was tall and full-framed. Her soft hair was swept back off one side of her face, which was heavily made up. He didn't like a lot of makeup on a woman, but Rita's skin was so lustrous it looked good on her. Every part of her face—her lips, her nose, her ears and eyes—fit just right with the other parts.

She was wearing a light cotton summer dress, and the designs on it—some kind of a yellow summer flower—reminded Obie of those rich and carefree white women in the old movies that ran on the classic movie channel.

Her eyes lit up when she saw the Bullock family, and they fairly sparkled when she looked at Obie.

"My, everybody looks so nice tonight. What's the occasion?"

Dora Lee told her and Rita turned to Sabaya. "I'm so happy for you. If I'd known, I'd have gotten you a present. As a matter of fact I will, I'll drop it over next week. Will somebody be around?"

Obie said, "Only me, I'm afraid. Sabaya's leaving for the South, and Dora Lee's going to be away for a few days."

"Okay, see you, then. Congratulations again, Sabaya. You look beautiful, darling."

Dora Lee tucked Obie's arm firmly in hers. "We have to be running now. Take care, Rita."

THE BULLOCK FAMILY HAD A QUIET RIDE back to Big Mama's house. Obie saw the old woman and the young woman to the door and said, "I'll see you in the morning, Sabaya. Your mama and I are going to be out at the Lenhardts' tonight, and we'll be down to pick you up at eight o'clock. That should give us plenty of time to get to the airport."

Sabaya said, "I wish you'd think this over one more time."

"Sorry, honey, but that's the way it's got to be."

She walked into the house and closed the door.

Obie nodded to the Puerto Rican family sitting on the steps next door and got back into the car with Dora Lee. At least they'd have a chance to be alone and make love tonight. He turned to her, kissed her, and put his right hand on her thighs.

"Well, we've done it. The child's out of high school. I couldn't be more proud of her."

Dora Lee put her hand over his. "The Lord's been really good to us, but I'm worried about Sabaya. I don't think we should leave her alone tonight with Big Mama, not in the state she's in. I think we should just go on back and stay with them tonight. Something's going on in that head of Sabaya's—I don't know what it is, but it's trouble."

"Baby..." Here was their first chance to be together in a month, and she wanted to spend the night babysitting Sabaya. He squeezed Dora Lee's thighs gently. "If we do that, it'll be one in the morning before we get to bed. We'll be talking with them all night. She's safe where she is."

"I know, but she's acting...I can't put my finger on it. We got to use our heads—I don't think she's using hers."

Obie had his hand all the way up her dress. It was past the garter line and pressing on warm flesh.

Two minutes passed in silence.

"All right, you win. But I think we should get up real early and try to be back down here around seven o'clock instead of eight."

"It's a promise." Obie started up the car and dropped his hand between her thighs. By the time they were on the Parkway headed towards Ardmore, he felt her fingers on his trousers. She rested her hand there, not moving it. Just there. It was the way they'd always driven when they came home from a good evening out. Sure was going to be nice.

"I just want to tell you something," he said. "I know we got some hard days ahead, baby, but we going to make it."

"I truly want to believe that, but I don't feel safe any more, and I really won't feel good until that girl is out of here and on that plane. And Obie, we got to start thinking about finding us another place to live."

"We got to build a wall around us tonight. Sabaya's going to be okay. Let this thing be."

Dora Lee sighed, curled her legs up under her in the old Chevy, and dropped her head onto Obie's shoulder like she'd done when they were courting. "Okay, but pray to God she'll be all right, because if she's not, I'll never forgive myself and I might never forgive you. Look, we have all day tomorrow to make love after she's gone."

"Doggone, you never do give up, do you? Here we are almost in Ardmore and you still talking that stuff. Forget it, baby."

Ten minutes later the car rolled into the Lenhardts' driveway, and Obie and Dora Lee got out of the car. Dora Lee held on tight to Obie's arm.

"It'll be all right, baby. Right now just remember, you just the most beautiful woman in the world. Can't nobody touch you."

Fifteen minutes later they were in bed, and an hour later, Obie was sleeping quietly.

Dora Lee stayed awake and stared at the ceiling. At three o'clock in the morning, she got out of bed, slipped on her bathrobe, and went into the Lenhardts' living room and turned on the television. Finally, she fell asleep in a chair.

It was there, on an overstuffed chair, the television guide in her lap, that Obie found her at seven-thirty when he woke up to go get his daughter.

"What you doing in here? I slept right through the alarm. You know I don't hear those things. You'd have heard it." He was already taking off his pajama top. "We ain't going to get there till eight-thirty now. We going to be late, baby. And what with those security lines down at the airport, we might not make it at all."

CHAPTER 7

SABAYA SAT ON THE EDGE OF HER BED and looked around the tiny room, which was filled with pictures of her mother as a little girl. In one she was in a pink ballet dress, in another she was posed with all of her Philly uncles from Barbados around her. Best of all was a picture of her dressed up in a red and yellow carnival costume at the West Indian Day parade over in Brooklyn, New York. She must have been fourteen years old and stood smiling with her arms around the shoulders of two girls who, like her, had smooth black skin and beautiful saucerlike eyes that could warm and charm the coldest-hearted person on earth. Sabaya took a leather-framed oval portrait in her hand and hugged it close to her heart.

Mama would understand everything. She always had. And all her parents would have to do was book a flight for the next day. It wasn't as if she'd really disobeyed them before. Sure, she'd partied with some kids her folks had told her to stay away from—they were fun and gave her a chance to relax—but she always left when they started doing drugs and talking trash. Nobody knew how hard it was to do piano all day and still keep up with your Algebra and English. And it wasn't easy trying to stay friendly with all the kids she'd grown up with when so many of them were either pregnant or in trouble with the law and felt that her music and good grades set her apart, made her too much like a white nerd.

She could tell from the way some of them acted when she stopped by to say hello at the bench where they all used to sit. Wasn't that long ago that Angela had jumped up and said, "Oh, that's Miss Bullock, she so smart we got to stand in her presence. Get your stupid black asses up for her!" Sabaya had burst into tears and fled to her apartment. Sometimes she felt her brains would burst from all the pressure. Yet she'd been a good daughter, she'd never done anything really wrong.

She didn't count sleeping with Hashim as wrong. After all, they'd known each forever, had gone to the same elementary school not far from the Temple University campus, had held hands on field trips to the Art Museum and Fels Planitarium downtown.

And he'd protected her from neighborhood bullies, both male and female, as they grew up, had continued to do so even as their lives grew apart. First he'd gone to the youth center upstate, then he'd failed to make it at an alternative high school in the city, and now some people were saying he was involved with drugs. Even her best friend, Rokina, had told her she'd seen him selling them in the stairwell down there on the third floor where all the trouble was.

Sabaya didn't want to believe it, so she never questioned Hashim about it and told Rokina that if she wanted to remain her friend, she'd never mention his name in her presence again. Sure, he might do a few things over the line, but the Hashim she knew would never do anything really bad, and drugs were bad. She did wonder sometimes about the clothes he wore, the gold necklaces around his neck, and his hints that he would be getting a lot of money soon, particularly since he didn't have a steady job.

But she loved him. She wished she didn't. Wished her music alone were enough, her love of God were enough to fill her. But no, the devil—and she knew very well it had to be Satan behind this—wouldn't let her alone. Two weeks away from Hashim's arms was worse than death. She couldn't go to sleep, couldn't touch her bed sheets without wanting him beside her, talking those sweet words to her.

Sabaya placed her hands on her breasts and moved both her nipples with her fingers. She shouldn't do this thing to her folks.

She walked over to the battered walnut bureau and eased open the drawers. She got out a little knapsack she kept for her music and put into it the clean underwear, makeup, and toilet articles she'd need for today. She just hoped Hashim would find them a better motel than the one they'd stayed in over in New Jersey the last time, before the Teagle shooting.

She quietly opened her door and held her shoes in her hand, then slipped out into the hall and softly placed her feet on the worn carpet. A floorboard creaked as she made her way down the hall into the dining room. She held her breath and stood still.

No sound from Big Mama's room.

Sabaya put down another foot. And another.

Finally, she saw the contours of the kitchen table. She turned on a reading light in the corner of the room and wrote a note to her parents and Big Mama.

When she finished, she slipped the big burglar bar out of the door—hesitating for a moment because she feared a thief might break in and hurt her granny—stepped out onto Bainbridge Street and quickly walked the one block up to South Street.to catch a bus. It was six-thirty in the morning.

No sooner had Sabaya started for the bus stop than she was approached by two prostitutes who told her she didn't belong there.

"I'm not in your business." She hurried past them.

But she was only half a block from them, walking quickly with her head down, when a car pulled up beside her.

"How much, honey bunch?"

Sabaya turned her head towards the car, a BMW with a white man sitting in the front seat, his body so fat it seemed to spread over both the driver's and the passenger's seats. He'd stopped the car and was leaning his head out of the street-side window. He wore a black cowboy-style shirt with white and gold piping on it. His face was pasty, and he needed a shave.

"I'm on my way to work, mister. I'm not available." She was sorry now she'd worn the red dress.

"Don't give me that shit, girl. What's the matter, too fat for you? I've got a fat wallet!"

Sabaya kept walking, but the man had one hand on the steering wheel and with the window down was slowly cruising along the street, keeping pace with her.

She wanted to scream, but then she remembered what she was doing and began to run down the block, only to stumble on her high heels.

She took off the shoes and began to run on the sidewalk. The cement, still warm from yesterday's heat, hurt her feet. She ran very fast.

The car kept up with her.

Should she go back to her grandmama's house? That was the only safe place to be. But the car would follow her whichever way she ran, and how could she explain to Big Mama what had happened? No, she'd better just keep on.

She ran along South Street, hating to think about what was under her feet. Suddenly, two men blocked her—one white and in dungarees and a torn yellow T-shirt, the other black with bell-bottom trousers and a weight-lifter's build. She tried darting to her right, but the black man gripped her arms in a vise.

Sabaya screamed. "Police!"

"Quiet, girl," the white man said, "we are the police." He showed her his badge. "Now do you want to tell us what was going on between that man in the BMW and you?"

"Nothing," Sabaya said. "I'm just on my way to see some friends. I was staying with my grandmama last night and wanted to get out early, and the first thing I know this man was following me."

The black man asked her for identification. When she gave him her learner's permit, he said, "What are you doing out here on these streets in that dress at this hour of the morning? Where's your grandmother live?"

Would they take her back there? "She's not home, she already left for work this morning, she works at a restaurant near Penn."

"And where," the white cop asked, "are your parents?"

"Down south on vacation, they won't be back for a few weeks."

The cops looked at each other. The black one said, "Young lady, I don't like your story too good, and I sure don't like you being out on the streets in that outfit at this time of the morning. We're going to have to take you down to the precinct and contact somebody to come get you. I'll feel better about it that way."

Her legs went limp.

In her purse was a program of the concert last night, and it had her picture on it. Sabaya pulled it out and showed it to the policemen.

"Here, this will prove who I am."

The white cop took the program, saw her picture, and read the caption: "Sabaya Bullock, valedictorian of the class of 2009." He looked at his partner, then back at her. "That's some honor."

The black cop looked her squarely in the face. "Sabaya, you're obviously smart, but use some common sense next time. Dressing like that at this time of day can cause you a lot of trouble."

She didn't relax until the cops had put her on the South Street bus.

"So long, kid," the white officer said. He flashed his badge at the driver. "Make sure she gets down there all right, she just had a pretty bad experience here."

The driver closed the door and nodded at Sabaya. "Sit behind me, young lady. Nobody's going to bother you."

She would get to see Hashim after all.

SABAYA SAT IN THE DINER at Seventh and South, drinking her third cup of coffee. The breakfast of bacon and eggs with hot buttered rye toast had restored her spirits. She felt comfortable in this diner, for it was here that she and her friends had often met after school. The waiter knew her well. He'd greeted her with a flourish and a bow when he saw how she was dressed.

"I get the feeling today's a special day in your life. If you don't mind an old man saying so, you look like a million dollars."

Sabaya thanked him and said, "You've got a ways to go before you should be calling yourself old."

As she lingered over her coffee, the Saturday morning regulars came in and the restaurant came alive with the sounds of Philadelphia. Behind the counter, a swarthy man loudly called out every order he received from the beautiful Puerto Rican waitress, turning her Spanish accent into a Greek one. At the counter three men argued about the Phillies' prospects.

A clattering of pots and pans and the smell of coffee and frying potatoes made Sabaya think of home and her folks. Maybe she should at least call Big Mama. She'd never met Hashim and wouldn't be as upset as her parents would be if they knew who she was with. Her dad said Hashim had no aim in life. His folks were a dentist and a schoolteacher who lived in a plush townhouse they owned three or four blocks away from the Hill project. "Anybody with the kind of privileges that kid's had who still ends up in reform school has got to have criminal ambitions. Don't you let me catch him around you."

And she remembered the end of the talk with her mama about Hashim. "Sabaya, that boy raises snakes for a hobby, which ought to tell you something about him. And don't let all that sweet-talking and 'yes ma'am, no ma'am' stuff when he's around me fool you. Underneath, he's trouble, and I don't want him anywhere around you, you hear me?"

"But Mama, why don't you let me make my own judgment about him? I'm practically a grown woman now, and I know him better than you do. He's sweet, really he is. And I hate this feeling that you don't trust me."

"Well, in this case, you're just going to have to trust me. I love you and don't want you hurt, and Hashim is nothing but trouble!" She took Sabaya's hands in hers. "Now I want your promise, that you'll never see him again." Sabaya loved her mother fiercely and knew, deep down, that she was right. She gave her solemn promise.

But she just couldn't keep her word—it seemed like the devil had taken possession of her soul, so she couldn't call up the spiritual strength to fight the temptations that were tearing her apart inside. Nevertheless, she'd had hours to think and had just about decided to get up and walk out of the restaurant when Hashim slid into the seat beside her.

"Sorry, I had some business to take care of uptown and I had a hard time finding a parking place around here."

The old waiter came over to the booth and asked for his order.

Hashim put his hand on hers and smiled. "Give me a little time, please, sir, I'd like to talk to my lady a minute."

Sabaya almost melted away with pleasure just from the way he looked at her.

He said, "Baby, I'm so glad you showed up. We going to have us a good time today, just wait and see." Sabaya looked at the waiter. "Just bring him a bagel and coffee. And make it to go, please."

The people at the counter who'd been talking away before Hashim came in were quiet now. Probably they'd taken an instant dislike to him. Gold earrings were in both of his ears, five in his left ear alone, and a small gold stud pierced his left nostril. His head was completely bald—he had it shaved once a week. A large gold bracelet was on his left arm, and the blue T-shirt practically molded to his upper body showed off a dazzling gold chain. Grownups were always judging people by appearances, stereotyping them just because of the way they dressed.

These people had never heard Hashim recite Keats to her—"She walks in beauty like the night"—or listened to him talk about the history of Africa, and how black people from Egypt had created Greek civilization. He could talk for hours about that history, he could make her truly believe that she, Sabaya Bullock of the Joseph E. Hill project in Philadelphia, Pennsylvania, was the direct descendant of Cleopatra. Hashim made her feel good about herself, and when he smiled at her the way he was smiling right now, she felt the sweetest, most delicious warmth spreading all the way up her body to her brain.

The old man returned with the order. She quickly paid him and put a two-dollar tip on the table. The waiter didn't look at Hashim.

"Thank you, miss." He hesitated for a minute. "Be careful, now."

Hashim looked at the man as if to say something, but Sabaya tugged at his arm. "Let's go, honey."

As they left, she looked back quickly and saw the waiter shaking his head.

THEY WALKED OUT onto South Street. It was ten o'clock, and the street was bustling with the faces and sounds of many nations: the Indians with their rich brown skin and swirling turbans; the lilting voices of the West Indians; the Hispanics who always made Sabaya think of sunshine, laughter, and guitar music; and then the whites, some wearing open-collared shirts, khaki shorts, and expensive cut-through moccasins—Philadelphia was becoming a very cosmopolitain city. Hashim had Sabaya by the hand and was pulling her through the crowd of people waiting to cross the street at a red light.

"Why are you rushing me?" she said. "We have the whole day to ourselves, let's just relax a little bit."

Hashim said nothing, just grasped her hand a little tighter, pulling her over to where his white Ford Expedition was parked.

Sabaya planted her feet on the ground and jerked her hand back. "What's gotten into you, I'm not breaking my neck getting over there. Can't you see I've got my high-heels on?"

Hashim smiled. "Baby, I just can't wait to love you—remember, it's been almost a month."

"I know. But that's still no excuse for you to try and kill me on this street." Her hands were on her hips, and her head was tilted to one side. "Please slow down."

"All right."

As they walked down the street, she heard a horn blaring away. Hashim had parked his car so tightly that it blocked in a red Honda Accord. A young white man sat in the car, a child strapped in the baby seat in the back. The man—typical Philadelphian—was blowing the horn over and over to tell whoever had blocked him in that he wanted to get out.

Hashim dropped Sabaya 's hand and ran down the street. He was a nice person, no matter what they said about him.

But Hashim didn't go to the Expedition. He walked over to the Honda and said, "Motherfucker, put your hand on that horn one more time and I'll kick your ass right here. Pull you right out of the car."

The little girl began to cry.

The man, about five-ten and solidly built, looked to Sabaya as if he could deal with Hashim in a fight, but these days only a fool would argue with a young black man. He looked at Hashim, glanced at Sabaya, then turned to his daughter.

"Please be quiet, honey. It's all right." He looked back at Hashim. "Kid, I don't know what's wrong with you, but you're looking for trouble and you're going to find it. Why don't you just get in your truck and go on out of here?"

Sabaya grabbed Hashim by the arm. "Come on, the man's right. Let's go."

He shook her arm off. "Just get in the truck, sit down and wait. Here's the keys."

"I'm not going anywhere—except home if you don't stop."

"You're going to do what? Ruin our whole day for this piece of shit?" What had gotten into Hashim, she'd never seen him act this way before. He was one of the politest boys she knew.

People had begun to gather around the scene. One of them, an older African-American woman, called to a man looking out a second-floor window.

"Jason, call the cops." The woman walked right up to Hashim and Sabaya. "Listen, you two. Just get right on out of here, we don't have any of that nonsense around here." She narrowed her eyes. "Young lady, don't I know you from somewhere, what church you belong to?"

Sabaya practically screamed at Hashim. "Get into that truck or I'm leaving!" The man upstairs had closed the window and by now had probably called the police.

Hashim stared hard at the black woman, looked at the man now sitting stony-faced in the Accord, and put his hand on its door handle.

"Sabaya, get in the truck." Sabaya didn't stir.

He moved away from the Honda and towards the Ford, looking back over at the man and the woman.

"Motherfuckers can kiss my black ass."

The woman looked at them. "Girl, I don't know what a nice-looking young lady like you is doing with him. You got any sense, you'll get out of that truck and go home."

Sabaya said, "Please mind your own business, ma'am." She turned to Hashim. "Let's get out of here—you've done it now, the police are coming and if they find me, my mother will skin me alive."

Hashim sped away, driving north towards the approaches to the bridge to New Jersey. But to Sabaya's surprise, he suddenly turned off and headed west up Market Street towards Broad as if he were headed for North or West Philly.

"What are you doing? I thought we were going over to Jersey."

"Changed my mind, we stopping at my place. I'm getting a little tired of going over there."

Sabaya sat bolt upright. "We can't go to North Philly, you know the Teagle gang is—"

"Don't worry about a thing." Hashim was on Market Street, close to Broad. "I always taken care of you, don't I?"

"I'm not going with you." Hashim had a hard look on his face, one she'd never seen before. "LET ME OUT! I'm getting the subway and going back to Big Mama's house!"

"We have to go to North Philly, baby, I got a very important reason for it." His voice sounded desperately sincere. He meant it. But what—

A subway stop. They were now heading up Broad Street—if she was going to get out, it would have to be now.

Hashim sat looking straight ahead as they waited at a red light. He wouldn't look at her.

"I'll see you around, I'm getting out here."

She pulled on the door handle. The door wouldn't open. She pulled again.

It still wouldn't open.

She turned toward Hashim.

"What have you done? Release those door locks, or I'll scream!"

She reached for the lever to roll the window down. If only

that light would stay red.

"Get your hand off that handle, Sabaya. I ain't playing, you going with me whether you like it or not."

Sabaya was thrown back in her seat as Hashim stepped down hard on the accelerator. He went straight through the red light. All around them, horns blew as he headed towards the center of North Philly.

Sabaya yelled, "You betrayed me! Say it!"

Dora Lee could barely keep still as she sat in the car. She'd have liked to put Obie into a pot of boiling oil. Here they were, stuck in highway traffic at eight-thirty in the morning, with no way of getting in touch with anybody to get that child off to North Carolina. Obie, as usual, had forgotten to charge up the cell phone. She'd have to call on King Jesus now. He'd know the problem and know just how to fix it.

She prayed silently, then looked at Obie and stifled an impulse to say something mean. Prayer did change things.

"Baby, it's all right. I told Mama to get Sabaya up, she'll have her ready to go when we get there."

Obie's hand was balled into a fist and he was pounding it on the steering wheel, keeping time to the music on the gospel station. There were beads of sweat on his brow. If he had to buy an old wreck of an automobile, Dora Lee sure wished he'd gotten one with working air conditioning.

She said, "Honey, what about getting off here and trying some of the side streets. At least we have some chance that way."

"Okay." Shortly thereafter, the car merged into lighter traffic. "Thanks, baby, it was a good idea, we just might make it."

Twenty minutes later, they were at Big Mama's. Obie double-parked, left Dora Lee in the car, and bounded up the stairs. Dora Lee sat back in the car seat and looked at her watch, the one Obie had given her on their fifteenth anniversary. He always did come through in the end. It was nine o'clock now, they'd just be able to make it to the airport in time.

She put her arm on the window edge of the car and smiled down at a little Puerto Rican boy who came wandering up to talk to her. "What's your name, sugar?"

He just had time to tell her "Roberto" when she heard something and looked up at the stoop. Obie stood at the door with her mother, who was crying. Obie was holding her by both her arms and saying something to her, while motioning with his head for Dora Lee to come up.

Dora Lee felt like her whole body had been plunged into an icy sea.

Still clutching the ticket tightly in her hand, she opened the car door and patted the little boy on the head. "Roberto, I'm very happy to meet you, darling."

She walked up to Obie and her mother.

"My baby's gone! I know it!" She took Obie's hand off her mother's shoulder and held her herself. "Mama, it wasn't your fault. You got to stop crying, we have to know what time she left and what she took with her. Don't worry about it, she surely will show up at the party tonight."

Dora Lee looked quickly at Obie—boiling oil would be too merciful for him—then turned her head away and grabbed her mother by the hand.

"Let's sit down here on the stoop for a minute. We always think better that way, remember?" She looked up at Obie. "I don't know how you're going to do it, but you got to find that child, you just got to."

CHAPTER 8

OBIE WAS GETTING NOWHERE fast. It was noontime, and he had no better idea now than he'd had three hours ago about where Sabaya was. All they had was that little note telling them not to worry, she loved them and she'd be home by Sunday.

He and Leroy had stopped for a beer at a bar in the center of North Philly.

"Dora Lee's saying we should call the police. What do you think?"

Leroy took a sip from the glass in front of him. "The Mau-Mau are turning this part of town upside down, I don't know what the police could do at this point. Besides, that new captain up there—shit, you know how he is, everything got to be by the book. So he ain't going to do a damn thing until forty-eight hours passes. Besides, we don't know for sure she ain't going to show up. She's only been gone a few hours. Let's give it a little time."

"I think we already given it enough. Look, man, you stay right here and take care of communications, I'm going to get into my car and start prowling around. I got a funny feeling about this thing." Obie's cell phone rang and he answered.

"I've called all her friends, and nobody's seen or heard from her," Dora Lee said. "But you know that black dress we bought her for the party? Well, it's still here. The red dress, the one she bought on her own and I told her not to wear any more—that's the dress that's gone." She began to cry. "Hashim liked that dress. I think she went to see him. That's what I think. She went to see that rotten kid. Obie, find her before it's too late."

"All right, baby, I'm on my way."

He grabbed a bottle of beer that had been left open on the counter and called to Leroy.

"I'm headed over to Hashim Mitchell's apartment. Any of the men call, tell them that's who we looking for. Driving that brand new white Ford Expedition. We got to get him, man. Got to get that punk before he messes up Sabaya."

TEN MINUTES LATER OBIE PULLED UP in front of a big apartment complex on one of North Philly's streets, parked his car at a meter, and walked quickly up to the building. The lock on the front door was broken, but the lock on the inner one was secure.

He stood in the lobby checking the names besides the buttons used to page occupants so they could open the doors. Most of the names were missing, and Hashim's wasn't among the ones that remained. Obie pushed five buttons on the panel. An angry jumble of voices answered on the speakers, all demanding to know who he was. And no one buzzed him into the building.

Just then an old woman carrying two paper bags of groceries walked up to the door.

"Let me help you with those packages, I got to get in here."

"I ain't letting you in this house, mister. Why, we just had a robbery the other night." She looked scared of him. Obie pulled out his identification badge from work.

"Look, lady, my daughter's in danger. I think she may be here with the Mitchell kid. He's trouble, and I got to find her. That's the Lord's truth."

She looked him up and down, then said, "You look like a Christian man. And that boy is bad, all right. Don't know what happened with him—Doc Mitchell's son, too! Go ahead, he on the fifth floor, rear apartment, him and some others just like him."

Obie took the key from the woman's hand, opened the door, and carried her bags over to the elevator. He put them down, thanked her, walked over to the stairwell, and began climbing up the stairs. Round each corner he went, higher and higher, climbing fast like the old ballplayer he was. He had to pause now and then to catch his breath—seemed he was a little out of shape. But his daughter might be up there. He pushed on!

When he reached the fifth floor, Obie stopped and waited a couple of minutes until his breathing was completely normal. Then he walked over to the scarred brown door with the tarnished brass knocker on it and rapped hard.

No one answered.

He knocked again.

Still no answer.

Behind him, he heard the sound of a door opening. He turned quickly around and saw a toothless old man peering at him.

"One of them left out early this morning," he said, "and Hashim and that other boy left ten minutes ago with some pretty young thing. That Hashim, he—"

"Sorry, sir, I don't have time to talk. When he left out of here, was that girl wearing a red dress?"

"It was red, all right. And come to think of it, she looked upset. Why you so—you a cop?"

"No, I'm a father."

"Oh, my God! You better call the cops, then."

Obie was already pulling out his cell phone.

His first call was to the police, where he spoke directly to Captain Palmer, the black officer who was replacing Sarnese at the precinct. Leroy was right about that guy. Everything by the book. Why don't I wait to see if she shows up at the reception tonight? The son of a bitch.

His next call was to Leroy. "Man, they took her, but we got one chance. They left out of here about ten minutes ago, so somebody should see the car. I'm coming over to pick you up and we going to drive up and down these streets till we find them."

•

HASHIM WAS DRIVING the white Ford Expedition up the spine of North Philly, Cecil B. Moore Avenue, and his breathing was shallow. Sabaya sat in the back seat, where a plump, light-complexioned man of about thirty named Khalid held a gun on her, all the while telling her she had nothing to worry about.

"Ain't going to hurt you, girl. So you can stop that crying. Just shut up, before I get mad or something."

Hashim hadn't known what he was getting himself into. With Trevon dead, he'd seen his chance to get in good with Raschid and take over the leadership of the Teagle gang's junior branch. And then there was all that money. But slowly he was beginning to realize the enormity of what he'd done, and he didn't like it. If he ever got free of this one, he'd get out of this business altogether. No amount of money would give him peace of mind when somebody as tough and unrelenting as Big Obie Bullock was after him. And the way these thugs were talking to Sabaya was really making him uncomfortable.

"He's telling you the truth, baby." Hashim turned quickly and looked hard at the man in the back seat. "He's not going to hurt you, the Teagle boys just want to ask you some questions, then I'll take you home."

"How could you have done this to me, to somebody you love?"

"I'll tell you why later." He hesitated, then said, "It was really all for you." He turned to Khalid. "How long you going to keep her up there at your place?"

"Just long enough for the boys to talk to her, tell her about the peace offering and things. That's all."

Hashim stopped for the red light and glanced around. Another two blocks and they'd be there.

A police car was in the bus stop space, a hatless cop behind the wheel reading a newspaper while his partner dozed. Hashim stared straight ahead.

Khalid said, "Make one move, bitch, and I promise you I'll kill you even before I off that cop."

"Yo, Khalid, don't be talking to her like that, she's my lady!"

"Sorry, man."

Hashim drove slowly down the next block. He looked in his rear view mirror and saw the cop had pulled out, and that the car was driving as slowly as he was. Seemed like it was keeping pace with him. Just one more block to Khalid's place, then he'd get the hell out of town—let them leave her off somewhere after they finished questioning her. He looked into the mirror and saw the police car had turned off into the next street.

They were home free.

He turned to Khalid. "Remember, I was promised you guys aren't going to hurt her. And don't forget, the Mau-Mau got some pretty rough dudes with them. And Big Obie is fierce."

"Yeah, yeah, now shut up and leave this shit to me. I'll take care of the girl. You drive up to that apartment house in the middle of the next block, the one with the big tree in front of it. That's the place. Just leave us off, and you can go."

In the back of the truck, Sabaya was crying, bawling like a baby, and it was hurting him real bad. This wasn't no joke, Sabaya was in the hands of her family's worst enemies, and he felt just the way Judas must have felt when he betrayed Jesus.

But ten thousand dollars would set him up good. That was the price the Teagle gang had put out as reward for delivery to them of any member of the Bullock family. Take it in cash or heroin. With that kind of money, he didn't even have to worry about being Trevon's successor, maybe he could go south, find him a small town, set up his own operation, stand up in his own right and be somebody. Shit, he might even cut him a DVD, Sabaya had always liked his rap songs. Or maybe he could start community college down there, become a veterinary assistant somewhere, do something peaceful and non life-threatening and play with his snakes.

He pulled up to the apartment building, let the two of them out of the SUV, and avoided looking at Sabaya, the little girl who'd sat beside him in Mrs. Baskerville's second-grade class.

Hashim watched as a smiling Khalid, his pistol hidden under his jacket and stuck into Sabaya's side, led her into the building. She turned around.

"Hashim, my daddy's going to catch you, and when he does, you'll be sorry you were ever born."

He pulled the truck away from the curb and headed crosstown towards his apartment. He'd wait until he got home to decide whether to call up Sheila or Barbara. Spending the night with one of them might make him feel better, because right now he was mighty low—his hands were trembling on the steering wheel and his stomach was churning something awful, like he'd have to throw up soon.

He turned up the radio, plugged his iPod into it, started playing some rap music, and pulled up to a stoplight on a one-way street.

When the light turned green, he drove off. He was halfway down the street when a car suddenly pulled in front of him. Hashim sensed trouble—he had to pull around that car, and quick.

Too late. Obie Bullock's Chevy had pulled alongside him, and that mean yellow nigger Leroy was staring at him. With a Mauser in his hand.

Hashim immediately shifted into reverse. But as he started to put his foot on the accelerator, he saw in the rearview mirror yet another car. It was full of men in white Muslim dress.

"Oh, shit!"

Inside of two minutes, Hashim found himself sitting, his right arm in Leroy's armlock, in the back of his own truck. Big Obie sat on the other side of him.

"Look here, boy, you done took my daughter somewhere, and I got to know where. Ain't got no time to play, so you going to tell me, and you going to tell me right now, you hear!"

Leroy began to twist Hashim's arm upwards. It hurt so bad he thought he might pass out. He turned to face Big Obie, who looked at him like nobody had ever looked at him in his life.

"All right, I'll tell you, if you just—"

"If, shit," Leroy said. "That's my goddaughter you got there." He twisted the arm even harder and smashed Hashim's face with a karate-cupped hand. "I'm going to tear your fucking arm right out of its socket."

Hashim screamed, but Leroy slapped him again and stuffed a handkerchief in his mouth.

He was going to die, here and now. He knew it. These men were going to kill him right on this street, in the middle of the day, in the very center of North Philly. And they'd toss his body out of the truck and leave him there—just another dead nigger on a street in the City of Brotherly Love.

His eyes filled with tears, and he smelled the sweet aroma of Sabaya's perfume. He nodded his head.

Shortly thereafter, three carloads of the Mau-Mau were headed towards Khalid's place, in a small apartment house. Leroy held a gun in the belly of Hashim, who was sobbing.

"I didn't want to do it," he said, over and over again.

Leroy, a look of limitless disgust on his face, hit him across the face with the Mauser.

"Shut up, you piece of shit. Shut the fuck up."

OBIE SPOKE OVER HIS SHOULDER to Leroy. "We're going up there with this good-for-nothing punk. He's going to get us in that apartment. Once we in, man, no messing around. Just clean them out."

"You sure you don't just want to surround the building and call the cops?"

"Man, you know that guy Palmer. By the time he asks all his questions and gets here, they might have gone and messed the child up good. We got to move. I tell you, I wouldn't even wait long enough for Sarnese to get here."

"All right," Leroy said. "Let's go. And you, Hashim, you want to live, you do just like I told you to, hear?"

Obie paused on the sidewalk in front of the three-story building and surveyed the situation. All of the windows were barred, and steel grates covered both the main door and that of the basement apartment. The Muslims were parked by the fire hydrant. They looked a little conspicuous, but that couldn't be helped. The men from the second car had moved down the alleys on either side of the building.

A few old folks were sitting on their stoops, but it was a hot day and not too many people were outside. Obie had forgotten how hot it really was.

He and Leroy, with Hashim between them, walked up to the front entrance. Obie pushed the buzzer.

A few seconds passed. A deep male voice said, "Yeah, who is it?"

Leroy pressed the gun into Hashim's ribs.

"Khalid, it's me, Hashim."

"What you want, man? Thought you were gone on home."

"Just want to talk with you for a minute, got something going on my way home. Might be worth about five k."

"I ain't got no time for your bright ideas now."

Obie's heart stopped.

Hashim said, "Hey, there's two k in it for you right now."

"You ain't shitting me? You got the money with you?"

"In fifties."

"That's cool. Come on up, but you only got about five minutes."

The buzzer rang, and Obie and Leroy opened the door, pushing Hashim ahead of them.

Obie pulled his pistol out, and the two men walked upstairs behind Hashim. They stayed close to the walls, but the wooden stairs creaked under the combined weight of the three men. Obie nudged Leroy on the shoulder and pointed to the stairs. Leroy nodded and put his feet down more carefully.

They reached the second-floor landing. Obie walked down the hall and spread-eagled his body alongside the wall outside the entrance to the Teagle apartment. Leroy did the same, and both men held their pistols on Hashim.

Obie nodded at Hashim. He knocked at the brown wooden door. Worn shellac was peeling off it. A voice came from inside:

"Hashim, that you?"

"It's me, man. Open up."

A sound of bars and chains being removed came from behind the door. But it only opened to the ten-inch length of the safety chain.

"Damn, man, open up!"

"Can't be too careful."

The man inside was trying to peek down the halls through the crack in the door.

The noise of loud rap music came through the opening.

Khalid looked at Hashim.

"Boy, why you got that shit-eating look on your face, something wrong with you? What that girl said about Bullock scare you or something?"

"It ain't nothing, come on, let me give you this bread and tell you about the deal."

The door opened fully, flooding the hall with the sound of hip-hop music.

Obie burst into the room and stuck his gun into Khalid's belly. The empty living room was full of beer bottles, leftover McDonald's containers, half-eaten cheeseburgers, and pieces of chicken wings.

Obie turned the drug dealer and Hashim over to Leroy, called softly into his cell phone for back-up, and moved quickly down the hallway towards the rear bedrooms.

He looked in one bedroom. No one.

He moved to the other door. Someone was talking in there.

He paused for a second in front of the door, then kicked it as hard as he could, holding the gun dead ahead.

There in a corner of the room, tied hand and foot, was Sabaya.

Stone Latimer, a leader of the Teagle gang, was kneeling on the floor in front of her, tightening the screws on a vise grip he was attaching to a table. His eyes popped wide when he saw Obie and his gun.

"Daddy!" Sabaya cried. "He said he was going to fix it so I'd never play the piano again!"

Bullock looked at Stone Latimer and said nothing. Just looked at him.

The short, brown-skinned man got up slowly from his kneeling position.

Obie's finger tightened on the trigger.

Still he said nothing.

He looked at Sabaya. "Wait a minute, honey. I'll be back soon as I get my friend Stone here tied up."

He marched the man to the living room, where Leroy stood guard over Hashim and Khalid, both of whom lay outstretched on the floor. Obie noticed that Khalid was slowly moving his hand.

He was about to warn Leroy when he raised his foot and crashed it down onto Khalid's hand, bringing a howl of pain from him.

Obie said, "Stone, get down there on the floor with them other assholes." He turned to Leroy. "I'm going to untie Sabaya, back in a minute."

He went to the bedroom and bent down to unloosen her bonds.

"Honey, don't ever do anything like this to your daddy again. It'll kill me."

He helped her to her feet, walked her into the living room, and told her to wait just outside in the hall for a minute. Then he nodded to Leroy.

"Tie their hands and feet, man. Use those sheets in the bedroom." Leroy bound the three while Obie held a gun on them. "Now just stick some gags in their mouths." That accomplished, he said, "Okay, bring me the vise."

Leroy brought the heavy metal vise into the living room.

"Okay," Obie said. "You hold this gun for a second."

He bent down beside Stone Latimer. "Hey, man, I loved you like a brother. Got you a job when you got back from upstate, didn't I? And you was going to break my daughter's hands? I'd say a little payback is called for, wouldn't you?"

He took the vise, opened its jaws wide and positioned it on Stone's right foot, then turned the grip until he could feel and hear it crushing the bones.

Stone's body twisted and jerked, and his face was a horror of pain, but no sound came from his gagged mouth. Suddenly, his body went limp. He was unconscious.

Obie turned his attention to Khalid. "You dared put your damn hands on my daughter, you must have been out of your mind—you know me from way back! Got to deal with your ass too." He removed the vise grip from Stone's foot, put it on

Khalid's right hand, and twisted. Then he took three or four hard, quick turns on the grip. Khalid's screams could be heard through the gag.

Obie said to Leroy, "Let's get Sabaya out of here, man. Cut that punk Hashim loose and let him go where he wants. The Teagle boys will get him anyhow."

Leaving the two barely moving bodies bound on the floor, Obie and Leroy gathered up Sabaya and Hashim and started down the stairs. Halfway down, Leroy stopped and turned around.

"Go ahead, I'll be right down."

A few seconds later, Obie heard noises—thuds? thumps? Leroy's foot must have banged into the ribs of the two men on the floor. He caught up with them at the bottom of the landing. "You know," he said, "we should of killed those guys. Iced them, man."

"We hurt them enough."

Sabaya clung to Obie—it took force to pry her arms away from his shoulder and lead her into the car.

The leader of the Muslims, a tall man with a white cap, got out of his car and came over to the Chevy.

"Everything all right, my brother?"

Obie said, "Thank your men. And tell them we got us a real war now. We got to take down this gang."

"We'll be behind you." The leader returned to his car, which cruised slowly down the street.

The remaining men returned from their posts on the sides of the building. They smiled at Obie, waved, piled into their car, and left.

"I AIN'T GOING TO GIVE YOU no sermon," Obie said when they were on Broad Street. You know your daddy, that's not my style. And I can't give you a whipping, because you too old and besides, you been scared enough, you don't need no more punishment. All I want to say is I love you and I'm mighty grateful to have you back. Lord knows you can do great things if you can only stay on the right track. Use the talents God gave you, baby, use them for good things, and don't let no jive-talking boys lead you astray."

"I'm so sorry, Daddy. All I ever saw in Hashim was the good side, the sweet side—because that's all he ever let me see. I feel so stupid. And so ashamed, I'd like to disappear into a hole somewhere and never come up for air."

"You ain't stupid, Sabaya, just too trusting. And it'll pass, honey, the way you feel now. Everything does, just keep your eye on the prize and your hands in God's hands!"

Obie turned into the street Sabaya had left in the morning at six-thirty. People were everywhere, and Frisbees were being tossed around in the street. Somebody had opened a hydrant, and cascades of water were splashing all over the girls and boys in their swimsuits and shorts. One toddler, dressed only in underwear, kept falling down and standing back up as the water poured into his little bucket, carrying both it and him to the street.

Seeing his persistence, Obie smiled for the first time that day.

Dora Lee and Big Mama had seen the car. They ran down the steps and into the street, hands waving in the air, meeting the Chevy halfway down the block.

Obie had no sooner pulled into a parking space than he sensed the door behind him opening and Sabaya getting out of the car. Dora Lee grasped her and held her close to her chest.

"Sabaya, darling!"

Obie got out of the car, Big Mama hugged him, and then Sabaya and Dora Lee joined in so all four were together, holding on to each other. Tears filled Obie's eyes. He held tight to his wife, his daughter, and his mother-in-law, who said:

"Now we pray, children. And thank God for his great and everlasting goodness and mercy."

They held each other's hands, closed their eyes, and prayed. Right there on the hot, steamy South Philadelphia street.

IT WAS SUNDAY AFTERNOON, and Dora Lee and Sabaya sat together in the Philadelphia International airport. Obie had gone to pick up the car, Sabaya's baggage had been checked, and she was just about to go into the secure area of the airport.

Dora Lee said, "Darling, we're going to put what's happened behind us, but I've got to tell you I'm really nervous about you and for one very good reason. You didn't—"

"I know, Mama. I kept a secret from you."

Dora Lee pressed her daughter's hands between hers. "That's it, and you know it's a natural thing now for me not to trust you any more, because here you are just about to go off to college and everything." She sighed. "Maybe it would be better if you stayed closer to home and tried to get into one of the state schools or Curtis—it shouldn't be too hard. I think your daddy would like that too. We talked about it last week."

"No, Mama, you're not going to have to worry about me any more—I learned my lesson."

"But how are we to know that? What kind of changes are you going to make in your life? Hashim was bad news once he got arrested, just like your daddy said, and you still went out with him."

Sabaya smiled. "See, Mama, there you go, you promised to put it behind us and now you brought up his name again—you're always doing that."

Dora Lee laughed. "I know I do, baby, but sometimes I just can't help it. What—"

Sabaya gently put her finger to her mama's lips. "Mama, I learned one incredibly powerful lesson from what happened. I'm still a growing woman, but I promise you now one thing, and I'm asking God to help me keep my word on this—I'm promising you I will never again sleep with a man unless he's my husband. The way you and Daddy are, that's just the way I'm going to be."

Dora Lee didn't say a word, knowing that Sabaya's resolution would be sorely tested in college, but she hugged her close. Now if only Obie and she could live up to the image her daughter had of them, if only they could hold it together themselves...Their marriage had been through some mighty rough patches lately, and Sabaya's escapade had just made things worse.

By one o'clock, Sabaya was safely off and Dora Lee and Obie were in a traffic jam just outside the airport.

"Well, baby," Obie said, "hasn't been much of a weekend, has it? But at least that child is safe and out of here."

Dora Lee, dressed in a blue blouse and white slacks, said, "We still have time left and it's only an hour and a half down to Wildwood. Let's drive down and walk the beaches for a while, then we can have dinner and go back to the Lenhardts' place. We can save something of the weekend, honey."

True, there were a lot of other things for her to do—study for the exams on Tuesday night, shop for next week's church dinner, take care of work left over from the office. But she and Obie needed some down time, a day of fun. She took his hand.

"Honey, turn on the radio and see if you can't get our gospel station."

In seconds the stirring yet soothing music she loved so much filled the car. A deep male voice sang:

I cried and I cried
Cried all night long
You know, I cried and I cried
Until I found the Lord!

The traffic thinned, and Obie began the drive down towards Wildwood. As the music played, he started up his rhythmic pounding of the steering wheel and began to sing along with the radio: "My soul just couldn't rest contented!"

Dora Lee joined in: "Lord knows it just couldn't be contented!" The blending of their voices with those of the singers on the radio turned the interior of their old broken-down Chevy with its torn seat cushions and its odometer long stopped at 125,872 into a temple of joy.

Dora Lee looked at Obie in his loud green shirt unbuttoned at the collar, his face shining, lost in the music—looked at her man and thanked God for him.

Another hymn started up. Obie smiled, humming the melody,

and Dora Lee just squeezed his hand tighter. Twice she did it, then chanted softly the words of the hymn:

"Yes, there's a cross for everyone, and there's a cross for me...."

They pulled into a municipal parking lot down at Wildwood and soon were walking together on the long beach. They found a quiet spot, and Obie spread out a section of the Sunday newspaper on the sand for them to sit. Out of the other pages of the newspaper he made two triangle-shaped hats to shade them from the sun.

Dora Lee still loved this place. It was here that Obie had first brought her when they were courting. She'd bring along a picnic bag full of fried chicken and potato salad, sit and read the Sunday Inquirer while Obie, barely stopping to eat, would be off and running with his fishing tackle towards the water.

Sometimes Dora Lee would sit and watch, enjoying the way he flung the long pole back, gave a quick flick of his wrist, and hurled the bait on its line far out towards the ocean, where it would hover for a moment in the air before its plunge into the foamy water.

Now, over the ocean, seagulls were swooping down from the sky, snatching their prey from the water, then flying off pursued by other gulls, shrieking for their share of the poor fish. Seemed like someone or something always had to suffer in this world.

Dora Lee turned to Obie. "I'm so glad you brought me down here. Funny, but even with everything, all my troubles want to flow away when we get here."

Their conversation was abruptly sabotaged by the loud blaring of heavy metal music. A group of teenagers dressed in shorts and no shirts walked down the beach.

Obie stopped trying to talk and watched them until they'd passed. Dora Lee stopped too and held his hand tight. She knew how much he hated the loud, screaming music with the high-pitched guitars and awful lyrics and all that shouting.

When the teenagers were fifty yards down the beach and there was peace again, she put her hand on Obie's arm and felt the strength in it.

"Baby, what are we going to do?"

"What you mean, Dora Lee? We going to do what we been doing. We going to make it safe where we live."

"But can't you see what's happening? I do nothing but worry all day long." She took her hand off his arm. "Last week I failed my examination in advanced algebra, I just didn't have the time or the concentration to study."

Obie moved closer and cradled her head against his chest. "Baby, I know we got a lot going on in our lives, and it ain't just the threats. There's all these pressures of college, and kids' clothes and things, and Jason being over there in Afghanistan and all, but one thing stays on my mind all the time, and that's poor little Shakeisha."

Dora Lee shuddered at the mention of the little girl's name.

"That child was on her way to being somebody and doing something in life, and Son's boys—don't care what they say about strangers doing it—were involved some way or other, and even if they wasn't directly connected with it, they've messed things up around here enough, made decent folks scared enough, that they set it up for her to be raped and left there the way those bastards left her."

Dora Lee remembered how he'd come into the apartment the night of the killing, told her what had happened, then gone into the bedroom and pounded their mattress with his fists till she feared he'd break the whole bed down with the force of his blows. He'd only stopped when he heard Timba shouting, "Mama, you better call the cops, Daddy's going out of his mind!"

Obie now tilted her chin up and looked her straight in the eyes. "You can leave if you want to, Dora Lee, but God has placed me here in these projects to protect and help these folks, and I ain't deserting them for nothing or nobody, much as I would lay down my life for you and Timba and Sabaya. I ain't going nowhere, baby, but you go if you feel you got to." He glanced down the beach a ways. "Shucks, might as well have asked Dr. King not to go to jail, or Malcolm not to make that speech at the Audubon. No, I ain't leaving."

"There you go again, Obie—comparing yourself to dead heroes! They're gone now, and we're running out of money. Sabaya's going to need something for college, and sending these kids by plane down to North Carolina has just about emptied the savings account. We only got eight hundred dollars left on the one credit card that's not maxed out. Then what we going to do?"

"Well, baby, I don't want to start nothing now, but you could stop buying fancy dresses."

Dora Lee got to her feet. "You know I need to look nice at work—no, let's stop it. I won't let us spoil our afternoon, honey, this is precious time."

Obie shrugged his shoulders, picked up a little twig from the sand, broke it, then threw the two pieces of wood away.

"Baby, I'm sorry I said that. I think we going to be okay. Look, in two more weeks we'll be in Carolina on vacation and we'll get a chance to get ourselves together."

"That seems a long way off."

"Nobody will know we're down there, and we'll be able to figure out what to do before the fall comes. In the meantime, I'll call Boat and tell him to find Sabaya a job down there. That'll help take the load off of us a little."

"But I still feel nervous."

"Don't worry, baby, God got us in the palm of his hands. Never failed us yet."

Dora Lee nodded, then put her head back on Obie's shoulder and began to cry quietly.

Soon, with Obie's arms tight around her, she calmed herself. That's the way it was with them. Argue and make up, argue again and make up again. But one time soon....

The two of them sat there for about an hour, and Dora Lee felt her love for Obie welling up. Just loved the closeness of his body, the warmth, the quiet strength he seemed to be able to give her even in times like today. She touched his pants and felt how hard and strong he'd become. She kept her hand there, then felt his left hand in her lap, kneading her through the stiffness of her dungarees.

She said, "Let's go up to the diner now and get something to eat."

"Sure, baby, we stay here much longer I'm liable to do something illegal right here on the beach."

"Oh, stop it," she said. "Why you acting like some young stud?"

"You make me young, baby." Obie got up, brushed the sand from Dora Lee's pants, and shook the sand off himself. Holding hands, they walked off down the beach and back to the car. By now it was standing almost alone in the parking lot. Behind them, the screaming of the sea gulls increased as they landed on the beaches to scavenge the scraps of food left by the Sunday afternoon visitors.

Twenty minutes later, the Bullocks pulled into the parking lot of the Greek-owned diner where they always stopped after their trips to the beach.

"You know we ought to drive right on back to Ardmore. Plenty of things I can fix us for dinner there."

Obie would have none of it. "Times like this, we got to take every chance we get to enjoy ourselves. Don't know what's coming next, baby."

"But the diner will cost us another thirty dollars on the charge, and—"

"Don't worry about it, baby, I'll just put in some more overtime next week."

And so Dora Lee and Obie were soon seated in a booth, looking at a huge menu. The diner was small and cozy, and behind the counter gleaming metal and glass shelves held rows of custard pies, fruit pies with shiny glazed crust, creamy puddings, and oversized muffins.

Dora Lee loved the smell of fresh baking. It made her think of long-ago Sunday mornings when her daddy used to hold her on his knee while they waited for her mother to bring the steaming hot biscuits to the table.

The waitress asked for their orders, and Dora Lee made a silent vow not to spoil Obie's meal by reminding him about his blood pressure.

It was just as well that she hadn't said anything. For soon Obie had in front of him a huge bowl of fragrant, steaming chicken noodle soup, and he was demolishing the basketful of home-made rolls.

Dora Lee contented herself with nibbling away at the green salad she'd ordered for herself.

Finally, the waitress, a middle-aged Italian lady with gray hair who seemed to have taken a liking to Obie, brought their main courses—chicken and dumplings for Obie, smothered in a creamy brown gravy, and a lightly browned filet of haddock for Dora Lee.

Dora Lee was amazed, even after so many years of marriage to this man of hers, to see how much he really enjoyed food. She sat carefully lifting piece after piece of fish to her mouth while Obie made first the chicken, then the dumplings, then the creamy Italian salad, then the remaining two rolls disappear.

Her man really loved his food. And Dora Lee liked to see him enjoy himself. But after he emptied the second coke, she had second thoughts about her vow of silence. Maybe he wouldn't eat dessert.

Obie ordered the peach cobbler a la mode.

Dora Lee laughed and shook her head. "I just don't know what I'm going to do with you."

"I do. You're going to make love to me, and you're going to do it in style. You remember that little motel down the road, the one we used to go to right after we got married? It's only five minutes away, and I just can't wait no longer, honey. Got to have my sweet loving."

Twenty minutes later they were at the motel and had rented a large room with a queen-sized bed, paneled in a dark wood veneer. A painting of children playing on a beach was on the wall, and the slightly worn carpet was dark red. It was a good room, because it was in this room, or one like it, that they'd passed many loving nights way back, before Sabaya and Timba, Obie's personal war on crime, and all their money troubles.

Dora Lee sat down on the bed and turned to Obie. "Just come over here, honey. Sit down beside me and hold me tight."

Obie went over and put his arm around her, his hand cupped over her breast.

Dora Lee shivered at the touch. "Just sing me a little song. You know that one you used to sing me all the time? You don't sing it to me no more, baby."

His fingers softly playing with her nipples, he began to hum the tune, as if to recapture the melody, then started singing the words of "Your Precious Love."

Her whole body rose to her man. "Don't stop singing."

She took his other hand and guided it down between her thighs. A deep and soothing warmth was rising in her body. She put her hand on Obie's and slowly began to rub it back and forth. She could feel the healing, loving warmth flow from her breast down through her stomach and between her thighs, sweeping the hurt and pain before it.

She felt Obie's mouth on hers, his tongue moving into her mouth. Oh, my goodness, she didn't know where she felt the best. Nipple feel good, thighs feel all good. She thrust her tongue deep into Obie's mouth, felt his tongue pushing back at hers, twirling up to the roof of her mouth, then playfully circling round and round her tongue. Lord, it felt good.

She tenderly broke off the kiss and said, "Lie down right here." Soon he was moving himself back and forth inside her while gently cradling her head in his arm.

"Oh, move, sweet man," she said. "Don't stop, honey." Her body began to arch back and forth, meeting his every thrust with her parry, so that their movements became ever tighter and more compressed.

Then Dora Lee was flying, soaring, screaming and hollering and grasping Obie tight to her.

"Higher, baby! Just take me a little bit higher....That's high enough!" Her feet pounded on the bed and her body exploded upwards to meet his last great thrust and draw his surging, wet power out of him and into her. She fell back on the bed, limp and calm.

Obie lay beside her, very still, and then she felt his lips on hers, felt him kissing her all over her body again.

"Love you, sweet man."

Obie looked at her and smiled. "Not half as much as I love you, baby." He wrapped her in his arms and drew her tight to him.

It was nine o'clock Sunday night when Dora Lee woke up in the motel room. She wriggled against Obie.

"We got to be going, honey. Work tomorrow, darn it."

"Okay, but you know what? I'm going to remember this evening for the rest of my life."

CHAPTER 9

TWO HOURS LATER, OBIE DROPPED DORA LEE OFF at the Lenhardts' house, then headed back to North Philly. He had a lot of work in front of him the next morning and would have to get to it early.

When he walked into his apartment, he immediately knew something was wrong. It was midnight, and both Leroy and the other guard were awake, sitting at the table, drinking coffee and waiting for him.

Leroy said, "Think we got us a problem, man—Stone Latimer. When I went back into the room, I must of kicked his sorry ass too hard, because he's in critical condition in the ICU at Temple Hospital. Was on the eleven o'clock news."

Obie said, "Get into a war with these dudes and somebody's going to get hurt. Did they say anything about suspects?"

"No, they said nobody would talk about it, there was no witnesses. You know how they like to make it seem nobody in the neighborhood cares. That kind of shit."

"Ain't nothing we can do about it now," Obie said. "Let's get us some sleep and deal with it in the morning. What about Khalid?"

"Said he was in the hospital under armed guard and had refused to say anything about what happened. Should have seen it. Showed him all in bandages in the hospital bed. Fucked his ass up, man."

"Good," Obie said. "I'm going to get me some sleep." He went into his room, poured himself a shot of bourbon, threw it down, and went to bed. Had good dreams, too, dreams of Dora Lee.

IT WAS THE NEXT MORNING. Acting precinct commander Zack Palmer was meeting with his plainclothes squad and the desk sergeant. The week's routine activities had been gone over, and

Palmer seemed satisfied with the order he'd laid out.

But Robbie Walker knew he was about to catch hell. He was now the temporary head of the squad and an acting sergeant. Palmer, once he finished talking with the desk sergeant, dismissed him. And sure enough, soon as he settled into his seat, he looked at Robbie.

"Talk to me about those assaults up at that Teagle apartment yesterday."

"Well, sir, we think it was drug-related, and—"

"You taking stupid pills, Walker? Any television commentator could have told me that." The lieutenant's eyes swept over the faces of the three men and two women in the squad. "I'm sick of all this shooting and violence going on in my precinct. People calling me all the time saying they're not safe. And you come talking like you don't know what's happening up there. That's why I have a plainclothes squad."

Robbie said, "Captain, we've had people working on this thing all weekend, and I think I'll have something for you soon."

The captain thrust his head forward across the desk. "Well, I have something now. I heard something, and if I can get it confirmed, I want the guys arrested today. Want their asses brought down here and arraigned."

"What'd you hear, sir?"

"The boys from uptown say the assaults weren't drug-related—those being the only damn words you know—but were done by the Mau-Mau. Don't ask me how they know, because they wouldn't tell me."

Robbie almost fell off his seat on the bench the captain had brought into his office to replace the wooden chairs that had been there when Sarnese was still in command. Robbie knew as well as Palmer that Obie Bullock and one of his men had got into that apartment and done a job on Teagle's boys. And he knew why, too.

He said, "Captain, if I was you, I wouldn't get into this thing unless I was dead sure who did it. I heard the same thing, but Bullock's still awfully popular around here, and there'll be hell to pay if you can't back this up. That guy in the hospital isn't going to talk, they take care of things themselves. And Bullock's no criminal. And they had his teenage daughter in there."

Palmer got out of his seat and turned his back to the five cops, then suddenly spun around to face them again. Like they were some school kids seated on the bench.

"I don't go for all this buddy-buddy shit with vigilantes. And I'm not going to stand for my precinct being a playground for gangs of private thugs. Do you know who Leroy is?"

Damn. Palmer knew a lot more than Robbie had thought.

"Have you ever seen his record, Walker? A real criminal!"

"That was before he went into the army,"

"That's right. Because after he got back from fighting, he became a damn drug addict and ended up in prison again. Look, I'm going to tell you guys this one time. We, the cops, run this precinct. We're responsible for law and order, and we'll provide it to the people who live here. All this violence, killing and brutality has got to cease. Now, you got any questions or objections?"

"No, sir."

"Then get out there and get me the evidence I need to arrest whoever tried to murder that dealer."

The prospect made Robbie feel sick to his stomach. The Bullock family were good people. Come showdown time, it would be the Mau-Mau—or what was left of them after Obie Bullock's television comments supporting Sarnese—and the Teagle gang. He didn't blame Bullock one bit. Shit, he'd have done the same thing if it had been his daughter. As a matter of fact, he'd have blown them both away. Where would the captain be when the Teagle gang came to destroy the Bullocks? Parading around the precinct in his shiny new Captain's Chevrolet?

But Robbie had to do something if he was going to keep his promotion to acting sergeant. Would have to find him a witness, then get a warrant. He didn't know when, if ever, Captain Sarnese would come back.

At seven o'clock that night, a call came over the radio for Robbie to return to the precinct. When he entered, the desk sergeant glanced up at him.

"There's a kid in the interrogation room wants to spill his guts. Says it's got something to do with that stuff up at the Teagle place. I called the captain, he's at a meeting and won't be able to get down here for a while."

A YOUNG BLACK MAN with more gold earrings in one ear than Robbie had ever seen in his life sat in a chair in the interrogation room. He wore a shiny blue T-shirt and white bell-bottoms. His head was between his hands. He didn't even move when Robbie came in and turned on the tape recorder.

"Okay, kid, what's the story? What you got to say?"

Slowly, the man raised his head and turned his eyes towards Robbie. "I know who fucked up those guys in the Teagle apartment the other night, and I'll tell you—"

"That's fine, but before you do that I have to warn you about your rights, and I want to know who you are."

The boy's hand was trembling. "My name's Hashim, Hashim Mitchell."

Robbie explained his rights, then said, "Okay, who did it?"

"They're going to kill me...."

"Who?"

"Teagle people going to kill me."

"Who did it?"

The boy slowly shook his head back and forth. "I got to be put in protective custody."

"Would you like a glass of water?"

"I haven't slept in two days."

"Look, kid, you're talking all crazy. Do you or don't you know who roughed up Latimer?"

Tears were in the young man's eyes. "I'm not telling you unless I get a promise of protection from you."

"I can't do that, that has to come from the D.A. How'd you get involved in this thing?"

"I did something terrible, lowdown. It's so awful I almost shot myself yesterday. I really want to die, but not the way the Teagle gang plans to kill me."

Robbie slowly nodded his head. "Okay, kid, I'll call the D.A. and we'll see what kind of a deal we can make."

He walked out of the room and slowly back down the hall. No way he could help Bullock now. He walked into his cubbyhall and telephoned.

"Philadelphia D.A.'s office, Deborah Saint-Claire speaking. How may I help you?"

Robbie immediately tagged the soft feminine voice as Haitian—Philly Haitian, but Haitian. He explained the situation, and Ms. Saint-Claire said she'd be at the precinct shortly.

He hung up the phone and returned to the interrogation room. He looked at the kid now sitting once again with his head in his hands. For this piece of crap, Big Obie Bullock had to go to jail.

"D.A.'ll be down shortly. We'll work something out for you."

....

"NO, I'M NOT GOING TO LET YOU do that, man, no way!" Obie said.

"You got no say in the matter, partner. Right is right, and you didn't put Latimer on the critical list—I did." Leroy looked up at the cell's bars and shook his head. "Besides, I know how to survive in here, you don't. And I ain't got no wife and kids crying their eyes out for me. No, I'm taking this rap. You'll be out on bail in a couple of days because you ain't got no record, but in the meantime, we got to figure out how we going to survive till then."

"You right about that," Obie said. Put there yesterday by that hard-nosed Haitian DA, here they were in prison, among dozens of Philly's meanest criminals. The warden had said there was no room in the regular blocks, so he'd put them in one with a bunch of crazy thugs, supposedly housing the two together for their own protection. Their lawyers had raised hell about it, but the warden said there was no place else to put them until some other prisoners were released to free up space. In the meantime, they were surrounded by men who had no fear of man or beast. Didn't want them contaminating the other prisoners. It was fine if they killed themselves or each other.

Except for Obie and Leroy, every man had his own cell. Every man was fed through bars. A half-hour mandatory recreation break every day allowed all the men to walk around in the cell block. Not in uniforms—they didn't have any. Walked in just about every kind of pants, shorts, and shirts, and all sweating in the 100-degree temperature.

It was their second day there and close to exercise period, the most dangerous time of the day. Obie knew he and Leroy were in for some hard fighting before the day was out. Some of the men they knew in there were people the Mau-Mau had helped put in prison. Some they had helped get busted two or three times, from the days when Sarnese had thrown the full weight of the precinct behind the anti-drug fight. Any one of those motherfuckers would kill them if they got a chance.

And then there were Teagle's guys, some of whom Obie also knew. Hell, Teagle would pay them ten grand for either one of their heads. Then there were the ordinary murderers and rapists, men who'd been anti-social since seven or eight years old—they were just plain vicious and might kill him and Leroy simply because they didn't like the way they walked or talked or combed their hair. And don't look at none of them the wrong way.

So far, Obie and Leroy's reputation as fighters had ensured that nobody had come within four feet of them. Nor said a word to them.

But they had to be ready for the unexpected. Only a half-hour recreation period—that's all they had to get over. Just stay alert, watch each other's backs, and pray that God would bring them through.

Funny, but since Iraq, nothing scared Obie no more. He'd never told Dora Lee this, but he counted every day with her and the children as a bonus gift from God, treasured every morning's sunrise, every robin's song in the springtime. He'd seen enough blood, mangled flesh, and torn limbs to last a lifetime—no room for fear inside him.

"Prisoners, break ranks. Half-hour break begins."

Within seconds, the ground floor of the cell block was covered with a mass of black and brown men, forming into groups, shouting at each other, striking open palms against open palms, and greeting each other as if it had been months instead of twenty-four hours since they'd been free to walk these very same floors.

Obie, dressed in a blue polo shirt, and Leroy, in white khakis and a red shirt, headed for their secure zone. It was against the wall and in full view of the guards who were looking down on the floor of the cell block from a spot close to their cell.

Obie and Leroy planted their backs firmly against the wall, folded their arms in front of them, and stood still as two ebony statues.

"Leroy, I ever tell you about the time I took a two-week leave in Jamaica while I was stationed in the Southern Florida Command?"

"I don't even want to hear it—you going to be telling me one of them lies again. Problem is, I always end up believing them and think I can do the same thing."

"No, man, this is the absolute truth. But since you ain't going to believe me, I ain't going to tell you about it." He scratched his arm—it still itched sometimes from where they'd taken the shrapnel out. "Won't tell you about this forty-foot yacht with this bevy of gorgeous island women came sailing into a marina one day while I was just sitting there, minding my own business and admiring the lines on the boats, no I ain't going to tell you about how they started asking me did I know how to run a motorboat, and would I like to come aboard and cruise around the island with them since I was looking at those pretty boats when I should of been looking at them. That's what they said. Would I rather look at the boats or come along with them?"

Obie stopped talking and surveyed the crowd.

"So what happened, man?"

"Aw, you don't want to know. It was just an afternoon, evening, and long night spent on a forty-foot yacht with a bunch of very intelligent and beautiful young Jamaican women. I learned a lot about their culture and geography."

Leroy jabbed him in the ribs with his elbow. "Man, you better tell me what happened!"

"Well, if you insist, you're not going to believe this, but..." As he talked, he realized that he was feeling a little lightheaded. The heat was getting to him, and it had to be getting to Leroy too. He just hoped it wouldn't make him collapse. If he did, it would be all over before those guards could even get down there with their batons. He'd be like a wounded lion facing a pack of jackals. One slip, and that's all she wrote.

Ten minutes passed with only the usual activity on the floor. Then four prisoners led by a tall, thin, very black man with a head shaped like an egg walked away from the main body of prisoners to a position about eight feet from them. Obie's eyes didn't move, but he began to take much deeper breaths.

He whispered to Leroy, "Get ready, old buddy."

"They got to bring ass to get ass!"

The tall man stood looking at them while the other three men staggered themselves in a semi-circle around the spot where Leroy and Obie stood. Then all of them took up a pose just like their leader.

The tall man brought his arms down from in front of his chest, put them behind his back, and began to walk up and down, always giving them four feet of space.

"Pieces of shit," he said. "Mama didn't have no boy childs, just girls."

"They sure look good to me, baby."

"Fucking faggots. How'd you all like to kiss my big black ass? You'd like that, wouldn't you?"

Across the room, towards the center of the cell block, a short, thin Puerto Rican of about eighteen began to clap his hands together. The other prisoners joined in.

The cell block resounded with the rhythm of the hands. The prisoners' legs began to move from one side to the other. The men would stand almost motionless on one foot until, with another collective clap of their hands, they all would shift to the other foot.

The Puerto Rican kid who'd started the clapping jumped into the middle of the floor, his body moving as if he were on ice skates as he darted first in one direction and then another. His arms moved counter to his legs, and his body would now dip down close to the floor and now up towards the guards, who were looking down without apparent interest.

The boy's body moved as if each limb were independent of the others, like the head bone wasn't connected to the neck bone, the neck bone not connected to the chest bone. Like all the bones in his body had their own existence, yet obeyed a single will. Another man—of medium height and thin too like the Puerto Rican—suddenly threw himself into the dance. The clapping of the men became louder, joined now by shouts of "Go, Juan! Go, Juan!"

The men directly in front of Obie and Leroy began to clap too and backed away from them, melting into the mass of shouting and clapping prisoners.

Leroy began to chant to himself. The chant rose above the sound of the break-dancing and seemed to hover over it—clear and distinct, because its pitch was higher than that of the shouts coming from the other prisoners.

Their sound became even louder as the tall man danced himself and his men into the center of the mass. The men collapsed onto the leader, surrounding him so that the guards above could see he was nowhere near the outside of the circle of men.

The circle stabilized itself. The noisy mass of men, like a swarm of bees, began to encroach slowly on Obie and Leroy's space, on the line they'd drawn for themselves on the gray concrete floor of the cell block.

Too late the guards reached for their walkie-talkies and began shouting into the loudspeakers for the prisoners to line up.

Obie said, "No sense in waiting no more, man, let's take it to them."

"Right!" Leroy said, and both men flung themselves into the crowd, punching with their fists and kicking with their feet and knees.

Then Obie leapt into the air, soaring over them till he landed on top of the ringleader, confident that he was protected in the middle of his men. When Obie had the man in his grip, he twisted his head hard and smiled, for the first time since he'd been incarcerated. They were on him in seconds, but he didn't care.

It was worth it.

CHAPTER 10

WALTER SHAPIRO SAT ON THE SUBWAY, his seersucker jacket falling loosely on his thin frame. His eyes focused on the tiny notebook computer in front of him, where he was jotting down the major points he wanted to cover in his analysis of the Bullock case. As the subway train rocked from side to side on its journey uptown to Cecil B. Moore Avenue, he reached into his pocket to get one of the little mints he chewed to relieve his nerves since he'd stopped smoking his pipe.

He quit writing, lifted his head, and thought for a moment about the Bullock family. The very man whose life he'd immersed himself in a year ago, honored in a special ceremony by the governor of the state, was now under threat of being put into the same prison system to which he'd sent so many members of the gang that had infested the Joseph E. Hill project.

Shapiro knew his series about the Bullock family and the Mau-Mau was the best work he'd ever done. And getting the story had been an unforgettable experience. Sundays, he'd gone to church with them; Saturday nights on patrols with the men in their old wrecks of cars and Radio Shack walkie-talkies; weekdays, wandering around the projects with Obie Bullock or his sidekick, Leroy Merriweather. He'd eaten the sweet potato pie Obie offered him and suggested that he visit his apartment for knishes. After a while, Rachel had told him he might as well move in with the Bullocks, for all she and the kids saw of him.

Now Obie, out on bail, had invited him up to accompany him, some of his men, and Reverend Johnson on one of their "harassment" patrols. After exiting the train in North Philly, Shapiro made his way down to the Hill project. He was so well known in the area that some of the men at the chess table called him by name. Shapiro returned their greetings and went up to the

Bullock apartment.

Obie, who must have weighed 220 pounds a year ago, had to be pushing 240 now. But he still had the build of one of those fast-moving Eagles linebackers. Like he could sweep away the whole left side of the New York Giants line if he got mad enough.

"Hey, little man," he said. "Sure has been a while. What's been happening?"

"Nothing," Shapiro said. "Nothing interesting, anyway. It's been a dull life since I stopped hanging out with you."

"How're the wife and kids?" Obie nodded for Shapiro to follow him out onto the terrace.

"Okay." Shapiro had decided he wasn't going to tell Obie that his youngest daughter, the twenty-year-old he loved with all his heart, had been diagnosed with leukemia.

Once they were comfortably settled on the terrace, Obie said, "I want to thank you for coming up tonight—might be a little dangerous for you what with all that's gone down recently, but I want people to know exactly what the situation is up here and how we're going to deal with it. Reverend Johnson and some of the boys should be along soon. In the meantime, I'll fill you in on anything you want to know about what's happening."

Shapiro got out his computer.

"Obie, what are you going to do now? I was mad as hell to find out the DA's office is thinking about indicting you. And what about Leroy? Just because he doesn't have a clean record like you, he's going to have to stay in jail unless he raises a hundred thousand dollars' bail?"

"Hey, man, you're a reporter." Obie reached into a cooler and brought out a beer for himself and a Pepsi for Shapiro. "You got to remember to keep your cool, your objectivity."

"You're right, Obie, so let's get down to it. This is for the record. What's your reaction and the reaction of the Mau-Mau to the D.A.'s decision? What are you going to do about it?"

"Look, Walt, there's not a lot I <u>can</u> do. Some people have put up funds for lawyers, and we're going to fight the charges all the way. I think the DA will wise up and realize that no jury would convict us. Those two will never talk. In the meantime, the only real problem this makes for me is, I can't travel out of state till this thing is over."

"Anything else for the record?"

"No," Obie said, "except you know me and you know the Mau-Mau by now, and we're not about to give up this fight."

"Okay, now tell me how things really are."

Obie popped the tab on his beer can and took a long pull. "You'll see for yourself tonight. We're in pretty lousy shape. Now that the cops are cracking down on our patrols—and particularly since they put Leroy away—our effectiveness is cut in half. You must have seen it yourself just now when you came in here. Dealers all over the place. We got about ten men left." He sighed heavily. "Lost more people than I figured when I supported Sarnese."

"See, it's hard for a black man to side with the police, even a good cop like Sarnese. Just don't sit right with the folks. Anyways, I got more support from around the city and country than I got right here in the projects. It hurts real bad, man."

"Anything you can do about it?"

"Tell you the truth, I don't know. They're scared of the Teagle gang too. And don't think I don't feel where they coming from. Seems like I been at war all my life. First, just to make my way out of North Carolina. I told you about that farm down there and the way my daddy was. A mean hard cruel son of a bitch. Then the army. And now this. Not a day without wounds."

Beer can in hand, Obie got up and walked to the balcony railing. Shapiro saw the change in his face as he looked out over the courtyard of the project.

"But I ain't going to stop now. Ain't noways tired. Going to run this race to the end. Count on it!"

He hiked up his trousers—they had a way of sitting low on him—and turned back.

"Tell you one thing. Ain't going to let no law keep me from protecting my family. I will surely die before I'll see one hair on the head of my wife or children touched. That's a promise. And you can quote that in the newspaper."

The doorbell rang. Obie answered it and Reverend Theodius Johnson stepped into the living room, followed by three members of the Mau-Mau.

"Good evening, gentleman," the minister said in his booming bass voice. "I believe it's about time for us to get moving if we're going to put our plan into action this evening." He shook Shapiro's hand. "Glad to see you again and glad to know you're going along with us tonight."

"Well, Reverend, they say there's nothing new under the sun, but I want to see just how effective this new tactic of the Mau-Mau is going to be. I mean, who ever heard of planning drug interdiction on a football pattern—man-to-man coverage?"

The reverend nodded his head in Obie's direction. "See that fellow there, see how many bruises he's got on his face from that scrape in the prison the other day? Well, it doesn't mean a thing to him. When he got home, first thing he did was call me up and tell me about this new idea he'd thought up while he was in the infirmary—that no matter how many men he had left, each one of them was to be a dealer's shadow every night, and each man would carry a walkie-talkie and one other little item he'll show you in a minute."

"See," Obie said, "this thing ain't going to be over till we strangle these connections, stop them from making a transaction, and we got one important weapon—I'm going to get it now."

He walked into his bedroom and emerged in a few seconds with an armful of boxes, then proceeded to pull out what Shapiro immediately recognized as cheap off-brand video recorders. He handed them out one by one to Reverend Johnson and the other men.

Shapiro was flabbergasted. He knew Obie had invited him up here for a reason but would never have dreamed that in the midst of all the uproar over the assaults, Obie and the Mau-Mau would go to the lengths of further provoking the dealers by videotaping them.

Obie said, "You have the reverend to thank for these cameras, they're borrowed from the church with the full approval of the trustees, all we have to do is see they're back in time for Sunday service, and that we surely will do. They're simple to use and can even shoot in the dark—you'll see in a few minutes. We operate just like a team, and those guys down in the courtyard are going to be auditioning for camera central. Let's get going."

Shapiro reached into his pocket to make sure his own digital camera was there—he wanted to be sure to catch as much as he could of this pioneering action.

TWO MINUTES LATER, Obie, Reverend Johnson, and their crew descended to the first floor of the apartment building. Obie stopped to greet the lovely policewoman on duty there.

"Hi, we going outside to get started on our man-to-man operation, and we just need a little communication help from you if things get sticky, ain't carrying no weapons, only thing we got is these cameras and walkie-talkies." He glanced at Reverend Johnson, who as always had on his white pastor's collar. "And the help of the Lord."

"I'll do whatever I can," she said, "but you know I can't leave my post here. If things get hot, I'll try and get help for you, but I'm not promising they'll come. Why don't you just let things cool down for a while? Look at yourself, face all messed up and everything, you need to be in bed."

"Lisa, just do your best." Obie nodded to the men and they walked outside into the courtyard, where he began calling out instructions, like he was deploying a squad for combat.

"Peyton, see Yusef over there, he's your man for the night. Long as he's in this yard, you keep that camera rolling. He going to be a sure-nuff star!"

Yusef, a boy of about sixteen with a bushy afro and blue dungarees worn low, glared at Peyton and Obie, then turned and walked away. Peyton didn't follow him physically but kept the camera trained on him.

"Don't matter how far you go, boy, this little thing can even see you in the dark." Peyton patted the camera. "Now you take your business out of this yard and you won't be in the picture, simple as that."

Obie called out, "Jabar, you take Clayton, give him his fifteen minutes of fame, like they say. Mitchell, you got Raschid, the big cheese. Me and the reverend here, we just going to stay right where we are and shoot the whole scene, just to show nothing illegal is going down."

Shapiro was amazed at the transformation that took place in the yard. When they'd come downstairs, there'd been a whole swarm of men, mostly young but some middle-aged, patently engaged in the selling of drugs. It was almost like an outdoor bazaar. But Obie had obviously zeroed in on the ringleaders, for now the group scattered to the far corners of the courtyard. Yet it was so small that the cameras stayed focused on them.

To Shapiro, there was something cruel and humiliating about the exercise. Certainly the dealers didn't deserve pity, but Obie, Reverend Johnson, and their crew were definitely acting like vigilantes. It reminded him of white southerners turning fire hoses on civil rights protesters back in the sixties.

Why the hell was he thinking like that? It was the rights of the law-abiding residents that were being invaded, not those of the dealers. But nonetheless what was going on was degrading to them, and he figured they wouldn't take it for long.

And he was right. Rather than flee into the street, they assembled together about fifty yards away, formed into almost military-like ranks, and began to advance on Obie and his picture takers.

Obie whispered into his walkie-talkie. "Everybody back to the Hill entrance, don't want nobody left out there all alone." As soon as the men had obeyed, he said, "Just stand firm and keep on shooting."

Shapiro pulled out his press card, pinned it on his jacket, and took up a position just behind Obie and his Mau-Maus. He turned around to see that Officer Martinez was standing right behind him, talking into the transmitter mounted on her shoulder.

A second later she shouted out to Obie, "Precinct says

unless there's flat-out violence, they're not sending anybody over here—stuff's happening all over the place tonight and they've got nobody available." She hesitated for a second. "And I've got to get back inside and cover the desk, so keep it cool."

Keep it cool? What planet was she living on? Obviously that gang of thugs marching on the Mau-Mau had more on their mind than peacefully negotiating an end to the video camera surveillance. There must be about ten of them, and as they marched towards the entrance, they began to chant a rap song. It was something to see. Their hats were askew, their hair done up in every fashion from braids to cornrows to bushes, their hands cocked in front of them with their fingers pointing out as if to fire at the members of the Mau-Mau.

Obie's men, a couple of whom were dressed just like their opponents, held their ground and kept on running their video cameras.

Suddenly the leader of the group, Raschid, commanded silence and the rap song ceased. He looked at Obie and nodded towards the door:

"We going up to our apartments now, and the ones who don't live here, they going up with us—they our guests." With that, he beckoned to his followers and they tramped inside, crowding the corridor, then walking one by one past Officer Martinez, who could do nothing but check the identification of those who didn't live in the building, then wave them on inside.

Obie's men were left outside with no targets for their surveillance.

Shapiro walked back to where they were standing. "Well, Obie, what are you going to do now—looks like the action's over for the night."

"No, it ain't, not by a long shot. They just trying to move the operation to the third floor, where they got their command center in Rachid's mama's apartment." He glanced around the courtyard. The old men had left, and the children had been called inside by their parents. "We going to take our cameras right up there and shadow every one of them comes in and out of those apartments.

Ain't going to give them no peace."

"You agree with this tactic, Reverend Johnson? Isn't this an attack on their privacy, an invasion of their basic rights as citizens?"

"You want to worry about somebody's rights, you worry about those old women living up there in those apartments. They thought they'd have some peace once their grandsons were sent off to prison, but they came back and built themselves drug nests up there—those folks are practically prisoners in their own homes." He pointed up the stairwells, "These guys peddle the stuff all day, kids, prostitutes, doesn't matter who. No, we have to follow them up there, badger them to death, till they have to go elsewhere. Come on."

Obie was already leading his crew into the elevator. Shapiro followed them.

They emerged on the third floor, only to be met by Raschid and his men, seated now on the floor of the landing. The way the building was laid out, there was almost no space left for the Mau-Mau.

Peyton said, "Let's call it a night."

Obie glared at Raschid. "We leaving now, but I'm going to follow your ass wherever you and these dudes go, ain't going to give a second's rest."

Raschid, with that smoothly slanted hat and a half-sneer, half-grin on his face, said, "Take your boys and this reporter with you and get the hell out of here before I make you do it." He looked at the minister. "Rev, I don't want to disrespect you, but you got to know that all this stuff with your church cameras is going to cause a lot of trouble, and I think you should back off of this thing, go to church and start praying, that's what you do best. Ain't right for no preachers to be mixed up in this kind of business."

Reverend Johnson said, "Raschid, is your mother home?"

"Why you want to know?"

"Because I'd like to stop in and see her. Me, Obie, and this reporter here." He threaded his way through the men on the floor, knocked on the door of apartment 3-B, then beckoned to Obie and Shapiro. "Come on, she hasn't been to church in two months and it's about time I visited her anyway."

Shapiro didn't really know what to do. Here he was in the midst of a situation where the slightest misstep might lead to an all-out fight right here in the hallway. He really wished he were home in his bed. Raschid's boys were muttering and making threatening gestures at Obie's crew, while Obie, in turn, was glaring back at them, and Reverend Johnson seemed intent on pursuing his ministerial duties. But suddenly, amidst the smell of marijuana, the door opened.

"Reverend, what a surprise! What you doing here? And what's all this going on in the hallway? Raschid, tell all your boys to just take themselves where they belong."

Raschid's mom was built tall, strong, and sturdy—almost incongruously so, Shapiro thought, for the daintily flower-printed dress she wore. She glared at her son and his crew.

"Git, now! And Raschid, you stay right over there with them tonight, I don't want them tramping around in here, messing up the floors and everything. I just mopped. Come in, Reverend, you welcome any time."

As they entered the room, Shapiro noted the large vaulted ceiling and the way every wall was decorated with tapestries or pictures of Jesus, or banners with religious homilies like "Jesus Saves," or the "Lord is My Light and My Salvation." A black Bible rested on a mahogany side table. The room was immaculate, with an oversized blue sofa and a matching blue recliner with an ottoman. On a large table stood framed high school diplomas amid pictures of weddings, and boys and girls in the marines and army. Mrs. Tucker had obviously done a fine job of raising what appeared to have been many children she could be proud of. Raschid, whom Shapiro knew had already done two stints in prison and was Teagle's number-one hit man, was another story.

Reverend Johnson introduced Shapiro and told Mrs. Williams exactly what was happening outside. She wasn't surprised in the least.

"See, Reverend, it's like this. Raschid is my oldest, and when he come home from prison, there was no place for him to go." She looked at Shapiro. "Don't expect you know what I'm talking about, mister, but your child is yours forever, no matter what sins he done, and there's no way I'm going to let him sleep on the streets while I sleep in a warm bed—it's against nature."

Reverend Johnson leaned over and took her hands in his. "But Hattie Mae, there's plenty of places for him to go, don't you see what's happening here? Why, just a moment ago, somebody could have got killed out there. And these dealers are like a plague, like the locusts in the Bible, spreading all over and stifling all of God's good work." He looked at Obie. "You should get Raschid out of here. If not for Obie's and Dora Lee's sake, then at least for the children's sakes who live here. God didn't intend for them to be raised with all this killing and violence around them."

Hattie Mae pointed at Obie. "But he's the one stirring up all the trouble. He's the one had Son's mama evicted from here on charges of harboring a drug dealer—didn't you, now, Obie?"

"Well, Hattie Mae—"

"Well, nothing, Obie Bullock, you been on everybody and everything, and don't tell me you don't have it in for my boy, and for Son, and everybody else who don't live up to your standards. You persecuted that poor Mammie Teagle till she could barely stand, might as well of took off all her clothes and whipped her right in the middle of the courtyard."

"Hattie Mae, we had to get Son out of there. And it wasn't me, but the housing committee—"

"Don't Hattie Mae me, you can talk about the committee did this, the committee did that, but when it was all over, you was the head of that committee and they done just what you said and don't try and tell me otherwise." She turned to Reverend Johnson. "Obie won't say so, but he done had it in for the Teagles and us ever since he got married to Dora Lee and that no good son of hers put him through the wringer."

Reverend Johnson said, "Now, Hattie Mae, we really just stopped in here to see how you were doing. We don't—"

"Tell them, Obie, tell them how that boy of Dora Lee's used to sass you and raise all kinds of hell in this place, tell them about that, and how you blamed it all on us poor folks instead on yourself and Dora Lee. And I know you told them about your junkie sister?"

Obie was biting his lip, obviously doing his best to restrain himself. But to Shapiro, Hattie Mae was making some kind of sense. Sometimes it did seem that Obie was really on a crusade, motivated not only by the truly bad situation in the project but also by some personal demons.

Reverend Johnson stood up. "Well, Hattie Mae, we got to be going now. Thanks for letting us in so this reporter fellow can see how things really are here." He clasped her hand tightly. "Maybe we don't know what you're going through every day with that diabetes of yours and all these problems, but God does know and he cares about you. Me and Obie, we have to keep after the dealers, no matter who they are—that's God's commandment to us. But I want you to know that there's no condemnation of you on our part. Like the old song says, 'No condemnation, no condemnation, no condemnation in my heart.' Let's have prayer before we leave."

A few moments later, on the way out, Shapiro handed his card to Hattie Mae. "Call me any time if you'd like to talk about anything that's going on here. I want what I'm writing about this project to be fair and accurate. Particularly if you know anything about what happened to Shakeisha."

The three men took the elevator down to the first floor. Officer Martinez was still there.

"Things have calmed down a lot outside, Obie, looks like you did run them off for the night. Your people are sitting outside waiting for you."

"Thanks, Lisa."

They went out into the courtyard, where Peyton and the other members of the Mau-Mau waited for them, video cameras now stowed in camera bags and slung over their shoulders.

"Well," Obie said, "looks like we can pack it in for the night. I'm going to take off for work, and you fellows can head on home too, nothing more to do."

Peyton said, "Makes sense, no use in just standing around

here. Hell, it's ten-thirty and the old men are already gone." He nodded toward the empty table where they usually congregated.

With that, the men scattered, leaving Obie, Reverend Johnson, and Shapiro alone.

"Mr. Shapiro, let me give you a lift," the reverend said. "My car's parked just outside and it'll spare you having to wait for the subway this hour of the night."

"I appreciate it, reverend, but won't it be taking you out of your way to take me up to Chestnut Hill?"

"Sure it will, I live right over the way. But I like driving and it'll give me a chance to tell you about other things the church is involved in besides this."

Shapiro looked up. All the lights from the building were on, a tower of light rising towards the sky. Behind it, he could see the full moon—it always surprised him how you could even see it in Philly with all its buildings, but there it was in all its full shining majesty, casting its light on the nearly empty courtyard where they were standing.

A prickle of fear slowly crept over him. Where had he felt it before? He remembered where and when—Iraq, in those deserted towns where everyone had fled. He didn't like the feeling and he could see that Obie didn't much like their situation either. His eyes were darting around the yard, trying to pierce the darkness. Emptiness in a place that should be teeming with life and activity—criminal or not—was a sign of danger to both men.

Obie said, "If you two don't mind, I think I'd like to take a little scout outside the courtyard, make sure you get into the car safe. Too quiet for me out here."

He'd no sooner said those words than a burst of automatic fire flared out from the street, close to the entrance gate to the courtyard.

Obie pointed to a concrete ring surrounding the toddlers' playground.

"Hit the ground and crawl behind that!" The other two men lost no time in following his command.

Another burst of fire split the air, the bullets whipping over their heads and splintering the glass in the entrance door of the project into a thousand pieces. The lights went out in the apartments above them as shouts came from the building windows.

"They shooting again!"

"Somebody call the cops!"

"When this shit going to stop?"

Then there was quiet in the courtyard. Whoever had done the shooting was gone, vanished into the darkness. Shapiro, Obie, and Reverend Johnson were on the ground, shaken but unhurt. Off in the distance they heard the sound of police sirens. Lisa Martinez emerged from the building, revolver in hand.

"Help's on the way, come on in here till they show up."

Shapiro had had enough for the evening. Here he'd just come up to see how things were going with the Mau-Mau and found himself in the middle of an ambush. Hell, it couldn't have been much worse in the Old West. He brushed his clothes off, got out his notebook, and went into the lounge to await the arrival of the police. He turned to Reverend Johnson.

"Where's Obie?"

"Said to tell you goodnight, he had to hurry so he could make it to work on time." He shook his head. "Those bullets don't faze that man one bit, couldn't scare him if you put him in a pit full of rattlesnakes. But maybe now you understand better what we're up against."

Shapiro nodded. He felt truly sorry for Obie and his family, for he saw no way that he and his small band of Mau-Mau could withstand the forces arrayed against them. He, for one, would give thanks to the Lord that night that he and his dear ones would rest safe and protected from the likes of Raschid and his followers. Here there was no law—it was like Baghdad in the aftermath of the invasion. Shapiro knew one thing: if Obie kept up his man-to-man campaign, attacking the dealers' bread and butter, he'd be dead in a matter of months if not weeks. It was sad, but true.

Then he had a bright thought. If he ratcheted up his investigation of O'Brien a notch, he just might be able to take a little pressure off of Obie. He was sure the relationship between

Raschid and O'Brien could bear close examination—he'd seen them talking once, and every instinct he had told him it wasn't an in-the-line-of-duty conversation. If he was right, he might be able to get them both put in jail.

CHAPTER 11

DORA LEE AND RUTH WALKED OUT of their office building together, both tired after a long day.

"Let's stop off and get something to drink," Dora Lee said. "I could really go for a white wine and soda."

"Me too. If I hear 'computer down' one more time this week, I'll go crazy."

The two women made their way to a little bar tucked away just off the main alcove of their building. Dora Lee could detect a slight smell of stale beer, at odds with the sleek decor of the cocktail lounge. The room was so attractive and comfortable that it made her feel—fifteen feet from her office building—like she was in a city where no one worked.

She was always struck by the amount of energy people saved up from the office to let out here. First it would be quiet. Then, as the waitresses in short red skirts and white blouses brought the drinks in tall, frosty glasses to the customers, the place would take on life—the executives would take off their jackets, and the secretaries would loosen the top buttons of their blouses. It was like their real lives began during this cocktail hour.

Dora Lee and Ruth rarely stopped in, but they were known here, and the Columbian bartender greeted them with a smile.

"Haven't seen you two in a long time. Come on in. Such beautiful ladies, I find you my best table." Still smiling, he came out from behind the bar, led them over to a table, and seated them with a little bow. Dora Lee and Ruth loved it. With cool and refreshing drinks before them, they relaxed and enjoyed the atmosphere. Then, after a few minutes, Dora Lee said, "I think I'll be going on my vacation by myself next week. Obie and I talked it over, and we agreed somebody ought to be there with the kids in Carolina. I'll be taking the bus down."

"What about Obie?"

"The judge won't give him permission to leave the state." She stirred a straw in her drink. "Tonight's my last English class, the exam's next week. I still haven't gotten over failing that math course. I'm just going to try and do better in this one."

"You should be all right, all you have to do to pass an English course is read."

"I know, but it's been awful hard keeping my mind on the books. I'm always worrying about the kids now, and..."

"What, Dora Lee?"

"About Obie."

"Oh, no."

"He's been awful moody lately. It's not like him. And we've been doing a lot of arguing on the phone. Over money and the way he's taken to drinking again. He won't admit it, but all this stuff is getting to him. We used to be able to make up by making love, once we were in bed together everything was okay again. But now..." She looked around the room. "I just don't see the end of this Teagle thing. I mean, even if Obie does get off on that assault charge, there's still the Teagle gang to deal with. They spray bullets in the projects, then the precinct cops come around afterwards—there's no way that one woman cop on duty at the desk can deal with it."

"Oh, honey, it sounds so hard. Isn't there anything you can do? I'd be going out of my mind."

"I've told Obie we should move from here. Go to his brother's home down south and make us a new life. Right now!"

"But that would be giving up, and—"

"That would just be common sense. I only have Timba left now, once Sabaya's in college, and I've got to protect him. Obie doesn't get that we're out here all by ourselves now. Leroy's in jail. And all the mayor does is talk about what he'd like to do. And the police..."

Ruth put her hand on Dora Lee's and squeezed.

"Besides, I can't just keep imposing on your hospitality. You have your own lives, I can't stay with you forever. And I can't go back to the project."

Ruth said, "Why don't you just think about it while you're down south? Give yourself some time. And as far as living with us goes, you can stay as long as you like. I mean it from my heart. That comes from the kids and Bill, too. As a matter of fact, especially from the kids."

"I really appreciate it." She looked down at her cocktail napkin, which was in tatters. "But hey, it's getting a little late now, we better be leaving if I'm going to make class."

Dora Lee and Ruth paid their checks, waved goodbye to the bartender, and went outside. Ruth walked towards Market Street, a few blocks away, and Dora Lee towards the subway to go uptown to the Nicetown extension center of the Community College of Philadelphia, many blocks north of where they lived.

As soon as she was down in the subway, she walked over to the track and looked up the tunnel to see if the train was coming. Nothing. At the newspaper stand, an Indian in a white turban was putting the magazines away and preparing to pull down the metal shutters that would protect his wares until the next morning.

At this late hour, only three other passengers stood on the platform. One was an old woman who, even in the heat and humidity, was wearing a white woolen sweater. A few feet away from her stood a young girl of about eighteen, reading the Inquirer. The other waiting passenger was a light-complexioned black man. He looked to be about forty-five, but he sure was carrying a lot of weight. It made him look older.

So many things to worry about. She'd have to clear her mind if she was going to do well in the discussion tonight. If only she'd had a chance to finish the reading. These summer school courses ran so fast.

Dora Lee was shaken out of her thoughts by the metallic click of the turnstile behind her. Another person had walked onto the platform. She didn't turn around. Instead she walked back to the edge of the platform to take another look up the tracks.

Still no train. If it didn't get here in another five minutes, she'd definitely be late for class, and the professor had promised to go over some possible exam questions tonight.

Down the platform, the older black man pulled out a blue and red handkerchief, then wiped his forehead. He looked towards Dora Lee and smiled. Although the man's smile seemed friendly, Dora Lee didn't return it. Never smile at anybody in the subway. Oh, where was that darn train?

She heard faintly the distant clatter that told her it was coming. The sound came closer and closer until suddenly the train, its searchlight probing the dark tracks in front of it, was filling the silent station with its roar and its wind.

Dora Lee stepped back from the yellow caution line as the train entered the station, its metal body swaying closer and closer to her. As she retreated from the edge she glanced behind her, and her eyes settled on the man who'd been the last to come onto the platform. Wait a minute. She recognized that walk from somewhere, but she couldn't remember where or when. His head was turned away from her, and he was walking towards the next car down from the one now pulling to a stop in front of her.

The doors opened, and Dora Lee got into the car and took a seat. The stout black man entered behind her, took a seat across from her, and unfolded a newspaper. The young girl and the old woman took seats not far from Dora Lee in the otherwise empty car.

She opened up her English literature textbook and buried her head in the dozens of poems she'd have to know before that exam next week. She needed to concentrate.

Slowly she let herself be carried away by the words in front of her. Swept up in the verses and rhythms of Langston Hughes, she felt herself going back to Africa with him as he wrote of the Nile and of the beauty of African women. She used to tell Obie he was lucky he'd come along after Hughes died, because she'd have dumped him for the poet in a heartbeat.

The train pulled into the next station. The man across from her folded his paper, tucked it under his arm, gave Dora Lee one last smile, and walked out the doors.

The train jerked into motion and headed for the next station.

Dora Lee looked up from her reading. She always did that when a train pulled out of a station. She saw the man who'd last come through the turnstile. He was standing at the doorway to the next car, and he was staring at her. When he saw she'd seen him, he pulled his head away from the window of the door.

She only had one look, but now she was sure there was something familiar about him. He wore a knit green shirt with little symbols on it and a black baseball hat that covered his hair and contrasted sharply with his yellowish-brown skin. Wait a minute—she knew who it was. Rufus, one of the hangers-on of the Teagle gang, he'd always been around Son before he went off to prison the last time. He had a beard now, but she'd swear on a stack of Bibles that it was him.

She looked quickly at the two other women in the car and suddenly wished she'd smiled back at the other man. Maybe he'd have stayed on until the next stop.

Dora Lee eyed the emergency box. Should she pull the handle? Where was the conductor? What car was he in? Fool girl, you forgot to look!

Then she remembered. He was in the far end of the next car. And Rufus was in the same car. To reach the conductor, she'd have to get past him.

The train was slowing down for the next stop. Should she get off there and be late for her class?

The train pulled into the station, the doors opened once again, and the old woman in the sweater and the teenager got out. Dora Lee prayed someone else would get on the train.

No one did.

She should get off—

Whoosh! The doors slammed shut.

She was alone, and it was five minutes to the next stop.

She looked straight ahead and began to rock slowly from side to side. In all circumstances, pray. Jesus, stay close!

She got up and walked towards the car door where she'd seen Rufus. If he was going to attack her, it would have to be right in there in the same car with the conductor.

So she just moved to the door, pulled it open, heard the roar of the tracks for a second, took a big step, grasped the handle of the door to the next car, pulled it hard, and burst in, running towards the car's other end right past Rufus, who sat lounged against the seat just inside the door.

Past him, and moving towards the conductor's cubicle. Didn't look back, either.

Dora Lee pounded at the conductor's door with her fists. A short black man with a mustache came out.

"What is it, miss? What's the trouble?"

"I'm Dora Lee Bullock, Big Obie Bullock's wife, and that man..." She pointed over her shoulder toward the other end of the car. "He was stalking me."

"What man, lady?" The conductor shook his head. "There's nobody down there."

"He must have run into the next car. Please, call the police! He's a gang member and he's likely to kill me."

"Lady, I can't call the police just because somebody looks suspicious. Probably that man wasn't even studying about you. Just sit down, and I'll make sure you get to your stop safely."

Dora Lee did as he asked and waited for the train to pull into the next stop. As it slowed, she said to the conductor, "At least do me one favor, just don't let the train pull out of the station till I get over to the gates."

"All right, ma'am."

When the train stopped, Dora Lee walked out into the station and looked down towards the other end of the train.

No one else got out.

She walked across to the gate and went through. The conductor yelled after her. "Mrs. Bullock, have a good evening!" Dora Lee heard the doors shut and the train move off.

She ran up the stairs two at a time and made it to the next level. Trains were letting off fellow students from other parts of the city. She spotted some friends and soon was on her way to her encounter with the English professor and Langston Hughes.

Nobody had threatened her—except with a look—nobody had bothered her. And she was terrified.

Class was over. Dora Lee had to get from the college to the Thirteeth Street station. Usually she just took the subway. But now she was too scared to even think about doing that.

Should she call Obie? No, he was supposed to be at a meeting tonight, and besides, he hadn't been that pleasant to her on the phone when she'd talked to him earlier. Grumbling about the charge bills that had come in after she'd bought that dress she really needed.

No, we'd probably just get into it again. Just won't admit that his personal war with Teagle is killing us. And that we're not prepared to pay for all those extras Sabaya will need if she goes off to Oberlin instead of a college here in the city. Can't take it much longer, no I can't.

She could take a cab. But she only had seven dollars in her pocket, not enough money for a taxi. She looked up the street but saw only one old junky car, and it seemed to be parked and not in service.

She was still standing on the steps of the college when she saw two of her classmates. They shouted over to her.

"Dora Lee, what's the matter with you, girl? You standing there like you don't know where you are. Come on, we taking the downtown subway."

"Well, I'll go with you far as City Hall, I'm going over to Thirteeth Street. I'm staying with some friends out in the suburbs until all this mess blows over."

"We know all about it," said the younger of the two women. She was short and plump, about thirty-five, and seemed to always have a smile on her face. She'd argued in class tonight that Langston Hughes was really not the most important writer of the Harlem Renaissance. Said she liked a man named Toomer, whose writing was chiseled and pure. Said it put shivers through her body just to read the man. The professor had laughed and said not to let academic analysis stand in the way of her judgment.

The three women began to walk down the steps. When they reached the sidewalk, Lurlene, the one with the smile, waved at the security guard, an older Hispanic man who was always giving the female students flowery compliments about their appearance. The women walked up the street towards the subway stop, which was in the next block and on the other side.

They stopped at the red light, then started across the street. Dora Lee was grateful to have company. After all, it would only be a fifteen-minute ride from City Hall. Once in Thirtieth Street—

Dora Lee sensed rather than heard the sound of a car.

She glanced to the left and saw that old car she'd noticed before coming fast towards them. The light was red, but the automobile ran right through it. The driver, a black man with dreadlocks, had his eyes set on Dora Lee.

"Hey, girls, watch out!" She pushed Lurlene, who was closest to the car, to shove her out of harm's way.

But Lurlene turned around, probably to find out who'd pushed her. It was just the opposite of what Dora Lee wanted her to do.

Dora Lee screamed, shoved Lurlene hard one more time—then, instinctively, threw herself forward between two parked cars. The third young woman followed her example and leapt for the safety of the sidewalk.

But Lurlene, overweight and confused by Dora Lee's shove, moved too little, too late.

Dora Lee, her head down against the warm pavement, heard a cry and then a thud.

Then screams, and the sound of the car accelerating down the street, its broken muffler rattling and clattering against its underbody.

Dora Lee lifted her head and took the hand of a bystander who reached down for her. She turned towards the street and saw what looked like a crumpled sleeping bag. But out of one end of the bag protruded the head of a woman who loved Toomer's poetry.

Her legs were thrown apart and twisted like a discarded baby doll's.

The street around the unmoving body was strewn with books, their pages open, so that white showed against the dark pavement. Lurlene's glasses, smashed, lay at Dora Lee's feet. Oh, my God, why hadn't she died with her!

She felt the street in front of her swirling. Then everything was dark.

A DAY LATER, having been checked out at the hospital and interrogated by the police, Dora Lee sat in a car with Obie as he drove her back out to Ardmore.

"Obie, I don't think I'm ever going to get over what happened yesterday, and the way I'm feeling right now, I just don't know what's going to happen to us."

Obie glanced over at her. "I don't blame you one minute for how you feeling and I ain't going to pretend this kind of life—killers after you, kids scattered, you and me living apart—is anything good for anybody. I got to think about a lot of things myself after all this."

"You got to do more than that, baby, I'm a strong woman and I've gone through a lot with you and a lot with our children, but when your crusade starts killing innocent folks, then we got to rethink everything. First it was Roy, now it's Lurlene. Who's next?" Dora Lee was staring straight ahead now. "We got to start weighing some other options."

"Baby," he said, "the next few days are going to be mighty rough, what with Lurlene's funeral and everything, maybe you should call up Reverend Johnson and see if you can't schedule a counseling session with him, talk this thing over before it gets settled in your mind and you can't get it out again. You—"

"Counseling session! I don't need a counseling session, I need for you to map a way out of our situation, and that means we either got to move or you, somehow or another, have to see your way to leaving Son Teagle and his people alone."

"What you say!" She would swear that if she'd been a man, Obie would have hit her, but instead he slammed his fist so hard on the armrest he almost tore it loose. "I love you more than life itself and I would lay it down for you and the kids, and I hurt for Lurlene and her family, but I will not give myself over to no group of thugs, and don't you ask me to do it, neither."

Dora Lee moved further over to her side of the car.

"'I,' you say. 'Myself,' you say.' 'Me,' you say. Oh, you will never understand, will you? It's not you in this fight, it's us. You've dragged us into this war with you, whether we like it or not. It's not fair."

"Life ain't fair, baby, you're dealt a deck of cards when you're born, and that's all you got to play with, but I still ain't about to play no losing hand, count on it." His jaw muscles tightened. "We can't stay up north if I quit—you too smart to think leaving that gang alone going to make them leave us alone. So we turn tail and run south, chased out of our home? That the life you want for our family? I feel so sorry about Lurlene, but I feel sorry too for all the decent folks in the Hill apartments who have to live with the fear of Teagle and his boys every day, and like I told you before, I ain't about to abandon them—you hear me, Dora Lee?"

"I do, Obie Bullock, loud and clear, I do hear you."

They rode the rest of the way to Ardmore in silence, and Dora Lee withdrew his hand from hers when he tried to put it there, an act she instantly regretted. She loved Obie, and it wasn't right to part from him with anger in her heart. But when he tried to kiss her on the mouth as they said goodnight, she turned her cheek to him.

Then she said, "See you at the funeral, Obie," and walked towards the house.

As she closed the door, she heard him say, "Oh, that's the way it is, huh?"

CHAPTER 12

MALIKA TEAGLE ROLLED OVER in her bed, shut off the alarm clock, and went into the next room to check on Ashanti. She cracked the door just wide enough so she could see her eight-year-old's head against the pillow, then quickly pulled it shut so as not to awaken him. Her sister, asleep in the third bedroom, would take care of him today.

Malika showered, then stepped out of the stall onto the thick pink carpeting that covered the floor and the toilet. She looked at herself in the mirrors that paneled all the walls of the room. Didn't look too bad for thirty, not bad at all.

After dressing hurriedly in a pair of designer jeans and a dark velvet blouse, she went into the kitchen and took two eggs and a package of bacon from the refrigerator. Soon the bacon was crackling in the frying pan, its smell mixed with that of browning toast and percolating coffee.

When she'd finished her breakfast, Malika smoked a cigarette and looked at the list she'd left on the table the night before to remind her what to take with her on the trip: two tubes of toothpaste, a copy of the African News, a book of Malcolm X's speeches, and two afro hair combs. Reassured that she'd not forgotten anything, she walked into the living room to make a last-minute check on the business figures. Son had a mind like a steel trap. Didn't forget one dime.

Malika flipped a switch on the wall, and the living room was flooded with light from the four torch lamps placed around the room. It seemed larger than it really was because of the mirrors that covered the walls on three sides. On the remaining wall was a blue satin cloth that matched the color of the heavily padded couch curved around two of the walls. The couch, like the other pieces of furniture in the room, was covered with clear plastic to protect it from dust. Against the other mirrored wall, running its full length, was a wide-screen TV and a stereo system with a burnished metal exterior. Malika had forgotten to turn the system off the night before, so its red lights were blinking. Shit. She clicked a button on the remote, and the lights went out.

She walked over to a panel in one of the mirrors and gave it a slight push. The panel pivoted open to reveal a small combination safe. Malika opened it and took out a white sheet of paper from among the rows and rows of crisp bills in the compartment. She looked intently at the sheet and memorized the total on it. Son would definitely not be a happy camper. She returned the sheet to the safe and closed it.

The door buzzer rang. She went over to it and talked into the speaker.

"Who is it?"

"It's me, Raschid."

"Be right down."

She rushed into the bedroom for her purse and a big brown shopping bag, returned to the kitchen and took some Kentucky Fried chicken boxes out of the refrigerator, rolls out of the bread box, and put the food into the bag. She gave the room where her boy lay sleeping a last look, then went into her sister's bedroom and woke her up.

"I'm leaving now, should be back around ten tonight. And baby, don't forget to make sure Ashanti gets his medicine exactly on time. Hear now?"

Her sister, barely awake, said, "I got it. Tell Son I said hello and I keep him in my prayers."

Malika went back into the kitchen, picked up the food and the other stuff, and left the apartment, taking care to re-arm the security system first. Downstairs in the lobby, Raschid stood talking to the night security guard, who smiled when he saw Malika.

"Good morning, Mrs. Teagle. You have a good trip." He unlocked the door so they could leave.

"Let me help you with some of that," Raschid said. "Looks like you packed for a week's visit."

They walked out into the still, warm air of a midtown Philadelphia summer morning. Raschid had on his white hat, its brim turned up on the side so it looked like one of those hats British hunters wore when the television showed them on safari in Africa.

Except no one would ever mistake Raschid for no British hunter. Not that skinny yellow man with his sleepy-looking eyes and red polo shirt. No, Raschid looked like he'd kill the British hunter and the lion too. Could probably do it with a look of his eyes. Son swore that Raschid had once stopped a mean-assed doberman pinscher—a dog he didn't even know—with a look. Dog stopped dead in its tracks, then backed away from him.

Raschid said, "Come on, baby, bus leaves in twenty minutes."

Malika got into the ugly old Ford Raschid used to get around the city and in a short time they arrived at their destination, a parking lot in North Philadelphia.

Three buses, their lights on, were parked in a line. Women, some leading small children, were walking from one bus to another, looking at the big white signs held up by the drivers. Each displayed the name of an upstate prison.

Raschid pulled up behind the last bus, took Malika's bags out, and opened the door for her.

The driver's sign said:Wiltshire, Buckingham, Chennault, and Delaware Correctional Facilities." Son was in Delaware. Raschid saw her onto the bus, waved goodbye, and left

MALIKA LOOKED OUT THE BUS WINDOW on the scene outside: a tall woman in a delicate white print dress and carrying two Target bags held a little girl's hand; behind her in the line waiting to board the bus was a short, squat woman dressed in jeans so tight that her stomach flowed out in rolls from under her blouse. A woman at the front of the bus said, "Hush, Abraham," as she held on to a sobbing child with one hand while she tried to take busfare out of her purse with the other.

Malika smiled every now and then as she recognized an acquaintance from a previous trip. Funny, but it was like they were all going on a church picnic.

There'd been a time when she and Son used to get on a big bus on a Saturday morning in August, and the boys and girls dressed in their light summer clothes would sit in the back, teasing each other, hiding each other's toys, and singing. The Sunday School teacher would always pay special attention to Son, give him something special to eat or some little airplane toy to play with, because Mammie Teagle was so hard on him.

That was before Son, his four brothers, and his mother had moved away from the old neighborhood and into the city homeless shelter system. Six years had passed before Mammie Teagle returned to North Philly to live in the Hill project. By that time Son, in his early teens, had changed. He wouldn't learn for nothing.

Malika remembered how she'd tried to help him with his arithmetic and English. But he just wouldn't pay attention. And the more he didn't learn and cut classes, the more Mammie Teagle whipped him. Until one day he got big enough to take the ironing cord out of her hand and almost turned it on her.

Soon after that, Son—for the first time—got sent away to a youth detention home. Ever since then, it seemed to Malika, he'd moved further north, into the youth homes and prisons upstate. The worse his crimes, the longer she had to travel to visit him, and the more she wondered why she'd ever married him. He could ooze the charm when he felt like it which wasn't often. No, she was wed to a foul-mouthed thug who beat her at the slightest provocation, once so badly that she needed fifteen stitches for a cut on her mouth, and who got out of bed the minute he'd satisfied himself with her.

Son swore he'd kill her if she ever so much as thought about leaving him. Said he'd break out of prison and track her down to the ends of the earth. And the bastard had even slapped Ashanti in the face for wetting the bed when he was two years old. No, it was better for her and Ashanti if they kept Son in prison—maybe one day somebody up there would get fed up with his arrogance and get up the nerve to kill him.

Then she'd have all the good things Son had given her—the

money in the bank, the furniture, the prestige in the community that came with being his woman—and not have to deal with his evil-assed self. She'd give up the apartment in center city, pack up her things, and take Ashanti down to Savannah, where they could live like decent folks and he could grow up to be something, maybe even a doctor or lawyer. After all, Malika had been one of the top students in her class when Son came along with his sweet talk, his Lexus, the fifteen-carat diamond ring, and the fine clothes he'd bought her when he was still courting her. Nothing had been too good for her then, and to tell the truth, he still treated her that way. All the material things she wanted, but then he'd beat on her whenever the notion came to his head. Just wasn't worth it.

"Young lady, looks like the seats in the back are all filled up. Mind if I sit down? My name's Pearl." It was a sweet-faced old woman Raschid had helped with her fare when she came up a few dollars short. She put her big brown bag down on the seat beside Malika.

"Put your bag up beside my stuff on the rack, and we'll be fine. Name's Malika."

"That's a real pretty name. Just need some place to get my legs stretched out. Couldn't do it in the back there. Besides, folks are always walking past you, waking you up because they got to go to the bathroom. Look, there's a line down there already."

She was right. So when the bus driver closed the door and suddenly drove off, several of the women were thrown into one another.

"Watch it, man."

"What the hell do he think he doing?"

The driver said nothing but did slow down a bit. Malika pulled out a small pillow from her bag, put it between the window and her seat, then turned to the woman beside her.

"I'm going to try and sleep."

Pearl, her head leaning toward her shoulder, was dozing.

Malika slept soundly and only woke up when the bus pulled into a rest stop with a restaurant. She got herself a sweet bun, quickly returned to her seat on the bus, and was asleep before it left. It was another three hours to the prison, and she needed the rest, had to be looking bright for Son.

When she woke up again, she saw they were at the outside sentry post at the prison. Malika looked up the aisle of the bus. A guard had boarded and was calling out names from a list the bus driver had given him.

"Tamatha Cripps, Rodney Cripps."

"Here."

"Beatrice Rodriguez."

"Here."

"Joyce Purvis, Lamont Purvis."

"Yeah, mister."

When he'd finished, the bus lumbered through the gates and up the long hill, bordered on both sides by coiled barbed wire, that led to the reception building. The morning sky was clear and blue, with only a few wispy clouds. From this road Malika could see way over to another range of mountains and to a small blue lake. She could even see the cars driving along the highway far below them.

She helped Pearl take her things down from the overhead rack, and all the women and children walked in a long, straggling line up the slope towards the reception hall. But visitors, arrivals on earlier buses, were already lined up in front of the locked doors. As always, the prison authorities could only process about ten people at a time. They made everyone walk through the metal detector, then swept their clothing with humming wands whose invisible beams probed even the most private parts of a person's body.

After about fifteen minutes of waiting, Malika and Pearl, along with eight others, were admitted to the entry room. Its walls were painted gray, and a large sign said in English and Spanish: "No Guns! No Drugs! No Prescription Drugs! No Knives!"

At the scarred wooden desk sat a guard who watched Malika and Pearl sign their names into a large blue register book. Three white female guards stood around the room. It was their job to make body searches of the women or children should the detectors reveal any concealed items.

Two white male guards sat on stools in a corner of the room.

They exchanged glances with each other when Malika walked through the metal detector. She felt dirty, like they were groping her with their hands.

Malika and Pearl entered another room, where five more guards stood in front of a long table onto which they were emptying the contents of the women's shopping bags, suitcases, and handbags. Everything was searched, including the bikini panties and filmy negligees some of the women who had conjugal visiting privileges had brought with them. Son had written to tell Malika they'd have no such privileges this time, since he'd been unjustly accused in some incident at the prison.

When the inspections were finally over and the backs of their hands stamped with marker ink, the women and children were escorted out of another door of the building and onto a waiting bus that would take them to the recreation hall, where the prisoners awaited them. Malika looked at her watch and saw that it was already twelve forty-five. Visiting hours had been under way for forty-five minutes and would be over at two o'clock.

Two guards at the door of the recreation building checked the identification tickets Malika and Pearl had been given. A guard gently motioned Pearl to the side—the old woman was to be given special transportation over to the infirmary, where her grandson was.

Malika walked into the main hall, which was full of black, yellow, and brown men in brown uniforms. The men, sitting at tables, jumped up quickly when their guests entered the room. A few barely managed to rise from their seats before their small children broke away from mothers or guardians and ran to them with shouts of "Daddy!"

EVERY OTHER TABLE had been filled with people, but only two sat with Son. One was that giant Homicide, the other was Jose, the leader of the Hispanic prisoners.

Son saw Malika, quickly stood and walked over to her. He'd aged a bit since she'd last seen him, seemed older than his thirty-five years.

But she didn't have long to think about that. In a second, he was holding her in his arms and she could feel him, even through her jeans. For several minutes they stood there in the middle of the floor, holding one another, gently rocking back and forth. Son started to say something, but Malika told him to be quiet, she just wanted him to hold her. Maybe deep down somewhere, she really did love him. But how come?

Finally, he let her go. "Come on over to the table, baby." The two men stood up and kissed Malika on the cheek.

Homicide said, "Been a long time between visits. What did you bring me?"

"Brought you those combs you asked for, that's what. And brought you some regards from Clara. Said she'd be up in another couple of months."

"I know about that. Always saying she'll be here." Homicide nodded his head at Jose. "We going to leave you folks alone, I think you only got about forty-five minutes left. I'll get one of the boys to bring your meals over."

Twenty minutes later, after a special visitors'-day meal of fried chicken, mashed potatoes, fresh-baked rolls, and apple pie, Malika and Son started to talk about the situation at home. Malika knew that no matter how serious things were, Son would never discuss anything over food. Eating, he said, was too important to be spoiled by a lot of talk.

Son motioned to a nearby prisoner to clear the table, then turned back to Malika.

"How's Ashanti?"

"Well, honey, I been taking him to the doctors once a week now for those shots, and he seems to be at least holding his own. Doctor say the sugar count ain't getting no better. But it's not getting worse. Sometimes he does seem a little tired.. They called me from the school the other day to come get him, he was so weak."

Son frowned.

"But he doing good in school," Malika said. "Teacher say he be the smartest boy in the class."

Son smiled. "She said that?"

"He doing real good. Come by it natural. Smart, like his daddy."

Malika knew what the next question would be.

"How about mama?"

"Well, Son..."

"You know better than to give me any of that 'well' stuff." His voice rose, and a guard looked in their direction. "How is she?"

"Not good. She just won't stop eating, and she eats stuff that's no good for her. You know how she likes pork chops. And she still eats her greens all soaked in fatback grease." Son shook his head. "Her weight's up to two hundred and ten. And her blood pressure's so high, no matter what kind of medicine the doctor gives her, it don't seem to do no good. Give her a call and tell her she going to kill herself if she don't stop eating. That's just what the doctor told her."

"Ain't going to do no good to call her. Truth is, she still mourning Trevon. Eating makes her feel better." He glanced at the clock on the wall. "How much we make last month?"

Malika took a deep breath. "Now, promise you ain't going to get mad, Son."

Already he looked mad. "About what?"

Malika looked down at the floor. "It wasn't a lot last month, Son, not much at all."

Son reached over and grabbed her arm. "What the hell does that mean?"

"Means our profits last month were only twenty-five thousand, two seventy-five."

"What the hell?"

"Ssshhhh, Son, look at the guards!"

His head was shaking back and forth. "Twenty-five thousand? You got to be kidding me, baby, somebody be stealing."

"See, I told Raschid it would be better not to tell you about the money and all, because first thing comes to your mind is, somebody's cheating on you. He told me about what you did to that man up here." She met his eyes for a couple of seconds. "Obie Bullock and the Mau-Mau, they the cause of everything, not nobody holding out on you."

"You mean to tell me our monthly profits have dropped from seventy-five to twenty-five thousand and change because of that bastard?"

"And you ain't even seen the results for this month, way the money's coming in, we be lucky to clear five thousand, just barely enough to take care of me and Ashanti. It's getting hard, Son. They using video cameras to stop deals, and some of your boys moving over to other posses, say it don't make no sense to get in the middle of a fight between you and Bullock. He's out to destroy us."

Son was silent, but Malika could see the wheels turning. He did not take kindly to losing money. He worshipped the stuff. And despite all the money they had in the Bahamas account, he was the only one who could get to it, and he was in jail. The very thought of her and Ashanti faced with the possibility of eviction from their co-op for nonpayment of the stiff maintenance fees would be excruciating to him. Coming on top of what Obie Bullock had already done to Mammie Teagle and Trevon...

Son's eyes had that crazed look she'd seen before. And on the mornings after she'd seen it, the papers would carry news of drive-by killings or mutilated bodies found floating in the Schuylkill or Delaware Rivers, bullet wounds in the backs of their heads.

He said, "I want you to go out and buy a new car. Nothing fancy, a Chevy Cavalier will do. Title it in your sister's name. Tell Raschid to park the car in the Pulaski Mall parking lot in Easton. He'll know where to leave the keys and papers. The car's got to be there two weeks from now. Tell him to leave it there for a week."

Malika felt sick to her stomach. "They'll kill you if you try to escape. You know that's what they want to do. Don't risk it, you'll—."

"Malika, don't start no shit now. You just do like I told you, you understand?"

She caught herself. "I'll tell him. I'm sorry, but I'm worried about you. I love you, baby."

Son tightened the grip on her wrist.

"Ain't that you beginning to enjoy the single life?"

"You know better than to even think like that."

"Just go ahead and tell Raschid exactly what I told you. Promise?"

"You got my word on it, baby."

Son slipped his arm around her waist, drew her close, and put his hand on her thigh. "Now, honey, we going to do the best we can with the time we got. You looking mighty good to me."

Malika relaxed into his warm embrace. It reminded her of how things used to be, before they got married. All too soon the bell rang.

"Five more minutes," a guard called out.

Son kissed Malika on her ear and whispered, "Baby, I love you. Now you take care of everything, and let me know what's happening with Mama and Ashanti. And don't be worrying about no money, Son Teagle going to take care of everything."

The bell rang again. Loud and shrill.

The prisoners stood up. A short Hispanic man tried to hold both his girlfriend and their two children in one big embrace.

Over in a corner of the room, a beautiful Puerto Rican woman, her long hair falling down her back, laid her head against the gray wall and wept. She was holding the hand of a lovely little girl in a white dress with her hair in perfectly braided plaits. Malika could just barely see the movement of the woman's body as she tried to hide her tears from the rest of the room. Her man, dark-haired like her, had his arm around her shoulders.

The final bell sounded. Seven guards, carrying billy clubs, came into the room and began moving the men towards the exit from the gym.

"Hey, sorry, you got to go now."

"Denny, it's time, man."

The prisoners, including Son, were gradually cleared from the room until the only people left were the women and children.

A guard called to them. "Hey, folks, Philly bus is leaving in ten minutes."

"WELL, HONEY," Pearl said as the bus slowly made its way down the mountain, "the news wasn't so good today. The boy is doing mighty poorly."

"That's too bad," Malika said. "What's the problem with him?"

She sighed and said, "Dying's the problem. Boy is dying, honey. And there be ten other mens in there with him. All be dying. AIDS, honey."

"I'm really sorry."

It was two o'clock. Malika had a four-hour trip back to Philly. She slept a little. But Son wanted out of prison, and her sleep wasn't peaceful. She dreamt he was coming after her. The dream frightened her so much she woke up.

She looked over at Pearl, fast asleep. She didn't know what was worse—to have a grandson dying of AIDS or to have somebody like Son coming after you.

CHAPTER 13

OBIE MIGHT HAVE KNOWN it was going to be a bad day from the way his left shoulder, the one that got separated in a high school football game decades ago, was aching when he got up Saturday morning. Might have known it because when he got into his car with Reverend Johnson to go up to Germantown to see how Justine was doing, the battery failed and he had to get a jump start from one of the neighbors.

And once out at Uncle Ward's, he found out Justine had relapsed and was back to stealing from his aunt and uncle to pay for her heroin habit. They were ready to throw her out, come hell or high water. What, they asked, could Obie do about it, and could he spare some money to help them out as they tried to deal with her? He gave them fifty dollars, money he badly needed for his own family. Reverend Johnson had prayed with them, but on the way back to North Philly, he told Obie there was nothing to do but let Justine go back to the streets.

"She can't be helped if she won't help herself," he said. And, he added, there was no way Obie could handle the added stress of taking Justine in—it would introduce a cancer into his life that would spread to Dora Lee and their children. "Obie," the pastor had said, "sometimes you just have to harden your heart and let God have his way."

But this was his beautiful baby sister, the one he'd been a father to when his dad died in that tractor rollover accident. No, there had to be a way out, some halfway house, some drug experimental group, something, anything, that might save her.

"If there was such an outfit," the pastor said, "I surely would have known about it by now. God and God alone can solve this one. Leave her be."

"Can't do it, I'll just have to find a way to get her institutionalized if that's the only way to keep her safe."

"She's not crazy, Obie, just sick, and I don't think you're going to find a place for her anywhere in this city."

IT WAS WITH THIS HEAVY BURDEN on his heart that Obie had arrived home, changed clothes, and tried to neaten things up for an unexpected visit from Dora Lee. She'd called that morning just after he got home from work and said she wanted to come up to the apartment that evening. Obie reminded her about the security problem, then said he'd have a couple of his men pick her up from work and bring her to North Philly. She could stay over for Saturday night, then they'd go to church together on Sunday morning and he'd drive her back to Ardmore that evening.

It seemed like a good plan, and Obie was looking forward to seeing her—they definitely needed some close time together, some warm loving to help ward off all the evil things happening around them. Yet even as he pictured them in bed together, he knew from that careful tone in her voice when she called that Dora Lee had things other than lovemaking on her mind. Still, he could always hope, couldn't he?

He heard the key in the latch, smelled the Popeye's chicken Dora Lee had brought for their dinner, then heard her say goodbye to her escorts.

"Hi, Obie, Lonnie and Rahim said hello and they'll be staying downstairs tonight with the Sutherlands in case you need them." Dora Lee was wearing a red sarong-like dress that showed off the fine curves of her hips, but from the look on her face, he knew he was in for trouble. Her eyes were focused dead on the glass of bourbon and water he held in his hand. She kissed him without enthusiasm and seemed distant and preoccupied, barely acknowledging him as she set the kitchen table and portioned out the fried chicken, baked beans, biscuits, and cole slaw onto paper plates.

"The place is really a mess, Obie, when's the last time you vacumed the rugs—you do know how to run it, don't you?"

"Baby, don't start up with me about that—I'm doing my best to keep things going while you're away. I just got back from seeing about Justine, give me a break, would you?" He reached across the table and put his hand on hers. "Let's try and have a nice peaceful evening tonight, maybe listen to some good soul music, relax ourselves a little, you know what I mean...."

She took her hand back.

"Not now, baby, not now."

"Dora Lee, what's the matter with you?"

She still looked to him like the most beautiful woman in the world, with her almond-shaped eyes perfectly set into a face that reminded him of a line from his favorite poem, one he'd learned in his first semester at community college: "And all that was best of light and love met in her aspect and her eyes."

"I love you, Obie, but I can't take it no more." Tears started to spill over from those eyes.

What had he done now? Hell, he was busting his butt trying to keep home and hearth together—kids away, wife away, sister in trouble, and Son's gang coming back like the damned Sunnis—and <u>she</u> can't take it no more? He leaned across the table.

"What you mean, Dora Lee? You my heart and soul!"

"Your drinking, for one. Visa's taking it to a collection agency if we don't come up with a hundred dollars in the next five days, and here you sit, drinking up your paycheck."

"Whoa, now, baby, a man got a right to relax sometime. And I'm looking for a second job, there's a managership opening up next month at Kentucky Fried, and—"

"Sabaya's off to college in a month. And where's the money coming from to pay for her books? They're not covered by that scholarship."

Obie tossed down the rest of his drink. He knew she was right, he should never have taken up drinking again, but he'd been the one to discover Shakeisha's body, he'd been the one to kill a boy who'd been like a son to him. And didn't he have to worry day and night about what Son's people would do to him and his family?

"And like I told you before, I'm tired of running scared," she said. "I got this awful fear in me. We got to get away from here before the Teagle gang destroys all of us. Everybody! You, me,

Sabaya, Timba."

Obie got up from the table and made himself another bourbon and water.

"You know I can't go nowhere in the midst of all this trouble, even if it was only a question of getting Justine's situation settled. But if you want to leave, go ahead and I'll just have to figure out a way of joining you soon as I can." Later he felt he should have left it at that, but something way down inside him made him blurt out: "I ain't deserting my post for nobody or nothing."

"There you go again! What the hell do you do you mean by that, Obie Bullock—you're not in no damn Iraq now. We're your family and we come first."

"Dora Lee, there's some things you got to understand. You—"

"Like what, Obie? That playing cops and robbers is more important than seeing your wife is safe and your children safe and fed and educated?"

"Dora Lee—"

"I came here to tell you I'm leaving for Carolina in the morning. And I may not be coming back."

"But you said you wasn't going down there till next week."

"That was before Lurlene got killed. I'm worried about my children now. Besides, you don't appreciate me standing beside you nohow. I'm leaving, and I hope you get yourself together, because if you don't change your ways, I don't want to be around you no more."

Obie felt sweat coming out all over him. He looked at Dora Lee, at the beautiful eyes and mouth. On that face he so loved, he saw—for the first time since he'd known her—disgust.

He finished his drink in one gulp and headed for the bedroom, his easy chair, and his fishing magazines. The booze and the anger were making him dizzy and he didn't want to hear one more word of chastisement out of his darling Dora Lee's mouth. Enough was enough!

DORA LEE SLEPT IN SABAYA'S BEDROOM that night. It didn't matter, because once he knew she had gone to bed, Obie went straight to the liquor cabinet, broke the seal on a new fifth of whiskey, made him a nightcap, and headed out to the balcony.

There he stood, looking down at that fountain, drinking, smoking, listening to the random pistol shots in the Philadelphia night, and feeling much put upon. Wasn't no justice in this world, you tried to do right and everybody thought you were doing wrong.

When he woke up in the morning, Dora Lee was gone. And she hadn't even left a note. Damn, didn't even say goodbye.

It was three o'clock in the afternoon and Walter Shapiro was stuck, along with Mayor Bascombe and his aide, in a car on the West River drive. The mayor, on his way downtown to a meeting of the chamber of commerce at four o'clock, had permitted Shapiro to accompany him for an interview about the Sarnese affair and the Bullock case.

Shapiro had known him for a long time, ever since they were up in Harrisburg together where he'd been in the legislature and Shapiro a cub reporter on the Gazette. As a matter of fact he'd given Shapiro one of his first scoops. Sometimes when things got a little rough in their conversations, he reminded him of that.

"Well," the mayor said, "looks like we're going to be stuck here for a while, so you got a captive audience. I know you want to talk about the stuff with the cops, so let's get to it. Everything's off the record. When we finish, I'll let you know what you can quote."

"Okay, Mr. Mayor. What are you going to do about Captain Sarnese and O'Brien?"

"Not a damn thing. Not when it's still before the police board of inquiry. When they finish, they'll make a recommendation to the commissioner. Whatever he decides, I'll back him up."

"The final decision is going to be seen as yours, one way or the other."

"True."

"Are you prepared to support the commissioner, even if he decides to fire both of them? You've got those negotiations coming up with the police union."

"I'll just have to cross that bridge when I come to it, but I'm known for my loyalty to my commissioners."

"If you cross the union, there's going to be trouble. The cops have lots of backing in the community nowadays. And Sarnese has been decorated time and again for bravery. Folks won't forget that."

"I know. Just about the best cop we've got." The mayor looked out of his window and saw the traffic was beginning to move. He spoke over the intercom to his driver. "You can put the light on now. Might help us get out of this mess."

"What about Bullock?" Shapiro said.

The mayor pounded his fist into the palm of his hand. "Don't you know the D.A. dropped charges against him after Leroy Merriweather took all the responsibility for what happened at that Teagle house on himself?"

"I know, but what else are you going to do about that family? All kinds of people out there are saying the city can't protect them and won't let them protect themselves. Particularly after that woman was run down."

The mayor stiffened. "Wait a minute, we don't really know she was killed by the Teagle people. All we know is that it was a stolen vehicle."

"Maybe you don't know who was behind it, but everybody else in the city does, and I can guarantee you if anything happens to the Bullocks, you're going to be in a heap of political trouble. Why don't you at least give them some police protection?"

"Because we really can't do that for a group of vigilantes."

Shapiro said, "We've known each other a long time. I think you're afraid the police couldn't or wouldn't protect the Bullock family. That's the truth, isn't it?"

The mayor took a long draw on his cigar, puffed out a stream of smoke, and twirled the Fisk University ring around his finger the way he always did when directly confronted.

"Sometimes you go a little too far, I think. Beyond journalistic limits. You really sound like you're beginning to take sides in this matter. You've been around the Bullocks too long, Walt. I'll let you off down at the Gazette building."

CHAPTER 14

DORA LEE WAS SWEATING as she stepped off the bus in Gastonia. Lord, it was hot! Felt just like somebody had brought a blast furnace down here and turned it up as high as it could go.

She walked into the terminal and strained her eyes for Sabaya and Timba in the throng of people holding up their hands and waving. Some of her fellow passengers were breaking into trots as they saw their relatives. Little clusters of people were gathering and hugging.

Dora Lee was beginning to worry when she heard a shout, "Mama!" She turned and saw a young man, who had to be her son, running towards her. She barely recognized him, he'd grown so big.

Timba's skin was now a darker brown from exposure to the southern sun, which had lightened his eyebrows. His muscular body had been made stronger and heavier by the grits, greens, cornbread, and fried meats she knew her sister-in-law had been cooking for him.

Then her son was hugging her and lifting her off her feet. "Timba! Let me down!"

"Sure, Mama," he said, before raising her up her one more time and setting her down.

Then she was hugged again. "Oh, Mama, I'm so glad to see you!" It was Sabaya, dressed in a too skimpy pair of black shorts and a white T-shirt that proclaimed, "To Know Me Is To Love Me."

Almost smothered by her children, Dora Lee felt tugs at her dress from little fingers. She freed herself from Sabaya and Timba and looked down to see her five-year-old niece.

"Auntie Dora Lee, it's me, your Melissa."

"'Lissa, baby." Dora Lee smiled and lifted her up in her arms. "How big you are now, darling. And so pretty, too. And in such a beautiful dress."

"It's 'specially for you, Auntie. Mama made it."

Dora Lee looked up to see Boatwright and his wife, Martha Ann, laughing and enjoying the welcome the children were giving her. When the children had finished, the adults came over and hugged and kissed her.

Boatwright held her at arm's length. "So good to have you down here again."

Martha Ann, a short chocolate-brown woman with dancing eyes, hugged Dora Lee tight. "Don't you ever stay away so long again. We've missed you, honey."

Dora Lee's eyes were moist. How good to be around loved ones, to be with plain country folks who let their feelings show. Folks who didn't have anybody after them.

BOATWRIGHT TOOK A TURN off the main highway running south from Gastonia onto a winding country road, the Blazer now passing only an occasional car coming from the other direction. The children kept up a nonstop conversation, mostly about how Timba had become the star pitcher and hitter for the Babe Ruth team—he was so good, some college scouts were looking at him.

Just beyond a bridge over a small stream, Boatwright took another turn off the secondary road and onto a dirt road that led uphill. It was muddy and barely passable in a few spots, at one point so bad he had to put the truck into four-wheel drive.

"Got to get a tractor up here soon, Dora Lee, level that ground out."

Then the Blazer was on flat ground and driving down a large alley formed by tall pine trees on both sides of the road. Beyond the trees she could see cornfields, and row upon row of tobacco plants and tomato vines.

At the end of the road, about a half-mile after the uphill climb ended, Boatwright took a left turn, and there stood a wooden log home he himself had constructed out of a kit. It restored Dora Lee's soul just to look at the house, standing there so erect and cleanly shaped in the middle of these country fields. Red and yellow flowers were planted in neat beds all across the front of the house.

The children piled out of the truck, each carrying a piece of Dora Lee's luggage. Even little Melissa insisted on carrying something, although Dora Lee had to bite her lip as the child—despite her heroic efforts—let her aunt's leather bag drag on the grass a few times.

Dora Lee entered the house, and as always thought she'd stumbled into a grove of cedar trees in the forest, so pungent was the scent given off from the planked wooden walls, the shining wooden floors, and the beamed ceilings.

An entire wall of the living room was dominated by pictures of the Bullock family, stretching back in time to the Civil War. Under each of the pictures was a neatly typed description of the vital statistics of each person. In the case of the dead, a Bible verse, engraved into a golden plate, was above the picture. It was a comfortable house and a place where Dora Lee knew she would be able to relax, but already she was missing Obie. She should never have left him the way she did. Sometimes the devil got into her!

Martha Ann said, "Just go into that bedroom upstairs, make yourself at home, and then come on down. We'll have us a light dinner tonight, 'cause Timba's pitching and we got to get over to the ball field."

An hour and a half later, after a "light" dinner of fried chicken, steaming fresh corn on the cob, sweet yams baked in molasses and cream, homemade rolls, and apple pie a la mode, Dora Lee was back in the truck and the Bullock family were entering the small village of Pine Hill. Boatwright, the windows on the Blazer down, drove slowly through the town, waving to folks, white and black, and even stopping once in the middle of the street to talk with a white policeman about the upcoming game.

When they reached the ball field, everybody piled out of the truck. Timba quickly kissed his mother and then—his old leather pitcher's mitt in hand—ran over to join his teammates.

He shouted back over his shoulder, "Just watch me tonight, Mama! I'm going to make you proud."

"You don't have to worry about that," Dora Lee said, though she knew he couldn't hear her. "I always feel that way about you."

The family sauntered over to the rickety wooden stands on the side of the field. Dora Lee let her eyes wander and noticed how whites and blacks were mingled together. There they were, the parents of both groups sitting together as if they'd grown up with each other. She smiled, sat back, and talked to Sabaya and her in-laws until the game started.

Timba walked over to the mound. Make her proud? Here he was, sixteen years old and an all-star in the tough North Carolina summer league competition.

Timba made his first pitches.

Zoom!

Zip!

Zoom!

He mowed down the starting lineup of the other team, and the audience shouted its appreciation.

"Way to go, Timba! Three up, three down!"

"Snuff em' out, Timba, just snuff 'em on out!"

Dora Lee watched every pitch and applauded every strikeout, of which there were plenty; cheered every ball Timba hit, and that included a single and a triple that went clear out of the field and into the woods nearby. Her boy could hit a ball!

Timba's team won the game, and afterwards he was mobbed by his teammates, tossed roughly around, and generally praised to the skies for the great game he'd pitched. When everything had calmed down, he came over to his family.

"Mama, I need a hot fudge and banana sundae. Uncle Boatwright knows a good place in town. Can we go?"

Despite the weariness in her body after the long trip down from Philly, Dora Lee said, "Of course."

That evening, after the children and assorted other youngsters had downed what seemed to her a mountain of ice cream washed down with root beer sodas, Dora Lee sat in the living room with Boatwright and Martha Ann. Boatwright was drowsing, looking at the ten o'clock news.

"How's Obie?" Martha Ann said. "Do you think he's going to get a chance to get down here?"

Dora Lee's legs were curled up under her on the couch where she too was almost falling asleep.

"No, too many things are going on up there for him to get away."

"And Justine?"

"Still at it, don't know what we going to do about her."

At the mention of her name, Boat looked up. "One of these days, I'm just going to jump in my truck and go up and get her, bring her right back here. Even smart as she is, I knew the city would be the death of her." He shook his head. "Just too delicate a flower to survive those mean streets. I love that poor girl better than myself."

Martha Ann said, "And Leroy, how's he doing? It's a sin and a shame they put that man in jail."

Boatwright stirred himself and took a sip of beer. "Wouldn't worry too much about Leroy. He'll take care of himself no matter where he be, but they did a job on him and Obie before the guards came." He looked at Dora Lee. "And you, sugar, how you taking all of this?"

"Tell the truth, it's getting to me. I'm scared all the time, but I'm more afraid for Obie now that we're all down here."

"How's he really doing, that no-good warlike brother of mine?"

Dora Lee laughed. "Oh, he's okay, but it's like he's only got one mission in life—to crush the Teagle gang. It's like nothing else matters to him, almost like he's on a crusade."

"He's been that way all his life, Dora Lee, ain't changed one lick. Did he ever tell you how he come to go in the army instead of college?"

"Said something about a little trouble down here."

Boat shook his head. "Little trouble, hell, he was run out! Had a cook's job down at the Richmond Hotel—and one of the white customers gets drunk and starts pawing one of the black waitresses."

Dora Lee said, "Don't tell me...."

"You can figure out what he did for yourself, you know him well as I do—comes running out of the kitchen, grabs the guy, nearabout kills him before the chefs pulled him off and hustled him out of there. Was in a car on his way north that very night, and that's how he ended up in the army." He took a sip of his beer. "Ain't changed none over the years, and I don't reckon he'll be leaving this action up in Philly no time soon."

Dora Lee sighed. "Not even for us, not even for his children. He's succeeding too well—with all these video cameras and things, he's practically shut down the drug operation in the project, and Son Teagle will not stand still for that. He runs everything from prison, Boat, and you know he's dead set on getting even."

"Well, you can sleep well tonight, sugar, ain't nobody going to bother you here." He drained the last swallow from his glass. "I reckon it's time we all turn in. Got a hard day tomorrow. Glad Timba's here to give me a hand with the crop—you all done raised a mighty fine young man. Respectable, strong boy."

Martha Ann said, "Amen!"

The sports news came on.

"Tonight, the Pine Hill Tigers won their tenth game. It was the third straight shutout for young Timba Bullock, a Philadelphia boy down here for the summer. College scouts from Duke, the University of South Carolina, and, of course, UNC have expressed interest in this young man. He's one to keep your eye on!"

Dora Lee's heart felt like a rock. She closed her eyes for a minute, then looked up at Boatwright.

"Where's that program broadcast from?"

"Charlotte, why?"

"Oh, it's nothing, Boat." She got up from the sofa and smiled at her in-laws. "It's been a long, nice day. I think I better go to bed now. And I want to thank you from the bottom of my heart for taking me and the children in."

Martha Ann hugged her. "You family, honey, and family's everything."

They all retired for the night. Tired as she was, Dora Lee

slept badly. She dreamed that Rufus, the man on the subway was chasing her....

JOHN SARNESE SAT WITH ANGELICA, preparing to watch the evening news. It was the way their life was most of the time. Eat a good meal—one day veal scaloppini, the next day chicken parmigina, all cooked with sauces made from home-grown tomatoes stewed and canned by Angie—then sit around together and do the day's reading while waiting for the news to come on. He'd read the Daily News and the Inquirer, anything about cops and politics, then look at the sports pages, focusing on the Philadelphia Eagles. The whole six months between the playing of the Super Bowl and the opening of the Eagles summer camp up at Hershey was an empty space he just barely managed to fill by watching an occasional Phillies or Flyers' game. But it was practically guaranteed that he'd doze off by the third inning of any baseball game.

And he'd practically never watch a basketball game—everybody was so tall, it took the skill out of the sport. Hell, if a guy was seven feet tall, how could he not hit the basket when it was right in front of him? Although he had to admit, Allen Iverson had really been something special to see, before management decided to trade him.

Angie, after doing the dishes and scrubbing down the Corian countertops in the kitchen, would come into the living room and settle on the blue velour couch, where she'd first read an article from Reader's Digest and then one from Cosmopolitan, never failing to bring to Sarnese's attention something she found interesting. Did he know, she'd say, that there really were hotels in Florida who rented out their entire facility for a swingers' weekend? Or that you could take off fifteen pounds in two months if you only added a half-hour's walk a day to your routine? "Think of that, John, just thirty minutes every day, and I could lose all of this weight in a year—you'd like that, wouldn't you?"

Sarnese would smile and nod his head without having heard a word. This particular evening, he was in a thoughtful mood, partially brought on by the prospect that soon—any day now—he expected to hear about the results of the riot inquiry and the ongoing corruption investigation into his precinct. It made him think about how far he and Angie had come together, putting both boys through college—one through Annapolis. No way he could have a better wife or mother than Angie. But all that mother instinct, all that hard work, all that striving to make the budget balance on a Philly cop's pay had taken its toll.

She looked nothing like the seventeen-year-old girl who'd sworn to love him forever when he'd enlisted in the marines at the middle of the Vietnam War. He could see her now, walking down the hallway at West Catholic High School in Philadelphia, hugging her school books, flanked by two girlfriends and pretending she didn't see the high school's football captain, the all-city halfback, trying to catch her eye.

Oh, she'd been pretty then. How he'd ached to hold her! Even now he could remember the first time she let him. Just pure heaven, that's what it had been.

Angie had been true to her word, and when he returned from Vietnam, a gunnery sergeant with a bronze star, they'd been married in the city and had decided to stay because he figured there were a lot of opportunities in the police department. They were right. A lot of opportunities—and pitfalls. So many crooked cops, so much crime, so many drug dealers. Made a man want to weep, give up on life sometimes. Thing was, as a cop you saw the bad side of folks each and every day, and it was hard to believe that most of them were still good deep down inside.

"John, what are you thinking about? You're awful quiet. It's not like you."

"I was kind of thinking back, honey, over all the good times and the bad times we've been through, and I just want you to know I wouldn't trade you for nobody."

It was true, though he wished she would find some way of dealing with her weight problem, for her huge hips and voluminous sagging breasts had long since made him lose interest in making love to her. He would attribute his lack of potency to his blood pressure pills, and she'd feel sorry for him, kiss him on the cheek, then turn over and go to sleep. Sarnese would feel bad because he did just fine with Bernadette, and he didn't need Viagra, either.

Angie looked over at him. "As long as you're in a looking-back mood...why don't you just retire? You work hard all your life, and then people don't appreciate it. Just quit now before the recommendations come out. You could get a job as a private security consultant. We'd make out all right, we'll have enough to—"

"You know me better than that, I'm not a quitter. And I'm not about to retire with my name not cleared. I'm going to make the mayor take a stand. He's either going to have to boot me off the force or be a man and do the right thing. He knows I did the best I could."

"Maybe the commission will clear your name."

"No way, too many minorities on it. I know how they're going to vote."

"But don't you think Obie's testimony about all the work you did with his organization will help?"

"I don't think so. But it really lifted my spirits when I saw the big guy come walking down that aisle to testify for me. And the thing was, he didn't have to do it. My lawyer said he just called him up and offered. Cost him plenty with his community, I hear. They tell me the black newspaper ran an editorial talking about Uncle Toms and race traitors."

He put the News down and punched his fist into his hand. "Call a stand-up guy like Bullock an Uncle Tom! I just can't understand it, same way I can't understand the way they make cooperating with the police something shameful. Some of those folks would rather let their kids buy dope than tell the cops who's selling it to them."

"I guess there's more sympathy for him since that poor woman got killed walking with his wife."

"Maybe, but it still pisses me off, how they low-rated him when he helped me out."

"Turn on the television, honey, the local news is coming on."

Sarnese punched the remote and they listened through

the theme music. Then a young black woman announcer said, "The commission investigating Captain John Sarnese of the Philadelphia Police Department and officer Kevin O'Brien has delivered its recommendations. We'll have the story right after the following announcements."

Son of a bitch. You'd have thought the least they could do for a man with all his years of service was let him know what happened before they called a press conference.

Angie left her seat on the couch, walked over to Sarnese's chair, sat down on the rug beside it, and reached up for his hand.

"It'll be all right, darling."

Buy a Hyundai Sonata, deal with the termites that are undermining the foundations of your home even as you watch this program, use your Mastercard to escape to Barbados, stop the onslaught of baldness, apply for our debt consolidation program!

The announcers, a white man and the black woman, finally came back on screen. Their faces were quickly replaced by a picture of Sarnese in full summer uniform of white blouse and blue cap. Immediately afterwards appeared a closeup of patrolman Kevin O'Brien.

"This afternoon at a news conference, the chairman of a departmental disciplinary hearing committee found that Captain John Sarnese, a much decorated veteran of the Philadelphia Police Department, was responsible for the police abuse in the riot of June ninth because he failed to exercise proper discipline over his men. The committee also found Sarnese negligent in the training of his command.

"Officer O'Brien was found responsible for precipitating the riot by virtue of wantonly and unreasonably striking a civilian. The committee has recommended to the commissioner that both officers be subjected to departmental disciplinary measures, up to and including removal from the force for Officer O'Brien and demotion or other measures for Captain Sarnese. That's our headline story, folks, we'll be back with the details right after this break."

Sarnese took the remote from Angie's hand and clicked off the TV.

His eyes were stinging.

Angie squeezed his hand. "I love you, Johnnie, it don't matter. And anybody who knows you knows the way it really is." That made Sarnese feel a little better inside himself, like he could weather this storm. The only thing was, he didn't know whether his bum ticker could do the same. A hell of a way to end a career.

CHAPTER 15

IT HADN'T BEEN TOO HARD for Son to get himself assigned to a minimum-supervision work gang. All you needed was the forged work assignment slip he'd bought from one of the guards. Sorry bastards with their forty thousand a year and working with a bunch of criminals all day, they were in prison for a lot longer stretch than him. As he stood painting the windows at a local elementary school along with the rest of a ten-member crew, he rehearsed in his mind what he had to do.

First of all, he had to get away from the unarmed school security guard supervising the detail and get himself a running start. Once he was moving, wasn't nobody going to catch him. He'd get himself to a road close to the river and follow it all the way south to Easton. Should take him about three days to make the fifty-mile trip, what with all the folks who'd be out looking for him.

He kept painting but put one hand down to check that he had the wad of money taped against one thigh and the knife against the other. The security guard, who'd been bantering with Son and two other inmates on his section of the scaffolding, finally broke off the conversation and wandered off around the other side of the building.

As soon as he disappeared, Son looked at the two prisoners near him.

"I'm long gone." He leapt off the six-foot scaffold and hit the ground running.

IT WAS EIGHT-THIRTY IN THE MORNING when Son ran out of the schoolyard and into the street. He took the brown prison shirt off and threw it into a nearby bush. Now it would look like he was just a laborer wearing a white T-shirt and a pair of brown work pants.

He veered off of the main street and began to walk very fast. He kept in his mind a map of the area he'd gotten from one of the few white prisoners and memorized.

In front of a big white house with a porch, Son saw three little girls playing under a tree. They had tiny buckets and were digging up the earth under the tree. Son waved to them. Damn, they got a pretty lawn like that, and they're messing it all up. Ought to go over there and tell them to stop. He kept on walking fast down the street.

There were very few houses, and most of them were set well back. But he couldn't keep walking much longer along the street—fucking cops would soon be out in force. Them and the dobermans.

He cut into a yard and began darting from lawn to lawn, concealed whenever possible by shrubbery as he headed east towards a mall the white prisoner had told him was on the other side of the main highway. He had to get to people, somewhere where his scent would be mixed with others so dogs couldn't track him.

As he ran, he heard a siren going off at the top of the mountain. It would go up high, then low, then high again, getting louder each time.

The prison siren was echoed by another siren, then another, all moving closer and closer to him, like they was coming down the mountain, trying to catch him in a web of sound. Another siren went off on the other side of the highway—it came from the direction of the mall where he was headed.

Down the road that lay some four hundred yards ahead of him, he heard the sound of a police car siren and saw, in the distance, the twirling of its red and blue lights. He had to hide, and quick. He'd run out of the residential area—no shrubbery.

He saw a small used car place maybe three hundred yards off. Between him and that little lot was a creek. Good. Get in the water, run up and down it for a while, follow it on up that little hill a bit, then double on back down to the used car lot and find him a place to hide. That would shake the dogs.

Son jumped into the cold water and ran up the creek, the

mud sucking at his shoes, once even pulling the left one halfway off his foot. A branch from a tree struck him full across the face. When he'd run a quarter-mile up the hill, heading back towards the prison, he stopped, crept behind a tree, and looked down towards the highway.

It was a sight to behold. Homicide would really dig this. At a roadblock were at least eight police cars, lights flashing, troopers and cops inspecting every car. Son could see cars backed up in both the northbound and southbound lanes. Wait till he told the boys back home how the fuckers had stopped all of that traffic just for him. But they wasn't going to get him noways.

He stepped from behind the tree and kept running up the creek. Another two hundred yards ought to do it. Then he'd turn around and head back down into that used car lot. Stay there until nightfall, then maybe head across the road to the mall....

"WE'VE BEEN THROUGH THIS AREA three times. What's the use of—"

"You never know. Just do it, and quit your bitching. He could of come in here after we went through."

"All right."

Son had waked up hungry and thirsty. He'd been asleep, maybe for three hours, in the tub of a foul-smelling, roach-infested bathroom in an abandoned mobile home behind the used car lot.

He could hear the footsteps coming closer and closer. He got up quickly from the tub and crept into the shower stall, closing the door with its rusted handle. He stuck the knife into his waistband. Cops come in here, I can't get away.

The door to the bathroom, already ajar, was pushed further open. It creaked. Son saw the beam of a flashlight hit the far wall.

"Holy shit, it stinks! Son-of-a-bitch wants to hide in there, he can have it." The cop backed out and his footsteps receded. Son could hear him talking to his partner.

"Man, I never smelled anything like it. Why the hell would they junk a home with all that mess in it? I'm going to write a citation."

The other cop said, "No, you're not, Jed's my hunting buddy. I'll tell him, he'll take care of it. I reckon Teagle's about made it out of here and headed south. Probably pick him up down the road ten miles or so, that's where they sent the dogs. Come on, let's get out of here."

Son got back into the tub and dozed off. When he woke up, he walked into the living room and shook his head at all the stains on the rug and the holes in the walls. He looked out the window towards the main clearing. He'd slept a long time.

Made for a clear head. When he got to Philly, he'd off Bullock, get his boys started back on the right track, then find himself a good hiding place down south till things cooled off. Some of his mama's brothers in the business down there would take good care of him.

THE SUN WAS SETTING, and the parking lot was empty of automobiles except for the used cars and the Chevy pickup that had been there in the morning. The truck had a couple of tarpaulins lying on its bed. The salesman was alone.

Son crept around the building, evening gnats buzzing in his ears, sized up the clearing, and made a dash to the Chevrolet. He pulled himself over the side of the truck, slid under the tarps, and settled in to wait, knife in hand.

It was some kind of hot under the heavy cloth. He could hardly breathe. Shit, the man ought to be coming soon. Time for him to go home.

Son heard the sound of the screen door opening, heard the man try the main door to be sure it was closed tight. He got into the truck, put it into reverse, then paused for a minute and turned on the radio. The powerful loudspeakers mounted in the truck's doors began playing a country music song, something—like most of them—about somebody done wrong by his woman. Son liked the song, he'd heard a lot of that kind of music in the prison. Guards played it all the time, wasn't bad.

The man drove off. If he knew who was back there, he'd shit his pants. Son smiled and relaxed. Might as well enjoy the ride. Got music, a nice truck ride, all the comforts of home. And this son of a bitch was going to get him out of here.

In about five minutes, the Chevy turned onto the main highway—Son figured it had to be, because in a few seconds he figured they must be going along at about eighty miles an hour.

But soon the truck slowed down. Son took a chance and peeked out from under the canvas. He saw flickering red lights and ducked back under.

The truck stopped. Forward a little. Stop.

"License, registration, and proof of insurance, please?'

"Sure, just a second. Still looking for that prisoner?"

"Thought we had him this morning, but he got away. A real smart one, I hear. All right, let me look in the back here."

Son hid the knife in the corner of the canvas. Didn't need no more raps.

"Hey, Jed, you just getting off from work? Damn, we both have had us a long day." Sounded like one of the troopers who'd come into the mobile home that morning.

The other cop said, "You know this guy?"

"Lives about fifteen miles outside of Easton. We go way back. And I can tell you, any inmate dumb enough to get in his truck would be in deep trouble. Jed's a black belt."

The trooper laughed and told the salesman he could go on. "But be careful—that's one mean bastard out there."

Son relaxed as the truck picked up speed. Twenty minutes later, it came to a stop. He heard the excited voices of two children running out to greet their daddy. The man said something, got out of the truck, and went into the house with the kids.

Son knew now that he was only fifteen miles from Easton. And he'd done it all in one day.

He needed clothes, food, and water. Jed had parked his truck right in front of his open garage. Son crept over lawnmowers, snowblowers, and rakes, then saw what he wanted. A red cotton work shirt hanging on a hook, along with two pairs of jeans.

And there were two baseball hats hanging from hooks: Phillies and Pittsburgh Steelers. He pulled on a pair of the jeans over his prison work pants, then put on the shirt and the Steelers cap.

He crept to the entrance to the garage and looked up and down the empty street to check the direction from which most of the cars were coming. Then he started walking, singing a rap tune he liked a lot. He walked past a church and a school, even passed a few people out for an evening stroll and carrying ice cream cones. Son smiled as he passed them, and they smiled back.

HE SAW A SIGN that said "Easton," and there on the other side of the big road he saw something that made him want to shout, "Hallelujah!"—a McDonald's, yellow and red arch gleaming in the hot summer night. He went into the bathroom. He washed his hands and face, took off the shirt and washed his torso, and finally stuck his head under the faucet, gulping cold water down in huge mouthfuls as it splashed into his hand.

All cleaned up and with the Steelers cap pulled down far over his face, he walked up to the counter, where a kid of about sixteen was watching a ball game on a small television set.

"Two big Macs, a large fries, two vanilla shakes, apple pie, and a large Coke."

The teenager smiled. "Boy, you must have worked up a big appetite from something."

"Sure did, been working construction all day long."

The attendant looked up as if to say something more, but after a glance at Son's face, kept his mouth shut. In a couple of minutes Son had his food and was seated in a corner of the room, away from an older couple and out of the teenager's sight.

On the walls of the restaurant were beautiful pictures of rafting on the Delaware. Nice. But the big Macs were even better. He washed them down with swigs of milkshake and Coke. Felt like he'd died and gone to heaven. He put ketchup on the crispy

French fries and stuffed them in his mouth. The prison fries were thick and gluey. Then he finished the apple pie in two big gulps.

He was ready now. All he had to do was to get to that mall in Easton and pick up his car. Son Teagle was coming back to the city, going to set everything right.

The low drone of the television baseball game was replaced by the sound of gongs on the set. The eleven o'clock news was coming on.

Son froze in his seat, mad that he hadn't just taken that food and walked on out of the restaurant.

"State and local police are intensifying their search for Son Teagle, the notorious drug dealer from Philadelphia who escaped yesterday from Delaware Correctional Facility."

They must have put his picture on. Son got up from the table and headed for the door.

"All citizens are warned to be on the lookout for this man. He is armed and dangerous. If you see him, call your local police. Do not approach him."

Son walked out the side entrance of the restaurant. He ran across a side road and down a hilly slope that curved up on both sides of the highway, crashing through trees and bushes into deep gullies.

He ran with all his might. Wasn't no man going to catch him now. Flying, baby! It was dark, and branches and vines pulled at his body, like they were trying to tear off his clothes and Pittsburgh Steelers cap. He pushed on, forcing himself to move fast even when it seemed almost impossible. Was going to the city, kill that damn Bullock.

At last he burst into an opening. He tried to run at full speed again, only to realize that his feet were wet and his shoes again being sucked at by mud. He was in a marsh.

Back there from the direction of the McDonald's, he again heard barking. He ran on into the marsh—he fucking would not sink into it. Far ahead of him, in the distance, he could see light reflected in the sky. Must be Easton. Just keep going and you'll make it.

At last, covered with mud and with mosquitoes at his head,

he broke out onto dry land once again. He slowed for a few seconds, because it seemed like the sound around him had changed. He stood stock still, an invitation to more mosquitoes and a swarm of gnats. They were on top of his head, in his ears and eyes and nostrils.

Son knew what had changed. There was no more sound of moving cars up on the highway. Only silence, and red lights reflecting off the night sky. They were probably trying to cut him off, sending troopers down into the gullies behind him.

Ahead, he could see houses. Must be about five hundred yards away. And the ground was solid. Just get over there, and the cops would have a hard time catching him. He ran like he'd never run in his life, better than that time at Magnum High when he'd broken through the line, juked one linebacker, run over the other one, levelled the cornerback with his shoulder pad, and stiff-armed the safety. Then sweet running, yes sir, right on down that sideline. Chicks going crazy.

"Stop, or I'll shoot!" A shadow emerged from the darkness. With a flashlight. And he could make out a hat. Had to be a cop.

Sun calculated the distance to the shadow. Maybe ten yards. And it was dark.

On you, motherfucker, like salt on rice! His body was galloping, legs working like pistons, fists raised like sledgehammers. Didn't slow down when a sharp crack whizzed past his ear.

The cop had missed.

Son just hurled his 190-pound body right into him, his knees connecting with the cop's balls.

"Oooof!" The cop hit the ground, writhing in pain. His gun fell from his hands and onto the grass a few feet from him.

Fool! Don't be telling me to stop when I'm on my way to the city.

Son picked up the gun and kept on running.

Didn't even look back. Knew that dude wasn't getting up for a few minutes, and when he did, Son would be nowheres around.

He made the row of houses and crept through a back fence onto the property of one that was unlit. All the houses in the row were dark. Seemed strange, it wasn't that late.

He slipped around to the front of the building and saw a river. These must be summer weekend homes, and that must be the Delaware River. That's why the houses were dark. Behind him, he heard once again the barking of the dogs. And he could just barely swim.

Son ran to the river bank and looked quickly up and down the shores of the river. Far away on the banks he saw red lights twirling!

But then he saw four or five docks. On them were tied all kinds of boats: a white cabin cruiser at least twenty-five feet long with a high fishing tower, a fifteen-foot runabout with a big outboard perched on its stern, two other outboard boats, and a small aluminum rowboat with wooden oars in its bottom.

Too bad he'd been sent home from every summer camp he'd ever gone to—his record for camp had been three days. Mama had to take off work and meet him at Thirtieth Street Station every time. And whipped him with the cord from the steam iron when she got his little butt home.

Didn't know how to run no outboard motor or row no boat. But it wasn't like he had a lot of fucking options here.

He ran down to the dock and stepped into the little rowboat. It pitched to one side, and Son fell into the bottom of the boat, his head striking the aluminum front seat.

He got carefully up—the boat still rocking back and forth—reached for the wooden oars with pins in them, and after some fumbling found the holes where the pins went. The oars dropped into the holes with a soft thump. He inched towards the front of the boat and cut the line that held it to the dock.

He pushed off and drifted into the Delaware. He pulled on the oars, and the boat moved some through the water, heading towards the other shore. He pulled on them again and began to feel comfortable. Wasn't too hard.

Way up the river, Son saw a white light moving slowly towards him. On the top of that white light there was another white light, a searchlight. It was probing the shore line, illuminating patches along the banks of the river.

Had to make it to the other side. He pulled hard.

The right oar popped out of its socket, flew up, and fell into the water. A soft splash and it was gone. Son could just glimpse it floating away from him and downstream.

He took the other oar out its socket, moved to the front of the boat, and began to paddle. But each time he pulled on the oar, the boat pitched. With one oar the damn boat didn't want to do what he wanted it to at all. Finally he sat back down lest he overturn it.

The lights from the police boat grew dim. His little rowboat was being pushed downstream by the current. The way things were going, he might just as well sit and wait until it ran ashore somewhere. He sure wasn't fool enough to try to swim for it.

The police light completely disappeared as the little rowboat rounded a bend in the river. He could breathe easier. Didn't see no lights.

But he could see the shore, about fifty yards away. Maybe he should give that one oar another try. He crawled back up to the bow of the boat and began to paddle, first on one side then on the other, slowly and carefully.

The shoreline came a little closer. Just keep this up, and he might make it. He took four more little strokes, then saw there was some kind of a sign posted right on a little island in the middle of the river. He strained his eyes to see what the sign said but couldn't make it out in the darkness.

Suddenly, it did no good to paddle—the current took over. The stern of the boat spun around quickly in the direction Son had been paddling, and the boat began to swing wildly back and forth.

He sat down in the bottom of the boat and held on to the sides with both hands as it veered back and forth in the current.

He heard a muffled drone. It grew louder and louder, becoming a roar as the current drove the rowboat downstream. Son raised his head up high and looked downriver in the direction of the sound. About twenty-five yards away, he could see ripples of white in the darkness. A fucking waterfall, and he was about to go over it! He grabbed a seat cushion and lay down in the bottom of the boat.

He wondered if they'd taught the kids in camp what to do if you hit white water.

TWO DAYS LATER, over on Lake Piney Grove, Sarnese was helping Angie clear the table after a supper of chicken parmigiana.

Angie said, "Bet Obie and Dora Lee are going to feel a lot better now that Son Teagle drowned in the Delaware."

"Well, hon, I've been in this business too long to trust in anything but facts. And the fact is, they've been dragging the river and still haven't found the body. I'll believe he's dead when they pull his corpse out of the water, not one second before. Believe me, Teagle is about the meanest, toughest guy I ever sent to prison. Wouldn't surprise me one bit if he's still alive."

"You really think so?"

He knew how much Angie liked Dora Lee. "Well, maybe not. I called the state police station up there. They say it's a pretty high falls and there's whirlpools at the bottom. Keeps the bodies down for a long time. They may fish him out in a day or two."

CHAPTER 16

OBIE WAS FEELING LOW, mighty low. First of all, he felt like Dora Lee had just about left him. Second, the rent was due. Third, he'd just received a bill for a deposit on Sabaya's dormitory fees for the fall. In three weeks she'd be going off to freshman week and he sure didn't want his baby embarrassed at registration. Didn't matter that she was going to be on scholarship—the college still needed a five-hundred dollar deposit for possible damage the students might do to the dormitory.

And the phone bill this month. What with the kids in Carolina calling and texting their friends in Philly on their cell phones and talking to him practically every night, it was almost as high as the rent. And money was something Dora Lee had always taken care of. He just gave her his paycheck and got his weekly lunch and gas money plus a few dollars for walking-around money. Now everything was on his shoulders. He just might have to sign on as a security guard somewhere during the day, since that job over at KFC had fallen through. Then there was the Teagle thing. Here it was five days after he busted out of prison, and the divers still hadn't recovered his body. The paper said there'd be one more day of searching and then they'd abandon the dragging because of the wicked currents.

Wasn't no sense in worrying himself to death over the dude. But there was no doubt in his mind that Son would be coming after him if he had even one breath left in his body. Hell, the way Obie was messing with his operation, he'd drag himself over burning coals to get to him. Well, his life insurance was paid up, so if he killed Obie the family would be all right, and the kids' college would be paid for.

The doorbell rang. Obie's bodyguard—Lonnie Chisholm, a short, heavily built man of about forty-five—got up from the other living room chair and pulled out his pistol. He walked over to the door, looked through the peephole, undid the chain and police lock, and opened it.

Four men came in. Two were dressed in African garb, one in Muslim, and the other in a white T-shirt and khaki shorts. They were members of the North Philadelphia Directorate of Black Men United, just coming from a meeting of the city-wide group that Obie had been unable to attend.

He smiled for the first time in many days. Knowing that the leaders of the other organizations frowned on the use of alcohol, he was even drinking coffee. Besides, it was seven o'clock, and he had to be off to work in a few hours.

"The house may seem a little rough since Dora Lee's been gone," he said, "but I got sodas in the refrigerator. We'll have us some crackers and cheese, get down to business."

Lonnie brought sodas and packages of snacks to Dora Lee's favorite table, which was looking the worse for wear. Obie felt better now that his guests were here. They were special people. The young fellow wearing the blue dashiki with white piping on it had come into the anti-drug movement because of his eighteen-year-old sister, a pretty girl with two baby boys. She'd been smart and wrote beautiful poetry—Dora Lee had read one of her poems to him.

That child, who should have been graduating from high school, had instead become hooked on drugs by her no-count boyfriend and was now hanging out down near the Ben Franklin Bridge, turning tricks for the men who came over from Jersey in their big cars. Her brother, the man seated on Obie's couch, had beaten her boyfriend nearly to death, taken in the two crack babies, and together with his mother was raising them. And he'd formed an organization to clean the drugs out of his project. The other men had come to Obie's house that evening with similar motives. They'd all just had enough. Time to raise the community.

They wanted to talk about Teagle, but Obie said, "We ain't got time to waste on him now. We got to get this rally together, figure out what we going to do and how we going to do it. First, I want to tell you guys how much I appreciate you sticking with me."

One said, "You did what you had to do with that Sarnese thing, man. We got to move on. Can't stay mired in no mud."

Obie said, "Here's the way I figure we should go. We need to keep the pressure up on these dealers. And we need to let these politicians know they got to help us, not hurt us with shit like railroading Leroy and me. No bullshit, no detours. So, my brothers, what I think we should do is set a Saturday afternoon march from Cecil B. Moore Avenue down to City Hall. Have the main rally there."

One man said, "I like that idea, but I think we should start from about three different points—you know we each have a lot of strength in our local spots—and then all converge on the plaza at City Hall. That way we hit lot more people, show these dealers what the folks in this community really think about them. We already got a lot of momentum going from the march on Harrisburg a couple of years back, and the problem has only gotten worse since then."

Obie nodded. "That's a great idea and I thank you for it. The more folks the better. Do you think we can get this together in three weeks? With marshals, security, entertainment— everything?"

The other men nodded. "A lot of my folks been on us to do something like this," one of them said. "We can make it."

Obie smiled. "Let's get the paper out and put the program together."

IN AN HOUR AND A HALF of hard work, the men finished the major plans for the march. It was set for a date in late August. When they'd left, Obie told Lonnie it was late, he should go home and get some rest.

Lonnie said, "Man, you know what we decided—security at all times."

"Don't worry about it, I'll be okay." Obie pointed to the .45 automatic pistol on the dining room table.

"Have it your way." The guard reached for his Philadelphia 76's hat and took a last sip of Coke. "See you tomorrow morning."

Obie let him out.

Truth was, he just needed some peace and quiet. He didn't have time to think, and the way things were going he didn't know when he would. Dora Lee was heavy on his mind. She was acting like she didn't want him to come down south—said she needed some personal space. She was even talking about leaving Timba down there for the whole next school year and hinting that she might stay too.

Obie had to admit, this war of his was wearing him down. One part of him said he should forget about the march, abandon the apartment, and ship everything down south to Boat's house. There was still land available on the family homestead for him to build on, and Boat and Martha Ann had long pleaded for them all to come "home" and help them farm. If farming didn't appeal to Obie, Boat said there might be some work at the Japanese car factory, not far away. As to Justine, they'd find some place to get her help, might be easier to do it down there than up in the big city.

Oh, the ties of family and thoughts of nice peaceful days out in the country were definitely enticing, but try as he might, he couldn't see himself abandoning all the good folks in the Hill project to their fates—the old retired cleaning women who daily stopped by the apartment with steaming dishes of down-home foods; the children who each day set off to school with bright faces that told the outside world—the rich world—that there was no way they could keep them down, stop them from having a share of the American dream; the young mothers with three of four kids who were still trying to get their equivalency exams; and the young African-American men with pulled-down pants, Sambo do rags, and caps twisted every way but straight on their heads. Prey for the thugs, fodder for the prison system and the faltering upstate economy!

No, he could not and would not abandon his post, not for anybody, not for anything. Shakeisha's ghost would cry out "Shame!" if he did. Nor could he leave his aunt and uncle to wrestle with Justine and her sickness.

And when all was said and done, the only way he could ensure the safety of his darling Dora Lee and Sabaya and Timba and their future was to stay right here in the thick of battle until the cops either caught Son or killed him. Obie didn't think for a minute that he'd drowned and it was just a coincidence that they couldn't find the body. Son was alive and free—and that meant he was a hundred times worse threat now. Obie could run to North Carolina, but although he wasn't about to tell Dora Lee, Teagle tentacles reached deep into the South—no such thing as safety until the head of the octopus was cut off. Obie shuddered when he thought of what Son's gang was capable of doing to those it targeted for revenge.

One girl, Monique, the twenty-two-year-old mother of two, had wanted to quit as a runner for the business and get a college degree. When Raschid couldn't persuade her otherwise, he'd turned her over to some of his underlings, who kept her bound and gagged in a crack house room and subjected her to every physical and sexual torment their demented minds could think of. Cops found her body, studded with cigarette burns, floating in a creek up near Souderton.

No, if Obie backed off so Son got his profits again, that would not be the end of it.

He felt like taking a drink but knew he'd be going in to work in an hour. The way they were about drinking these days, he might find himself out of a job. He settled for another Coke, his third of the night.

He'd just sat down to watch the ten o'clock news when the buzzer at the front door sounded. Obie reached for his pistol, pulled off its safety, went to the door, and looked through the peephole. Who the hell could it be at this hour of the night?

It was Rita. He hadn't seen her since that night she stopped over briefly to leave Sabaya's graduation gift. He put the pistol down and let her in.

She walked into the room like she was trying to take possession of it. It was in her walk, in the movement of her arms, in the way her eyes darted from the soda cans on the tables to the old newspapers on the dining room table to the pizza boxes, left open with half-eaten crusts still in them.

She looked Obie in the eye and laughed. "You look like you could stand some help."

Before he could protest, she was in the kitchen, had found garbage bags, and was sweeping the cans and boxes into them. Obie just stood there.

"Since your whole family's away, I thought I'd come over and lend a hand. I just got back home and wanted to catch you before you left for work. Still on the night shift, right?"

"Look, you don't have to do any of that. We clean the place up pretty good every few days or so. You quit that and sit down. I only got a few minutes before I have to get out of here."

She finished clearing the debris off of the tables and sat down on the couch, snuggled into one corner.

"The real reason I stopped is because I thought you might be able to use some help in the organization. You've done too much to have things go downhill now. And it must really be rough on you with the family away." She adjusted her skirt. "I'm not playing about this. I can type, stuff envelopes, deliver messages...."

He hesitated, then said, "Come to think of it, we could use some help in the next few weeks. We got a big march coming up, means a lot of mailing and telephoning."

"When can I start? I get home from work around five-thirty, I can be over here by seven. How's that?"

The phone rang.

Obie, who was sitting in his favorite easy chair, had to get up to go into the kitchen and answer the phone. He sure wished he didn't have to get up, because he was embarrassed—his dick was hard enough to show through his pants. He couldn't help himself, it had been a long time since he'd made love. Rita kept her eyes on him.

"Bullock residence."

"Hi, honey, you getting ready to go to work? I was just thinking about you."

"Was just sitting here watching the news. How're the kids doing?"

"Good as ever, only one piece of news since you talked to them. Timba's started working out with the football team at the high school."

"What? You told me we were going to talk about that. You can't treat the boy like a yo-yo, get him started playing ball down there then expect him to come back up here and learn the system at this school. I sure wish you hadn't done that. Pisses me off."

"We didn't have a lot of time to think about this thing, Obie. The deadline was Wednesday, and I just found out about it two days before. I didn't have time to talk with you about it."

Obie glanced into the other room. Rita had picked up an Ebony magazine, but he could tell she wasn't letting a word of this conversation escape her. And that she'd hiked her skirt up a little higher. Damn it. He was getting another hard-on—it had dropped when he heard Dora Lee's voice on the phone.

He stared out of the kitchen window, trying to regain control of the situation.

"Obie, are you still there? Why aren't you talking to me?"

"Because I'm too mad to talk. Beginning to look to me like you made up your mind about our future. And I ain't got no say in the matter."

"I'm sorry you feel that way about it. I just had to make a decision, and I did it. I'm still not saying anything about us. I got two weeks of vacation time left."

"But how can we get this straightened out when you know I can't come down there now? And you don't even want me to come down. It just ain't right."

"Look, I just called you up to tell you I love you and miss you. If you're going to get all upset about this football thing, then I don't feel like talking to you any more. I'll call you back tomorrow when you've calmed down some."

"You just do that thing. The kids around?"

"Timba's sleeping over at a friend's during the first week of practice. They're at it all day long, and it's kind of a long trip out here from town. Wait a second and I'll get Sabaya. I love you."

"Sure."

Sabaya came to the phone. "I miss you and I worry about you a lot, Daddy. Don't let anything happen to you."

Obie said,"I'll be seeing you pretty soon, one way or another, sweetness. Are you practicing? You don't want to let that get away from you, now."

"Don't worry, I'll be fine. And I'm making money with my job over at Wendy's. But I feel awful scared about school, it's going to be hard."

"Not for my baby. Don't even give it a second thought. Listen, honey, I got to get out of here and get to the job. Tell Timba I said hey."

Rita sneezed.

Sabaya said, "Who's there, Dad?"

"One of the bodyguards, that's all."

He hung up the phone and turned towards Rita. She was still looking at Ebony magazine. And Obie still had a hard-on. Lord, she was one fine-looking woman.

Hands in his pockets, he walked back into the living room. "Listen, thanks for the offer, you can get started tomorrow night. I got to get moving now if I'm going to make it on time, so I guess I have to throw you out."

Rita laughed, uncoiled her long legs from the couch, got up, and walked towards the door. Once there, she turned so that her full body faced Obie.

"Once I get started working, you may find it a little harder to get rid of me. After all, you just made me a bodyguard, didn't you?"

Obie laughed, and felt a warmth going right through him. He hadn't had that happen with a woman since he'd met Dora Lee.

He opened the door for her. "We'll see what tomorrow brings."

THE IMAGE OF RITA'S GORGEOUS BODY as she walked out his door was on his mind when he first got into the car, but it was soon replaced by his number-one worry—when, where, and how was he going to get the money for Sabaya's dormitory deposit? It stayed on his mind all during the shift, and by morning he had to have some kind of solution. Hell, how could he save the folks in the project when he couldn't even save his own family?

CHAPTER 17

ASHANTI WOULDN'T STOP coughing. It was three o'clock in the morning, and for the sixth time that night, Malika pushed the covers off, slipped into a bathrobe, and went into the room where the boy lay sleeping. Her sister had gone away for the weekend, leaving her to deal with him alone, and she was tired.

She saw that he had turned the lamp by his bed on and was sitting up.

"Mama, what took you so long? I need some water and some more medicine."

"No, baby, you can't have no more medicine. Not till six o'clock this morning. I'll get you some more water now and turn on the vaporizer, that should help some."

Malika could hear the coughing even as she was in the kitchen filling the humidifier with water. The doctor had told her to call him if the cough couldn't be controlled by the medicine. "Malika, asthma is a funny kind of sickness—part hereditary, part stress. Try to keep the boy calm."

Easy enough to say. She tried to control things, but it had been rough. Particularly with Ashanti at the age where he could watch television and see all those things people were saying about his daddy on TV.

She set up the humidifier and sat down on his bed. "Want to hear a story?"

He coughed, then nodded his head. Malika took down Zamani in Africa, an illustrated adventure book, and began to read. Under the influence of his mother's voice and the steamy air circulating in the room, Ashanti's coughing spasms died down. As she kept reading, they finally stopped altogether.

Hours later, she woke to the sound of the telephone ringing in the living room. Ashanti was shaking her.

"It's Granny on the phone—she wants to talk to you."

"Tell her I be there in a minute."

"WHAT TAKE YOU SO LONG to get to the phone?" Mammie Teagle said as soon as Ashanti handed Malika the receiver. "You should of been up by now. It's late, boy should of had his breakfast. No wonder he always sick."

"This is my house, he's my son. Don't be telling me what to do. You ain't my mama."

"If Son was here, you wouldn't be talking like that to me. He'd whip your black ass, and you know it."

"But he ain't here now, what do you want?"

"Did you forget? I'm supposed to come over there today and babysit so you can go shopping. What time you want me to come?"

"You don't got to do me no favors. I can find me somebody else to come over here."

"You ain't going to keep me from my grandchild, so don't you even try. I be there at ten-thirty, you hear?"

"I don't feel like arguing with you no more, so goodbye, see you then."

As Malika hung the phone up, she noticed that Ashanti, who usually couldn't be distracted from his Saturday morning television shows, was standing in his bedroom doorway, holding his space man holster with its toy gun in his hand and looking at her. His light brown legs were sticking out of the shorts he'd slept in.

"I don't want Granny to stay with me. I don't need a babysitter and Granny's mean to me. Just let me come with you."

"Don't talk that way about her. I'll knock your block off, boy."

Malika saw his wounded expression and walked over, arms outstretched, to hug him. But it was too late. He started to cough, turned back into his room, and closed the door behind him. She hesitated for a minute, then decided not to break their privacy rule.

TWO HOURS LATER, Malika opened the door to her mother-in-law, a short, dark-skinned woman with a full, round face and softly curled black hair that fell over her forehead in bangs. Ashanti, who by habit would open his door when he heard the entrance chimes, stayed in his room.

Malika said, "Sorry I lost my temper over the phone. I just been a little tired lately, what with Ashanti's sickness keeping me up and all this stuff about Son."

"Don't even pretend you sorry. Where's Ashanti? He don't have enough manners to come say hello to his granny? Get that boy in here."

"Mammie Teagle, please don't be starting up again. I'll go get him." She knocked at Ashanti's door.

No answer.

She knocked again. Ashanti poked his head out and said, "I'm busy, can't you just leave me be? Please?"

"No, you got to stop whatever you doing right now and come in and say hello to your grandmama. And don't argue with me about it, neither."

"But, Mama," he said, trying to push the door shut, "I don't want to see her."

Malika shoved her way into his room, closed the door, shut off his television, and grabbed Ashanti by his arm. "Now listen here, you ain't going to be embarrassing me in front of that woman. She's your grandmama, and you going to treat her with respect or I'll have to whip you here and now. You hear me?"

She raised her hand as if to slap his face, then moved it down to grasp his arm..

Ashanti eyes glittered with anger, and he tried to pull away. She tightened her grip.

"Stop, you're hurting me!"

Malika let go. "All right, now just get in there and say hello, you done already made me late."

Mammie Teagle, who was seated in one of the chrome-framed leather chairs in the living room, smiled big when they walked in. Then she saw her grandson's face.

"Ashanti, what's the matter? Why you looking so mean?"

"I was watching 'Star Planet,' and Mama made me come in here. That's why."

"Well, that's just too bad. Come over here and give your granny a kiss, I ain't seen you for a long time."

"Don't want to."

Mammie Teagle got up from her chair, walked over to Ashanti, and grabbed his ear and twisted it.

He yelled.

"Get your hands off my child," Malika said.

Mammie Teagle let loose of Ashanti's ear.

Malika turned to him. "Kiss your grandmama. She's your daddy's mother, and you going to respect her. Now do it before I get that cord out of the kitchen."

MommaTeagle returned to her seat, folded her arms across her ample breasts, turned her head sideways, and stuck out a cheek.

Ashanti walked over, pecked her on the cheek, then ran back through the living room and down the hall to his bedroom. He slammed his door.

Fifteen minutes later, when his mother left, she had to say goodbye to him through that door....

MALIKA BURST ONTO THE COURTYARD of Parkwood Village with a smile on her face. Even though she'd had to leave Ashanti with that evil-assed old lady, she now had a day of freedom to enjoy. Before she left, she'd warned Mammie Teagle once again to keep her hands to herself. It was beyond her how that woman could expect Ashanti to like her when she hit him.

Malika sat down on a playground bench for a minute while she thought about what she had to get done that day. A little Indian girl in a seersucker playsuit with her hair braided in long plaits came over to her. She was accompanied by a young black girl and two white children.

"Hi, Mrs. Teagle," the girl said. "Where's Ashanti? We've been waiting for him all morning long. He promised he was going to come down and play baseball with us."

"He should be down in a little bit, Rajee. I got to go shopping now, and his grandmama's over babysitting."

Two hours later, having finished her grocery shopping and paid the boy to deliver the groceries, she was on her way over to her friend Linda's apartment. She lived just a block away.

Malika, dressed in a pair of white slacks that accentuated her bottom and a black blouse that plunged to show the top of her breasts, took the elevator to the tenth floor, where Linda lived with her two little girls. This weekend, the girls were away with their daddy.

Linda, a light-complexioned, tall woman with long braids, answered the door. "Been ages since I seen you."

Malika hugged her friend, whose body smelled of expensive perfume she'd just used in the shower. "Been busy times."

"Well, we don't have to worry about nothing this afternoon. Going to go out and have us some fun, girl. How much time you got?"

"I told Mammie Teagle I'd be back around six."

"Come on in and make yourself comfortable. I'll get us something to drink and a little weed. Take your shoes off. We going to the Last Stop."

The apartment was a mess. An ironing board that seemed to never have been taken down stood in the center of the living room, which was strewn with newspapers and magazines. An unplugged iron stood on end on the scorched white cover of the board. Malika had to push aside the girls' washed but unironed clothes to make herself a place to sit down on the living room couch.

In a few minutes Linda was back in the room with a bottle of white wine, two glasses, wrappings for marijuana cigarettes, and a container full of the brown weed. She turned on the jazz FM stereo station, then threw a pillow onto the floor in front of the couch.

"You got to tell me everything. I been reading the papers and hearing all this stuff about Son—I'm real sorry he died. How's Ashanti taking it?"

"I can't tell, he don't believe his daddy's dead. But he's a little moody, staying in his room a lot more than he used to."

"And how you taking it, Lika?"

"Truth is, it don't make me no difference. Leastwise, I don't feel no different. Son been gone so long, seemed like he was dead anyhow."

"But what you going to do now? How you going to live?"

"We got plenty of money, so I'm thinking about selling our condo and moving back to South Carolina with my sister and Ashanti. Mama said she be glad to have us come home, and it's a lot safer down there."

Linda said, "You right about that, girl. I worry about my children every second they out of my sight. All these perverts and sex fiends out there, you don't know what's going to happen. Just wish I could move down south. But I ain't got no relatives there, and I sure wouldn't have a job. No, I got to stay here."

Malika said, "It's funny, but sometimes I like the city and sometimes I don't...."

Linda noticed that Malika's glass was empty, so she got up and refilled it. Malika had already finished one of the joints. She said, "I don't think I want another drink—you know how I get. And we going out. And Mammie Teagle's home."

"Oh, don't worry about her. What difference do it make now? Son's dead. Enjoy yourself, honey. Life's short."

"I'll take one more, but that's it. It's already two-thirty, and you know how the time passes once we get over to the Last Stop."

Linda handed Malika the glass of wine. "I'll get myself ready, and we can get out of here now."

"Don't talk so much about Son being dead. You know I loved that man. And he's the father of my child. Now, no matter what nobody say about him, he did provide for us, we ain't never wanted for nothing. Gave me everything a man could give a woman." She looked down at her hands. "See these rings? Son gave them to me. Look at this necklace, these earrings. All from Son."

A tear slipped down her face. She got up, walked over to the stereo, and turned up the volume. Then she began to move her body back and forth, her arms poised like someone about to run a race, her thighs and hips moving in opposite directions in time to the music. Tears still in her eyes, she would shuffle a few steps forward, stop for a second, then slide a few steps backwards.

"Let's get out of here, girlfriend," she said.

By the time Linda returned from her bedroom with her handbag, Malika had drunk another glass of wine, her third. The tears had been replaced with a half-smile that was fixed on her face.

Linda looked at her. "You sure you want to go over there now? You looking like that wine and weed done got to you a bit. We can just stay here and—"

"No, " Malika said, shaking her head in rhythm to the music, "let's go. I feel like enjoying myself."

IT WAS SEVEN O'CLOCK when Malika finally opened the door into her apartment. She was woozy from wine, marijuana, and dancing. And she'd met a nice man, a financial consultant down on Walnut Street who was a good dancer and had a sweet rap. Body wasn't too bad either. While they were sitting at the table, he'd run his hands up and down her legs, and her juices had started to flow. One more drink of that wine, and she might of accepted his invite to come home with him. Was she supposed to sacrifice herself for the rest of her life?

Before she could turn the key she'd put in the door, Mammie Teagle opened it and stood there staring her right in the face.

"I smell liquor on you. You know Son didn't like you drinking nowhere without him. And you late. I got to go all the way back uptown and get over to Sister Jones's house for Saturday night prayer meeting, and here you come late."

"Let me in—"

"I always knew you was no-count. Son barely in his grave, and you running around like some hussy."

Malika stepped past her, turned around, and stared her right back in the eye. "Mammie Teagle, if you can't treat me right, then you just don't have to come over here no more, you hear?"

Ashanti came running out of his room and threw his arms around

Malika's waist. "Granny was mean to me. She slapped me twice this morning just because I forget to say 'please.' And she been twisting my ear all day long. And she wouldn't let me go out and play."

"Go back to your room for a minute, I want to talk to your granny alone."

He ran off.

She turned to Mammie Teagle, who had picked up her purse and Bible from the kitchen table:

"I borned that child and I done told you a million times not to hit him. Now, don't make me disrespect you here in my house. You just leave, and I don't want to see you back here no more till you ready to treat him right. Ashanti ain't going to be hit the way you hit Son, that's all there is to it. I don't want him turning out like his daddy."

Mammie Teagle was reaching for the door, in a royal huff, when the chimes sounded.

Who could that be? Malika wasn't expecting company, and even if it was company, they'd have had to be buzzed in downstairs.

She walked to the door and looked through the peephole.

She felt lightheaded, wished she'd been drinking coffee instead of wine.

It was Son.

HE WALKED INTO THE ROOM like he'd never been gone, dressed in a white summer shirt open at the collar, blue slacks, and sandals.

Malika couldn't say a word.

Mammie Teagle threw herself into his arms. "I knowed my boy wasn't dead. Hallelujah! Praise the Lord!"

Malika ran to her son's bedroom. "Ashanti, your daddy's home!"

Ashanti ran into the living room, crying, "Daddy!" When he reached his father, he leapt into his arms and hugged him tight around the neck.

Malika rushed into the bathroom, where she scrubbed her

face like it was a pot and the washcloth was a Brillo pad. She found some mouthwash and gargled. Looking at herself in the mirror, she quickly brushed her hair into place, spritzed herself with Allure, then hurried back into the living room. Son, in a group hug, was just lifting up his head in search of her.

As Malika threw herself into his arms, he released the two others, hugged her tight, and gave her a long kiss. If he noticed she smelled of pot and alcohol, he said nothing about it. He pushed her away from him so she was at arm's length.

"Mighty good to see you again, baby. I been many a hard mile to make it back home, believe me."

Mammie Teagle stood with her hands on her hips, head cocked to the side. With a smirk on her face. Could barely wait to tell Son his wife'd been out drinking.

Son said, "Honey, I'm hungry. Get me something to eat?"

"She can get you a drink," Mammie Teagle said. "That's what she's best at doing. I'll go in there and fry you up some chicken, make you some biscuits right quick. Now get in the bathroom and get yourself cleaned up."

Son smiled at Malika. "Guess I could do with a drink. I know you got that bourbon in the cabinet, right?"

She said, "I'll get it, and while I'm at it, I'll pour myself a glass of wine. It's dangerous for you here, Son, the cops been stopping by every other day."

"Be gone in the morning, baby."

He sat himself down on his easy chair and put Ashanti on his lap. "Hey, little man, how you been since your daddy's been gone?"

"Good, except I had a lot of coughing attacks."

Son frowned. "They ain't been giving you your medicine?"

"No, Daddy, it's just the medicine don't work all the time."

"Well, we'll have to see about that." He lifted the boy off his lap and walked into the kitchen, where Malika was getting his drink. "What's wrong with these doctors? They ain't been giving Ashanti the right medicine? What's the name of the motherfucker?"

Mammie Teagle turned from where she stood bent over the kitchen table, rolling the biscuits. "Don't you be bringing that nasty language in here. I done raised you better than that, boy."

"Honey, I told you about the money running short," Malika said. "But he got the best doctor we could find, and to tell the truth, he's doing better now than he ever done."

Mammie Teagle muttered, "Malika stay home more, boy be a lot better."

"What'd you say, Mama?'"

"Nothing."

Malika put a full glass of bourbon in Son's hand, led him back into the living room, and pushed him gently into his chair. "You sit down there for a second." She turned to Ashanti, who'd been following his father's every step. "Go get your report card for your daddy. I want to show him what a smart son he has."

When he'd left the room, she walked over to the gleaming black stereo, pushed the ipod controls, and selected a playlist by Beyonce, Son's favorite singer.

As the music filled the room, Son seemed to relax in his chair. He loosened up even more and smiled when Ashanti returned and showed him a report card with all A's in his academic subjects. But then Son turned the report card over, saw Ashanti had gotten a C in conduct, and read a note about an incident in which he'd talked back to a teacher. Too late Malika remembered what the teacher had written.

Before she could get the report card back, Son had grabbed the boy by his arms. "What the hell you doing, talking back to a fucking teacher?" He drew back his right hand and struck Ashanti full in the face, so hard the blow sent him sprawling across the room. Ashanti lay motionless on the floor for a few seconds.

Malika screamed. Mammie Teagle, her rolling pin covered with small patches of dough, came into the living room and shouted, "Son Teagle, sit your black ass back down in that seat!"

Ashanti, his eyes fixed on his father, slowly got up from the floor. The whole left side of his face was already darkening. Without a tear in his eye, he walked back to his bedroom.

Malika went into the kitchen, got a long, thin butcher knife, and came right back into the living room. Son was on his feet and headed toward Ashanti's room. She blocked him with her body and spoke in a deadly quiet voice.

"I will kill you if you even think about hitting that boy again. I promise you that."

Son, stopped in his tracks, his mouth open, looked at the two women. He turned around, walked back to his chair, and sat down.

"Mama, hurry and get the food done. And bring me your cell phone—they sure to be tapping the apartment line. I got me some calls to make."

BY ELEVEN THAT NIGHT Son had eaten a good meal, drunk almost a half-bottle of whiskey, and changed into a clean set of clothes. He told Malika to go to the bedroom and get ready for him. He'd already called a cab to take Mammie Teagle home to her place in West Philly.

Ashanti hadn't come out of his room. When Malika took some food to him, he was huddled in a blanket on the floor in a corner. His thumb was in his mouth, and he was holding a teddy bear.

At eleven-fifteen the chimes rang, and Son, after the usual precautions, opened the door. Malika, having taken her shower, left the door of her bedroom ajar so she could overhear the conversation. Already she was wishing Son had been killed in the escape.

Sitting in the chair and drinking glass after glass of bourbon, he'd become increasingly angry—now cursing the guards at Delaware Prison, now boasting how he'd outwitted the state police, now saying what he was going to do to Obie Bullock, and then—suddenly fixing his eyes on Malika—demanding to know what the hell she'd been doing all day before he got there. Only the intervention of a phone call by Raschid had spared her from answering that question. Malika knew now that she'd either have to leave Philly with her child or kill her husband.

Raschid had been talking to Son for several minutes in tones she couldn't hear. She opened the door a little wider.

"When is it scheduled for?" Son said.

"Two weeks from now. City Hall Plaza."

"Gives us plenty of time to get it together. Way I figure it, I'll stay here tonight and tomorrow morning I'll be on my way...." He lowered his voice as if he knew Malika was listening. Then she heard him say, "You have the car outside at six. And I need some heat, man."

There was further talk, but Malika had heard enough. She crawled into her bed and waited for Son to come in. She was scared to death. Maybe he'd contracted AIDS in the prison. She'd never known him to like men, but all kinds of strange things happened in there, and she was sure plenty of inmates in that place had diseases. For the first time in many years, she closed her eyes and prayed.

She heard the door open.

"Open them eyes—don't you be making like you asleep. I want me some loving, and I want it now."

WHEN THE MORNING RAYS were just coming through the blinds, Malika felt Son slip out of the bed and heard him go into the bathroom. She kept her head tightly pressed into the pillow. It didn't save her.

Dressed now in a light summer suit with an open-collar shirt, he came over to her, grabbed her hair, pulled her face up to his, kissed her sweet, then slapped her—hard.

"That's so you won't pull no more of that shit you did yesterday. I'll be in touch. And don't be acting smart with my mama, you hear? She told me how you been dissing her."

Malika waited until she heard the front door shut, then left the bedroom. Ashanti was standing in the hallway in his shorts.

"Mama," he said, "what are we going to do? Is he going to kill us?"

"Don't you worry," Malika said, "your mama going to take care of you and herself too. He ain't killing nobody, leastwise not in this house. I guarantee you that." She put her arms around him, bent down and kissed him. "Go watch television for a while. It's

Sunday morning, remember? I'm going to put the waffles on."

Ashanti smiled. "And don't forget the sausage, hear?"

"And don't you forget to wash your hands and face, hear?"

She went into the kitchen to make the waffles. But first she checked up behind the spice tins, to make sure the revolver Raschid had gotten for her was still there. It was, and the cold metal felt comforting to her touch. Son wasn't going to be beating on her the way he did before they took him to prison. No way!

CHAPTER 18

LIFE WAS FORCING DORA LEE to make an awful lot of important decisions. The swirling activity of buying clothes for the children, running back and forth to the various malls in the Gastonia area, had worn her down. Her inlaws had been great and the children all helpful, but they missed their daddy. Especially Sabaya, who'd have to go off to college without seeing him.

It had been decided that Boatwright would drive Sabaya and Dora Lee out to the college in Ohio. It was only about a fifteen-hour drive, Boatwright said, and that was nothing for southern folks used to the long highway cruises to visit relatives up north. Still, to Dora Lee it didn't seem right that Obie would be completely left out from his daughter's departure to college. But there was no room on the credit card for airfare.

And what she was to do with her own life? She'd decided Timba would stay here in Gastonia, at least for the fall. But what of her and Obie? Where did she belong, here with her son in the south or up north with her husband? She had to decide soon, what with her vacation coming to an end in a few days.

And the news from the city wasn't good. Obie's march was coming up soon, and Son Teagle's body still hadn't been recovered. That's what scared her most of all. Why hadn't the police done more? A mad dog might be loose in the city, yet life was going on as usual. And Obie, her Obie, the man who'd come home bone-tired day after day and who'd singlehandedly started a new baseball league for kids, who'd created a new Pop Warner football league when they said there was no place for African-American city kids to play—this man who'd tried even to save the children of the Teagle family itself, he was now Son Teagle's personal target along with all the other Teagle drug dealers and the police instead of protecting him had treated him like a criminal.

Dora Lee prayed nightly for Obie and for guidance in her life. She also prayed that he'd be kept away from temptation—the last three times she'd called him, the phone had been answered by Rita: "Philly Drug March Committee."

Lying in her bed on this August night, she replayed the first time it had happened:

"What?" Dora Lee had said when she heard the woman's voice. "Is this the Bullock residence?"

"Yes, it is."

"Well, who is this?"

"May I ask who's calling?"

"Dora Lee Bullock, that's who."

"I'm sorry, Dora Lee, it's Rita. I'm helping Obie get ready for the march."

"Oh, that's very kind of you," Dora Lee said. "Would you put him on the line, please?"

"Would it be all right if he called you back later? He's taking his shower and getting ready for work."

"I don't care what he's doing. Tell him to come to the phone, please."

"Well, if you insist, we've been working round the clock on the march, and he's real tired. And you know he's working four hours a morning as an assistant manager over at McDonald's now."

A couple of minutes later, Obie came to the phone.

"Baby, I really been missing you. It's been real hectic around here what with the committee trying to get the march together."

"Just how many members of the committee are there right now?"

"Everybody's gone now because it's late and I have to get off to work. Rita just stayed around so's I could have a hot meal."

"Suit yourself. But I just want to let you know I'm nobody's fool. I don't feel like talking to you any more. Goodnight."

She hung up the phone on Obie. It was the first time she'd ever done that. For a few minutes, she thought about calling him back. But the more she thought about it, the madder she got. That night she'd slept as if on a bed of boards. No matter what position she got into, she couldn't drift off. All she could think about was Obie and Rita making love. In her bed.

IT WAS EIGHT O'CLOCK on a midsummer's evening. Obie had just walked back into his apartment after surveying the demonstration site down at City Hall. The front room was milling with workers making placards. Paint containers lay all around, as did lists of churches, ministers, and community organizations.

Rita yelled from the kitchen, "Big Obie, that you? I've been keeping your dinner on the stove. It's good and hot."

Jason, a bodyguard, smiled at Obie. "Man, you got it made. Couldn't live better if you was a king."

Obie laughed. "Well, some of us got it and some of us don't."

Rita, whose white cotton knit blouse and form-fitting jeans accentuated the high pointed tips of her breasts and the sweet curve of her butt and thighs, came into the living room.

"Obie, if you want to get any rest before you go to work, you go on down to my apartment, because you're not going to get any peace here. Phone's been ringing all day. And these folks around here don't know how to be quiet. I'll bring your dinner and work uniform down."

Obie hesitated for a minute—the bodyguard's eyes were on him. But tired as he was, what she said made sense.

"Tell you the truth, it's been pretty rough on me all day long. Didn't get a chance to sleep this morning, so I'll accept your kind invitation."

As he gathered up a few of his things, the guard said, "You sure you don't want me to go down there with you, man?"

Obie laughed. "If they going to hit any place, it'll be here, not down at Rita's. Don't you worry none, I'll be fine, just so long as I get a chance to get me a little nap."

He left with Rita, who was carrying a tray with a plate of ham hocks, greens, boiled potatoes, and biscuits she'd made for his dinner. It was only one flight and a short ways down the hall to her apartment.

They came up to the door, and Rita said, "Reach into my pants pocket and get the keys out, would you? They're in the right-hand side."

Obie reached down. The jeans she was wearing were really tight, so he felt the firm flesh of her thigh. And the keys were at the bottom of the pocket, so that in trying to get them out he touched her in a sensitive spot. Like a fool, he let his hand linger there for a second.

Rita turned to him and smiled. "The keys, remember?"

Embarrassed, Obie took them out and opened the door into her apartment. It was painted light blue, and the furniture was old-fashioned and beautiful. If he hadn't known better, he'd have thought he was in the home of an interior decorator. In the corner was an antique oak chair with hand-carved wooden flowers on its back. And he'd bet anything the couch was custom-upholstered. At each end of it were decorated china lamps.

The entire floor was covered with a deep luxurious white pile rug. The walls were hung with oil paintings of original African art, and pieces of African sculpture were placed around the apartment. Obie was really impressed by a finely wrought bronze African head of a warrior with a sword held high, like he was ready to strike a death blow to an enemy. How had Rita gotten into this place under the middle-income quota for the building?

Before they walked into the living room, she asked him to take off his shoes so as not to soil the rug. She did the same.

"Sit down any place you'll be comfortable. I'll go put this food on some plates, be back in a jiffy. You want anything to drink?"

"Just some water."

"I've got some beer here if you'd like it, Obie."

"No thanks. But I wouldn't mind a ginger ale. Dora Lee was right—liquor and me don't agree."

He carefully sat down in the big red armchair. It was made of a fabric so fine he just didn't feel comfortable sitting on it. Rita returned with the dinner.

"What kind of music do you want to listen to?"

"I'm not particular long as it's not hard rap. Stuff gets on my nerves. Luther van Dross is more my style."

Rita turned on a local FM station that featured just that kind of music. She picked up a big pillow from the couch, brought it over to where Obie was sitting, dropped it on the floor, and sat down.

"You make yourself as comfortable as you can, honey. You've been under a lot of pressure, and I just want you to relax yourself while you're here."

Obie was busy eating the ham hocks and greens. This woman could really cook. And the biscuits tasted homemade, like the kind Dora Lee used to make before she started going to night school. It was a good meal, and he started to feel very comfortable.

While he ate, Rita talked about about the final arrangements for the march.

"Would you believe the other day I called sixteen churches and ended up having to leave answering machine messages at fifteen of them?" she said. "I was so discouraged I wanted to give up, then I called the sixteenth church, it was Bethany Baptist, and a Reverend Shawcross answered. When I told him about what we needed—the posters, the organizations, the folks, and everything, and the trouble I was having reaching people—he said, 'Don't you worry about a thing, child, because the quarterly conference of ministers is meeting for breakfast on Monday morning at Macedonia Baptist church, all seventy-five pastors will be there, and I'll personally make it my business to see to it that time is set aside to deal with the march. It's too important to let fall by the wayside.'"

"That's great news," Obie said.

"Except for one thing," Rita said with a sigh. "You'll have to tell them what you need, and you're going to have to go there right from work."

"Hey," Obie said, " that's my day off from McDonald's and the Lord will give me the strength to do it, and there definitely will be good eating—Reverend Jones has told me about all the grits, hot biscuits, scrambled eggs, and salmon cakes they got for those breakfasts." He smiled. "Oh, yes, I'll make it there all right, and Reverend Johnson is going to make announcements at the big mid-city revival over at Shiloh AME next week, and I'm going to get the city-wide ushers' boards of as many churches in the city to endorse this march as I can at our meeting next Wednesday night. If we can get them there, they'd all be coming out to the march in their Sunday usher uniforms. God's sentinels marching to protect his children—oh, that will be something to see!"

"Obie, with some more hard work by me and the others, it's really going to come off the way we want it to." Rita went on to tell him how she had input lists of churches, self-help organizations, YMCA's and YWCA's, school principals, and PTA presidents into computers with the help of her church's women's guild—they'd stayed up most of three nights running to finish their task, humming "Blessed Assurance" as they sat at the computers down in the Sunday School room typing away.

When she finished, Obie felt sure everything was totally under control. She'd even taken two days off from her job—she worked as an office manager in an insurance claims processing office—to make sure no ends would remain untied.

After the meal, Rita asked him whether he wanted more water before he went in to take his nap. He said no, he'd just go in and lie down now since he had to be up and ready for work in an hour.

"I'll draw the covers back for you, then you can come on in and sleep." She went into the other room. In a few seconds, she said, "Everything's ready."

The bedroom, decorated in the same colors as the living room, was dominated by a white queen-sized bed. The room was neat but comfortable. Rita had drawn back both the expensive-looking satiny sheets and a red quilt that covered the bed. The door to the bathroom was open, and Obie could hear water running in the tub.

She got up. "I'm going back into the living room. You'll find everything you need here. I hung your uniform up in my closet, and you'll find towels and washcloths in the bathroom. If you need anything else, you give me a shout, hear?"

Obie was in the throes of the most powerful temptation of his married life. Why had Dora Lee let him fall into this situation by leaving him in the city alone? What did she think he was? Superman? Not to be tempted by a woman like Rita with her warm smile and carefree manner and...never mind her body.

And what enthusiasm and organizational skills she had brought to the planning for the march! By now, people from all around the city were beginning to think she was the mastermind of the event. And she hadn't asked anything of him, either. Just the opportunity to join in the fight against drugs and gangs.

Obie got into the bathtub. He didn't really know who this woman was, whether she had kids, a husband, a boyfriend. But he did know that he really wanted to make love to her. And he knew it was wrong.

He took a long shower after his bath, then prayed to God to give him the strength to withstand this temptation that would wreck the union he and Dora Lee had built with so much love and such hard work over the years. But Rita's image was replacing Dora Lee's in his mind.

He turned the faucets in the shower to cold and let the water run over him. He prayed hard, with all his heart and every bit of his faith. And when he got out of the shower, the temptation was gone.

MORE TIRED THAN HE KNEW, he fell right off as soon as he stretched out in the bed.

He woke up an hour later, startled by the strangeness of the surroundings and by the distinct and powerfully seductive smell of Rita's perfumes and toilet waters. He felt a hand on his shoulder.

"Time to get up now. I put a pot of coffee on for you."

She had on a black negligee just barely visible under a light white summer robe. She'd sat down on the bed to waken him, and like a fool he let his hand fall onto her thigh. She snuggled up closer to him .

"I've been in the other room, spent the whole hour keeping myself from coming in here and getting in this bed with you. Only thing stopped me was I thought you needed the rest more than you needed me."

"You got to understand, Rita. I do need you, but the problem is I'm married, and I long ago promised myself this was one African-American man who would not cheat on his wife."

He tried to keep his hand motionless on her thigh. "It's true, Dora Lee and me having a lot of trouble. No disputing that. But we'll work it out—we just got to—and I'm not going to do anything to hurt us. And that don't mean I don't want you, because the truth is, you can see by looking at me that I do. But right now, I'm going to have to get over that. And you got to help me, Rita, because we got a big thing to do in a few days, and this ain't no time to be messing up."

"Do you want cream or skimmed milk in the coffee?"

"Cream, baby, I got to indulge myself somehow—now, don't I?"

Rita laughed, gently took his hand off her, stood up, and went into the kitchen to get his coffee.

CHAPTER 19

TODAY, SATURDAY, was Obie Bullock's march. Shapiro figured it was likely to be an even bigger event with the unexpected announcement yesterday that the district attorney had failed to indict Leroy Merriweather. Stone Latimer, still recovering slowly in the hospital, had refused to say anything, so had Khalid. And Hashim, the one Shapiro knew had set up the kidnapping, had disappeared from the safe house where the district attorney had secluded him. Shapiro wouldn't want to be in his shoes when the Teagle gang caught up with him, as they surely would.

Shapiro took the bus and subway, then walked over to Obie's projects, the real starting point for the march which would then proceed up to Broad Street and Cecil B. Moore Avenue, then down Broad to City Hall. It was a warm day—must be ninety degrees—and he was sweating heavily by the time he reached the project. He considered taking off his suit jacket, then decided to keep it on. He was a reporter, not a participant.

He walked onto the courtyard of the Hill Projects and was immediately impressed. There had to be at least five hundred people here, and more arriving every minute. Blacks and Latinos were everywhere. Vans lettered "Mt. Calvary Baptist Church," "Mt. Moriah Church of God in Christ," or "Sweet Pilgrim Baptist Church" were parked all up and down the avenue that bordered the courtyard. Close to Shapiro was a white-haired old lady, bent over by age and wearing gold-rimmed glasses suspended from her neck with an elastic cord. He walked over to her.

"Ma'am, are you marching down there in your condition?"

She looked at him as if he were not very bright. "Ain't everybody?"

He shook his head and circulated in the crowd.

Music was everywhere. Drum and bugle corps were tuning

up their trumpets and trombones, while men carrying long African drums and dressed in the clothing of Africa were all over the place, their thumping instruments the dominant sound. On a landing at the edge of the courtyard, a rap group was performing anti-drug lyrics. Neighborhood kids stood around them, clapping and dancing and showing off special steps in hopes of being caught by one of the many television cameras present.

Shapiro threaded his way through the crowd to the main building. Inside its lobby, he found a group of men and women gathered around a long table, making last-minute arrangements for the march. Big Obie Bullock, his hair newly done in cornrows, stood listening intently to a very attractive woman telling him something. Shapiro looked around the lobby for Dora Lee but didn't see her. She was probably outside in the crowd.

Obie let out a shout. "Hey, come on over here. Glad to see they had the sense to send their best reporter. Meet Rita Simpson, she's really the one put the march together. Rita, this is Walt Shapiro."

The woman, dressed in white slacks and a gold dashiki with red embroidery, turned towards him. She had light brown skin and wore her plaited hair swept up around her head like a turban. She was tall, self-possessed, and so stunning she would bring silence to any crowded room she walked into. She smiled at Shapiro.

"Obie's told me about you, Walt. Are you going to be with us all day?"

"If my feet hold up." He wanted to ask Obie where Dora Lee was, but after observing him with Rita, he thought maybe not. Instead, he asked Obie, "What does the police security look like?"

"Well, you already seen what there is outside. We notified the police about the routes, they going to give us as much help as they can. We're also providing our own."

"With even money Teagle's still on the loose, you'd think they'd have cops all over the place."

"Captain said he'd do his best, and we'll have regular traffic and crowd control cops from downtown." Obie got up from his chair. "We got to get the show on the road. See you later, Walt. We set up a special section up front for the press. Just show your credentials to the marshals, they'll let you through."

Shapiro went back outside, where marchers under their organizations' banners were already forming along the length of the street. He moved to a spot where he could look down on them.

All along the street, he could see people dressed in a dizzying variety of colors interspersed with solid stretches of yellow and white that marked the positions of the marching bands. Obie and Rita and some of the men and women who'd been inside the building walked up to the head of the line.

As they moved off, the marching band directly behind them struck up the strains of "We Shall Overcome," and the lines of marchers shuffled off, first slowly, then picking up speed as group after group joined in.

The marchers passed Shapiro, then fell in step with a group whose banner proclaimed them to be from the Mt. Moriah Baptist Church. The group was mainly composed of women, the younger ones wearing T-shirts with anti-violence slogans. An older woman was holding a sign high above her head displaying a life-size picture of a girl with a smile on her face that showed she was enjoying the opportunity to be photographed. Just a regular teenage cut-up. Under her photograph were the lines: "My Daughter, Fatasha, Killed by Drug Dealers. Age 16. Safe Now in the Arms of Jesus."

Most of the other women carried large black Bibles, well-worn and with creases on their covers from being opened so often. A few men were sprinkled throughout the group. One was about forty-five years old and dressed in white, with a red bandanna around his head and a red kerchief tucked into the collar of his shirt. Holding his arm was a blind woman carrying a white cane. She had a high soprano voice, and whenever the singing faded, she'd sing a little louder and the rough-hewn yet clear tones of her voice would soar high above the sounds around her, until the others, as if challenged by the clarity and strength flowing from her soul, lifted their voices a little higher too.

As Shapiro's group moved along, men and women from the small side streets came out and joined the march. He soon found that the people from the church were being separated from each other, so he decided to stay with the blind singing woman and her husband.

As the march reached the intersection of Broad and Cecil B. Moore Avenue, then moved down Broad Street, it passed a corner notorious for drug trafficking. Years ago, Shapiro had written an article about it, and when he updated the story every few years, he found that the problem was even worse.

Today he saw eight or so young black men standing on the corner. They weren't dealing, but their body language was defiant, cocky. One thing was sure—they weren't going to give up their corner without a fight.

A short, stout woman, part of Shapiro's adopted church group, broke away from the march line and called out to one of the young men.

"Hey you, Malik! You, boy. What you doing out here? Ain't it enough they done killed two of your brothers? All last night, your mama was crying for you. Been looking for you for two days. Come on, child—do right. Come with us."

The boy she was talking to, short and thin with a clean-shaven head and stubble on his chin, couldn't have been more than eighteen. He looked from the woman to the group he was with, then back to the woman.

"Mrs. Watkins, just leave me be. You tell Mama I'm fine and I'll be home in a few days."

The woman put her hands on her hips and shook her head. "You going to be home, all right. In a great big black funeral car." Some of her fellow church members were pulling at her arms, and a marshal, distinguished by a red and green sash across his chest, came up to coax her away from the corner.

She walked away, but not until she delivered her parting shot. "I be praying for you children. Malik, you breaking your mama's heart, going to put that poor woman in the grave."

BY THE TIME THE MARCHERS reached City Hall, forty-five minutes later, Shapiro was astounded by the size of the crowd.

By God! There was no room in the plaza. Everywhere he turned there were people. He thought he'd be crushed to death if he tried to make it to the press area, but he had to give it a shot, so he said goodbye to his newly made friends from Mt. Moriah's and struck off through the crowd in the direction a marshal pointed him.

It took a while, but he made it to the press area. The planners of the march had constructed an elevated stand that gave the reporters a good view. Shapiro greeted his colleagues and looked out over the vast sea of people filling the entire plaza as well as the streets that bounded it.

The leaders of the march gradually made their way up to the podium through the crowd. On stage a gospel choir—the women dressed in white blouses and black skirts, the men in black pants and shirts—began to sway back and forth. Then, as their leader brought her hand down in a signal to begin, they started to sing:

We will not, we will not be moved,
We shall not, we shall not be moved.
Just like a tree that's planted by the water
We shall not be moved.

The crowd began to take up the verses, and the singing spread out over the plaza, gathering volume and power as the thousands of blending voices created their own unique sound. The singers in the choir, black faces glistening from sweat, seemed to draw energy from the crowd. Their swaying motion became even more pronounced, their voices ever louder. And then—led by a woman with her head tilted to the side, eyes fixed on high—the singers began clapping, soon joined by the throng in the plaza. Shapiro watched a little girl in a pink dress with white lace around her sleeves begin to clap too, her tiny hands keeping exact time and her mouth voicing the words of the song as if she'd been born singing it. She couldn't have been more than three years old.

Now a tall, light brown-skinned man even bigger than Obie came to the center of the stage, took the portable microphone out of its holder, and began to pace back and forth, starting the first lines of each stanza of the song.

Shapiro recognized him as Brother Carter James, a famous gospel singer. Even if he hadn't recognized the face, he'd have known the voice. The song just poured out of him, his voice now dipping low, now soaring high, now smooth and melodious, now rough and guttural.

It made Shapiro think of strong trees, bent low by stormy winds but springing upward every time the gusts relented; of cresting waves, swirling and foaming and reaching high just before they crashed on a beach; of those moments when a lightning storm bursts out on a summer's night, its flashing bolts so close together they illuminate the entire landscape.

He found himself clapping and singing along with the crowd, then noticed that several of his fellow reporters were looking at him oddly. He stopped and typed a few phrases on his notebook screen, as if his participation had been part of his coverage of the story.

After about ten minutes, the choir took their seats on the platform and a short, chubby man came to the podium—Larry Grimes, a well-known talk-show host who announced he would serve as the master of ceremonies for the day.

The enthusiastic crowd loudly welcomed preacher after preacher delivering anti-violence messages, as did the local politicians who were interspersed with the preachers. But it was obvious to Shapiro that the people were waiting for Obie to speak. And after another selection by the gospel singer, the talk-show host advanced once again to the lectern.

"Folks, I'd like to introduce our main speaker for this afternoon, Brother Obie Bullock. Now, there's no need for me to go into a lot of detail about him. This is a man who finished high school in a small town in North Carolina and then served honorably in the U.S. Army. Then he came to Philadelphia, where he met his beloved wife Dora Lee one Sunday morning at a chicken dinner after church service, and began to raise a family. He's lived in North

Philly ever since, except when he was called back into the service for Iraq and was wounded there. He's dedicated all of his adult life to his God and to the salvation of our black youth. The Good Book says 'by their deeds ye shall know them.' And it is by his deeds that we know Big Obie. Ladies and gentlemen, I present him to you."

The crowd burst into applause. Obie pushed himself up from his chair, walked to the podium, and shook hands with the talk-show host. His white shirt was soaked from the heat and humidity, and he carried a white handkerchief that even from this distance Shapiro could see was already wet.

On the large platform, Obie seemed almost small. He stood silent at the lectern for a moment, then as the applause grew he stepped to the side of the platform and began to clap, as if to thank the crowd for their support. He raised one hand, and as the applause died down and the crowd stilled, began to speak.

"First of all I want to thank Almighty God for life and for bringing us together here this afternoon. Those of you who know me know I ain't much of a speaker, but I believe God is going to help me say what I got to say today.

"Don't take no fancy words to say why we're here. We want to get the drug dealers out of our community and take charge of our own lives. Children being wasted. Hearses rolling out of churches every week with our boy children. Twenty-two children killed last year, nineteen of them black and all but one of them a male. Four hundred and six homicides last year and close to eighty percent of them black males! Mamas be weeping all the time.

"Look like the only way we see ourselves serious is on television, only time we be wearing suits and ties is when we mourning, when the gospel choir is singing and some preacher is asking 'Why, oh Lord, did you have to take such a young life?' Our favorite scripture is Job and his tribulations.

"In the last month, I been to two funerals of boys killed because of drugs. Oh, I don't guess I have to tell you what it's like, because you surely been there too, if you black and if you poor.

"And you stood in that pew facing the cross, heard the preacher coming up the aisle chanting 'Thou art the resurrection and the life, holding the Bible in his hand and leading the family into the church.

"And you stood over them caskets to see our boy children all dressed up for churchgoing, but their faces can't move, hands can't clap, tongues can't sing God's praises.

"Only time a preacher gets to talk to most of our young people is when they come to the church to bury one of their friends.

"Oh, I don't know about you, but I ain't noways tired! Going to stay on this battlefield, ain't going to let nobody turn me round.

"Not no Teagle gang.

"Not no falsely accusing D.A.

"And surely not no devil.

"My God rides shotgun for me, yes he does."

Obie paused, and shouts came from the crowd.

"Hallelujah!"

"Say so, Brother!"

"Preach it!"

Obie's face became ever more serious and his voice more powerful and cadenced.

"Now, you all know I was under threat of indictment for defending my own family. Me and my friend Leroy. Now, don't our God work in mysterious ways?

"Didn't he deliver Daniel?"

"Yes!" the crowd shouted.

"Didn't he deliver the Hebrew children?"

"Yes!"

"Didn't he deliver Leroy Merriweather?"

"Yes!"

"And didn't he deliver Obie Bullock?"

"Yes, he did!"

Some women from the choir broke ranks and ran down to throw their arms around Obie. Others jumped and stomped up and down on the stage, some going into a holy dance, their bodies twisting and turning in rhythmic jerks across the wooden floor. Shapiro was afraid the motion of so many bodies might cause the platform to collapse.

SON TEAGLE, a rifle with a scope in his hands, was across the street with two of his men—Raschid and Rufus, the tall, thin man who'd followed Dora Lee into the subway.

The three were in the Municipal Services Building, in an upper story office with a window that looked out on the plaza. They'd reached it by posing as a cleaning crew, complete with buckets and mops, then killing the two weekend security guards who became suspicious of the men's I.D. They brought the dead bodies up the elevator with them, then stashed them under a conference table.

Son was calm and secure. Everything had gone right. And Raschid's idea to make an anti-drug banner and unfurl it from the office window as a cover was perfect. When the time came to shoot Bullock, they'd just make a hole in that sheet and fire away. Then make their way out through the panicked crowd.

He turned to Rufus. "Now remember, car's in that garage up at Twelfth and Race. We split, then meet down there. Ain't far, and we may be able to make it without shooting. Ain't that many cops out there."

They could hear all the sounds coming from the plaza. Son actually started clapping his hands in time to the gospel music at one point.

Bullock came on and began to talk. Son stood at the side of the window and viewed the scene below. Thousands of folks down there shouting their lungs out about how they was going to run the drug dealers out of town. And Bullock standing there, looking fit, maybe some heavier than he was before Son went to prison, still a big tall dude always trying to tell folks what to do.

Son returned to his place behind the banner, rested the rifle on the window sill, pulled out a knife, and cut a hole in the sheet. He pushed the rifle through the hole, looked through the periscope sights of the Ruger mini 9., and adjusted them with the knob so that the crosshairs lay right on Bullock's head.

But just then choir members ran up and surrounded the fucker. Couldn't hardly see him. But he heard him say, "Well, that's it, folks, we'll end things right here."

He'd get a good bead on him in a minute. Didn't want to kill any of those folks around him if he didn't have to. But he'd definitely get Bullock. He'd had enough of this shit—motherfucker crowding him everywhere he went, thinking ahead of him every time he tried to make a dollar, disrespecting his family, making life miserable for them. See how he liked it when Dora Lee, Sabaya, and Timba suffered just like Son's family had suffered!

ON THE MORNING OF THE MARCH, Leroy had told Obie, "I think we got to act like Teagle's alive. I'll be there during the speech. You know me, old recon patrol."

Obie had laughed at the expression. "All right, you go on over there. But after it's all over, promise you'll have dinner with me and Rita tonight. We going to eat over at Martha's restaurant."

Leroy had agreed but he didn't feel comfortable about it. What was happening to Obie and Dora Lee? The Obie he knew would never cast a sideways glance at another woman. Wasn't like him at all, and when all this was over, he'd sure talk to him about it. Friends were supposed to help each other when they got off the right path.

Early that morning, Leroy had made a few strategic phone calls to some people who owed him and finally managed to scare up an old friend who worked in City Hall in an office directly overlooking the Plaza. He agreed to come into his office and sign in Leroy as his guest for the morning. The man said he had a lot of paperwork anyhow, and Leroy could do his surveillance while he got a head start on his next week's work. So it was that now the bureaucrat sat in his inner office working while Leroy, equipped with a pair of binoculars and a walkie-talkie through which he could talk to the security command post of the Mau-Mau, kept watch over the windows of the buildings that looked onto the plaza.

There were plenty of armed security people from the Mau-Mau scattered through the crowd, and even a few dozen policemen on the fringes of the plaza, but nobody was up high. If he'd been around during the planning of the march, he wouldn't have let them make that kind of mistake.

So now, while the ceremony went on below him, he was casting a close eye on everything He kept alert by sipping coffee from a cracked thermos mug he'd brought with him. He also had a little portable radio over which he could follow the proceedings—the talk-show host's radio station,WURD, was broadcasting the rally live.

He settled himself down for a long morning and turned the walkie-talkie on just to hear what was going on. Every few minutes, voices would come on indicating that the security men were indeed on the job.

Just as the second or third minister—he was losing count, they all seemed to want to "say a few words"—wound down, Leroy saw the tiny figures of first one man, then another, then a third in a big office picture window of the Municipal Services Building overlooking the plaza.

He grabbed his binoculars. The men in the window unfurled a big white banner that had been rolled up on two sticks. The sign, visible even without his binoculars, said, "No More Dope, Save Our African Children!"

Leroy settled back into the easy chair and poured himself another cup of coffee. Twenty minutes later Obie was coming to the end of his speech, and it had been a good one. Leroy, just for the hell of it, took a walk over to the window again. He raised the binoculars and swept them slowly over the windows of all the buildings, including the one with the sign. Nothing.

He brought the glasses to bear directly on the window with the sign and carefully adjusted the focus.

The sign was still there, but the men who'd been standing in the window were nowhere in sight. Why? And something had changed about the sign. What the hell was it?

He focused the binoculars dead on the sign and saw what was different.

Right there where the sign—really a sheet—met the top of the window sill was a big hole in the cloth.

It hadn't been there before.

Leroy steadied his glasses on the window sill and looked intently at the tear in the sheet.

A piece of metal protruded through it. It glinted and moved.

He picked up the walkie-talkie and called the command post.

No answer. Only the crackling voices of the men who continued to talk as if they hadn't heard him.

"Come in!"

No answer.

Leroy knew what the trouble was. This cheap-assed walkie-talkie could receive but didn't have enough output to break through the insulating barriers caused by the building's structure.

Lord!

Had to get down there and warn the people.

He yelled into the bureaucrat's office, "Call the cops, tell them there's a sniper in a window of the Municipal Services Building across from the speakers' stand!"

Then Leroy was out in the hall and running to the elevator bank. He pushed the button, then waited. The bronze arrow on the elevator door remained still. He pressed it again. Still nothing. He ran to the end of the hall, where a red sign indicated a fire exit door:

For Use in Emergency Only.

Will Trigger Burglar and Fire Alarm

Leroy opened the door and hobbled down the steps, one at a time, his torn left tendon paining him with every movement. Those prisoners had really done a job on him. And the clanging of the burglar alarm was now echoing up and down the stairwell.

Good. Two security men , pistols drawn, were looking straight up at him.

"Get out there and tell them folks to get off the stage! There's a sniper across the street"

The cops both ran out the door, with Leroy limping behind them.

"Sniper!"

The cop who reached the stage first shouted and motioned for everybody to get down.

But the people panicked and began running to get off the stage. There was only one staircase, quickly clogged with people as the members of the gospel choir tried to escape. Their uniforms mixed in a black and white pile as they fell over each other on the floor just above the jammed stairs. Many of the singers began to leap from the stage onto the ground, as did some members of the platform party.

Even as they leapt, a minister wearing a gray shirt with a stiff white collar fell to the ground. A bullet had hit him as he bent down to help one of the choir members, a stout woman with gray hair and spectacles who'd been knocked to the floor by the crowd. Another singer, a short, round man who'd just been pounding Obie on the back and congratulating him, fell to the platform floor, blood pouring from his head.

Leroy heard people shouting.

"Mercy, mercy!"

"Jesus, save me!"

"Help me, somebody!"

Sobs, screams, shrieks, and cries came from the women.

Chairs lay tumbled and sprawled all across the floor.

In the center of the stage, crouching behind the lectern, Leroy saw Obie. He had the portable microphone.

"Folks, don't panic. Don't run. Keep calm. There's a sniper across the street, but the police will get him."

A bullet smashed into the top of the lectern right by Obie. Leroy yelled to him across the stage.

"Get out of there, the man wants to kill you! It's got to be Teagle."

Leroy beckoned Obie to come towards him, thinking they and others might escape back into City Hall. But he looked and saw there was no one to let them in—the doors only opened from the inside on weekends.

It didn't matter, Obie wouldn't go anyhow. But he did crouch way down behind the lectern.

"Well, he's just going to have to kill me, because I'm not going to have that crowd panicking."

It was already too late for that. At the fringes of the crowd, clusters of people broke away into the streets, then the rest began surging this way and that way. Looked like a herd of African wildebeest in flight from a lion. First the people would surge towards one street, than towards another.

Crack! Crack!

The bullets from the high-powered rifle smashed into the lectern, tearing away the top part. Obie went right on pleading for calm.

The shooting stopped.

Leroy looked across at the window where the men had been and saw four cops signaling to others down in the street—they'd found the location of the sniper. Obie slowly raised his head up, walked over to where the minister lay dead amid some choir members, then got down on his knees and prayed silently for a couple of minutes.

Leroy put his arm around his friend's shoulder. "Come on, soldier, there's folks need our help."

The crowd in the plaza slowly resolved itself into knots of people who stood in stunned, silent circles around the spots where folks had been trampled by the crowd trying to escape from the plaza. Police cars and ambulances, their sirens wailing, converged on the area. Soon police helicopters arrived, called in to evacuate the wounded.

Sure hadn't been no day of triumph.

SON TEAGLE WAS IN THE SUBWAY STATION. And pissed. Hadn't been for those choir members, motherfucker be dead by now. He went up to the cashier, bought a card, and went through the turnstile, turning his face to avoid the cop on duty.

Everything depended on time now. Shit! They'd made a bloody mess of the stage, now the cops would be all over his ass. He just hoped Raschid and Rufus would get to the car. Where was that damn train?

On his heels, people from the rally were flooding into the subway, many jumping right over the turnstile in their haste to escape the massacre scene. They'd do some hard thinking before they went to another anti-drug rally.

The lights of the train appeared up the track. Son boarded the coach, protected by the chaos all around him. He felt the automatic pistol inside his breast pocket, slumped down in a seat, pulled his cap down over his face, and pretended to be asleep. It was just one subway stop up to the garage where they'd parked the car.

A few minutes after the train pulled out of the station, it slowed, then crept to a dead stop. The car was packed, and there was no air conditioning. In the eight years he'd been away, city services had really gone down while the fare went up.

With a series of jerks, the train lurched forward. Only to stop again.

The conductor's voice came over the loudspeaker. "Sorry, folks, there'll be a delay. We should be moving in a few minutes, though."

Son knew what the trouble was. The cops were getting their forces together in the next subway station so they could search the train when it came in. They'd let one car come in at a time, search it, then have the next one inch into the station. And by now every cop in the city knew his face.

Son got up from his seat and started moving forward through the coaches. The car with the conductor was where he thought it would be, about two back from the front. He knocked on the door. A slim Chinese man with a goatee opened the door. Son pushed him back into the compartment, closed the door, and stuck his pistol under his chin.

"Now, listen to me, mister, I'm Son Teagle and I've killed a lot of people already today, and I hope I don't have to kill you. Do what I say and you be all right. Understand?"

The man nodded.

"You and me together, we're going up to the motorman's compartment. You get on that radio and tell him you're coming. This gun be in your back all the way up there, so don't try no shit. I'm one crazy motherfucker, and you look like you got a nice family. Now get on the phone."

The conductor obeyed, and in short order they were pushing their way through the crowd with the conductor saying, "Make way, we've got an emergency."

At the engineer's compartment the conductor gave the coded knock, and the door opened. The engineer, a short white man with aviator-type glasses, took one look at the conductor's face and tried to shut the door. Too late! Son had pushed the conductor into the cubicle and had his gun trained on both men.

To the conductor, he said, "Get down on the floor and just stay there. Ain't no room in here. And remember what I said about your family." He turned to the engineer. "Now, you got a real simple job. Just step down on that accelerator or whatever it is makes this thing go, and you run right on by that station coming up. You hear me?"

"But mister, we got signals, we have to follow them. There's probably something wrong with the track in the station."

Son slapped him dead up aside his head with the pistol. "Don't even think about lying to me, man. Just do what I said. Get going."

The engineer obeyed, and when the train pulled into the station where some twenty-five armed cops were waiting, it just kept on going.

"Nothing wrong with the tracks," Son said, and slapped the engineer aside the head one more time with the pistol. "You see what you almost got me into, man?"

Blood streamed down the side of the engineer's face. From his spot on the floor, the conductor said, "Hey, mister, he's got a family too. Two little daughters. Give him a break."

"Give you both a break if I get out of here all right," Son said. "And if I don't, I'm going to kill you both. Don't make me no difference noways."

In five minutes, the train approached the next station. Son looked out the window at the platform and saw no cops. He looked at the engineer.

"Okay," he said, "just let her in here real easy and everything's cool."

The man wiped his face with his blue kerchief, slowly applied the brakes, and brought the train to a halt. Son pointed to a microphone.

"This the radio cord?" The engineer nodded his head, and Son ripped the cord from its housing. "All right, you two get out of here and just sit down on one of those seats after you open the door. Move and you're dead."

The men obeyed, and Son hurried out of the car, mingling with the mass of people getting off the train. Some were grumbling because it had passed their stop.

He started to run up the subway stairs, only to look up and see two policemen standing at the top. They were scanning every face that went past. He'd have to take his chances right here. He stopped running and walked right up the middle of the steps.

He was almost past the policemen when one of them said, "Hey, you, the guy in the white jacket, just a second there."

"Yeah, officer, what can I do for you?"

The cop stepped up close to Son. "You look familiar. What's your name?"

The other officer kept on scanning the other passengers.

"My name's Mitch Rouse."

The cop took Son by the arm and pulled him away from the crowd. "Where are you going, Mr. Rouse?"

"Home, I been working all night. "

"Up against that car there."

"Man, why you got to be starting up with me?"

"No back-talk, mister, just do like I say." The cop was tall and had red, blue, and green ribbons on his summer shirt.

There was a commotion in the stairwell. The engineer and the conductor must be coming up the stairs to find a cop. The policeman turned his face away from Son for a second to locate the cause of the disturbance.

Son took off running. Once on the street he dashed across the roadway so recklessly that several cars skidded to a stop to avoid hitting him. Then he was into the shelter of trees and bushes of a large city park. Now he really began to run, breathing hard as he tried to make his way towards his neighborhood in North Philly.

Even as he cut through the park, he could hear the police sirens on all sides of him. They were trying to cut him off in the park. He wouldn't want to be the cop who had the bad luck to catch him.

A pretty young woman in blue shorts and a red T-top looked up as she saw Son coming towards her, screamed, and picked up her three-year-old girl, who was playing with a tiny tennis racquet. A male jogger, thin and dressed in matching gray shorts and top, veered off the path and into the woods the minute he saw Son.

Son kept running, forced ever deeper into the park by the sounds around him. Cops on foot patrol were blowing their whistles. And he could hear dobermans barking and yelping.

He found himself in an open clearing.

Thirty-five feet away, mounted on a brown horse and framed against the backdrop of a large white granite rock that dwarfed him, sat a cop in a white plastic helmet. He drew his gun, put his head down alongside the mane of the horse, and charged across the clearing straight at Son.

Son fell flat to the ground and pulled the German-made machine pistol from the holster concealed under his white suit jacket.

No time to aim. Just pull the damn trigger and hope.

The air was filled with the sound of gunfire and the smell of gunpowder.

The horse and rider crumpled and collapsed, like a kneeling horse in a circus act. Right in front of Son.

Terrible sounds came from the horse.

The cop, blood pouring over his white shirt, struggled to get from beneath the horse. Son stood straight up and fired the Schmeisser into the horse and the cop.

Silence came to the glade.

Son cut in a straight line across the park. Any more cops get in my way, I kill the motherfuckers or they kill me. Kill one cop, might as well kill them all.

Finally he came to a wall surrounding the park and pressed his body down into a space between it and a small hedge of bushes. He raised his head up above the wall and looked up and down the block. There was no traffic on the street.

But there was a cop car at either end of the block, and two armed cops on foot stationed along the block between the cars.

Son dropped down again into his hiding place.

He could stay where he was and wait until darkness to try and cross the street. But the dobermans might find him. Or he could make a break for it—try to get across the street now.

He reached into his pocket, pulled out an ammunition clip, and reloaded the Schmeisser. No sense in staying here. Think long, think wrong. He'd attack the cops right at their strength, just shoot up the fucking police car and try to break through to the projects. Shit, they'd been smoking cigarettes anyhow. By the time the cops up the block got down to the car, he'd be either dead or gone.

Son looked out of his hiding place to where some kids about ten years old were climbing on a big wooden jungle gym maybe a hundred yards away from him. The kids were having a real good time, and he remembered for a second how his mama had brought him out to the park to play when he was a little boy. One of the few times. Soon after daddy beat her one night and left.

Son leapt over the wall and ran directly at the police car, firing burst after burst from the Schmeisser. Just do or die!

CHAPTER 21

When Sarnese walked up the stairs to headquarters, the two guards at the door snapped to attention and saluted him even though he was in civilian clothes. He returned the salute. One guard said, "Good luck, Captain, we're with you." The other nodded his agreement.

"Appreciate it a lot, fellows."

He received the same warm greetings when he entered the building and checked in at the reception desk. He took the elevator, got off at the second floor, and walked into the commissioner's outer office. There, at the invitation of the secretary, he took a seat.

Usually he bantered with her. This was a very pretty lady, and she always wanted to talk, but after a few brief exchanges he fell silent.

He didn't have long to wait. A couple of minutes later, the commissioner came out of his office.

"Chief Inspector Branson's inside, John. We're ready for you."

Sarnese followed the short, paunchy commissioner into his office and greeted the chief.

The commissioner said, "O'Brien's off the force. When it comes to consequences for your failure of supervision, I've decided to give you a choice. You understand how grave a matter it was. Because you failed to adequately control your people, peaceful protesting citizens were hurt. But there's something else. You've been a fine cop all your career, and this is the only blemish on your record."

Sarnese wished he'd get to the point.

"In light of that, I'm going to permit you to retire voluntarily from the force. I have the papers here on the desk, all you have to do is sign them. The chief will be a witness, and the whole matter will be closed."

"You mean I'll get my full pension?"

"Everything you've got coming to you, plus the accumulated sick days." He looked at the papers and said, "You've got nearly a year's worth of vacation time and sick time, comes to about a sixty-thousand-dollar cash payout at the time you retire. In addition to that, your annual retirement will come to about seventy-five thousand a year."

"That's pretty good."

The chief said, "You worked for it, every bit of it."

"And if I don't accept it?"

The commissioner lifted his eyes from the papers on the desk. The chief leaned forward in his chair and put his hand on Sarnese's knee.

"John, I've known you a long time. Believe me, I've thought this thing out. It's what's best for you and Angie. Take the offer."

"I think, for old time's sake, I at least deserve a straight answer to my question."

The chief nodded at the commissioner, who said, "If you don't retire, you'll be demoted to the rank of lieutenant and placed on two months' suspension without pay."

Sarnese looked at the chief for a long moment. Finally he said, "I always respected you, thought it was mutual. Now I'm hearing an offer to buy me out, bribe me, make me admit I did something wrong when I didn't do a damm thing wrong and you know it. How could you be a part of this?"

The chief's face turned red.

"John, believe me—"

"Chief, don't even bother to say anything. You'll make me feel sorry for you." He turned to face the commissioner. "I'm not retiring. Not me, not John Sarnese. You want to punish me for doing my job, you go right ahead. When does the suspension start?"

The chief said, "At least for your wife's sake, think about what you're doing. Think about the kids. Why end a great career like this, when you've got a chance to go out with a spotless record?"

"I've already talked this over with Angie, and you know what? She agrees I shouldn't take you guys off the hook. As for the kids,

Chief, I think mine will be a lot prouder of their old man than yours will when they hear what you did to me."

The commissioner got up and walked back around the table so that he was right in front of Sarnese.

"All right, John, I was trying to give you a break, but you won't let me. O'Brien's not only being dismissed, a grand jury's about to bring charges against him and three other men in your precinct. All four have been taking money and sex to let the dealers—including Teagle's boys—operate in your bailiwick. What do you say to that?'

Sarnese half-rose in his seat. "What? Why didn't—"

"And one of them has already agreed to turn state's evidence."

Sarnese had never seen such a mournful look on the chief's face. "I tried to tell you, John, told you to just pack it in and go on up to the lake."

The commissioner had returned to his seat. "You're dismissed, captain. The punishment will be effective at twelve midnight today. If you change your mind before then, you can reach either the chief or me. The secretary will give you our itineraries for the rest of the day."

The chief walked towards the door as if he wanted to accompany Sarnese down the elevator, but Sarnese waved him off. He'd deal with this in his own way. Thirty-some odd years and not even a hint of a bribe, ever. And now this! All of the strength seemed to go out of his body, he could barely trust his legs as he walked down the outside steps of the building. When he set out on his career he'd been determined to bring nothing but honor and respect to his people, Italian people. He wasn't going to let one bit of that Mafia stuff touch him—he'd be an example to Italian kids that there was a better way to make your mark here in America. Over the years, through everything, somehow, he'd believed that integrity couldn't be totally defeated by corruption. Now, O'Brien and whoever else was involved in these schemes had trashed the one thing he treasured most, his reputation as a good cop.

More than that, he was thoroughly pissed because he'd truly believed that no one could ever pull the wool over his eyes—not his kids, not the criminals, nobody! And now O'Brien, probably with the help of some desk officers in the precinct, had done exactly that. Just how was he ever going to hold his head up high again, or face his friends or neighbors—for surely everybody would believe that he himself had been on the take.

SARNESE WAS DRIVING UP BROAD STREET on the way to his Frankford home. It was two o'clock in the morning, and he was going to have some tall explaining to do. The truth was that he hated to lie, and it pained him every time he had to tell Angie some story about having been out with the boys when he'd really been with Bernadette.

When he was still the precinct captain it had been easy to find excuses—he'd just told her he was making the rounds to check on things. And she never questioned him, even though he sometimes came in at five in the morning, having gone to Bernadette around six-thirty, had a good dinner, good sex afterwards, and then a decent seven hours of sleep.

He still hadn't come up with a good excuse when he turned on the police scanner he kept in his private car. Things had really changed since the cops had started the "blue flu" four days ago, protesting the measures taken against him. Hastily assembled National Guard units—mainly composed of upstaters—patrolled the streets. Unfamiliar with the city and the way its streets were laid out, they were no match for the roving gangs of teenagers committing hit and run robberies all over the town. It went without saying that the National Guard units were totally lost in the subway system. And most of the police work in the city was being done by supervisory personnel—sergeants and above.

It really was breaking Sarnese's heart. Especially considering that he was the cause of all this trouble. It was a mess, and he wished with all his soul it was over. That and the coming disclosure about the scandal. Still didn't know how he'd be able to look his kids in the eye when the news broke.

As he approached North Philly and his old precinct, he felt another twinge of sadness—this time caused by the fact that he was not on the job. Then, over the scanner, he heard the voice of a female sergeant from his precinct saying, "All units to 787 Windsor Street. It's a brownstone. Officer down, Sergeant Walker is down. Send a bus. They've got Teagle cornered in the house, urgently need backup. And hurry! The guy has an arsenal inside and there are only three officers over there."

Sarnese figured he was maybe five minutes from the house. He instinctively hit his side to check that the gun was there. It was, and he thanked God that he'd not left it home when Angie said, "Listen, Johnnie, you're suspended. You don't have to carry a gun."

He floored the accelerator of the Buick sedan and took off up the highway at eighty miles an hour. He braked at Cecil B. Moore Avenue, then swerved onto that street and drove crosstown, narrowly missing some early morning drivers.

He turned into Windsor Street and saw what to an old-time cop was a terrible sight. There were two police cars in the street where there should have been fifteen. The call he'd heard was supposed to bring all available help to the spot. Looked like it was just him and three cops to take on Son Teagle and whoever was with him.

So be it!

Sarnese drove slowly down the street and pulled his car behind one of the other police cars. As he came to a stop, a burst of automatic weapon fire blew out all the windows on the passenger side of the car and showered his face with splinters of glass, a few of which drew blood. He opened his door and rolled out of the car and onto the street.

On the sidewalk, directly in front of the house the fire was coming from, lay Robbie Walker. Two sergeants Sarnese didn't know were pinned down behind their cars, in the same situation he was.

He yelled over to them, "That's my man down there."

"We know, captain. Are we glad to see you! Teagle's in that house, but we've only got one man around back."

Sarnese said, "Let's not worry about Teagle now. First thing we got to do is get Robbie out of there." He yelled, "Robbie! It's me, you hit bad?"

"Yeah, in the side, lost a lot of blood."

"Hang on," Sarnese said, peering around the front tire of his car. "I'm going to get you out of there. Paramedics should be here in a minute." He looked over at the two policemen. "Hey, you guys, you got to give me some covering fire."

One of the sergeants, an older man with gray hair and a stomach that suggested he hadn't stayed in good shape, said, "Give us a second to reload."

A white ambulance with luminescent orange markings, its siren on and its lights flashing, rolled slowly into the end of the street. Not one house had its lights on. But the windows of some had been thrown open, and the sound of rap music poured out into the street. Robbie moaned.

Sarnese said, "You guys get loaded up or I'm going out there without you."

"All right, Captain, we're ready," the woman sergeant said. "Just give the word."

"Now! Open up!"

The two sergeants crouched down behind the fenders of their cars and fired in rapid bursts at the second-floor windows the automatic fire had come from.

Sarnese waited two seconds, then leapt out onto the sidewalk. He'd barely reached Robbie before a withering fire from the third-floor window broke out. From that higher angle the shooter got the woman sergeant, who screamed as she went down.

The other sergeant continued to fire, but now the entire second and third floors' windows were ablaze with flashing bursts of fire.

Sarnese saw it would be damn near impossible to get Robbie back to safety under the circumstances. But marines didn't leave nobody out like that. Never had and never will! He might die doing it, but he was going to give it a try. So he put his arms under Robbie, who lay sprawled across the front steps of the building, lifted him up, and staggered the ten feet to the shelter of the police car. When he got there, he nearly collapsed under the dead weight of his former driver. His heart was pounding pretty bad.

Across from him behind the other car lay the dead sergeant, her body sprawled in the street. He looked down at Robbie, lying now with his head propped up on a pillow Sarnese had made out of his suit jacket.

"You're going to be okay, don't worry."

Sarnese barely heard the shouts of encouragement and applause coming from the people in the block.

"Captain, you shouldn't have done that, but I thank you for it." Robbie closed his eyes and died.

Down the street Sarnese saw the emergency vehicle, its driver afraid to venture deeper into the street. And still there were no other police vehicles in the block. Where the hell was the fucking National Guard? Probably couldn't find the street.

He called over to the remaining sergeant, a short man of about forty who had his back up against the side of the squad car and was reloading his revolver.

"Can you still contact that man you got around back?"

"Sure, he's out there, but God help him if Teagle and those guys with him decide to come out."

"Think we can get the shotguns out of the cars?"

"You can't be thinking we can get Teagle with just us three. We got to have backup, Captain."

He was right—under ordinary circumstances—but the backup might not come any time soon, and Teagle might break out and escape any minute, and Sarnese could see the headlines: "Cop-killer Escapes Sarnese!" He would not have that on top of everything else.

"It's not here, and we've got Teagle cornered. He's not going to stay in there all day, and we've got a hell of a better chance of surviving if we go in after him before he comes out after us."

"All right, Captain." The sergeant put his pistol in his holster, reached into the front of the car, and unlocked the shotgun from its rack. He crawled over the body of his companion and got the shotgun from the other car. Then he bent down over the dead sergeant, took her bullet-proof vest off, and tossed it to Sarnese, who shook his head, then laid it on the ground. It wouldn't fit him.

Sarnese said, "Let me have that walkie-talkie, would you?"

The sergeant handed it and a shotgun to him. He loaded the gun, then called the policeman who was guarding the rear entrance of the house

"This is Captain John Sarnese. We've been catching hell out front here, but we got to get this guy. Any activity back there yet?"

"No, Captain." From his voice, Sarnese could tell he was young and scared.

"Tell me, son, does it look like there's more than one exit out there?"

"No, Captain."

"How long have you been a sergeant?"

"Only about a month."

"Well, they don't give those stripes away for nothing—you must be pretty sharp to have earned them so fast. Okay, me and Sergeant Bowman out here, we're going in. You just cover that back door and everything will be fine. Any bastard comes out, open up with everything you got. We're going to get that son of a bitch today."

He turned to the sergeant beside him. "Cover me—I'm going to break for that door. When I get there, I'm going to start firing straight up into that window. When I start shooting, you come on. Once we get into the front vestibule, we'll reload and start up the steps."

"Captain...I could lose my rank, much less my life, obeying your orders. You're still suspended, you know."

"Yeah, I know that, Bowman, so what're you going to do? Because I'm telling you—"

"I know, Captain, you'll go in by yourself. Let's move."

The sergeant returned to his post by the fender and opened up on the second-floor window. Sarnese made it to the shelter of the small alcove at the top of the steps. He put the shotgun down, stepped out a bit from the alcove, then aimed his revolver at the window and fired four shots, smashing out the remaining panes and causing a momentary pause in the firing from the second floor.

The sergeant, carrying his shotgun and a beltful of ammunition, broke from behind the car, ran across the street, and leapt up the steps, taking them two at a time.

"Let's go," Sarnese said. "You know the drill."

He blew open the front door with shots from his revolver, and he and the sergeant burst onto the first-floor landing. Silence.

Sarnese didn't wait. While the sergeant posted himself against the banister, his shotgun pointed at the head of the staircase, Sarnese, holding his shotgun balanced over his left elbow, crept slowly up the stairs. What would be would be, but he was not letting Teagle get away.

A tall, thin, yellow man leapt into the hallway and landed on the second floor. A blast from Sergeant Bowman's shotgun blew the man's head apart even as his finger was closing on the trigger of his Schmeisser automatic pistol. He toppled down, his body thumping from stair to stair. Sarnese moved aside quickly lest he be been knocked down by the falling body, and as he did so, he took his gaze off the landing above for just a second.

"Captain, watch out!"

Son Teagle stood at the head of the stairs, eyes red and mean, machine pistol aimed directly at Sarnese. Behind him stood Raschid in his white Safari hat.

Son said, "Welcome, motherfuckers." Both men opened up with their machine pistols.

Sarnese knew Teagle was hit—in the upper arm or shoulder—but not killed. Running right out the door, and firing.

Knew he himself was hit but not killed.

Way he felt, he wasn't sure which he was sorriest about.

CHAPTER 22

IT WAS EARLY OF A FALL Carolina morning, and the sky was blue as could be. Dora Lee got out of her bed, put on a pair of slacks and a blouse, started a pot of coffee to percolating, and walked out of Boatwright's house as she often did when she was troubled to the point of despair.

She began walking down the long dirt road that led to the main highway. The trees were full of singing birds, and Dora Lee saw one squirrel running along a power line, balancing itself like a trapeze artist. He seemed to want to keep pace with her. When she stopped, he stopped too and rose up on two legs. Then she'd begin walking again, and the squirrel would drop back on all fours and keep up with her.

The dust of the road was very red here, reminded her of all the blood shed over the years in the city where she'd grown up laughing and playing hopscotch on hot sidewalks with Jewish, Hispanic, Irish, and Chinese children. Dora Lee felt just like she did when Obie got called up to serve in Iraq. Like she was a wife on the home front, waiting for the battles to be over up there in Philly.

With Boatwright driving the van, Sabaya had been safely delivered to Oberlin College. And here they were back in Carolina with Timba's first day of classes coming up tomorrow. It would also be Dora Lee's first day as a secretary at a hospital in Gastonia. She'd even managed to buy an old Dodge Colt to get her back and forth to the job. But she had no peace in her soul.

As Dora Lee walked along the red dirt road she began to sing a hymn she loved:

Are you weak and heavy-laden,
'Cumbered with a world of care?
Precious savior, still my refuge
Take it to the Lord in prayer.

As at so many other times in her life, a sense of fullness and satisfaction began to replace the heaviness and emptiness in her chest. She talked out loud, first telling God about her situation, how torn up she was, how frightened....

And so this tall, ebony-skinned woman walked on and on down the road with her hips moving slowly back and forth in a timeless African rhythm, asking that God somehow reunite her with her husband, remove the danger that pervaded all their lives, assuage her desperate, sickening fear....

WALKING AND PRAYING AND SINGING, Dora Lee must have gone a mile down that red country road before she reached the main highway. A car flashed by. She turned and went back to the house. When she reached the driveway, Timba was sitting on the steps, dressed only in his pajama bottoms.

"Mama, where you been? I was about ready to come looking for you."

Dora Lee laughed as he came up to her. "You hadn't waked up so early, you wouldn't even of known I was gone."

"Auntie already cooking breakfast, be ready in about ten minutes."

"Well, then, why don't you just walk down the road with me for a little bit? Do you good."

"Don't feel like it, I'm sore from all that tackling yesterday. These southern boys are rough, they're some ferocious people."

"Come on anyhow. After tomorrow, we won't have that much time to talk, what with the new job and all."

Timba started down the road, his mother's arm around his shoulder. "I really did want to ask you something, guess I might as well do it now." He was looking down, like he was worried about the answer to his question. "What's going to happen to Daddy and you?"

"I really can't tell you a whole lot, honey. Right now, your daddy's got to stay up north because he's not sure he can get a job here, and we need the money for Sabaya's education. Jobs up north pay a lot more than down here. And maybe you won't understand this, but he's the big brother and he doesn't want to have to come down here and depend on Uncle Boat to tide us over till he gets a job. It's a pride thing."

She pulled him a little closer. "And it's just too dangerous up there for us to live. We wouldn't have an hour of peace up there."

"But why hasn't Daddy at least come down and visited us? Just for a few days, anyhow?"

Children always knew how to ask hurting questions.

"Baby, your daddy's doing the best he can. He's carrying a big load up there in the city what with all that trouble. His people need him, and long as Teagle isn't caught, he just can't walk away, not even for a few days. Even if we had the plane fare, which we don't. And Aunt Justine needs him too." She smiled. "He talks to you every day, honey. He still loves you just as much, believe me. And so does your mama."

BY TEN O'CLOCK, the family was pulling up in the Blazer to a white wooden church way out in the country. It could only be reached by traveling five miles down a dirt road, and it had been the Bullock family church since shortly after the Civil War. In a graveyard behind the church were tombstones marking the burial places of the Bullock parents, grandparents, and great-grandparents. The church had been founded by Great-grandfather Nathaniel Bullock when he'd returned after fighting in a Union regiment during the war. Whenever Dora Lee came down here, she placed fresh flowers on the graves of Nathaniel Bullock and his wife, Sarah, on whose tombstone was inscribed, "Traveling Days Are Over."

The clearing in front of the church was filled with people, the men all dressed in suits despite the heat, the women wearing wide-brimmed straw hats and bright-colored dresses that set off their shining dark skin. In the yard of the church, little children just let out of Sunday School ran back and forth in a game of hide-and-go-seek. One boy, about four years old, hid behind Dora

Lee's skirts from a little girl who was "it." Dora Lee laughed and tried to act like she didn't know he was there.

A deacon, his light brown face creased with lines, came out of the church and stood on its top step. Dressed in a neat but worn old black suit and a black tie, he looked out over the crowd of worshippers.

"Folks, it's time. Time to enter unto the house of the Lord."

Slowly the worshippers walked up the church's creaking yet solid wooden steps. The children stopped playing and ran to reattach themselves to their families. Timba took Dora Lee's arm and guided her up the stairs, the way he'd seen his daddy do so many times.

The church was paneled with polished birchwood—Boatwright and some of the men had spent a week of evenings plus a weekend doing the job. A golden cross stood before the altar, and the wall that formed the background was covered with a purple cloth on which a Latin sentence was embossed in gold leaf. The frosted glass windows were always kept open to the outdoors in the summer and fall. You could look through them as Dora Lee often did and see the seasons change Sunday by Sunday. The pews were sturdy oak benches, and as Dora Lee had learned over the years of visits, each pew by custom belonged to a particular family. As members of the founding family, Dora Lee and Timba sat with Martha Ann in a front pew.

Boatwright sat across from them with the other four deacons. Being their head, he stood up and broke into a song that started the service:

Jesus is a rock....

He was joined by the congregation— female voices high, some steady, some quavering and breaking; male voices deep and gravelly as the rough dirt roads:

In a weary laaaand,
Weary land,
Weeeeary laaaand!

Boatwright began a slow, rhythmic clapping. By the time the last line of the hymn was reached, everybody in the church right down to the two-year-olds was clapping in rhythm, using the time and space between claps to accentuate the power of the music. They made of emptiness an accompanying instrument.

He's a shelter in the time of trial...

As Dora Lee clapped, her body began to sway from side to side in time with the rhythm. Boatwright raised the pitch of his voice just a little bit higher, and the congregation moved up with him: "Jesus is a rock...."

Dora Lee saw Son Teagle's face. "Jesus is a rock!" Son's face was gone, wiped out. She saw Sabaya coming home that morning after her abduction. "Jesus is a rock." Son vanished again. Her mind rested for a second on her man, Obie, and she heard Rita's voice answering the phone when she called. "Jesus is a rock!"

Her mind must have floated away, because Boatwright was saying, "All rise. We're now turning our service over to the minister of music."

A middle-aged woman in a yellow dress with a red flower pinned to its front sat down at the piano, then looked towards the rear of the church, where the choir was gathered. Satisfied they were ready, she dropped her head in a signal to them and began to play, "Walk in the Light, Beautiful Light." Dora Lee looked up at the front of the church, where a shaft of sunshine was falling directly into the space before the altar.

The choir, the women in black skirts and white cotton blouses, the men in black pants and white shirts, started marching down the aisle, their bodies moving in the same swaying cadence towards the front of the church.

Down where the dewdrops of heaven shine bright....

Every voice was distinct to Dora Lee as they passed her, and each seemed to have been honed and given its own peculiar tones of sorrow and joy. It was as if they were vessels through which poured the spirits of the slaves who'd tilled the fields around the church for over a hundred years before the Civil War.

Shine all around me by day and by night....

The choir took its place in the pews down front, and the entire church joined in the singing of the song. Dora Lee thought her heart would burst with joy, for she knew with great certainty that no evil could come nigh her in the midst of such power. Oh, I want to thank you, Jesus, for this song, and for this morning, and for this church.

Boatwright prayed out loud about "Hard trials, cruel tribulations," and Dora Lee clasped Timba's hand and prayed that God would put a fence of protection around her family. The choir began to sing, low now, the song that had sustained her through all of her life:

Sweet hour of prayer, sweet hour of prayer
That calls me from a world of care...

She was a four-year-old girl, and Big Mama, after a night of weeping when she heard that her husband had died of an heart attack while on duty, was sitting beside her just as Dora Lee was now sitting beside Timba. She remembered the grace that had filled her soul then as she heard the words:

In seasons of distress and grief,
My soul hath often found relief.

A short, round woman wearing thick glasses jumped up and shouted, "Thank you, Jesus!"

Without a thought, Dora Lee stood up herself and began shouting, "Can't stand it no more, Master! But I want to thank you, anyhow!"

She fell back into her seat, her head between her hands.

Great sobs came from her, even when Timba and Martha Ann embraced her. The choir and congregation just kept on singing the song, repeating verse after verse.

Dora Lee opened her mouth and the praise poured out. The fear and sorrow that weighted her soul seemed to leave with the words, "My soul hath often found relief."

The minister, a tall, light brown-skinned man with a beard, was standing behind the small wooden lectern. He looked out over the congregation.

"Oh, what a mighty God we serve! Ain't he all right, now? If he saved somebody in here, just put your hand up and say thank you."

Everybody raised their hand, and the people waved them back and forth to show that God had touched their lives, just like the preacher was saying.

He began slowly to hum the melody of another one of Dora Lee's favorites, "Just a Closer Walk with Thee, Grant It Jesus If You Please." The preacher's eyes closed, and his voice quavered on each note of the music. When he'd finished the last line of the song, he fell silent for a moment, then started talking, his voice low and earnest.

Dora Lee's soul was rested. She could hear the preacher's words, but it was like God had cleared her mind of the world and all the troubles of her life.

"Yes, sir, yes, ma'am," the minister was saying, "we got us a black president now, but we are still in deep trouble as a people. Folks ain't got jobs and some young black boys would as soon kill you as look at you. Kill you for looking, same way them white people down in Mississippi killed Emmet Till. Why, I heard that in Philadelphia, the children got some saying they'll all either be Carried by Six or Tried by Twelve. Have Mercy! Young men think they either going to be killed or sent to the penitentiary. Mercy!

"Can I get a witness?"

"Amen!" came right back at him.

"I don't know how we got here. But I know what's going to get us out of this mess.

"We got a God!

"Oh, yes we do!
"Who sits high!
"Yes, he do!
"And looks low,
"That's my Lord!
"He's a father,
"Yes, he is.
"To the fatherless
"Mmmmmmmmmmmmmmmmmmmmmm.
"And a mother
To the motherless
"Mmmmmmmmmmmmmmmmmmmmmmmmmmmm.
"He's so wide you can't get around him
"MMMMMMMMMMMMMMMMMMMMMMMM!
"So tall you can't get over him
"Mmmmmmmmmmmmmmmmmmmmmmmmmmmmmmmmm.
"So deep you can't get under him
"Mmmmmmmmmmmmmmmmmmmmmmmmmmmmmmmmm!
"Amen, mighty God, amen!"

The choir director got up from her seat in the congregation, moved back to the piano, and began to sing in a low, rich voice:

That's all right, that's all right,
That's all right, it will be all right!

And it was. Dora Lee just knew it. It was <u>all</u> all right.

CHAPTER 23

SON WAS SITTING UP in a bed in Raschid's girlfriend's apartment in Nicetown. A bandage was around his shoulder where the bullets from the shotgun had injured it. It was forty-eight hours since he'd shot those cops, and as he looked at the television he saw he'd managed all by himself, bad nigger that he was, to make the cops come back to work. Well, maybe that wasn't quite true, it was really because he'd shot the wrong one, Sarnese. Not fatally—but bad enough to land him on the critical list.

The cops were not only back, they were working voluntary overtime trying to find Son. Wouldn't be long before they came looking for Raschid, but there was no place else to go.

Raschid, sitting at a round dinner table in the studio apartment, was cleaning his AR-15 carbine and drinking a bottle of beer. As always, there was very little expression on his face. Nothing would make him happier than to see a bunch of cops break through the door of their ground-floor apartment.

In the little alcove that served as a kitchen, Carlyne, Raschid's girlfriend, was cooking some bacon and eggs. It was the last food in the apartment. Son didn't trust her to go out and buy more. Raschid had only been going with the girl for a month or so, and that wasn't long enough to trust anyone.

"Yo, Raschid, we got to get some food in here, man."

"Tell me about it."

"We know they got Malika's line tapped. I'm thinking now we got to call Rita."

"What? Man, you promised her long time ago she could live free."

"That was then—eight years ago. She made a lot of money when she was working for us. And I didn't mean for her to be starting up with all this anti-drug crap and hanging out with Obie Bullock.

That wasn't no part of the deal. Told her if she helped us with getting that coke in from Nigeria, she could live on easy street. So fine, that's what she been doing. Now it's payback time."

Son pushed himself further up in the bed and felt a slight dizziness, but it passed. "Hand me the phone. We should be ready to get out of here tomorrow, and I got me a few more little ideas. We been through a lot lately."

From the kitchen the smell of eggs and bacon wafted through the apartment. Carlyne had her head stuck close to the radio, trying to listen to a black talk show on WURD over the sound of the television in the living room.

"Hey, Son, they talking about you on the radio station."

Son nodded to Raschid, who cut off the television. Carlyne turned up the radio and they heard the voice of a call-in listener.

"...see it, Son Teagle is really a freedom fighter. This racist society made him. He wasn't nothing but a shelter child, every time he was in a school, they'd move him to another hotel in a few weeks. Had him and his mama sitting up in chairs till ten o'clock at night waiting for shelter space, then send him off to some strange school in the morning and expect him to learn and behave. Living with nothing but drug dealers around him all his life? Now, what's he supposed to be? What do he see all day long? Boy see evil all his life, it bound to become a part of him."

Son nodded his agreement with the caller. Felt kind of funny having people talk about you on the radio.

"And they shouldn't never have put that boy's mama out on no street, the way they done it. It's a sin and a shame the way they treated her. All that man be doing is demanding some respect for his mother."

"Whoa, there, my good sister," the talk-show host said. "I grant you some points, but here this man is putting poison into the veins of our children, and you call him some kind of freedom fighter. Here he is shooting down black people, and you calling him a freedom fighter. He's shooting black cops, and you calling him a freedom fighter. And just yesterday they got the DNA results on his brother, Trevon—turns out he was the one killed and raped Shakeisha. Whatever happened to him when he was a boy, he's sure enough a criminal as a man, and I hope they catch him and electrocute his butt."

Son yelled, "Turn that motherfucking radio off! I ain't listening to that shit." He couldn't believe what he'd just heard. Didn't think Trevon could do a thing like that—never would believe it, no matter how many DNA tests they ran. But it hurt him pretty bad, right down there in the gut, because nobody should ever harm a child, just wasn't right.

Carlyne, now serving the breakfast, ran into the kitchen area and clicked the radio off. She came back to the main room, sat down on the couch, and watched a television quiz show while the two men ate and talked.

Son noticed that she was constantly shifting position on the couch. "Give the bitch some more coke, Raschid. Acting like she scared of us, or something. What kind of women you go out with, man?"

Raschid laughed and went over to a kitchen cabinet, where he got out a supply of the powder. He nodded to Carlyne, who came over and took a small amount into the bathroom.

Son had finished his meal. "Now I'm calling Rita."

"Suppose she tells the cops? What we going to do then?"

"She ain't about to do that. All the shit I got against her, and Malika got it in the safe. No, Rita ain't going to do nothing but what we tell her. Bring me the phone over here."

Son dialed her number. He waited for a moment as the phone rang at the other end, then suddenly hunched forward and said, "Rita, that you, baby? It's Son."

Silence.

"What's the matter? Can't you say nothing?"

"What you doing calling me? You promised you'd let me be."

"That was a long time ago. Things changed. I need you now."

"I've gone straight, I got a new life now."

"With Bullock, right?"

"There's nothing between us. I'm just a new person now, God has come into my life. Leave me alone."

"No way. You got to do some things for me, and you got to do them now. Thought I was safe and away up in that jail, didn't you? You going to do what I want, won't take long, then I'll let you be."

"I won't, Son. I don't care what you do to me."

"Cut the shit out, Malika has enough stuff to put you away for twenty-five years. How would your darling daughter in college and Big Obie Bullock like that? As a matter of fact, I might have my boys pay a little visit to your daughter. And you know how Raschid is, now don't you?"

There was silence on the other end of the phone. Then Rita began to cry.

"What you want me to do?"

IT WAS FOUR O'CLOCK in the afternoon when the chimes in the doorway of the studio apartment sounded. Son reached over to the table and grabbed the Schmeisser pistol. Raschid picked up his semi-automatic, went to the door, and looked through the peephole.

"It's her, it's Rita."

"Be careful, look like anybody else out there?"

"She by herself."

"Okay, open the door," Son said.

Rita was just as good-looking as she'd been years ago when she was Son's secret girlfriend. She had two bags of groceries in her arms and was dressed in a red blouse and a white suit.

Raschid pulled her into the room with a quick jerk of his arm, then slammed the door behind her.

"That's not necessary. Treat me like a lady." Rita walked over to the kitchen area and put the bags down on the counter. "You did some nasty things in your life, but this is the worst."

"Don't say shit to me."

While Carlyne was putting the groceries away, Rita sat down at the table with Raschid and Son. She reached into her pocketbook, took out an envelope, and threw it and a pair of car keys onto the table. She reached back into the pocketbook and pulled out five thousand dollars in fresh one-hundred-dollar bills. She put the money on the table beside the other items.

"This is everything you asked for. I parked the car outside."

She got up from the table and headed towards the door.

She had her hand on the knob when Son said, "Come back here, bitch. You don't think you're going to walk out on me like that, do you? I ain't done with you yet."

Rita kept her face towards the door. "I got everything you asked me to. And I'm not crazy enough to tell the cops after I went and brought these things over here. Just let me go. I'm leaving town."

"No you ain't, not yet. You got to give me one more little thing."

"Son, you know I ain't going to sleep with you, so you can forget it."

"That ain't no bad idea, but it's not what was on my mind." He smiled. "I need to know where the Bullock family is."

Rita froze. Just like she did when he used to checkmate her king when they played chess together.

"You tell me. Now. Exactly where his kids and wife are hiding."

"I don't know. And if I did I wouldn't tell you—it would be just like murdering them."

"And what you think he done to my brother?"

"Son, they didn't do it, Obie did."

"I'm going to get his ass too, but first I'm going to find his family and kill them, so he can see just how it feels deep down inside to have your kin shot down in cold blood. Let him suffer a while, shed some tears, do some praying in church about that, then I'll finish him off."

Rita had walked over to the couch where she now slumped down. Carlyne sat trembling at the other end, her eyes wild and dilated.

"I don't know, Son. That's the gospel truth. Obie won't tell nobody, sure didn't tell me."

Son walked over to her and slapped her across the face. The force of the blow knocked her to the floor, where she lay with a trickle of blood flowing from her mouth.

Son reached down his left hand and grabbed her by the hair, lifting her up so that she was in a sitting position on the floor. Once she was upright, he slapped her again, knocking her again to the floor.

Carlyne began to cry softly. Son turned to her.

"Bitch, shut up, before I do you the same." He stood over Rita. "You know me, and you know I will get the whereabouts of Dora Lee and those children. And you won't lie to me, because you know if you lie I'll have your sweet daughter killed. Now, you just better save yourself some trouble . You seen what I do to people, and that ain't even to folks that call Bullock a friend."

He looked at Raschid. "Man, get some of that coke out of there. We'll just inject this bitch with it a little bit before we beat up on her some more."

Rita sat upright on the floor, tears running down her cheeks and mingling with the blood coming from her nose and mouth.

"His wife and kids are staying with his brother, Boatwright Bullock, on a farm in North Carolina about fifteen miles outside of Gastonia."

"Better not be lying to me, Rita, because I'm a man of my word. Now make yourself comfortable here—you ain't going nowhere till me and Raschid is ready to go, and that won't be for a while. What's the phone number down there?"

"I don't know, but it's probably listed."

Son got the number, then asked the operator, "That's in Gastonia, right, ma'am?"

"No, sir, it's in Pine Hill, about fifteen miles south of Gastonia."

Son dialed the number. A woman answered.

"Hello, Mrs. Bullock, this is FedEx in Gastonia. We have a package here for you from Philadelphia and need directions out to your place. I see here by the address that you're right outside of Pine Hill, but how do we find the house?"

"Oh, that's easy enough," said the woman, who proceeded to

give him exact directions to the Bullock place.

Three hours later, after making several other phone calls and eating again, Son and Raschid were ready to leave.

Raschid said, "I think we ought to get rid of Rita. Much as she meant to you one time, man, that bitch is going to cause us some pain. She'll mess us up, you watch."

"No, Rita ain't going to do nothing, because she done heard me tell Rollo to kill her daughter if the cops catch me. Besides, she damn sure don't feel like going to jail for no twenty-five years. Shit, even Bullock ain't worth that—is he, Rita?"

Rita was sitting in the middle of the couch, watching the television with Carlyne. She hadn't said a word but had smoked nearly half a pack of cigarettes while waiting for Son to leave.

"I'm not a fool. I just wish you'd get out of here."

"We're leaving now. But come here just for a second. I want to see how bad I hurt you."

Rita got up and walked over to where Son was standing at the door with Raschid.

"Come a little closer, it's getting dark and I can't see your face."

Rita moved to within an arm's length of Son. He hit her hard across her face, this time with his fist closed. The blow knocked her into the kitchen area, where her head slammed against the refrigerator door. She fell to the floor and lay sprawled at the bottom of the stove.

Son turned to Raschid. "Tie both of them up."

When Raschid was finished, Son took the keys and the rental car forms off the table and said, "So long, Rita. You better thank your lucky stars I still feel something for you."

He and Raschid walked out. Son, immaculately dressed in a suit and looking just like a businessman, was whistling....

OBIE SAT WITH LEROY and two of his bodyguards watching the Saturday evening college football game. It helped take his mind off the loneliness and sadness he felt, being away from his family and all. Today had been a little better than most. Reverend

Johnson had pulled a miracle and found a drug rehabilitation place willing to accept Justine for treatment. They'd dropped her off the day before, and he was determined to hope for the best and stop tormenting himself with thoughts about what his baby sister's life could have been like.

Syracuse, Obie's favorite team—because it had been the team of Philadelphia's own Bernie Custis from John Bartram High, Ernie Davis, Floyd Little, Larry Csonka, Jim Nance, Jim Brown, and Donovan McNabb—was leading Alabama, by a touchdown and a field goal. Looked like they had a chance of scoring an upset.

A beer in his hand, Obie cheered as a swift quarterback swept towards the right end behind two huge linemen, then stopped, eyed his receiver in the end zone, and threw a pass that hit the flanker dead in his numbers. Touchdown, Syracuse!

In the commercial break afterwards, Obie turned to his companions. "Looks like we're going to have us a good one tonight. What say let's get in some fried chicken for the halftime?" He'd just finished ordering a big bucket when the gong at the front door sounded. He put his hand over the telephone mouthpiece. "Hey, Leroy, see who it is, would you?"

He went back to the telephone, and the chicken place asked if he wanted biscuits with the order. Obie hesitated, remembering what the doctor had said, but then who was he to deprive his buddies of good hot bread? "Send us about a dozen biscuits, extra butter." He put the phone back on the hook and had just reached for the bowl of potato chips when he heard Leroy calling.

"Obie, you better get in here!"

He ran into the living room. Rita lay on the couch, her face almost unrecognizable. Her lips were swollen, both of her eyes were black, and red welts ran across her face, like someone had lashed it with a whip.

Obie said, "We got to get her to a hospital, and quick."

Rita, her voice just barely above a whisper, said, "Don't worry about the doctors yet. I'll be all right—it's you who's in trouble. Son Teagle did this to me."

Obie said, "Son? How the hell did he find you?"

"Doesn't matter—"

"Hey, Rita, the whole damn police force is looking for him and you come in here all beat up and say you don't want to tell me how it happened? Come on, we got to know."

"I'll tell you, but get them out of here."

Obie nodded at Leroy and the bodyguards, who left the room.

"Okay, let's have it."

Rita twisted her head to the side, so as not to face him. "Please don't question me, I'll tell you everything later, but right now you have to listen."

"Just talk."

"Teagle knows where your family is. He threatened to kill my daughter and beat it out of me. He left here about two hours ago, on his way to North Carolina to kill your family."

Obie yelled, "Leroy, Jerome, Preston, come back here!" He didn't look at Rita. "Teagle's on his way south to kill Dora Lee and Timba. We got a lot to do—and quick."

OBIE'S MIND WAS RACING. Could he pick up the time on Teagle? Maybe, since he would definitely not be speeding on the way down and he might have to stop to rest and eat—it was a good nine- to eleven-hour trip, and a fast-moving car was likely to attract police attention when traffic was light, which it would be in the middle of the night. No, Son might be in a hurry but he'd be careful not to draw attention to himself, might even be smart and try to get off the road after one or two o'clock in the morning. That gave him a chance that he could beat Son to his family. In the meantime, he'd call the police and let them alert the North Carolina state troopers. Maybe they could even pick up the son of a bitch before he got down there.

He said, "Rita, I don't care how all this happened. But you got to give us all the information. Now answer me careful, you hear?"

Rita, her eyes by now closing from pain and fatigue, nodded.

"What kind of a car is he driving?"

"Chevrolet Malibu," she whispered. "Red...new. I rented it for him."

Leroy and the bodyguards glared at her but said nothing.

"What company? It's important, although that sneaky son-of-a bitch might switch cars on the way down."

"MLM."

"How's he dressed?"

"In a gray...businessman's suit."

"And Raschid?"

"White suit and a white hat."

Obie's heart was beating fast, and he could feel that familiar ring forming around his head from the elevation in his blood pressure.

"How long ago you say they left?"

"About an hour and a half ago, they left me tied up, me and Raschid's girlfriend. We helped each other...get loose. I'm sorry."

Obie nodded at the bodyguards. "Get her over to the hospital, me and Leroy got to get going."

Rita said, "There's one more thing you got to know...before you go."

"What is it?" said Obie, heading towards the phone.

"Son said his men would kill my daughter if I told anybody about the car and where he is."

"I'm sorry to hear that, Rita, and it took a lot of courage for you to come here, and I thank you for it. The way I see it, you and me got a common interest right now in stopping Son. We'll let the police know about your daughter." He glanced at the guards. "Get Rita on over to the emergency room, get the information where her daughter is and pass it to the cops so they can protect her."

Before she was out the door, Obie was on the phone giving the police a description of the car Son was driving and his destination. In the living room, Leroy was busy throwing clothes, weapons, and ammunition into bags.

Obie called Boatwright in North Carolina. The phone rang and rang on the other end. Obie looked at his watch. It was nine o'clock on a Saturday night. They must be out on one of those movie evenings Boatwright liked so much. Or they might be at a skating rink. In any case, chances were they wouldn't be home until eleven or twelve o'clock.

So Son was already two hours down the road on a trip that could have him in Gastonia by seven in the morning, but only if he drove it straight through, which Obie had already figured out wasn't likely. At least, he hoped it wasn't. He dialed the operator for Randolph County, North Carolina, and asked for the number of the sheriff's department. The operator put him straight through:

"How can we help you?"

"This is a big emergency matter I'm calling you on, ma'am, There's a killer headed for the Boatwright Bullock place, and you got to give the family there some protection. Have the Philadelphia police gotten in touch with you about this yet?"

"Wait a minute, mister, I'm on another call. Please hold." In about two minutes, the woman was back. "What's this about a killer coming down here from Philadelphia?"

"Yes, ma'am. The man's a drug dealer, we're an anti-drug group, and he wants to kill my family. I'm Boatwright's Bullock's brother, Obie."

"Oh, why didn't you say so? I remember you. You used to drive your daddy's tractor into town with the tobacco. How you been? I'm ZaLee Thurston."

"Oh, ZaLee, I'm so glad it's you there. Listen now, you got a lot of trouble headed your way. You better get the state police in, because this man Son Teagle has already killed a couple of cops up here and he's dead set on getting my wife and boy. The family's out for the evening, you just got to find them."

"I'll get on it right—wait a minute, some information is coming in on the fax machine. from Philadelphia." She was silent for a few moments. "Boy, you were right. There's an all-points alert on this guy. They're loading the road right up and down from Pennsylvania with state troopers and everything. He'll never get through all that. Okay, Obie, goodbye. Don't you worry about a thing, now."

He was plenty worried. Shit, if the whole United States intelligence service hadn't been able to stop those Arab dudes from blowing up the World Trade Center, how could he trust the cops to keep slick Son from slipping through them? He turned to Leroy.

"Hey man, we ready to go?"

"Always ready. Let's hit it."

IT WAS CLOSE TO ELEVEN O'CLOCK when Boatwright turned the Blazer off the country road and began the one-mile drive up to the farm. It had been a long, happy evening, three enjoyable hours rolling around the rink, eating popcorn, talking and joking with friends, and sometimes just relaxing on the benches and watching the folks skating by. It had taken Dora Lee's mind off everything. A handsome man, about forty-five years old, had asked her if she'd skate around with him a few times, but she smiled and pointed at Timba and said she already had an escort. The man laughed and skated away.

As the Blazer finished the climb to the top of the hill and its headlights fell on the roadway in front of the house, they saw a car parked in the driveway.

Dora Lee's heart sank. Timba's athletic exploits had been getting too much publicity in the area.

"Boat, can you turn around and drive back to town?"

"Come on, ain't nothing to be scared of down here. Them city folks got better sense than to mess with Boatwright Bullock."

"Stop the joking, I'm serious, just turn around and go back."

There must have been something in Dora Lee's tone of voice that put caution into Boatwright's heart. Not fear, because he feared nobody.

He braked the truck, swung quickly into the driveway behind the parked car, threw the truck into reverse, got it turned around, and started back down the hill.

As he began the descent, the taillights of the car in the driveway lit up, its headlights flashed against the garage wall, and it too turned around and started down the hill.

Boatwright drove as fast as he could. Martha Ann said, "Take it easy, you'll turn us over."

"Quiet, sugar."

Another car appeared, its headlights coming directly up the road at them. Its high beams were on, and blinding.

Dora Lee took a deep breath and silently said a prayer.

The roadway in front and behind them burst into flashing blue lights.

Boat braked hard, just before he would have crashed into the state trooper's car. Five minutes later, the family sat in the living room of the house, listening to a state police lieutenant explain the situation.

"Mrs. Bullock, you won't have to worry about a thing. We'll have this house sealed up tighter than a bottle, and we're prepared to give you and the boy all the protection you'll need until we get this guy. And we will get him."

Dora Lee looked at Boatwright. "I don't want to bring all this trouble on you. I think me and Timba should find another place to hide."

Boatwright said, "It's been hard enough on the boy and his schooling the way things are now. Here at least you got me and you got Martha Ann, and I guarantee you we not going to fail you. I think you just better do like the good book says, stay in one place and wait on the Lord."

The lieutenant, a short, heavy-set white man, said, "I don't want to influence you one way or another, ma'am, so I want you to know we'll see you get safely to any place you want to go. But this man is a cop killer, and I can tell you that every policeman from Pennsylvania to Alabama is looking for him. He doesn't stand much of a chance of getting here, if that's his intention. But the decision is yours."

Dora Lee was so tired. Where was Obie? Why, for the first time in her life, was she having to make these kinds of decisions alone? Boat had called him as soon as they walked into the house, and there'd been no answer. And he never kept his cell phone on.

She jerked her mind back to the problem at hand. She was tired of running, tired of drug dealers directing her life, forcing her here and there like some cornered rat. Now was as good a time as any to make her stand.

She looked at Boatwright and Martha Ann, sitting together on the couch and holding hands.

"We'll stay here."

The lieutenant got up. "I'll be leaving, then. We're going to post one car down at the turn-in from the main road, and we'll have another one parked right outside of your house, the way it was when you drove up."

Boatwright saw him out, then returned to the living room and said to Dora Lee, "Sugar, I got an arsenal in this place. Now you just go on to sleep. Wouldn't hurt you to have a little bit of whiskey before you do."

Dora Lee smiled. "I don't think that's such a bad idea. I believe I will."

It was now twelve o'clock at night. The words of an old spiritual went through Dora Lee's mind: "Dark midnight was my cry!"

CHAPTER 24

SON HAD THE RADIO TURNED UP just about as loud as it would go. It was past midnight, and he and Raschid had pulled up to sleep for a few hours at a truck stop in the mountains. The road they were traveling was far from the turnpikes being patrolled by the state troopers. Son was coming into Gastonia through the back door, from the west, not the north. Instead of heading due south, he'd driven out to Harrisburg to pick up Route 81, then headed into Maryland. He lost a few hours that way, but the few troopers he saw weren't after him.

And he wasn't coming in no MLM rental car. They'd ditched it, along with the body of the traveling salesman who'd been so unfortunate as to show up at the rest stop just outside of Gettysburg when Son and Raschid pulled in. His spanking-clean Lincoln had caught Son's eye, and in a matter of minutes the man's body was in the trunk of the Malibu.

At five o'clock in the morning, Son—mad at himself for sleeping so long—shook Raschid, who instinctively reached into his suit jacket pocket for his machine pistol. Son grabbed his arm.

"Hey, man, it's me. Don't be reaching for no gun!"

Raschid shook his head and rubbed his eyes. "Where the hell are we?"

"I been looking at this map, figure we about two hours away from where the Bullocks are. They going to call this the Sunday morning massacre."

"You know, it's bad luck to be killing folks on Sunday. My mama used to say to honor the sabbath and keep it holy."

Son turned on the radio and after fiddling with the pushbuttons finally settled on a gospel music station. He looked over at the convenience store across from the truck parking lot where their car was sitting. He was hungry and knew they'd be better able to take care of business if they had something to eat.

He put his suit jacket on to conceal his weapon and went over to the store. A look of fear crossed the face of the young white man behind the counter. Shit, man, if you knew who I really was, you'd know I wouldn't be fucking around robbing no cheap store like yours.

"Can I help you with something?"

Son walked over to the coffee self-server. "Just going to get me some coffee and a few of these fresh rolls."

"Help yourself. Where you heading?"

"Gastonia, my brother just died and we going to bury him tomorrow."

"Too bad."

"Yeah." Son put his purchases on the counter so he could pay and get out of here. A radio was playing country and western music. Damn, these white folks down here and them prison guards up north, they all like the same thing.

As he walked out the door, he heard the radio announcer say that a widespread search was on for two cop killers driving a late-model Chevrolet Malibu. Son went back to the Lincoln and got in.

"We got to eat fast and be on our way—that bitch told on us. I'm calling Malika soon as we off these folks."

Raschid spread his rolls out on the windshield ledge. "Don't you think we ought to get us a car? Them cops sure to find the Chevvy before too long, they may be looking for this one soon. I forgot to take the guy's license—soon as they find out who he is, they'll know what we driving."

"We just got to be on the lookout for something. Anything turns up, it's ours. Here, hold my coffee, we got to get on the road." Son switched on the ignition, turned the radio up still louder, and pulled out of the rest stop and onto the main road to Gastonia.

HE AND RASCHID PULLED into an empty high school parking lot about eight-thirty so Son could check the map and figure out the way to the Bullock farm. The city was just coming alive to Sunday morning. Black people, walking a lot slower than they did in Philadelphia and dressed in their best, were on their way to worship. Many of the men Son saw going into the church that stood across from the school were carrying Bibles. Son remembered how his daddy had done the same thing when Son was a little boy. That was before he'd left Son's mama. Son hadn't had much in the way of good thoughts about the church since that time. Still, he felt sad. Maybe the gospel music was getting to him. He shut off the radio and wrote directions on the dead salesman's pad that was attached beneath the windshield.

Raschid said, "You know they got cops around the Bullock place. All around, man. How we going to get close, much less in?"

Son looked at the church, its parking lot, the sidewalk in front. "That's our ticket, right there." He pointed to a small yellow church van that was unloading a group of elderly African-Americans.

"What?"

"The van been pulling up, then driving away again to pick up more passengers. All we got to do is to follow it, and next time it stops to pick up a passenger, it's all ours. Ain't no cops going to be stopping no black folks' church van on no Sunday morning."

"You is smart!"

Son followed the van, lettered "Lebanon Baptist Church," as soon as it drove away.

Raschid said, "Let it pick up some passengers. That way it'll look a lot more natural when we get to the Bullock place. Give us more protection, too—you know, hostages, in case shit go wrong."

"You smart too." The Lincoln continued following the van as it picked up its load of elderly and handicapped passengers.

When the van had made its fourth stop, Son said, "That's enough folks in there now, man. Let's get it. Be sure you got all the weapons and shit. I'll go in first." He pulled the Lincoln in front of the van, which was still standing at the curbside. The driver blew his horn. Son got out of the car.

"Open the door," he said. "I got to tell you something. It's important."

As soon as the elderly driver opened the door, Son leapt up the stairs, drew his pistol, and put it against the man's head.

"Folks, I'm real sorry to mess up your Sunday, but me and my partner need this particular kind of transportation for something we got to do this morning. And I'll need your company, too."

While he was talking Raschid had boarded the bus, all loaded down with ammunition clips and machine pistols.

Son said, "Now, I don't want no trouble out of you. Just be quiet and nobody going to be hurt. Move to the back of the bus. Just keep on praying and reading your Bibles, everything be fine."

"Young man," said an old lady in a white usher's uniform, "God going to punish you. Going to strike you dead for what you doing. You messing with his people, and he don't tolerate that one bit."

An old man who was moving with some difficulty to a seat in the rear said, "Amen, sister, the deacons consecrated this van to God's service. You do far better, son, to put them guns away, fall on your knees, and beg his forgiveness. God love a sinner man who repents. Come on back to church with us."

As Raschid held a gun against the head of the driver, Son said, "Listen, I'm going to tell you who I am, so you won't give me no more trouble. I'm Son Teagle from Philadelphia, and the police want me from the Canadian border to the end of Florida. Now, you all do what I say."

The old man in the rear seat said, "All right, sisters, obey him, God won't let him harm us."

The three women in the van did as they were told, but one said, "I don't care who you are, boy, you are surely going to burn in hell, and it won't be long before you get there. Pulling a gun on poor old colored folks like us."

Son and Raschid positioned themselves in the seats directly behind the driver. Son put his gun into the man's back.

"Just start driving, mister, I'll give you the directions. And don't play no tricks—I ain't got no quarrel with you."

ABOUT TWENTY-FIVE MILES AWAY, still north of Gastonia, Obie and Leroy were flying down the road doing a flat-out seventy miles an hour. It was as fast as the old Chevy would go.

Obie had already had to put three quarts of oil into the car between Philly and North Carolina.

"Man, you know it did my heart good to talk to Dora Lee this morning," he said. "All that stuff been going down between us don't really mean a thing. Once we get rid of Teagle, we going to put our lives back together."

"I been meaning to pull your coat on that thing, my friend. They don't come no better than Dora Lee." Leroy looked at the speedometer. "You can slow down a little bit now. The cops are out there by now and if some cop stops us with all the stuff we're carrying we going to be in some deep trouble."

Obie eased his foot off the accelerator, but not much. "You know Son Teagle as well as I do, ain't no cops ever stopped him yet except when they came and got him when he was sleeping. Took a whole squad to get him then. No, buddy, we got to get there fast as we can. I reckon we about a hour away now."

He turned on the radio to a gospel music station and began humming along with the songs. He felt sad, mad, and frustrated. The news about Trevon and Shakeisha had almost been the last straw. He'd failed them both! But he wasn't about to fail his family.

AT THE BULLOCK HOUSE, Dora Lee was in the kitchen helping Martha Ann with the Sunday breakfast dishes. Boatwright was saying he thought he'd stay home from church today, give Dora Lee and Timba the company and protection they needed.

Dora Lee said, "No, Boat, I think you and Martha Ann ought to go on to church. We got the two police cars here, and you know they'll have patrols all along the road. We'll be all right."

Martha Ann said, "Dora Lee, we're not going anywhere today. Obie and Leroy should be getting in soon, and it wouldn't be right for us to be away when they get here. So soon's we get these dishes cleaned up, we'll have prayer meeting here. That's the way the old folks used to do when they couldn't get to church."

"All right, I like that idea."

Timba came into the kitchen. "Uncle Boat, can you just check me out on that shotgun one more time? I want to be ready if I got to be."

Dora Lee looked at her young man. He was wearing the University of North Carolina gray baseball shorts he'd gotten from a coach trying to recruit him. His hair was short, with afro cuts on the side. He was a handsome boy, even if Dora Lee said so herself.

Boat pushed himself away from the breakfast table and walked into the recreation room, where his collection of shotguns and rifles were locked in a mahogany and glass case.

"Come on in here, Timba, I forgot which shotgun you was using the other day."

Timba pointed to a Remington double-barreled gun. His uncle unlocked the case.

"Get it out, son, and we'll go into the garage and go through that loading exercise a couple of more times."

"Thanks a lot, I just want to be real sure."

"That's the way a man should be, especially when he got to defend his family. You know you getting to be a man now, and sometime soon when this thing is all over, I'll tell you how your granddaddy, your daddy, and me had to defend this very same farm against some real bad men. And I was a lot younger than you, Timba. Scared, too, but once we got to shooting, I growed up mighty fast. Come on, now."

They went into the garage. Fifteen minutes later they came back into the main house and Boatwright called the family together for prayer.

OBIE'S CHEVY WAS THROUGH GASTONIA and on its way to the farm, but the gas gauge was on empty. Not just a little above, not below, but exactly on empty. And that was giving Obie a fit. The Bullock house was about seventeen miles away, and usually when that gauge was on empty, he had exactly one gallon of gas left.

But God was speaking to Obie through the music on the radio. Hadn't the Beulah Baptist Church choir just sung the words, "We ain't got long to stay here"? It was telling him something, he just wasn't sure what.

He turned to Leroy. "If we go on, we may run out of gas a mile or two from the house. If we stop for gas, we going to lose at least five minutes. What you think?"

"I say we stop, I got the cash right here in my pocket. Put in three gallons, we can be in and out of that station in two minutes flat. We might have to do some more driving once we get there."

There was a gasoline station about a quarter of a mile down the road. Obie pulled the Chevy into the station. But there were two cars already ahead of them at the one pump. Even if the folks in front of them were kind enough to move their cars, they were still going to lose time here. Obie could feel his blood pressure rising, but right now he had no choice. They sure couldn't afford to run out of gas.

THE LEBANON BAPTIST CHURCH van, its yellow body shining from the wash and wax job the church deacons had applied to it Saturday morning, was now about a mile from the turn-in to the Bullock house.

"Let those who refuse to sing..."

"Shut up that singing before I have to hit one of you." The old folks acted like they didn't even hear Son. They were practically at the Bullocks', and there'd be cops there. He had to think!

"Let those who refuse to sing..."

Raschid said, "Look down the road—cop car right by the crossroads. Must be the turn-in."

"Slow down, man," Son said to the driver.

The van decelerated to about fifteen miles an hour.

"Let those who refuse to sing..."

Son cracked his pistol across the head of the old man who'd been slow to move to the rear of the bus earlier. He fell against the lap of one of the old ladies. His head lay just below the gold cross that was hanging around her neck.

The singing stopped.

"Boy, you done hit Deacon Farley. You done hit a holy man. May God have mercy on your sorry soul!"

"Another word from any of you, and you get the same thing. When we get up to that cop car, don't none of you say a word. I'm going to kill him, and I'll do the same to you folks too if I have to. Count on it." Son nudged the driver. "Just pull up slow, and when that man ask you what you doing, you just open that door so I can talk to him. Don't you say one word, I do the talking."

The van pulled into the roadway that led up to the Bullock house and stopped.

The state trooper, a young white man with blond hair, was sitting in his car reading the Sunday paper. From his angle in the van, Son could see the various sections of the paper strewn across the front seat of the patrol car. He could also see that the shotgun rack was unlocked.

The trooper waved his hand from his window for the driver to stop, then pulled his microphone from its bracket and said something into it. He got out of the car, put on his cap, walked up to the van door, and motioned the driver to open up.

The driver opened the door, and in the instant before the force of the Schmeisser automatic's bullets knocked the trooper's body back against the hood of his vehicle, Son saw on his face that he recognized his killer. The body crumpled beside the still open door of the police car.

Women in the van screamed. From his spot outside the car, Son looked back at Raschid, who was standing in the stairway of the van, his pistol trained on the driver.

"I'm going to drag him over to that ditch there," Son said. "Soon's I do that and cut the telephone wires, I'll get in that car and drive it up the hill behind you. When you get to the top, wait for me."

Son disposed of the body, but not until he'd stripped the blouse and tie off the trooper and put them on. He donned the trooper's hat, got into the car, and jerked his thumb at Raschid.

"Get going, and remember, slow down at the top of the hill. If they got more cops up there, I want it to look like I'm escorting you to pick up some folks for church. Go ahead now, and shoot this lot if they mess with you."

Up the hill went the procession of the church van and the state police car. When they reached the summit of the hill, the van slowed down. Son could see the other blue patrol car parked in the driveway of the house.

The state trooper, a tall black man wearing dark sunglasses, got out of his car and motioned the van to stop. He had a smile on his face like either the van or the name of the church on it was familiar to him. Maybe he knew the driver.

Too bad for you.

Son floored the accelerator of the police cruiser and ran it into the trooper, hitting him so hard that his body was thrown a good ten yards down the long driveway, where it bounced, then became perfectly still.

Son stayed in the police car, waiting to see if any alarm had been raised inside the house. After a few seconds, satisfied that no one had heard, he got out of the car and walked over to the van. Raschid had the driver open the door to let him in.

Son motioned the driver and his women passengers to get out of the van. The old man was still unconscious, so he left him inside. He marched the others over to the police cruiser and at gunpoint pushed them all into the back seat and locked the door on them. That's one thing he knew pretty good, how the back seat of a police car locked.

"Now you folks can sing all you want, won't bother me none."

Son turned his attention to the large patio door with its picture window at the front of the house. The curtains were still drawn, as they would be on an early Sunday morning.

Raschid was in the driver's seat. Son got back into the van and reached for the ammunition clips.

"We going in the front door, man. Right on through that plate glass window. Don't leave nobody alive. Kill every motherfucking Bullock."

Raschid nodded his head and checked his weapon. "Here we go."

....

AT THE SOUND OF THE ACCELERATING CAR outside the house, Boatwright had immediately reached for his shotgun, which lay on the table across from where he sat watching a gospel quartet from Charlotte perform on television. Dora Lee, sitting with him, had also been startled by the sound.

Boatwright walked over to the blue curtain and looked out of the picture window. He saw the body of the trooper lying prone on the driveway and watched Son, in his weird-looking combination of civilian pants and trooper jacket, put sisters Evans, Childs, and Trimble into the police car.

Boat yelled to Martha Ann, "Call the state police, tell them Teagle's killed their cops. Then take everybody and get going down that old slave path back there. You'll make it to the Ferguson's house in about fifteen minutes. Call the police again from there."

He turned to Timba. "Everything's on you now. You got to take care of your mama, your aunt, and your little cousin. Take that shotgun and stay in the rear. It's a narrow path. Anybody coming after you got to come single file. Remember what I showed you, and remember what kind of folks you come from. Get going now."

Martha Ann called from the kitchen. "Phone's dead, they must of cut the wires."

"All right," Boat said. "Just get going now. And use your cell phone on the way. I love you."

"But what'll happen to you?"

"You're wasting time, get going. I be fine."

BOATWRIGHT WATCHED DORA LEE follow the others out of the kitchen door, down the hill, and onto the old path. Timba took up his position in the rear of the group.

Left alone, Boat ran through the ground floor of the house, overturning chairs and couches to serve as barricades against the bullets that would be flying any second now. Then he walked up to the side of the picture window and pulled the curtain back just a little bit. He was in time to see the yellow church van lurch across his recently reseeded lawn, headed right for the window and him.

Boat threw himself behind a chair and released the safety on the shotgun.

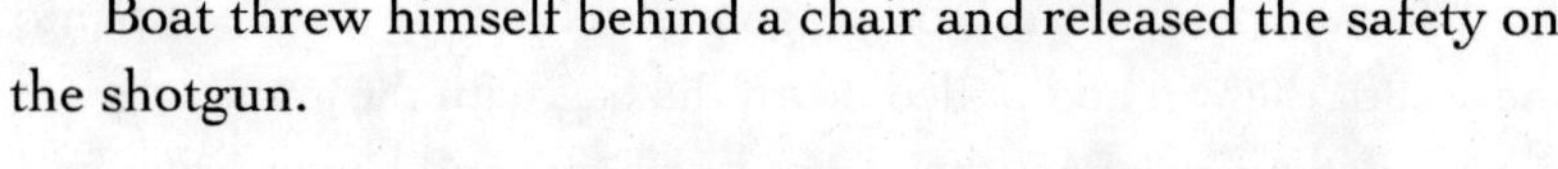

AS SOON AS THE VAN CRASHED through the window and into the big family room, Son jumped out, his automatic weapon firing. He sprayed the machine pistol back and forth.

He paused for a second.

He heard a loud report and saw Raschid's head explode before his eyes into a bloody mess. Pieces of him splattered all over Son's stolen police jacket. Son fell to the floor onto the deep blue pile rug and stationed himself behind the right front tire.

The only sound in the room was a gospel quartet on the television. They were singing:

> Life is in his hands,
> Don't you know?
> Life is in his hands
> I say,
> All life is in his hands!

Son peeked around the tire. Couldn't see or hear a thing. He fired four quick bursts from the machine pistol, spraying the whole recreation room with bullets, including the leather sofa he figured the guy with the shotgun was behind.

"Oh, shit!" A man's cry of pain, followed by the sound of a jerky, uneven movement on the floor as he ran out of the room and down the hallway, told Son he'd wounded whoever had fired that two-barreled shotgun. Lucky for Son—and bad for Raschid—that the guy had made a mistake and emptied both of those first barrels at Raschid.

Silence again.

Raschid was gone. Cops would be here in a few minutes, soon as they couldn't get the dead cops on the radio. How the fuck was he to get out of here?

Didn't care no more, blood rage was in him. He reached up into the seat of the van and pulled down the bag with the ammo clips in it, reloaded his weapon, then leapt to his feet and began firing into the hallway that led down to the living room and the kitchen.

As he turned a corner and started for the kitchen, he saw the barrel of the shotgun protruding from around the base of a kitchen island. And glimpsed the face of a man who looked a lot like Big Obie Bullock.

One shotgun barrel exploded, and then the other, and Son felt a sharp pain in his thigh. He yelled, then leapt across the room, firing a burst of Schmeisser bullets into the man. Then he dropped behind a cabinet, stuck the remaining clips of bullets into his pockets, and sat still for a moment.

He looked at his leg. It was bleeding awful bad. And some of those big pellets from the shotgun had grazed him up top, ripping away the epaulet from the North Carolina state trooper's jacket and opening up the old wound again. He'd survive long enough to get the rest of these fucking Bullocks. One down, a lot to go.

The man moaned, but Son had to move on. Had to get the rest of the family first.

He'd come back for him. The quartet was still singing: "My life is in his hands."

He'd like to shut them up. Hearing no other sounds in the house, he cautiously stood up and tested his leg, then moved slowly from room to room, nudging the doors open with the barrel of the Schmeisser and firing short bursts to kill anybody alive in the rooms.

Finally he came to a room with flowery decorations on the door and a sign that said, "This is Melissa's room. Enter with joy in your heart."

Son nudged that door open and heard a movement just behind it. He jumped back from the door and emptied half a magazine of bullets into the room. He stepped in and saw the remains of what had been a cat. Had been lying in a toy rocking cradle.

Where the fuck were the Bullock children and women?

He ran to the back door of the house, which led off from the kitchen. Son opened the door and found himself on a big deck that overlooked woods and a small creek that flowed down past the house before disappearing into the trees.

The raised patio stood about thirty feet off the ground. Steps at one end of it led down to the ground.

About half a mile away, in the woods, he glimpsed people heading away from the house.

Bullocks.

Son reloaded and started down the steps. He couldn't sing worth a lick, but by now he knew the tune, and he gave it a try:

I say, your lives are in my hands.

OBIE WAS AT THE BOTTOM of the hill. The first thing he'd seen as the car turned up the roadway to the house was the body of a state trooper thrown into the ditch.

Great God almighty, Teagle was there and didn't care who knew it!

He turned to Leroy. "Get ready for anything, man. You loaded up?"

"Yo, let's go!"

Obie stomped down on the accelerator. The Chevy swerved from side to side as the rear tires spun and finally gripped the dirt and gravel, then leapt up the dusty road.

Then he was in the clearing at the top of the hill and saw the log house and the two police cars parked in the driveway. The body of the other state trooper was lying in the road, and some old people were locked in the back of one of the police cars. A van stood where his brother's picture window used to be.

Leroy got out and in a few seconds had opened the front door of the trooper's car, pulled the security lock, and unlocked the rear door. One by one, he helped the weeping old women out of the car.

One said, "There's two evil men in that house. Done beat Deacon Farley bad—he in the van—and killed them troopers. And they going to murder everybody in the house."

Obie was out of the Chevy and already on the radio to the state police.

"Somebody come in. You got two dead troopers and at least one injured civilian out at the Bullock place. Son Teagle's here."

"I read you, mister. Who are you? Identify yourself."

"Obie Bullock, Boatwright's brother, and Leroy Merriweather, a friend. We're both in red shirts and dungarees. We got guns and we going after Teagle. See you soon."

"Over and out, help is on the way. Good luck!"

Obie looked at the old women. "You ladies get back in the police car, lock the doors, and sit tight till the police get here."

As he and Leroy headed for the house, one of the women called out, "God bless and keep you, mister, because the men you're going after is surely Satan's chief henchmen."

ENTERING CAUTIOUSLY through the picture window, Obie saw Raschid's body slumped across the front seat of the van. He and Leroy, covering each other, moved first into the living room, then into the kitchen.

Boatwright's body lay on the blood-covered linoleum. No doubt that he was dead.

Damn, they were too late! What about the others?

He and Raschid quickly made their way through the rest of the house and finally to the patio, from which they could see—about two hundred yards away—Son limping his way down the path to the Fergusons.

Obie said, "Let's hit it, man. He after them, they must still be alive." They ran down the wooden steps.

BRAMBLES AND BRANCHES TORE at Dora Lee's clothing and scratched her face. Seemed to her it must have been centuries since anyone had used the path. Ahead of her, Martha Ann and little Melissa struggled to clear the way. Behind her was Timba. He'd follow them for a few minutes, then turn around and face the rear. He had his Eagles baseball cap on backwards and seemed calm and sure of himself.

Dora Lee touched Martha Ann's arm. "How much further we got to go?"

"We about five minutes away now."

They heard gunfire from the house. Then silence. They walked up a slight rise to a clearing. From there they could look back.

Martha Ann touched Dora Lee. "Wait a second." She shaded her eyes with her hand and looked back at the house. "That ain't Boat on the deck. We got to run for our lives now."

She shouted back to Timba. "You can't hope for no help now. Do just like your uncle said."

"You know I'm not going to let anything happen—"

"All right, everybody," Dora Lee said, "let's just get going and stop talking."

For a couple of minutes, the little band hurried along the path. Martha Ann carried her crying child in her arms, followed by Dora Lee and Timba.

As Dora Lee grabbed for a branch to help her over a rock in the path, the limb gave way, and she fell. A sharp pain shot through her ankle.

In an instant, Timba was by her side. "Mama, you okay?"

"Just give me a hand getting up, I'll be all right."

Martha Ann put Melissa down and walked back to Dora Lee.

"Timba and me'll get you up."

"Thanks, I'm just sorry I'm causing all this trouble."

"Hush your mouth, child, we in this mess together."

Dora Lee stood up, supported on one side by Martha Ann and on the other by Timba. She put her right foot forward. It was okay. Then she put her weight on her left foot—

No way she could walk on it. Jesus, have mercy. Now her whole family was going to die because of her, for they surely would not leave her there alone.

She looked up at Martha Ann. "I can shoot a shotgun good as any man. Just leave me the gun, and you all and Timba get to the Ferguson place fast as you can."

"What kind of man would I be to do something like that?"

Timba said. "Auntie and Melissa can go ahead, I'll stay here and protect you. We'll be okay."

Martha Ann said, "Stop all this talk about anybody leaving. We'll all stay. Here, Dora Lee, put your arm around my shoulder. We going to hide off in the bush. Timba, you know what you got to do."

He nodded, then walked over to a rock, rested the shotgun barrel on it, and sighted back along the path. The women and little girl had barely taken cover before Timba called over his shoulder to them.

"I can see him—about fifty yards back. He's got a machine pistol and a revolver. And he's hurt, blood all over his shirt and legs."

Master, if it be thy will, spare my people.

SON'S THIGH AND SHOULDER BURNED with pain. And the blood seemed to be flowing more freely. He used his knife to cut a piece of cloth from the trooper's jacket, crunched it in his hands, then held it for a few seconds to his leg. He might be hurting, but he would surely destroy those Bullocks this day. Don't nobody fuck with Son Teagle and live to talk about it. Catch these motherfuckers, kill them, and get on out of here.

He kept walking through the woods. The sun's beams pierced the branches intermittently, now making the path bright, now making it dark. A slight breeze, hinting of the fall coming on, kept the leaves rustling.

Just ahead, Son saw that the path took a slight bend. He cautiously approached it, then looked ahead. Seeing nothing suspicious, he kept on walking.

Then he saw a glint of metal—and the barrel of a shotgun exploded. The pellets cut a path through the leaves about a foot away from him. He dropped to the ground. So somebody had them a shotgun.

He began to crawl on his hands and knees through the woods, brushing the undergrowth aside with the barrel of the Schmeisser. After about three minutes, he saw a fallen cottonwood tree, its bark moist and green from the lack of sun. Son crept behind the tree. From it he could see that he'd worked himself to a position from which he could come up on his prey from the side.

He slowly raised his head and looked.

About ten yards away from him was a fucking kid holding a shotgun and aiming down the path, waiting to kill him. Too bad.

Son looked at the trees around where the boy was and noticed some patches of color—blues and reds—showing through the leaves and brush. Why, the whole Bullock family must be hiding from him here.

Had them where he wanted them. He stood up, his Schmeisser trained on the boy.

"Hey, kid, just drop that fucking shotgun or I'll blow your head off."

The boy turned his head towards Son, saw what he was facing, and slowly took his hands off of the shotgun.

"Stay where you are, boy. Timba, ain't it? And don't move a muscle."

Son pointed his gun at the bushes where he'd seen the colors. "You people, come on out in the open where I can see you."

Dora Lee crept out from the underbrush, followed by another woman and a little girl. The child had her hands over her eyes, but neither woman looked frightened. What Son saw in their eyes was contempt.

"Well, what have we here? I got the whole Bullock family, right?"

"Wrong!" The voice came from behind Son. "You ain't got the daddy. And he's behind your black ass with a shotgun. So drop that pistol."

Fire burned up through the body and soul of Son Teagle.

His finger tightened on the trigger of the Schmeisser. He whirled around, threw himself to the ground, and fired, all at the same time. But not fast enough.

His body was cut to pieces by shotgun slugs as both Leroy and Obie fired at him.

He saw darkness, then stars. Then Son Teagle said his last "Motherfucker!" right there on the old slave path.

CHAPTER 25

OBIE WAS DOWN AT THAT SPECIAL BEACH in Wildwood, looking out over the water. For a moment, he wished he'd brought his fishing tackle along. No day that couldn't be made a little better by getting in a bit of fishing. Poor Captain Sarnese, he'd talked about retiring up to that small place on the lake and insulating it so he and Angie could live there all year round. Funny, but in a way Obie was glad the captain hadn't lived to see O'Brien and those other rotten cops put away for fifteen years. Would have broken his heart. Well, Captain, all that don't matter much now, I'm sure you someplace where the fishing's good and the sun never sets.

He walked down a little closer to the water's edge, thinking of the day last summer when he and Dora Lee had come down here. Seemed so long ago, and so many things had happened. Boatwright dead and gone, Dora Lee and Timba down south without him for seven months so the boy could finish the school year out and they could help Martha Ann deal with her grief and get the farm ready for sale. She was going to buy a townhouse with the proceeds and go and live with her relatives.

And now it was June. School was over, the farm sold, and Timba was already registered for the summer baseball league. The kids would sure be glad to see him back, they'd had a disappointing year without him.

Obie watched a seagull swoop low over the water and skim along its surface for almost thirty yards, its wings beating against the rippling waves, causing spray to foam out in sparkling white streams behind it. Suddenly the bird spread its wings wide, flapped them once or twice, and soared back into the clear blue sky.

He looked out over the water, said a silent prayer for the souls of Boatwright, Captain Sarnese, Dora Lee's friend Lurlene, that young black detective, the sergeant, and Shakeisha. Oh, he'd never forget to pray for the soul of that child.

He looked up at the fast disappearing gull.

Better pray for Son, Raschid, and Trevon, too. They were God's children, one and all. He bowed his head briefly.

He turned away from the water, got back into his car, and hit the road for North Carolina to bring his family home.

Allen Ballard, a graduate of Philadelphia's Central High School, Kenyon College, and Harvard University, was formerly a professor of government at City College of New York. He presently teaches history and Africana Studies at the University of Albany. His previous works on African-American history—including the renown *One More Day's Journey*, a history of Black Philadelphia, have been praised by such literary greats as Ralph Ellison, John A. Williams, and Alex Haley. His first novel—about the very first about African-American troops in the Civil War —*Where I'm Bound*, (Simon and Schuster, 2000) won the "First Novelist" prize of the Black Caucus of the American Library Association, and was named a "Notable Book of the Year" by the *Washington Post*.